HEARTS OF GOLD

HEARTS OF GOLD

Jessica Stirling

GUILD PUBLISHING LONDON

This edition published 1988 by
Guild Publishing
by arrangement with Hodder and Stoughton Ltd

Printed and bound in Great Britain by
Mackays of Chatham Ltd, Chatham, Kent

The poor labour under a natural stigma; they are *naturally* despised.

William Hazlitt

Contents

PART ONE

ONE

The Runaway Wife

The winter of 1814 was reluctant to give way to spring. In March its icy trademarks remained stamped upon the hills and the squalls that snaked across the river, broad as a lake below the Kincardine crossings, were of sleet not rain. Between flurries, however, the sky cleared to a huge, washed-blue sheet that stretched taut as gauze above the distant estuary and made the lands that penned the Forth seem hard and new and clean.

Elspeth Patterson no longer cared where she was. She had no notion where the cart would finally trundle to a halt, in which hamlet on which headland she would be obliged to spend the night, to find food and shelter for herself and her child. She knew only that she was travelling again, moving on again, riding further and further from the place that she had once called home.

She was worried about Mary Jean. During a night in the open the baby had caught a cold and mewed and snuffled fretfully in the shawl in Elspeth's arms. She was worried too about the cost of the ride for every mile that the cart travelled cost another penny from her purse. But she did not have the courage to call to the carrier to set her down. Each mile that rolled away took her further from Balnesmoor, from James Moodie, her husband, her father.

She had fled his house in the autumn, had foolishly supposed that, once settled in the city, she would be lost among its citizens and safe from pursuit. She had reckoned without James's ingenuity and perseverance. He had distributed handbills describing her, offering reward for news of her whereabouts, and there were plenty of sharp-eyed opportunists in the weaving trades, women and men who would sell their own mothers for a crown. Three times she had been recognised.

Three times she had been challenged and handled, and had escaped. In hindsight Elspeth realised that she had betrayed herself. She had refused to jettison all of her past. She had retained the name that her foster-mother, Gaddy Patterson, had given her, and that was a grave mistake. Everything that connected her with Balnesmoor and James Simpson Moodie should have been left behind in the ruins of her marriage. From the first she had compromised and the compromises, one by one, had brought her down.

The cart was a long four-wheeled affair drawn by a pair of burly Clevelands. Given rein the horses could have pulled it along at a tidy lick but its cargo was apparently too valuable to risk at speed. Ten large glass bottles, bedded in straw, gave off a stench of corrosive chemicals. Exactly what the bottles contained and where they were being taken were questions that Elspeth did not dare ask, for the carrier was a wet-mouthed, slovenly old man who would give her no answer but a snarl. However, she had been lucky with her other rides that day. Only this last slow cart would cost her precious pence since the others out from Stirling had been driven by cheerful, charitable men who had waived passenger charges for a pretty young woman with a bairn in arms.

All day long she had trundled along the hem of three shires. She had eaten nothing since dawn. Now her head swam and her muscles ached. She drowsed in the twilight and might have fallen asleep if it had not been for the clanking carboys and the baby's coughing. Jerked awake, Elspeth would peer at the broad-running river and gigantic sky, and wonder if she had at last passed out of James Moodie's reach.

"Whoa-whoah!"

Abruptly the horses came to a halt. The carboys lurched and gurgled menacingly.

Bolt upright, Elspeth clutched Mary Jean protectively to her breast.

"What is it?" she asked. "What's wrong?"

"Get down," the carrier growled.

"But – but where are we?"

"We've come as far as I'll tak' ye. Get down when you're told."

There was nothing to be seen but flat shore and, above the road, a bank of leafless trees.

Elspeth had no strength left to challenge the man. Meekly she hoisted Mary Jean into the crook of one arm. She reached for the oat sack, her bundle, which contained all her belongings. The carrier would have none of it. Perhaps he thought that she might skip into the trees and cheat him of payment. He craned over the board and tapped her wrist with his willow switch.

"Ye can have that after I've been paid."

Elspeth climbed over the side of the cart and, using the wheel as a ladder, clambered stiffly to the ground. She walked to the driver's step and fumbled in the waist of her skirt for the leather purse in which she kept her travelling money, three shillings and some coppers. Four one-guinea banknotes and two half-crowns, the last of her funds, were tucked into the toe of a shoe in the oat sack.

She untied the purse string with her teeth.

"How much do I owe you?"

"Fifteen pence," said the carrier.

"What? We haven't made fifteen miles."

"I say we have."

"No, it's eight at most."

"How would you know since you sleppit most o' the way? It's fifteen mile at a penny a mile. Pay me, damn you."

Elspeth bit her lip, shook a shilling and coppers from the purse into the palm of her hand, then tipped out the rest of the silver and showed it to the carrier.

"See, I can pay for more miles. Will you not take us on to a town?" she pleaded.

The carrier squinted from under bushy brows.

Elsepth had no warning as to his intention.

Suddenly he lashed her arm with the willow switch. Coins, the purse too, leapt from her grasp into the well of the cart. Elspeth cried out and darted forward. But the carrier cracked the reins and cried the horses into motion and Elspeth had to step back, swinging Mary Jean away, or she would have been crushed beneath the wheels.

The old man stood upright and slashed at the Clevelands. They surged forward and the cart was off and away, carboys clanking. Clasping the baby, Elspeth ran frantically after it.

"*Thief*," she screamed. "*You thief. Stop, you thief.*"

The carrier no longer cared about the fragility of his cargo. The cart clashed on, dipping down the slope of a little hill out of Elspeth's sight.

She ran after it for thirty or forty yards, then realised that it was hopeless. She stood stock-still watching the cart appear briefly a quarter of a mile away then vanish around a turn in the road.

Rocking the wailing child against her body, Elspeth stumbled to the verge. She was numb with exhaustion and, trembling, seated herself on the grass, aghast at what had occurred. She had been abandoned in an unknown part of the country without so much as a penny to buy bread, and neither she nor Mary Jean would survive unscathed another night in the open.

She sat there for some time, crooning to and soothing Mary Jean until the baby quieted.

It was late now, almost dusk. The lavender sky had cooled to pale yellow. Long feathers of cloud, stained rust and rose, soared across the estuary. Rooks cawed in distant trees and a solitary gull flapped overhead, solid and unhurried against the night's first stars. The river no longer reflected the colours of the sky but ran heavy and cold as mercury.

If, at that moment, James had come riding out of the gloom Elspeth might have been tempted to surrender to him, to return to Balnesmoor and pretend to be 'his wife'. It would cost no more than the price of a lie, public acknowledgement that Mary Jean was his daughter. James knew that it could not be so, for he had never lain with her. He had married her not out of incestuous passion but only to possess her, to own her under law.

Elspeth stared into the gloom. How could she burden Mary Jean with her father's guilt? Did her father truly believe that he could wipe away his shame by compounding it, that, in course of time, pretence would become reality and that the past would somehow be altered and renewed?

She wiped Mary Jean's face, dried her own eyes. She could not sit here for ever. She must do something. The night was growing colder by the minute and the forlorn shore of the

14

Forth was no place to rest for long. She must not give in to despair. She had arrived at a crucial moment in her life when nothing but determination would sustain her, when she must prove herself to be Gaddy Patterson's daughter in spirit as well as law.

Elspeth pushed herself to her feet. She turned her face from the direction of Stirling and set off along the shore road, heading east, Mary Jean against her shoulder.

As she walked, unsteadily at first, she could hear Gaddy's voice jogging and cajoling her along.

"Come along, m'luckie," Gaddy would say. "Step it out. You're well rid o' that oat sack. It was naught but a burden to a traveller. Come on now, 'Pet, step it out. There will soon be a light t' guide you."

She had gone no more than a mile before a light did come into view, the glimmer of a lantern in the gloaming. She caught too the sound of voices on the wind. Quickening, she rounded a dog-leg in the road and saw the lights of a village on the hillside above her. Relieved, she hurried on towards a humpback bridge that led up the hill to the dwellings.

The cottages had lime-washed walls. The steeple of a kirk was visible against the afterglow. From that angle the village appeared neat and self-possessed. She had run into company too. Along the shore road came men, women and children, quite a procession. They threaded their way across the bridge and into the cobbled lane that led to the heart of the village.

Although the landscape did not remind Elspeth of Balnes-moor, the community seemed homely. She noticed that the girls wore gaudy ribbons and bright clothes. Some sported snow-white pantaloons under knee-length skirts. Only a few of the younger ones were barefoot. The menfolk too were trim in dress, not slouched and ill-kempt. They strolled along in threes and fours with their hands in their pockets, jabbering and laughing as men will, separate from the women and girls.

Elspeth did not head directly into the village. She hesitated on the road at the bridge-end. Common sense told her that a penniless stranger would hardly be welcome. She was wary lest she had stumbled into a mill-town where James might have contacts and connections. She glanced down the shore road. Peculiar shapes loomed in the fields that curved towards the headland, indistinct in the dusk. What held the folk here? she wondered. She was sure that it was not a farming community. Uncertain as to what to do next, she loitered, watching.

The man was about forty years of age and he walked apart from the other men. By the hand he held a girl of ten or eleven and was preceded by a younger girl and a boy. It was the young girl, no older than eight, whose quick, assessing gaze first fixed on Elspeth, who gave her brother, for so the boy appeared to be, a nudge with her elbow.

"I wonder, sir," Elspeth stepped forward and addressed herself to the father of the family, "if you would tell me the name of this place. I'm a stranger to these parts."

He wore tweed and moleskins and a hat dyed azure blue. A cotton scarf was knotted in the gullet of his shirt and his half-length boots, Elspeth noted, were of calf leather not cheap hessian.

The girl who clung to her father's hand was tiny. She rubbed herself daintily against his flank and stared up at him to see what her response to the stranger should be.

It was, however, the youngest child who gave Elspeth an answer.

"This is Placket."

The man admonished her without anger. "Sarah, hold your damned tongue."

"Aye, Daddy."

He studied Elspeth carefully then nodded at Mary Jean.

"She's not sick wi' the contagion, is she?"

"No, sir, it's only a cold."

"Is that the God's truth?"

"I've no reason to lie."

The man nodded. "This is Placket, as she says."

The girl-child by his side giggled.

"Are you – are you weavers here?" said Elspeth.

The man tipped back his head and bellowed with laughter. The sound of his mirth attracted the attention of four men who hung about the bridge on the far side.

"What's all your roarin' for, Jock Bennet?" one enquired.

"Hear this, this lassie takes us for weavers."

"Weavers, b'God. She'd as well tak' us for dancin'-masters."

"By the look o' her, Jock, she might be worth weavin' with, eh?"

Sarah, the solemn child, explained. "Placket belongs to the pit."

"What pit?" said Elspeth.

"Mr Bolderon's pit. The Abbeyfield," Sarah answered.

"The best damned pit in Christ's own kingdom," the boy put in. His father did not chide him for the blasphemy. "Where have you come from that's never heard o' Placket or the Abbeyfield?"

Elspeth had learned not to give direct answers to questions about her place of origin.

She said, "I'm here in search of work."

The man, Jock Bennet, suddenly lost interest in the banter of his friends. He snapped his head round and scrutinised Elspeth with a frown, as if he found some puzzle in her.

"Davy," he said, "take Sarah up t' Mr Nicol's an' wait inside until I come."

"But, Da—"

"Go on wi' ye."

Sarah turned on her heel and walked, prim and obedient, away across the bridge. Davy, grumbling, trailed her. The elder girl seemed favoured. She was not dismissed. To secure her position she scrambled on to the bridge post and transferred herself to her father's shoulders. Arms about his neck, she clung to him. He ignored her.

"Work?" he said. "So you're in search o' work, are ye? And what sort o' work are you fit to do?"

"I can tend cattle, milk, thresh, plant—"

"Nah, nah, lass. Nothin' grows on the Abbeyfield."

"I can also cook. Plain fare. I can sew."

"Where's your man?"

"I have no man."

"What about the bairn? Has she no father?"

"Her father's dead."

"Dead – or run off?"

"Dead, a full year ago."

"Was he a weaver?" Jock Bennet asked.

"He was – a drover."

"Aye, so you're a drover's wife?"

"I was."

"Drovers are a hardy breed."

"Hardy enough," said Elspeth, guardedly.

"Step closer to me, girl," Jock Bennet said.

She came forward a step or two, enduring his close inspection.

The years with James Moodie, as mistress of Moss House, had softened and refined her and, even after months of hardship, much of that refinement remained. But Elspeth had the woman's instinct that told her that the pitman was not interested in her looks, that, whatever else he might have in mind, it was not his intention to wheedle her instantly into his bed.

"Can ye cook good meat?" he asked.

"Meat of all sorts," Elspeth replied.

"We eat meat in our family. Ham and mutton. On Sundays, prime beef," Jock Bennet said. "No skink for coal-hewers." He paused. "Look, I've a corner in my cottage if ye want it. There's a hot fire in the grate an' food on the table. As you can see I've three livin' children who need tended."

"But no wife?" said Elspeth.

"I buried her two years since. Aye, an' one before her."

Elspeth could not afford to hesitate.

"I'll tend for you," she said. "In return I ask only food and shelter for me an' my child."

"I see you've no baggage."

"You see right, sir."

"Is it only work you're anxious for?" Jock Bennet said.

"What do you mean?"

"It's not a place in a man's bed, is it?"

"If that's your offer, sir, I'll thank you an' be on my way."

"Nah, nah," said the pitman. "That's *not* part of it. I want it clear from the start I'm lookin' for neither wife nor strife."

"An' I'm not after a husband," said Elspeth.

The girl-child hitched herself up on her father's back. She leaned her chin against his cheek and scowled at Elspeth.

"She's no' comin' home wi' us, is she?"

"Would ye not like that, Mousie?" the man said.

"We're no' needin' her, Daddy."

The pitman did not argue with his clinging daughter. Ignoring her complaint he peeped into the folds of the shawl at Mary Jean, who had fallen into a light, wheezing sleep.

"I hope she's not a bawler," he said.

"Not when she's warm and fed."

"How old is she, pray?"

"Twelve months." Elspeth lied to save further explanation. "My husband never looked upon her face. He was gone before she was born."

She told only half a lie. Mary Jean's father had died before her birth. But he had not been a drover and he had not been her husband. She seldom thought of Michael Blaven now. He belonged to an unclouded past, like a dream only dimly remembered.

Jock Bennet shrugged, unimpressed by such ordinary tragedy.

"Well, girl, if you've a mind to accept my offer," he said, "I'll give you room in my cottage in exchange for fair work."

"Daddy, we're no' *needin'* the likes o' her," the girl-child protested. "Sarah looks after us fine."

"Mousie, hold your damned tongue."

Elspeth said, "I'll accept, sir, an' gladly."

"Very well," said Jock Bennet. "Come wi' me."

"Where are we going?"

"To Nicol's, to the grocery shop."

Without another word the pitman stalked across the bridge, his daughter still clinging like a jackanapes to his back. He paused at the bridge-end just long enough to allow the group of miners an opportunity to admire his new acquisition.

"By God, Jock, ye've found a fair treasure there."

"She's too bloody good for a crabbit old devil like you."

"Man, I'd steal her for m'self – if it wasn't for the wife."

"Well, she's exactly what I've been lookin' for," Jock Bennet declared and, dismissing with a wave of his hand the great hoot of ribald laughter that went up from the men, strode on into the lane.

Trustingly Elspeth followed him into Placket which, in that raw March gloaming, seemed so warm and welcoming, and hid its pain so well.

* * *

From time to time Anna Sinclair might pretend that she was wasting away from unrequited love but the truth was that 'the arrangement' at Strachan Castle suited her down to the ground. Never before had she possessed the right to have things all her own way. The shape and proceeding of her life to that point, which seemed so strange to outsiders, was to Anna quite plain and simple.

She had been born to Gaddy Patterson and Coll Cochran, was sister of sorts to Elspeth, had been forced into marriage with Matt Sinclair, had become the mistress of the laird of Ottershaw, had conceived a child and, when her husband had finally shown his true colours and become an outlaw sought by the law officers, she had been absorbed into the Sinclair family and moved with them from Ottershaw to Strachan Castle as part of the domestic staff of the laird's brother, Gilbert.

It was – all that – no more than the drift of circumstances, and Anna did not question it or relate it to the outlandish things that had happened to her sister, Elspeth, who, in Anna's candid opinion, deserved all the trouble that she had brought upon herself.

The birth of her son gave Anna even more power. She fell to manipulating those around her secure in the knowledge that she would not be flung out, that because Gibbie was answerable to Randall and Randall, laird of Ottershaw, would never let her down, her place in the servants' hall was as safe as the Bank of England.

Gilbert Bontine had acquired the lease of the ramshackle little castle soon after Randall limped home from the war to claim the ancestral estates of Ottershaw for his own exclusive use. But a bargain had been struck between the brothers. Gibbie had been given Lachlan Sinclair, the grieve of Ottershaw, to aid him in developing the land around Strachan, in exchange for which favour he had agreed to tend the welfare of Randall's mistress, Anna, and the child that she would bear.

The beauty of it all, as far as Anna was concerned, was that nobody was quite sure which of the two men who had loved her had fathered the child, whether indeed she had given birth to a 'genuine' Sinclair or to a bastard son of Ottershaw. Anna was perfectly willing to let Bontines and Sinclairs fret over the mystery of her son's paternity. She firmly believed that he had been conceived during a matching with Randall Bontine for, if passion was a proper criterion for conception, little Robert Cochran Sinclair was most certainly the laird's natural son, whatever the parish register showed to the contrary.

In February, when it came time for the baby to be formally christened in the dismal kirk at Rothwell, Anna steadfastly refused to consider any name that might tip the delicate balance of uncertainty. She picked the nice unaffiliated name of Robert, added to it her father's surname, Cochran, to make the weight, and thus revealed no prejudice. To the Sinclairs, however, she confided her belief that Robert was really the son of Matt, her husband, while to Mr Gilbert she hinted that the blood of the Bontines flowed in the little chap's veins.

There were folk in Balnesmoor and Ottershaw who gleefully declared that Anna had been abandoned by the laird of Ottershaw and sent to stay with Gibbie at Strachan as a punishment for her sins. Anna did not see it in that light. Her days in the sun had been fleeting but Strachan was no jail and she was no more confined there than she had been in the hut on the hill of Drumglass or, indeed, in the cottage in the pine wood that she had shared with Matt. She still had her dreams and fantasies and being drawn into the bosom of a family as tightly knit as that of the Sinclairs, under the protection of the vague but benevolent Gilbert Bontine, allowed her to cherish the illusion that, one day, Sir Randall would send for her, marry her, make her into a fine lady with servants and carriages and closets full of silken gowns. To the realisation of that end Anna regarded her son, Robert Cochran Sinclair, as essential.

Over and above his value as a bargaining pawn, however, Anna adored Robbie for his own sake. She could not deny her feelings for her son and was surprised that motherhood had so swept her away. Though she did not plan that particular manipulation it was her honest worship of the child that gradually turned the Sinclairs' resentment into toleration and, in time, into guarded affection. The menfolk, in particular, were willing to forgive her anything for, in contrast to Aileen and Catriona Sinclair, Anna was quick-witted, bold and lively, and had the knack of warming men with her attentions.

Lachlan Sinclair had now faced up to the fact that his elder son had behaved foolishly and he was inclined to regard Anna as a victim of that foolish behaviour and not a partner in it. Besides, Lachlan badly needed a place to put his pride and a grandson was an ideal repository, and in the grieve Anna found an ally.

Strachan Castle, however, did at times seem very far away from Ottershaw, though it was no more than seven miles on dry roads, and there were moments when Anna felt herself to be under siege there, haunted by the past and its uncertainties and by things that she did not quite understand about the workings of her destiny and its connection with Elspeth.

In flickering winter nights, in the melancholy mists of dreary winter dawns, in the shadowless twilight of short winter afternoons, Anna sometimes imagined the lurking shades of retribution, saw Matt and Elspeth, Elspeth and Matt, twined, not like lovers but like wraiths.

The servants' hall at Strachan did not have the rigid demarcations of authority that were to be found in the halls of other grand mansions. The Bontines were an incongruous mixture of extravagance and parsimony and, in spite of Mistress Alicia's ambition to raise the castle to the equal of Ottershaw in Lennox society, the manning of the estate showed up the niggardly aspect.

Lachlan Sinclair was certainly in charge of all groundsmen, a group that consisted mainly of day-labourers hired by the piece from farms round about. Aileen had charge of the house, under Alicia's command, of course, and also attended to the cooking. Catriona was both day maid and nursery helper, though a poor wight, Edith Simmons, was employed to keep the Bontine brood from wreaking too much havoc about the place.

Anna's tasks were varied. She milked a bit in the evening, collected laundry for the boiling-tubs, trimmed candles and filled oil lamps and acted as a 'spider-chaser' when nothing else offered itself. She was also expected to 'assist' her father-in-law in the fields when he required it of her, though the long winter season had thrown up little work that a woman could do since the breaking of the ground was considered too heavy for a female.

Even so, Anna used this appointment to take time out of

doors where Aileen could not drop a broom or duster into her hand and steer her towards the dining-room or the downstairs parlour or even into the 'long hall' which had the proportions of a byre and was impossible to keep clean.

The Bontines lived in the 'east wing', which meant a warren of small apartments beyond the hall. The resident servants, that is the Sinclairs, had beds in neuks and presses about the kitchen, warm and snug enough in that well-fired region of the house. In fact the Sinclairs had the best foothold in the castle, with ready access to the yard's log and coal cellars, the water-pump and a privy fashioned out of stone and which flushed by a tug on a handle and was certainly the most modern appurtenance on the estate.

It was about ten of the clock of a crisp March morning when Anna, with Robbie slung in a shawl at her hip, popped out of the laundry door and headed in the direction of the privy. She did not visit there, however, but darted round the corner out of sight of the castle's windows, went on over the bridge that straddled the stream into the ten-acre field. Here a handful of cattle grazed on tumbledown grass and her father-in-law, quite alone, was pacing out a rectangular area which would be fenced for ploughing-out and re-seeding, come spring.

Though Lachlan never said as much, Anna suspected that he was not sorry to be back with his feet in the muck, an earth-labourer instead of a supervisor. He had left much of his dignity behind at Ottershaw, though he still held his shoulders square and had that stern solemn gaze to him. He had been handsome once, Anna supposed. He was handsome enough now for an old man of fifty-three or four. She could see traces of that handsomeness in Sandy, though, at eighteen, with his growth full, Sandy was not so tall as his father and not so broad in chest and shoulder as his brother Matt had been.

The baby bounced quiet and happy by Anna's hip. She hardly noticed the weight of him, though his limbs fleshed out more every day and his infant features had character and his hair was coming in thicker and darker in hue. She grinned and clucked at him as she opened the wicket gate into the field.

The ground underfoot was lumpy, cut up by cattle, but the frost had not come out of it yet and the sharp morning had laid a fine white fur upon the tussocks and coarse leys. Arm wrapped about Robbie, Anna trod carefully across the field.

Mr Sinclair, intent upon his calculations, did not notice the young woman at first. He wore a knee-length coat of brown whipcord and a fan-brimmed hat that had faded with weather from black to slate grey. The coat flapped about his shanks as he paced out the distance from one marker to the next. In both hands, like an offering, he carried a large white stone, the size and shape of a quartern loaf, and his breath made little white puffs in the cold clean air as he audibly counted out his steps.

Anna waited until he had reached the point of the rectangle, until he stooped and placed the stone upon the grass. He straightened, a mite stiffly, drew a long billet of paper from his pocket and, with a pencil from behind his ear, still muttering, jotted down yardage and made a calculation.

"Mr Sinclair." She still called him that, in spite of their intimacy. "Mr Sinclair, see who's here."

Cattle in a corner by the willows lifted their heads and blinked as if she had asked the question of them. Lachlan Sinclair turned. The muttering ceased immediately. He stuffed the paper away and hastened towards her.

Anna lifted the baby, shawl-wrapped, from her hip and held him up, a form of handling to which Robbie did not seem to object in the slightest. There was little enough of him exposed. In the swaddle of soft wools, only his eyes and the tip of his nose could be seen, but when he caught sight of his grandpa he became animated and excited, struggled, girned angrily, and craned out from Anna to greet the man.

"It's as well if you take him, Mr Sinclair," said Anna. "He'll not be content wi' me when he can have you to hold him."

Flattered, Sinclair untied the knot of the shawl at Anna's shoulder and swung the baby-bundle into his arms. Robbie blew a bubble, gave a milky hiccup then kicked his legs within the bindings to show his grandpa how he would pace a field in a year or two.

Mr Sinclair's cheeks creased; a smile.

"Have you started the wash?" he asked.

Anna answered, "I've built an' lit the fire an' filled the tub to the brim. The water'll take a while to boil on a cold day like this, though."

24

"Aye, but if it stays dry Mrs Sinclair will be anxious to see the spring wash begun."

It was as close as the formidable Sinclair dared come to a reprimand.

Anna knew all about the importance of the spring wash. God knows, there was hardly a clean kerchief left in cupboards and chests. Even her own bedding, in the boxed bed tucked between kitchen and stillroom, had a stale odour to it and, she suspected, might even harbour a flea or two.

March and early April, given dry days, would see a flowering of cloths and clothing on every lawn, hedge and bush. Even the autocratic Bontine children would be press-ganged into lugging baskets of laundry hither and thither and the evenings would be hot with the smell of flat-irons and smoothing stones. Anna, however, would limit her involvement as much as possible, except when it came to the ironing which was one domestic occupation that gave her pleasure.

"Robbie wanted to see his grandpa," Anna said, in a tone of sweet apology, as if household commands were miraculously issued by her son. "I'll go back in five minutes, I promise, Mr Sinclair."

Sinclair grunted then adjusted the baby against his shoulder while he did a shuffling dance and sang a snatch of a psalm tune to entertain him. Robbie hiccuped again, unimpressed.

"When will the strip be ready for the ploughin'?" Anna asked.

Sinclair broke off his song. "When the frost comes out."

"Are there strong horses t'rent hereabouts?"

Strachan did not possess one let alone a pair of the draught-horses that were needed for heavy ploughing. The work could be done with ponies but a light blade would not penetrate far into the soil and the resulting grass layer, however well sown, would not smother the weeds that lay hidden below.

So intent was he on romping about with Robbie that Mr Sinclair hardly heard Anna's question. In a year or so, when the wee chap was toddling, old Lachlan might get no work done at all.

Anna was not sure that it would matter if the fields remained untended, as they had been for decades. Mr Gilbert did not seem to need the revenue that the acres would bring in. He had departed from the age-old Bontine tradition of transforming property into pounds and had gone into banking.

Strachan had no rent book to speak of, four cottages, and a flour-mill hardly bigger than a toadstool, and a grazing-patch between the low road and the river which was leased for sheep, at a peppercorn rent, to one of the local tenants. Everybody knew, though, that Mr Gibbie had had his fair share of old Sir Gilbert's legacies and none of the servants doubted that they would be secure under Young Gibbie's protection for the rest of their lives.

"Robert," Lachlan Sinclair was saying to his grandson, "Robert was the name of a king of the Scots. He fought a great battle against the English, not ten miles from here. An' he beat them hollow, so he did. Will you be a brave warrior when you're grown, m' lad?"

The menfolk of Ottershaw, over whom Sinclair had ruled with rod of iron for so many years, would have been amazed at the change in the man, would have thought that grief instead of grandfatherhood had stolen his reason.

"He's a prince, Anna, is he not?"

"He is indeed, Mr Sinclair."

"I wonder if his father will ever see him?"

Anna's enjoyment of the morning diminished instantly. Lachlan's reference to his outlawed son – who dared not return home at peril of his life – had come unexpectedly. The grieve seldom mentioned Matt's name. Even Aileen had given up snivelling in corners at the thought of her lad driven out of Scotland into lifelong exile.

"He – he might," said Anna lamely.

"It would be a fine thing for us all to be together," said Mr Sinclair with a sigh.

"Aye," Anna diplomatically agreed. "Aye, it would."

Mercifully Robbie took a hand in the conversation and gave out that champing sound which meant he wanted all the attention and not just a part of it. Mr Sinclair discarded wishful thinking and bucked off like a thoroughbred to give the bairn a ride down to look at the cattle.

Anna did not follow him.

She watched, half smiling, and stretched her arms above her head and breathed deeply of the milder air that the sun had brought with it. She smelled the unthawing and, she thought, the first faint sappiness of the spring season unlocked after the long dour winter; then she turned her head and saw it.

The thing was black, glinting black, like a coffin carved from ebony, an image that rose in Anna's mind the moment she caught sight of it above the hedges that separated the low road from the field. It seemed hideously out of place in the bright, white morning. Its menace, and the fact that she did not know what it was or what its appearance signified, made her cry out under her breath and crouch down slightly as if to hide.

Sinclair had also stopped some fifty yards away, half-way between the thing and Anna. He too must have been startled by the carriage's abrupt appearance. He lowered Robbie against his chest and wrapped both arms about the baby in a gesture of protection.

Neither the grieve nor his daughter-in-law had heard the carriage approach, and the horses, high and handsome though they were, were hidden by the hedge. Only the raised, black-painted hood of the cabriolet was visible above the thorn. So out of place did that unique Frenchified vehicle seem on the low road that Anna, even as she recognised it, could not believe the evidence of her own eyes. The jingle of harness trappings came to her, the whinny of one of the horses, and then she saw a figure she could identify – Tom Tolland, James Simpson Moodie's steward and, this past six months or so, his keeper and his nurse.

Anna moved forward over the rutted ground until she stood behind her father-in-law who, having recognised Tolland too, did not hasten to greet the man, though grieve and steward had been acquaintances for many years.

"What – what can he want with us?" Anna whispered.

"Perhaps he brings us news of Matt."

"Of Matt?" said Anna, thinking that it was more likely to be news of Elspeth.

Once it became clear that James Moodie's story that his wife had been sent away to spend time with his sister was naught but a face-saving lie, there had been much speculation in Balnesmoor. Some claimed that Elspeth had gone chasing after Matt Sinclair. Anna did not subscribe to that calumny. Elspeth's childish infatuation with Matt had been long ago dispelled.

Anna could not understand why Elspeth had fled from Moss House where she had had everything that a woman could desire: servants, fine clothes, carriages and the devotion of a wealthy husband; yet Elspeth had torn herself from James Moodie, and from Balnesmoor, without a word to anyone. Moodie had gone quite mad with grief at the loss of his beloved wife and baby daughter. The grim, resolute, pragmatic Moodie had been turned by love into a pathetic idiot. Hard to swallow – yet true, as every gossip in the district could attest.

Now the cabriolet, which had been seen not at all upon the roads since autumn, had appeared on a string road below Strachan, and Tom Tolland, in his rusty black suit and Sabbath hat, was climbing down from it. It could only mean that an event of some magnitude had taken place, and Tolland brought news of it. Logically Anna thought of her sister, Mr Sinclair thought of his lost son – and both were afraid.

"Sinclair, do you not recognise me?" Tolland called out, taking off his hat and waving it.

"I see you, Tom Tolland. What brings you here?"

Bobbing behind the thorn, Tolland cried, "How do I get through this cursed hedge?"

Sinclair and Anna remained rooted in the centre of the field while the cattle, startled by the sound of a strange voice, louped away in a straggling line to the far side of the pasture where they congregated and swung round as if to make a stand against an unseen threat.

"Walk down a piece," Mr Sinclair called. "There's a stile of sorts yonder."

The hedge had been spread by the insertion of two stout posts with turves ramped against them on the lane side and a crossbar roped across their tops.

While Tolland waddled down the road in search of the entrance Mr Sinclair handed the baby back to his daughter-in-law and told her to return to the house.

"No, I will not," Anna retorted.

"It is not your business, Anna."

"How do you know it's not?"

Tolland had found the stile and was cautiously mounting it, the round black hat tipped to the back of his head.

Mr Sinclair frowned.

"It – it may be nothin'," he said, "but a sociable call."

"In which case there'll be no harm in me stayin'."

Robbie had fallen silent inside the swaddle. It was almost as if he was listening to the argument and had determined to take no part in it.

"Come, man, give me a hand," Tolland shouted.

Lachlan Sinclair, who was normally courteous, hurried off to extricate the plump steward from the thorns.

Anna followed. She could see the shape of the cabriolet and the horses through the hedge now and thought that she could even make out another person within the carriage. She lifted herself on tiptoe but had no clearer view and had to wait until Tolland was hoisted into the field and the grieve and the old steward picked over the grass to her.

Tolland had aged. He wore no wig under the hat and his sparse hair was snow-white. Though he was still on the round side, his features had sagged, and hung pale as dough upon the bones, his eyes circled with grey, as if he had not slept much all that long winter season.

Impetuously, Anna blurted out, "Who's that with you, Mr Tolland?"

The steward did not answer. He had never approved of Anna Sinclair, thought her a wild, dark-haired slut and no fit relative for the former mistress of Moss House.

Softly, sadly, Mr Sinclair said, "It's not about Matt, Anna."

Anna let out her breath but put no second question to the visitor from Balnesmoor. It was obvious by his manner, though, that Tolland had questions for her.

Wasting no time in asking politely after the health of the 'new arrival' or to peep into the shawl at the baby, Tolland said, "Have you heard word from her?"

"If you mean my sister," said Anna, "no, I have heard nothin'."

"Have you heard from your husband then?"

"He would not dare even t' send a letter," said Anna, "in case the Excise officers found it."

"Why do you ask these questions, Tom?" said Sinclair.

"Because I am instructit so to do."

"By your master?" said Sinclair.

"Aye."

"Is he himself again?" said Sinclair.

"He will never be himself again."

"But is he still as – as distressed as he was?" said Anna.

The last time she had clapped eyes on James Simpson Moodie he had been wandering about the roads like a lunatic, wailing and crying across the empty fields for Elspeth to return to him. He had been knocked off his mental pedestal by the shock of her departure and, Anna suspected, by the skein of events that had tangled murder to Moodie's weaving-mill at Kennart. Since then she had heard occasional news from the big houses of Balnesmoor and Ottershaw – though she was much more interested in the doings of the laird than the weaver – for Sandy made trips back to the villages when Mr Gilbert required a driver. But James Moodie had become reclusive and had not been seen about the mill or the parish these many months.

"No, he is better," said Tolland curtly.

It was known that most of the servants of Moss House had deserted the weaver mannie. Kerr was gone, and Betty. Even the cook had found another post, with Mr Eshner in the manse. Only Tolland had remained, loyal through the time of trial – and what Tolland knew of the truth he was not telling, not even to the Sinclairs.

"How is he better?" said Anna.

Mr Sinclair might chide her for her sharpness but she did not care. She could not forget how high-handed Tolland had been with her when Elspeth had been his mistress and she had been nothing but a humble dairy lass on Ottershaw. Now that the authority of James Moodie had been undermined, now that she was mother to a natural son of Ottershaw, she felt herself to be Tolland's equal.

"Tell us, Tom," Sinclair urged. "Whatever passes between us will not become gossip, I promise you."

"He has heard that she's in Stirling."

"Stirling!" Anna exclaimed. "What's she doin' there, so close to home?"

"Apparently she was employed in the bleachfields."

"I thought Elspeth had more sense," said Anna.

"Mr Moodie issued handbills invitin' information," said Tolland. "This is a result."

"It would be your idea, Tom, was it not?"

"What if it was? We've paid out many guineas to charlatans and frauds; also to some honest folk who did bring us word of the mistress."

"We knew nothin' of this," said Anna. "Why did you not tell us?"

"Why should you be told?" Tolland snapped.

"Because I'm her sister, her kin."

The sneer on Tolland's lips informed Anna that nothing had changed. The pompous steward still regarded her as inferior to her righteous sister. The knowledge rankled sore. What did she care where Elspeth had gone to? She, Anna, was the last person in the world that Elspeth would come to in time of trouble.

Tolland said, "I'm here under instruction. It's not my wish to involve you, Mistress Cochran."

"Sinclair. My name is Sinclair."

"Aye, whatever your name may be, madam—"

Lachlan Sinclair intervened. "Come, Tom, do not be so sharp wi' the lass. She has lost a husband as well as a sister."

Tolland sniffed, screwed the scorn off his face with an effort and pressed on. "Since the mistress has never been far awa' from us, since she has been seen in Glasgow as well as Stirling, Mr Moodie believes she's bein' keepit away by persuasion."

"By persuasion?" said Sinclair. "By whom?"

"By your son."

Sinclair's nostrils flared. For an instant Anna thought that he might boil over with temper and run the steward off Strachan land.

"My son's sought by the law for a crime that would mean his neck in a noose," said Sinclair thinly. "Tell your master, Mr Tolland, that my Matt's not stupid enough to tarry in Glasgow or in Stirling just for the sake of a pretty face. *No, they are not together.*"

"Can you be sure? Have you heard as much?"

31

"Damn you, Tom Tolland, fine well you know I've heard not a word from Matt. He's gone far away. Surely you canna believe that he would do otherwise?"

Stepping closer, Tom Tolland said, "It's not me, Lachlan. It's Mr Moodie. He's not sound in his faculties. He has it fixed in his head that Matt an' his wife are in hidin' together."

"That is, indeed, madness."

"It is, it is," Tolland agreed. "But it's a reasonable sort of madness. Better than the lunacy of the autumn months when I feared he would do himself an injury. At least he has hopes now." The steward placed a hand on the grieve's arm. "I tell you this, though, Lachlan, if the mistress does not return soon it'll be the death of him an' no mistake."

"Is he so far gone, Tom?"

"The apartments in Moss House have all been sealed. He gave me rantin' orders just before Christmas, orders which I was compelled to obey. If he takes it into his noddle to dismiss me, he'll be left quite alone. Do ye see?"

Sinclair nodded sympathetically.

Tolland went on, "He has shrunk back into the wee room behind the stairs. He spends his days there, an' his nights. He sleeps in a cot not fit for a stable boy. Sups his food there too, though he hardly pecks enough to keep a sparrow alive."

"An' drinks his brandy, I'll warrant."

"Aye, in quantity," Tolland confessed. "I tried to bring in a doctor but he would have none of it. Besides, what good would a sawbones do him? It's obvious he is deranged in his wits."

"Can he not be repaired?"

"How can you repair a broken heart?" said Tom Tolland.

Anna spoke up. "What does it have to do wi' us, Mr Tolland? We can no more cure the weaver Moodie than you can."

"Have you no idea where she might be?"

"None," said Anna. "She has no kinfolk to run to."

"What of Coll Cochran's other children?"

"Elspeth never met them. I doubt if she even knows they exist."

Sinclair said, "What of the mill, Tom?"

"The business ticks over," Tolland answered. "Mr Rudge

an' Scarf manage it between them. Some other enterprises too. I took the liberty of makin' an approach to them to do so."

"Do they know the true state of affairs?"

"You can keep nothin' from Rudge," said Tolland. "He'll have his skin off the top of the profits; Scarf too. But they buy an' sell an' scratch out markets."

"An' the sheep? The Cheviots?"

"The Macfarlanes look after them well enough."

"How long can it go on thus?"

Tolland shrugged. "Until Elspeth returns."

"What if she never returns?"

"Until Mr Moodie dies."

It was Anna who put the question. The words were out of her mouth before she even realised that she had formed the thought. "If the weaver dies who'll inherit his wealth?"

Tolland seemed taken aback by the question, Lachlan Sinclair dismayed by the girl's mendacity.

"His sisters, I suppose," Tolland said.

"Not Elspeth?"

"Not if she canna be found," said Tolland.

Embarrassed by the turn of the conversation and its implications, Lachlan Sinclair took the steward by the arm and guided him towards the stile once more, saying, "If you've come down from Balnesmoor just for this, Tom, it's been a fruitless journey. Will you have a taste o' something in the kitchens before you return home?"

Tolland said, "He is with me."

Sinclair glanced towards the cabriolet. "Is he? He's given no sign of his presence."

"Nor will he," said Tom Tolland.

"Can he not speak?"

"He's ashamed," Tom Tolland said. "Shame keeps him silent, I think."

The men strolled out of earshot. Anna did not follow. She had heard enough to set her imagination spinning like a teetotum.

Robbie girned in her arms for attention but for once Anna was not all devoted to pleasing her infant. Abstractedly she *wheeshed* him, knotted the shawl ends at her shoulder and lowered the baby to her side. She turned and walked up the sweep of the field, abreast of the cattle herd, until she could see over the hedge to the narrow road and make out the weaver. He was hunched within the shelter of the carriage hood, haggard, unshaven and as shabby as an old tinker. He did not seem to notice her there on the slope. He crouched over, hands clasped in his lap as if he was praying, praying for a miracle, for Elspeth to materialise before him, all loving and forgiving.

Sinclair and Tolland still chatted by the stile. Anna eyed them with vague concern. Were they talking of money? Were they too speculating on what might happen if the weaver mannie died without a notorised will? Anna could not grasp the value of paper holdings. But she could clearly visualise the mill at Kennart, the mansion of Moss House and, being a drover's daughter, the fat flocks that roamed the three-hundred acres of hill land that ran west from Dyers' Dyke.

Land, property, grazing stock: James Moodie was near as rich as Randall Bontine. If he died before his enterprises could be ruined by pilfering and neglect the inheritor would be fabulously wealthy. If he died before Elspeth could be traced, however, it would all vanish in the stroke of a pen, would be gone to sisters who had abandoned Balnesmoor and their brother years and years ago.

The prospect of such injustice hallowed Anna's greed. It made her fantasy seem righteous, brought sudden ghastly concern for Elspeth's welfare. Somehow her sister must be run to earth, persuaded to return to claim her inheritance and, out of respect for the family tie, to hoist Anna out of humble service and lift her and her son on to a plane equal to that of the laird of Ottershaw.

Wherever her sister had gone to ground, Anna told herself, as she walked back towards the castle with Robbie at her hip, she must be found.

On that March morning Elspeth's loss had become Anna's loss too.

The courtship – the seduction – began within a week of Elspeth's arrival in Jock Bennet's humble cottage.

The Bennets' house stood apart from the torn canvas shacks of the out-workers and the rows of permanent stone-built dwellings of the other coal-hewers. It had a little patch of its own on the west side of the Rutherford burn, a tidal channel five or six feet wide which served as a communal sewer. At one time, so Jock Bennet told her, it had been an oversman's house and they were lucky to get it. Mr Hector Fotheringham, owner of the lands of Placket, had acquired the accommodations several years ago when the Preston Island pit closed down.

Regardless of the size of the dwelling or how many people crowded into it, rent of a shilling a week was charged. The sum was deducted from the fortnightly wage by 'Snippets' Smith, the Abbeyfield's paymaster. That, however, was the only piece of money taken at source, for the manager of the Abbeyfield, Mr Keir Bolderon, was vehemently opposed to truck systems of any kind and adhered to the philosophy that a man got in his hand what he had earned on his knees.

Jock Bennet also informed Elspeth, on more than one occasion, that wages on the Abbeyfield were the highest in the kingdom, at least for deep-seam men, and that a collier could do no better in hard cash anywhere. Such 'lectures' on the benefits of labour were part of Jock Bennet's wooing of the pretty stranger, though Elspeth did not realise what the collier intended until his persuasion had taken effect.

Living cheek by jowl with a parcel of strangers was, initially, difficult for Elspeth. The cottage was no smaller than the sheep hut on the Nettleburn where she had been born and brought up but the Bennet children were lively and quarrelsome and there was a general air of confusion which made the place seem, at times, as cramped as a cattle pen.

Elspeth and Mary Jean were allocated a corner. A canvas curtain draped from a rope provided a modicum of privacy. Elspeth's bed was on the floor. Mary Jean slept in a wooden cot which had served the Bennet children until each in turn outgrew it. Pegs in the wall held clothing and, as soon as she acquired a little money of her own, Elspeth intended to buy a tin box to hold her small belongings. The trouble was that she had no belongings now. The black-hearted carrier had stolen them and she and Mary Jean had nothing to call their own except the clothes on their backs.

No cheat, Jock Bennet lived up to his part of the bargain.

He fed Elspeth and her baby, gave them shelter and a place by his hearth. But he did not dole out one farthing in cold cash for that had not been part of their 'contract'. Sarah was charitable enough to unearth some soft cloths which Elspeth boiled and trimmed to make napkins for her daughter but, that apart, nothing was brought forth to make her existence more comfortable. In her desperation it had not occurred to Elspeth that once she had secured shelter and nourishment the absence of any sort of income, no matter how meagre, would accentuate the fact that she had passed down into poverty.

To rub it in – though Elspeth was not sufficiently cynical to read Jock Bennet's motive – every other Sunday the collier paid out 'wages' to his son and daughters around the communal table. It was quite a ceremony. The children gave no sign that the ritual was new to them and not a normal thing for Daddy to do. Elspeth was obliged to watch and, in spite of herself, coveted the children's shillings.

From the purse in his trousers Jock Bennet would tip out a heap of silver coins, would announce with pride that he and Mouse had hauled that money from the bowels of the earth in the course of ten shifts.

"Fifty-two shillin's," he would declare, stirring the pile with his fingers. The children would sit forward in their chairs like orphans waiting to be fed. "An' Davy's twelve. Amazin' how it mounts up, eh? Sixty-four shillin's."

Elspeth would pretend that she was impervious to the sight of the money spread out among the crocks. But she could not keep her eyes off it, transforming it mentally into new boots and a new light dress for Mary Jean, a little lace bonnet, and a pair of underdrawers to replace the patched and scratchy items she wore now.

"Two shillin's for you, Davy."

"Thank ye, Daddy."

"Four for Mousie."

"I'm goin' to buy ribbon an' a pie," Mouse would declare smugly. "An' put the rest away for rainy days."

"An' for my wee Sarah, a shillin' to spend how she likes."

The performance was skilled enough to have been rehearsed. Elspeth saw with her own eyes where the money went. It rankled her that Mouse would fritter so much on geegaws and cheap trinkets or that Davy would succumb to outrageous gluttony and fill a whole bag with sticky cakes and sweetmeats up at Nicol's shop and, in an orgy of stuffing, would devour the lot in one sitting.

Elspeth was, of course, given money. Jock would press the big, solid, silver coins into her hand, pat her on the shoulder and tell her what he fancied to eat, admonish her not to be rash in her purchases but to shop wisely – and to return to him any money that was left over.

In the confusion of Mr Nicol's shop in Placket Elspeth was tempted to skin from the housekeeping a penny or two for herself. She resisted. She was fearful that Mr Bennet's trust was naught but a test of her honesty, that if she succumbed to pilfering he would throw her back on the open road.

The only crumbs that fell from the table of the Bennets' apparent affluence came the way of Mary Jean. Sarah would share her sweet things with the baby throughout the week and seemed, indeed, to budget for such acts of charity. To Elspeth came nothing that would stick to her fingers, nothing that could be secretly accumulated and put to use to replenish worn-out clothes or provide the basis of another 'travelling fund'.

"By God, Mousie, we did well this fortnight, did we not?"

"Aye, Daddy, so we did."

"Sixty-eight shillin's we took."

"I'm buyin' beads an' almond cake, an' yon pretty pink lace hankie in Mr Nicol's box."

"Well, ye'll be needin' some extra," Jock Bennet would say magnanimously. He would select a shiny shilling from the heap and hold it up for Mouse to snap away with her tiny fingers. "You workit hard for that, Mousie. An' ye deserve it."

March passed into April, April into a warm and windy May. Pay-night succeeded pay-night. The pattern of days was pegged to the Abbeyfield's shifts, an hour before dawn until dusk, with the notorious 'Saturday shift' to end the working week.

Elspeth was not idle. She worked hard to make herself needed by the Bennet family. She spent all day on chores. Twice in the week she cleared out the furniture and scrubbed the cottage from corner to corner. She wrestled with the quantity of soiled clothes that seemed to accumulate in direct proportion to her ability to keep them clean. She devoted hours to preparing evening meals, a hot dish supplemented with the products of griddle and baking-oven. Her efforts were appreciated, but not applauded. So weary were Mouse, Davy and the father of the flock on their return from the pit that it hardly seemed to matter what they stuffed into their mouths or that their blankets were clean and fresh-smelling and the cottage was whisked free of that clinging grit which found its way into everything. Jock Bennet preferred ale to soup. Mouse complained that the bread tasted too much of soda and was not as 'stiff', whatever that meant, as the loaves sold by Mr Nicol. Davy ate what was put before him, every dish drenched in either vinegar or warm treacle.

With solemn little Sarah to assist her, Elspeth could wade through a day's work in five or six hours. If she had not been beset by anxiety about her continued penury and a lingering fear that, even here, James might track her down, she might have settled to enjoy her periods of leisure, particularly in the balmy days of young summer. Settle, however, she could not. She was obsessed by the need to justify herself to Jock Bennet, to win his respect for her qualities as a servant. She remained oblivious to the fact that Jock Bennet needed and wanted no servant, that the hearth and the table were not the hub of his existence and that, to the pitman, all that mattered was the daily haul.

All along, from the moment of first meeting, Jock Bennet had wanted her as a stable-mate for Mouse. He might have taken Sarah below ground with him; it was not decency or conscience that prevented him. She was old enough, was Sarah, to earn a shilling or two. But Jock Bennet wanted more than a pennyweight. He needed a strong, sensible woman to haul out for him. Elspeth Patterson was perfect for the job.

"Fifty-four shillin's. Plus twelve from Davy."

By now Elspeth had forgotten that her father, James Simpson Moodie, would spend that much on a vest or a cravat or a pair of silver-buckled shoes without turning a hair; that such a sum would hardly buy one of the Cheviot rams that cropped the pastures along the ridge of Drumglass. Wealth had become relative: a shilling was a fortune; a half-crown a king's ransom.

"Mr Bennet?"

"What is it, girl?"

"I – I need – I need somethin' of my own."

"What's this?"

"Sixpence. Sixpence each week will do."

Arms square upon the table, making a little fortress about his hard-earned cash, the pitman stared incredulously at Elspeth.

"Somethin' of your own?"

"I must buy – things. To wear."

"Did Sarah not lend you thread?"

"I've nothin', Mr Bennet."

"You had nothin' when I took you on, Patterson. Now you have a roof, a warm bed, food in your belly. Both you an' the bairn."

"I'm grateful, Mr Bennet, believe me. But I need—"

"Tell me, Patterson, d'you think ye earn it?"

"I do what's required."

Mouse gave a squeak of derision. "Sarah can do all that, so she can."

"Are you askin' me for a wage as well as keep?" said Mr Bennet.

"If I had anythin', I would not ask. But—"

"Aye, the money has turned you, has it?" Jock Bennet said. "You suppose it's easy come by because I'm generous wi' it."

"Easy come by!" Mouse squeaked again.

"No, no. I know how hard it's come by. But what more can I do?" said Elspeth. "I need a few pence, that's all."

"Work for it, then."

"I do work for it."

"Och, you're no idler," said Jock Bennet, "an' you're worth the price o' feed t' me. But you're not worth more."

"How can I earn—"

Suddenly, shockingly, she saw what he had led her to.

She stepped back from the table and glanced at Mary Jean who was crawling about, quite happily, in a pile of blankets under the dresser, playing with a broken string of wooden beads that she had found under Mouse's pillow.

"I'll take ye below," Jock Bennet said.

He did not meet her eye. None of them did, not even Mouse.

"Below?"

"Into the seams. I can use another pair o' arms t' haul for me, since you press for it."

Jock Bennet was beginning to make it sound as if she, Elspeth, had suggested that he find work for her in the depths of the pit, almost as if she had begged him to take her below ground.

"What about Mary Jean?" she protested. "I canna take her down with me."

"Sarah will tend her," Jock Bennet said. "Sarah's a sensible lassie."

Elspeth could not deny that, young though she might be, Sarah was the 'sanest' of all the Bennets and had a certain affection for little Mary Jean which was returned in kind by her daughter.

"Who'll keep the house clean?"

"Sarah kept it fine," Mouse put in, "afore you came."

In her weeks on the edge of the Abbeyfield Elspeth had observed much but had learned surprisingly little about the nature of the underground labour. She realised, of course, that it was bullying work, physically demanding and very punishing to the weak. She had a sketchy idea of its routines, acquired from conversations between Mouse and her father and from Davy's complaints about the grinding monotony of tugging a rope on a ventilator flap for twelve hours each day.

Among the women who crowded Mr Nicol's shop there was evidence of the cost of such labour: chronic coughs, rheumatic spines and gout-swollen hands and feet, wounds healed and unhealed, scars and deformities hidden under stoicism and by gaudy scarves and skirts and shawls. Every trade had its 'warpings', though, and Elspeth had paid no particular heed to details of the colliers' craft since she did not remotely associate herself with it.

Money, the fortnightly yield, glinted on the table.

She could associate herself with that, however, with colliers' pay, the rake, the take, the haul: present comfort and future security.

"I – I know nothing of diggin' coal," she said.

"Diggin' coal," Davy hooted. "Women dinna dig. Men dig."

"Women haul," said Mouse.

"Haul?"

"Bring out the coals the hewer cuts. In basket loads, on sleds," Jock Bennet explained.

He fixed his eyes on Elspeth, in contrast to his previous shyness. He sensed that she was interested, that, like a river fish, she was nosing at the bait.

Capitulation was swift. The pitman would never know what, apart from the sight of the money, swayed her.

"How much would I be paid?" said Elspeth.

"One tenth o' my take."

"How much would that amount to?"

"With two haulers," Jock Bennet said, "I can bring out eighty shillin's in the fortnight."

"Eight would be my share then?"

"Sometimes more."

Eight shillings for herself. Eight shillings to spend on clothes for Mary Jean. Eight shillings to divide up, to budget, to save and to spend. First she would buy a cotton dress, then stout new boots, then new underdrawers; then she would begin to put away, say, four shillings every week, and in a year would have a fat nest-egg of a hundred shillings or more, a 'travelling fund' worth the name.

"One tenth of the take, an' my keep?" Elspeth said.

"By God, lady, you're the sharp one."

"You said I was just what you were lookin' for, remember?"

The pitman grinned. "Food but not clothes."

"I'll clothe from my own earnin'."

"You'll have to work hard."

"I'm not shy o' hard work, Mr Bennet."

He hesitated then reached across the money pile and offered Elspeth his hand. She shook it, sealing the bargain.

"Done?" she said.

"Done," Jock Bennet said.

And Elspeth Patterson Moodie, mistress of Moss House and wife of the wealthiest weaver in the Lennox, became that day a collier's mate.

TWO

A Word to the Wise

Whatever it was that Keir Bolderon believed in, apart from the value of capital investment, he would not at that time have subscribed to the theory that he was being guided along life's highway by anything as intransigent as fate.

Manager of the coal-pit on the Abbeyfield Mr Bolderon might be but he was not yet master of his destiny. Chance had long ago inaugurated a shaping process and, whether he knew it or not, Keir Bolderon's future had been cast in the melting-pot and, by the spring of 1816, two years after Elspeth Patterson first wandered into Placket, had at last begun to assume what would become its final, irrevocable form.

None of this mystical nonsense mattered a hoot to Mr Bolderon. Indeed, if Nemesis had writ the names of her protagonists in fiery letters in the sky, most of them would have meant nothing to the mining engineer. He was concerned with policy and practice, with squaring a situation which, not for the first time, seemed to be all at sixes and sevens and left him precariously dependent upon another man's whim. The 'other man' was Mr Hector Fotheringham, heritor of the lands of Placket, owner of the mineral rights to the Abbeyfield, and partner in the business of digging and marketing coal.

Keir Bolderon heartily detested Mr Fotheringham. He suspected that the antipathy was mutual. Both Bolderon and Fotheringham were, however, gentlemen, though of markedly different stamp, and hid their true feelings well, particularly as each remained in need of the other to help wrest profits from the haggard shore of the Forth. Restraint had led to reticence and, during their infrequent meetings to discuss matters of business, conversation hardly rose above a murmur. Only Margaret Fotheringham, Hector's saintly wife, showed any animation over the supper table, and the men were content to let her prattle on inconsequentially until the stroke of ten signalled her bedtime.

Margaret, who longed to please, bade her guest goodnight, curtsied to her husband and retired to her bedchamber where, she claimed, she would 'meditate' for half an hour upon *Christian Truths*, a recent work by Ebenezer M'Gilp, the Edinburgh divine. Bolderon could well imagine that a half-hour spent with a theological book would be the high-water mark of Margaret's day.

Margaret Fotheringham was a woman of exquisite beauty, with hair like spun gold and skin like alabaster, yet Keir Bolderon, who normally enjoyed the company of ladies, had never experienced the slightest twinge of desire for her. Her beauty, like her piety, seemed bloodless. Three children indicated that Margaret and Hector had on occasion put chastity in the closet, though Keir Bolderon preferred to believe that the little heirs of Placket had been found among bulrushes or delivered in napkins dangling from the beaks of swans; the mating habits of such ethereal panjandrums as the Fotheringhams were beyond the scope of his imagination.

At thirty-eight Keir Bolderon was a fine specimen of manhood. He had thick dark brown hair which needed no tongs to enhance it and dark brown eyes which, if not perplexed by some problem or other, had just a hint of roguishness in them and certainly a glint of humour. His features were broad and regular and, to go by the lore of tavern and croft, the cleft in the middle of his chin hinted that he was unusually virile. On the whole, Mr Bolderon had little to complain about when he squinted into the looking-glass on top of his dressing-table. But Keir Bolderon paled in comparison with Mr Hector Fotheringham whose chiselled features and unblemished brow elevated him to a realm of male beauty that most women found irresistible and that most men, Bolderon among them, found repulsive.

Such an ideal couple as the Fotheringhams required an ideal receptacle, and Monksfoot Priory was all of that. Sheltered by sycamores and stately elms it nestled on a promontory east of St Austin's Bay and provided uncluttered views across the river to the parklands of the Grange, the saltpans of Bo'ness and the dim, blue, dimpled hills of the Pentlands dipping towards Edinburgh.

From the lawn below the south façade Mr Fotheringham could enjoy the sight of keel-boats and collier brigs plying the trade that nicely topped up his income from rents and leases. Now and again he was treated to a glimpse of a spanking-new steamship from the yard at Kincardine, the *Morning Star*, say, as it puttered between Alloa and Leith. Though he professed otherwise, Hector Fotheringham did not understand the basic mechanical principles by which steamships were propelled. In them, however, he recognised a future in which he must have a share.

If the prospect of river traffic stimulated the gentleman of Monksfoot he was careful to ensure that his domestic estate was not tainted by too close a contact with the trappings of commercialism. Piers and lading quays were not permitted on the peninsula and diligent planting of shrubs screened out the grubby cottages that marred the half-moon curve of the bay. Nonetheless, from one shady corner of the garden, close by the old sundial, Mr Fotheringham could not help but see something of commercial import, a sight that made his heart shrink within his breast – the ruins of the pit that had once graced Preston Island.

Silhouetted against the fish-skin shimmer of the tidal flats, the ruins served to remind Mr Fotheringham that clay and water could devour money faster than even steamboats could haul it in, that mineral speculation could bring a fellow to ruin faster than whisky, politics or the gaming tables.

Keir Bolderon, manager and partner, did not share the landowner's caution. He was brimful of promises and blandishments, siren songs to which Mr Fotheringham tried to turn a deaf ear.

Anyone who branded Keir Bolderon a mere prattling fool, however, was much mistaken. Bolderon had taken on operation of the Abbeyfield in the middle of a lease period after the previous appointee, a slack and scurrilous rogue named Agnew, had all but brought it to ruin. Agnew had finally absconded by dead of night, taking all the ready cash, including the fortnight's wage packet, with him. For the sake of putting the pit immediately into production Mr Fotheringham had been forced to find a substitute for Agnew rather quickly, and Keir Bolderon had been on his doorstep, so to speak, almost before Agnew had ridden over the hill.

Bolderon was available. Bolderon had letters of recommendation as to his ability and his honesty from no less a personage than Lord Mulgrew. Bolderon was on the spot and, then as now, full of extravagant promises. He had driven a hard bargain, though, by demanding not salary or fee for his services but a share of the pit's net monthly profits. Mr Fotheringham had reluctantly agreed to Bolderon's demands. But the heritor of Placket had a memory that would shame an elephant and had not forgotten the man's impertinence, even if the transaction had proved to be of benefit in the long run.

Monksfoot's dining-room was situated in the basement. The vaulted cellar was almost all that remained of the original priory for three generations of Fotheringhams had modified and 'improved' the building to conform with the popular view of antiquity. Even the cellar had been tampered with, the fireplace embellished with facings of new Italian marble carved with plump cherubim whose bottoms blushed in the glow of the good Scotch coals that growled in the hearth below.

The supper, though, had been no better than adequate and the wine was an inferior claret fished from a tub in the back of the butler's pantry.

As soon as the butler had supervised the clearing of the table – a massive piece of Elizabethan oak – Keir Bolderon braced himself and got down to business.

"I trust, sir, you'll not think it premature," he began, "if I enquire as to your intention in respect of the Abbeyfield?"

"Oh, I have no intention, as you put it, Bolderon, no intention at all."

Keir Bolderon was used to the heritor's slippery ways. He pressed on undaunted. "Coal digging is a sluggish process and I feel it's incumbent upon me to remind you, Mr Fotheringham, that the lease runs out next year."

"I am aware of that fact, Mr Bolderon."

"Boring operations must be put under way soon, if—"

"*What* operations?"

Fotheringham was being deliberately obtuse. Bolderon had

submitted several reports on his plan to discover fresh seams and to expand the line of existing ones.

"To chart new seams," Keir Bolderon said patiently.

"The Abbeyfield is a veritable warren of seams."

"Only down to twenty-six fathoms, sir."

"Is that not deep enough for you, Bolderon?"

"The seams are almost worked out. They'll yield great coal only for a limited period."

"What evidence do you have that there is coal below that depth?" said Hector Fotheringham.

"None. But my instinct tells me that we have not had the best out of the bearing strata."

"Thomas Rance's 'instinct' tells him that the site is finished," said Hector Fotheringham.

Thomas Rance was the Abbeyfield's oversman. He had been found and hired by Keir Bolderon who could not disparage Rance's judgement without bringing his own into question. Fotheringham had snared him rather cleverly. Bolderon hesitated. He had to tread with care. He did not wish to antagonise the heritor of Placket at this early stage in negotiations. It galled him, though, that he had to tackle the fellow as if he was an opponent and not a partner.

Seven years ago Keir Bolderon had been so desperate to obtain a piece of the lease that he had not given due regard to the small clauses in the document. He had sunk his own savings into the pit to make it yield profitably on the assumption that Mr Fotheringham would retain him as manager and sharing partner at the end of the seven-year period. Now it was beginning to seem as if the heritor might discard him.

"Thomas Rance is not a manager. He's not paid to take responsibility for expansion schemes," said Bolderon.

"Is Rance not a sound and experienced man?"

"Indeed, indeed he is. But what he has given you, sir, is only an opinion."

"And what is it that you have given me, Bolderon?"

It was he, not Fotheringham, who had organised river transport to tap the Edinburgh markets. It was he, not Fotheringham, who had drummed up the capital vitally required to repair the vents and drainage systems and to replenish the stock of dray-horses. To accomplish all of this in short order

Keir Bolderon had pledged away percentages of his share of the profits. Did bloody Fotheringham now expect him to finance exploration without the assurance of a new contract at the end of it?

Keir Bolderon said, "I'm suggesting, sir, that the modest cost of exploration might repay itself tenfold if bearing seams can be accurately charted."

"Good Lord, Bolderon! Surely you cannot expect me to throw money into expensive schemes on nothing more substantial than your instinct." Fotheringham shook his head. "My father, God rest him, had the best out of the Abbeyfield. He extracted only what could be readily redeemed, lightly hauled and sold in Alloa, without all this unseemly clamour for a city market and carping for costly machinery."

"Your father, sir, with all due respect, had miners bonded to his service," Keir Bolderon said. "Slaves, in other words."

"Idle blackguards they were too."

"They are not idle now, sir, I assure you."

"Indeed they are not, not at the wages you see fit to pay them. Highest rate in all the land, so I'm informed."

"Highest rate for the finest colliers."

"Balderdash!" Fotheringham exclaimed. "I do not believe the myth that claims coal-hewing is a trade into which a man must be born. In my book colliers are not special people."

It was all Keir Bolderon could do to keep his temper. What did this pampered provincial lairdie know of the brutal labour of the pits, of labour of any kind? To Bolderon's knowledge he had never set foot below ground.

Bristling, Keir Bolderon said, "*My* colliers *are* special people, Mr Fotheringham. Few men not born to it would dare work the base seams of the Abbeyfield. Why, most of the colliery owners in Scotland would poach our crews if they could."

"In which case, may I ask, why do the crews stay?"

"Because they are loyal, sir."

"And grossly overpaid?"

Never before had Keir Bolderon heard Fotheringham express such candid opinions. In evading the issue of the new lease Hector Fotheringham had revealed himself with startling clarity. There was no enlightenment in Monksfoot, it seemed, Christian or otherwise.

Keir Bolderon said, "I came to talk of new winnings, Mr Fotheringham, not of old scores."

"What exactly do you want of me, Bolderon?"

"Permission to employ a company of master borers."

"What would these so-called 'master' borers do – apart from soaking me for money in fees?"

"Sink a line of holes to discover the depth and direction of new seams of coal," Keir Bolderon answered.

"Can you not podge up a crew to undertake the work?"

"No, Mr Fotheringham. I do not have the equipment or the expertise."

"If coal *is* discovered, I suppose that will mean the expense of digging new shafts?"

"Not necessarily," said Keir Bolderon. "We might be able to reach the new seams through existing tunnels. In addition there is the old, closed shaft – the Dead Man – which might, by modest repairs, be restored to use."

"It all sounds so terribly – fraught, Bolderon."

"Fraught?"

"Expensive."

Keir Bolderon bit his lip. It infuriated him not to be able to tell if the heritor of Placket really understood the principles of coal-mining or if his indifference was calculated to throw the new lease into confusion.

"I must know soon, sir, if the work is to be costed."

Smiling, Hector Fotheringham said, "Mining has been done here for three hundred years, since first the abbots put spade to turf. I do not think, Bolderon, that we need rush headlong into wild speculations. Let us proceed circumspectly."

"Boring is best done in summer."

"Each year brings a summer."

Mr Fotheringham got to his feet. The meeting was over. Nothing had been decided. No positive conclusion had been reached. Keir Bolderon was not one step further forward. He too rose from his chair, fingers clenched by his sides lest he succumb to the temptation to take the beautiful Hector Fotheringham by his beautiful white neck and shake sense into him.

As Fotheringham escorted the manager towards the steps that led from the cellar to the ground-floor hallway, the heritor

48

said casually, "Of course, it might spur me somewhat if there was evidence."

"Evidence?"

"That these fat new seams exist."

Keir Bolderon hesitated, a foot on the bottom step. He was shorter in stature than the heritor of Placket and he lifted himself deliberately on to the step so that, for once, he would not have to look up to the man.

"What if I find evidence?" Bolderon said. "What if I discover a layer of new coal? Will you then invest in the cost of line boring?"

"I might very well do so, yes."

"So, sir, you are not against boring in principle?"

"Find coal how you will, Bolderon."

"Providing the finding does not cost you money?"

The remark was tart enough to sting Fotheringham. For a fleeting moment there was anger in his hazy blue eyes and a dusky flush marred the purity of his complexion. He regained control of himself swiftly, however, and placed an affable hand on Bolderon's shoulder.

"Rest assured, Mr Bolderon, that I will not let your enterprise go to waste."

The promise was riddled with ambiguities, but Keir Bolderon did not press for clarification. He had the feeling that he would wring no more change from Hector Fotheringham that night.

Servants were all decently abed, for the hour was late, and the heritor of Placket opened the front door for his guest with his own fair hand but, after bidding the manager a good night, closed it again rapidly to prevent vapours from the workings from stealing into his house.

Keir Bolderon stood on the stoup for a minute or so listening to the rattle of bolts and chains as Fotheringham made his place secure, then, with a shrug, he filled his lungs with sweet fresh air.

He was relieved to be out of the stuffy basement chamber and felt weary with the effort of badgering the elusive Fotheringham into making decisions. He trudged around the gravel path as if he was emerging from a back-breaking shift in the seams and not from supper with a gentleman. Sometimes he wondered if the hard but simple life of a working collier would not be preferable to what he did now. Sometimes he wondered if the ungrateful devils who toiled in the tunnels ever spared a thought for the tribulations of their manager. He doubted it greatly. Colliers spared no thought for anyone but themselves. They lived from week to week, from pay-night to pay-night, with no regard for what tomorrow might bring or for the efforts that he and his kind put into securing their future employments.

The grooms had left a lighted lantern by the stable door and by its glow Keir Bolderon untethered his horse and led it along the path that backed the Priory and on to the track that wound away through the shrubbery to the road. Once the road was reached Keir Bolderon mounted and set the horse to a walk. He was in no hurry to be home; he enjoyed the fresh March night and wished to clear his head of the abysmal fumes of Fotheringham's cheap claret.

Riding on the east wind Mr Bolderon fancied he could hear the shriek of the winding-rope and the suspirations of the vent-shaft's furnace. He loved the sounds of industry. He could visualise the activity of the Saturday shift in the tunnels below ground, the burrowing and the hammering, the hauling and the heaving and the flap-flap-flap of the ventilator doors sending breath down into the lungs of the earth.

In the darkness of the young spring night Keir Bolderon experienced a dour sort of affection for the broad busy river and its black-faced shore, for all the men and women who laboured under it, under his protection. What would he do without them? What, in turn, would they do without him, at the mercy of fellows like Hector Fotheringham who would wreck the continuity of their labour just to save a few miserable pounds?

Keir Bolderon spurred his horse to a trot and soon his mind was engaged in plotting his next move in his bid to secure the Abbeyfield's future, and his own, for another fifteen or twenty years.

Tomorrow he had engagements in Leith and in Edinburgh. He must rise with the lark if he was to catch one of Neil McNeil's keel-boats down river, for the keels would be loading by torchlight and would be gunnelled down early to seize advantage of wind and tide. He could not be caught napping if he was to satisfy his passion to share in the coalfield's future, to have his mess of profit as well as power.

For a full, assured partnership in the Abbeyfield, signed, sealed and delivered, Keir Bolderon would sell his soul to the devil, in Hell, in Hanover Street, or wherever the devil was to be found.

Where the coal seam narrowed and bent beneath a ledge of sandstone little Allison Bennet stopped and sat back on her heels. She fumbled with the handle of the sled and, encumbered by heavy skirts and calico pantaloons, manoeuvred the rope between her thighs and gave it a tentative tug.

Obediently the sled grated along the floor behind her, its iron runners emitting a high-pitched *skree* that, even after twenty-two months as Jock Bennet's hauler, still set Elspeth's teeth on edge.

Taller by a head than her tiny companion, Elspeth could not move freely in the tunnel that breasted the 30-inch seam. She was obliged to crouch on all fours, chin tucked to her chest. In her time below ground, however, she had learned a trick or two to allay cramp and acute discomfort. She arched her back and pressed the crown of her head, protected by a canvas hood, against the tunnel roof, squeezed firmly until the ache in her shoulder-blades eased and the bones of her spine clicked and sent tingling warmth into the nape of her neck. Elspeth groaned with pleasurable relief. She stretched her arms out in front of her like a cat to coax the stiffness out of her hips then she too groped for the sled-rope, nuzzled the handle against her belly and made ready for the final, breathless crawl down to Jock Bennet's room.

It was the twenty-first trip back from ladder level. Return journeys were less arduous, of course, than hauls from the face when laden sleds scraped the walls as if the coal was reluctant to be drawn from the bosom of the earth. Even so, the rigours of the night-long Saturday shift were beginning to take their toll.

At this depth the slopes were more taxing than on the upper levels where most main roads had been widened and shored to accommodate the huge, box-sided hods that were dragged

51

along by women shackled in leather harnesses. There were no auld wives at this depth, for a woman had to be supple to negotiate the twists and corkscrew turns of the base seams. Besides, the Abbeyfield's upper levels were all but burned out and provided work mainly for folk who were not willing or able to earn big money hewing and hauling 'by the piece' but had to settle for payment of a fixed wage. This past two years the take of great coal had dwindled and the upper rooms yielded only 'chows', small, drossy coals for which there was little demand on the lucrative domestic markets.

Certain hewers, Jock Bennet among them, would not squander sweat on cutting chows. Jock had been born and bred to difficulty and risk. He had served his time in the foul wet seams of the Calderhead, had survived the gases of Braemore and been lured away from the Crabbe pit near Alloa, which he claimed was too tame for him, by Mr Bolderon's promise of big money for dangerous digging. He had been brought here to scour the seams at the roots of the Abbeyfield, seams that wandered far below the boulder-clays of St Austin's Bay and out under the river, and he loved it.

Jock Bennet vowed that he would have none of snug working, not for himself, not for his servant and certainly not for his children. Jock's bond was to the pit and their bond was to Daddy – and Daddy made them like it whether they willed or not.

Elspeth crept forward. "What is it, Mouse? What's wrong?"

Mouse shook her head in perplexity. "I canna hear anythin'."

Crawling over the sleds Elspeth rested her chin against Mouse's back and listened intently. It was true; no sound at all filtered out of the tunnel ahead of them.

"God save us!" Mouse hissed. "Where's Daddy gone?"

Silence below ground was nerve-racking. Usually the workings were alive with noises. Old pillars creaked under the weight of the overlay. Roof timbers groaned pitifully. Water guddled in the drainage channels and, in the echoing shafts, falling stones gave out fierce, heart-stopping whistles and loads shed from broken creels would rumble like thunder down and down the ladder holes.

Mouse whimpered, "Where's m' Daddy?"

"He'll just be restin'," Elspeth said.

The tunnel's remoteness and the awkward dimensions of the room in which Jock Bennet cut coal combined to magnify every tiny sound, even the intimate, unwitting grunts and wheezes that the hewer uttered as he wriggled under the live black shelf. Elspeth was too experienced to ignore the possibility that, in the twenty-minute period since their last trip to the room, Jock Bennet had met with an accident.

"He isn't even breathin'," Mouse cried.

There were only two rooms in the low seam. The Ogilvie family worked the other, seven or eight minutes back towards the ladder bottom. Elspeth strained her ears. She could just discern the *chak-chak* of Willie Ogilvie's pick but no mutter of voices to suggest that Jock Bennet had left his place and gone down to converse with his neighbour. Besides, they had come past the mouth of Willie Ogilvie's dig and would surely have noticed if Mr Bennet had been there.

"Give him a wee shout, Mouse," Elspeth suggested.

"Da? Are ye there, Daddy?"

No answer came from the tunnel.

Mouse's agitation increased. She had been employed in pit work since she was eight years old, half her life, in fact, and experience told her to look for certain signs and signals that might indicate the nature of disaster.

She inspected the candle flame, its hue and shape. Sudden changes in colour or a rainbow mist about the wick would mean a concentration of water vapours in the air. But the flame rose wan and steady, smoke melting into the soot stain on the wall.

"Would you like me to go in first?" said Elspeth.

"Aye."

Unhitching herself from the sled, Elspeth crawled over Mouse and, on hands and knees, peered with trepidation into the narrowing. A single tallow, stuck in a tin cup at the corner of the room, glimmered wanly but cast no shadows and gave no suggestion of movement.

"Mr Bennet, are you there?"

By now she expected no reply.

She sucked in a deep breath, bent her head and pushed herself under the rock ledge into the narrow tunnel.

Mouse continued to whimper. It was no mystery as to why the girl was so desperately afraid. If Jock Bennet died the family would be left at the mercy of circumstances. In Bolderon's pit there were no 'societies' or institutions to dole out bread to orphans or attend the welfare of the sick. It was the harsh law of this big-money mine that you fended for yourself or you did not fend at all.

Elspeth wormed down the tunnel as quickly as she dared, her hood brushing on the roof, her breath, shortening in the scarce air, coming in curt panting grunts.

She felt slag prick and jab at her knees, debris pushed out of the cutting. At this depth a hewer had no 'sweepers' to do the chores for him and an hour of every shift was wasted on clearing the work space. The room was hardly more than a tuck in the coal seam, like a fold in brocade. And it was empty.

The slanted stool was still in place under the cut but Jock Bennet's spade and wooden wedges were strewn on the floor as if he had flung them aside in a fit of temper. His clothing curled in a corner like a shed snakeskin.

"Is he dead, is he?"

Mouse had crept along the tunnel hard on Elspeth's heels. She thrust her face under Elspeth's arm and stared into the room and, seeing that it was indeed empty, wailed hysterically.

"Allison, stop it. Stop your noise this minute."

Whatever had taken Jock Bennet might be lurking nearby.

Elspeth shook her head to be shot of such silly thoughts. She was no superstitious colliery lass. She must be practical, positive, must find an explanation for the occurrence.

"Willie Ogilvie might know what's happened," she said.

Mouse sobbed and clung to the young woman in despair.

Elspeth twisted round and put an arm about her, to offer comfort. Poor Mouse: she was neither ugly nor pretty. Plain was the only word to describe her, yet she had a certain appealing daintiness that the callous labour of the pit had not yet managed to erase.

"Da would never leave his room in workin' hours."

Elspeth could not deny it. Jock Bennet worked as if demon-driven, pausing only for a bite of bread or a sup from his bottle or to relieve himself. Elspeth separated herself from the girl-child and inched closer to the coal. The cuts that Jock

54

Bennet had made were as uninformative as Roman inscriptions. Clearly nothing was to be gained by loitering here. She must fetch Willie Ogilvie. He would know what to do. Elspeth crept backwards into the butt of the tunnel, pressed against the mound of slag that had been flung there; and then she saw it. She uttered a cry of fear. A hand, a human hand protruded from the marl.

Elspeth threw herself away from it, cowering, but Mouse, who had seen it too, uttered an uncertain giggle.

"Daddy?" she said. "Is that you?"

As if in response to the question, the fingers of the protruding hand seemed to wave and, as Elspeth watched in fascination, scooped away loose dirt and made space for an arm, a shoulder and, finally, Jock Bennet's head.

The pitman grinned.

"So there ye are at last," he said, as if nothing in the world was more natural than for him to emerge from behind a heap of slag. "What ails the pair o' ye? By God, Patterson, you look as if you'd seen a ghost!"

Mouse's fears vanished at the first sight of her father, alive and apparently in one piece. "We thought you were done for, Daddy."

"Nah, nah, Mousie, it'll take more than a slide to carry me away." He heaved the upper portion of his body forward and groped, beckoningly, with his right hand. "Give me the tallow, Patterson."

Jock Bennet was as naked as Adam. All hewers worked in a state of nature and Elspeth had long since grown used to it. She picked up the tin cup and extended it towards the man, who took it in both hands and, bobbing his head, squinted up the tunnel.

He said, "Rance isn't down here, is he?"

"No, Daddy."

"We can do wi'out his company tonight."

Mouse giggled again and wiped her nose on her sleeve. She was quicker to appreciate the situation than Elspeth.

"What've you discovered, Daddy?"

"A cavity of some sort."

"Where does it go?"

"It runs east, below this level."

"Is it a fresh seam, Daddy?"

"Aye, I do believe it is, Mouse."

Elspeth said, "I thought all the coal lines petered out here."

"Mr Rance says they do," Mouse added.

"Give Rance a wheel an' chain an' he can build you a bloody hoist in ten minutes but he's as ignorant as a pig about pit bottoms," Jock Bennet said. "It's a seam sure enough. What hour is it?"

"Close to midnight, I think," said Elspeth.

"We've not a moment to lose," Jock Bennet said. "I'm goin' down there again, now you two are here. I'm takin' a light this time."

With his elbows Jock Bennet enlarged the hole. Elspeth could see now that the filling of soft marl had been deliberately heaped against the tunnel butt to act as a cover. Jock Bennet did not want the 'natural cavity' found by prying eyes, especially by the oversman. It seemed, that oblong crack, to be a find of considerable importance to the hewer but Elspeth did not immediately grasp the reason for the Bennets' excitement.

"Where's Willie Ogilvie?" Jock Bennet asked.

"Tight in his room," Elspeth answered.

"Where did ye leave the sleds?"

"At the end o' the broad tunnel, Da."

"Well, if Willie spots them he'll think you've just tapped off for a bite o' supper. It's about that time o' night."

Bennets and Ogilvies had come down within an hour of dawn on Friday and would work without surfacing until dawn on Saturday. It was the dreaded 'long shift', a straight twenty-two hours, a tradition in most Scottish pits and one which Mr Bolderon, in his quest for a top take, honoured and encouraged.

Bennets and Ogilvies did not work in harmony. No more, though, was there open rivalry between the families as there was in other twin rooms on higher levels. Neither Elspeth nor Mouse kept tally of the Ogilvies' haul and there were few exchanges between the Bennet women and Willie Ogilvie's burly daughters when they encountered each other in the broad tunnel or at the ladder foot.

"Did ye see any coal down there, Daddy?"

When he grinned Jock Bennet's tongue showed red as a poppy in his black face.

"Truth is, Mousie, I couldna see a blessed thing. But I could smell it. Aye, I could feel it with my hands. Oh, there's coal below us, an' this hole's the way in."

"How close is it?" said Elspeth.

"It's close. Ten or twelve feet down. I'll not need t' dig far t' bare it for cuttin'."

"Can I see?" said Mouse eagerly.

"Why not?"

Jock Bennet enlarged the opening with his arm and, lifting the candle-cup carefully after him, withdrew into the cavity and vanished from sight.

Mouse went after him and, kicking her heels, also disappeared into the hole in the marl.

Still shaking, Elspeth crept forward and drew herself up the ramp to peer warily into the cavity. She could see the glimmer of Jock Bennet's candle, hear the sounds of his breathing but saw nothing of either man or girl. Presumably they already had climbed below the level of sight.

Even now Elspeth could not grasp the reason for the Bennets' excitement. She assumed that Jock Bennet had in mind the 'reward' of ten pounds that Mr Bolderon had offered to any miner who uncovered a bearing seam. In spite of Jock Bennet's claim that there was coal below, Elspeth harboured doubts on that score. She had more faith in the judgement of the oversman, Thomas Rance, than had any of the male colliers. Mr Bolderon, the manager, was desperate for new winnings, now that the functioning levels were burning out, and she could not believe that Thomas Rance had not thoroughly probed this tunnel as he and his aides had probed every inch of the rest of the workings in the search for coal lines.

Curious, Elspeth dragged herself further up the ramp and put her head into the cavity.

She did not have the wealth of experience that Jock Bennet had accumulated over a lifetime of pit labour but she was free of accumulated prejudices and superstitions. What was more, she had acquired two interesting volumes from a packman, a traveller in books, who had found no sale for his wares in Placket apart from her purchases. She had read enough of the 'new sciences' in the literature which abounded on the shelves of Moss House to be able to comprehend a fair part of the treatises on the formation of the bodies which formed the natural constituents of the globe, of 'fossils' and their meaning, and of the wayward history of mineral mining. She kept the volumes hidden in her chest, had not read aloud from them to the children, as she did with the storybooks in her possession. She realised that the Bennets would pour scorn on such high-flown 'scientific' nonsense and boast that they, as colliers, knew better than any grey-powed professor what secrets the earth contained.

It had occurred to Elspeth as it had not, apparently, to the Bennets, that the 'cavity' might not be a natural fault at all but might be some ancient, decayed tunnel cut out by a miner from a previous era. The Abbeyfield, after all, had been yielding coal for hundreds of years and even the bottom levels had been in part explored in the past.

The fissure did not have the configurations of a tunnel, however. It was more like a cave. There was a steep, short drop to a shoulder-width space and a bottom rimed with fine brown sand. The rock, less compact than sandstone, had a peculiar rough nap that rasped on Elspeth's fingertips.

Something about the crack disturbed Elspeth. Perhaps it was superstition after all, memory of the tales of a lost channel to the river which pitmen recounted to round-eyed novices on their first day down, stories of limestone no thicker than eggshell beyond which the river coiled and slithered secretly, waiting for some innocent to fracture the restraining wall and give it roaring access to the seams. She could hear Jock Bennet's hammer tapping rock. The sound made her flinch.

Mouse giggled in the space below, and Jock Bennet gave a muffled whoop of glee.

Nervously Elspeth whispered, "Mouse, where are you? Mr Bennet, are you there?"

"Aye, aye, girl."

"Mr Bennet, what sort of rock is this?"

"It's millstone grit, lass."

"I haven't seen its like before."

"It's rare on shore fields. The crown of the shire is lidded wi' it, though. Farmers call it the moor rock. Gives damned poor tillage, I'm told.''

"But why is there none elsewhere on the Abbeyfield?"

"There isn't, that's all," Mr Bennet answered.

"How did it get down so deep?" Elspeth persisted.

"Liftit on the lava or a torrent o' ice in days long ago," said Jock Bennet. "Listen, lady, it's no' for the likes o' us to question why Nature did things, or how. This slab o' millstone hides a fat seam o' coal, an' that's all that concerns us. Am I not right, Mousie?"

"Aye, Daddy," said Mouse, and added, "Elspeth, the seam's taller than me, I swear."

After a hesitation, Elspeth asked, "Can we get coal out of it?"

"I'll widen the hole, fix a ramp or some steps," Jock Bennet said. "A couple of hours' work."

"Will Mr Rance not send down carpenters to do it?" said Elspeth.

Instantly, Jock Bennet's angry face appeared in the space below the hole.

He shouted, "This is *our* seam, girl. Thomas Rance will *not* be told of it. No, nor anybody else for that matter."

"How can you keep it secret?"

"I can, an' I bloody-well will," Jock Bennet declared. 'I'll fit a trap to the hole an' cover it with loose marl. It'll not be seen, I promise."

"Mr Bennet—"

"There's a bloody fortune in great coal down here, Patterson, an' I intend to share it with no man, not until I've had my skim. Do you understand?"

"But Mr Bolderon promised ten pounds—"

"Ten pounds! Hah! What do ye suppose Mr Bolderon'll make out o' such a fat seam? A hundred times ten. Bolderon may have his share, but only at my rate."

"Rate?" said Elspeth.

"Twenty full baskets to the shift."

"Mr Bennet, Mouse an' I canna manage so much."

"You'll manage."

"But can you cut twenty baskets in a shift?"

She should not have asked the question of a man like Jock

Bennet. By impugning his skill she angered him still further.

The pitman spat in disgust. He wiped his mouth with his wrist, leaving a smear of white flesh like a scar across his cheek.

"If I find I canna do it m'self," he vowed, "I'll bring our Davy down to help me."

"Davy?"

"An' Sarah too, if I must."

"Sarah's too young for bottom work, Mr Bennet."

"She's strong enough t' help me load."

Elspeth was silenced. How could she hope to penetrate the pitman's ingrained prejudices, make him understand that Davy would be unlikely to last a month in the foul air of the deep seam? Hard labour at this level would destroy the boy, who was pushed to fulfil his stints as a trapper in the air current just below the ventilator shaft.

Jock Bennet climbed from the hole, leaving Mouse to scramble behind him in darkness.

Elspeth would have beaten a retreat but, confined by the narrowness of the tunnel, she could not even turn around. Jock Bennet caught her by the wrist and thrust his face close to hers, his eyes sullen.

"Listen, Patterson, I know what's right for me an' mine. You're not my bloody wife, remember."

"I just thought – Davy's so young."

"God, I'd been bound to the face for three years when I was his age. He's thirteen. It's high bloody time he learned t' hew coal for his livin'. He canna go on just tuggin' a rope all his days, can he? Cuttin' will make a man o' him. Am I not right, Mousie?"

Mouse had emerged from the hole and pulled herself off the marl with an arm about her father's chest. She draped herself against him, lovingly.

"Aye, Daddy," she said.

"Keep your neb out o' Bennet business, Mistress Patterson."

"I – I will, Mr Bennet."

He did not release her wrist just yet but drew her closer still, so close that their noses touched and she could taste his breath on her lips. "One word to anybody about what we've found here an' I'll break your bloody neck." He dunted her brow with his. "Do ye hear me, lady?"

"I hear you, Mr Bennet."

"Fine. Now that's settled you'd best fetch the sleds."

Wriggling away from the pitman, Elspeth turned and crawled into the narrow tunnel, trembling.

It was not just speculation on what hard labour might do to Davy Bennet or the thought of solemn little Sarah Bennet brought down into the tunnels that distressed her. She could not properly explain her coiling dread, dread of the fissure, of that slanting crack under the millstone which, according to her knowledge of natural laws, should not have been there at all.

It was two years almost to the day since the last positive 'sighting' of the wayward wife had been relayed to Moss House and had caused James Simpson Moodie to shed his melancholia and live in a glow of hope for a week or two.

The weaver's right-hand men, Robert Rudge and John Scarf, had both been despatched to Stirling to take report from the woman who had seen and recognised Elspeth and had so foolishly challenged her.

Rudge and Scarf were cynics. They did not for a moment believe that Jamie Moodie would ever hold his young wife in his arms again and had privately agreed that it was some dark secret of the bedchamber that had driven Elspeth to forsake their employer. Even so, Rudge and Scarf were thorough. They questioned the woman, made written note of all she had to say – which was precious little really – and judged that she had indeed encountered Elspeth Moodie upon the Stirling bridge. They paid out the guineas that the handbill promised, and rode out together along the five turnpikes that stretched away from the town to question innkeepers and the like. Scarf discovered a carrier who had picked the woman and child from the roadside and had taken them four miles east, to the crossroads at Gaines, and left them there. And it was there that the trail finally petered out.

In spite of Elspeth's belief that her father had spies in every quarter of Scotland, this was not so. The range of James Moodie's influence was limited. It did not extend upwards into Fife or eastward into the Lothians, though John Scarf, agent and wool-buyer, scattered the yellow-paper handbills liberally in all directions and kept up his personal enquiries until the end of that year.

Throughout the summer of 1814 there had been odd reports, none reliable enough to bear investigation and the paying out of reward money. Tinkers would chance their arm from time to time. Tricksters hither and yon would have a letter penned claiming that, for a sum, they could put a hand on the runaway. But Scarf and Rudge parried the more obvious frauds and Tom Tolland, without telling his master, disposed of the rest. To all intents and purposes Elspeth Moodie had vanished as if the earth had swallowed her up.

After the passage of two full years Tolland no longer believed that salvation for the House of Moodie would come in the shape of Elspeth's return to Balnesmoor. By then the steward had more to worry him than his master's 'madness'.

By the light of late-night candles, tucked away in his cubby, Tom Tolland read of market fluctuations, the steep rise in prices, falling wages, of riots and restrictions, failures and financial disasters. He had already pared the domestic economy to the bone by paying off gardeners and grooms. There were no longer 'appearances' to be kept up and, with most of the rooms closed, he ran the house with just two servants, a cook who lived out and a resident day-maid. He kept on two gardeners and two horse-men, including Luke McWilliams who had been with Moodie since he was no taller than a riding-boot.

Gradually James Moodie sank deeper into himself. Days, weeks, would go by when he appeared to be both deaf and dumb. He would answer no question put to him, would skulk in his room under the stairs, would not take a razor to his chin or a comb to his hair, would not change his linen or his stockings, and certainly would not open himself to 'business' of any kind at all. In these prolonged moods he would pick at the food put before him but drank spirits as if they were water, a pleasure that Tolland did not deny him.

Once each month Robert Rudge would ride up from the woollen-mill at Kennart. Tolland would admit him to Mr Moodie's room. Rudge would vainly endeavour to converse with his employer, would leave upon the table the trading figures and a summary, written in his own upright hand, of fluctuations in market prices. But James Simpson Moodie would not so much as cast his eye upon the documents, would not turn a page, or make a comment that might give a hint as to his wish and his opinion.

What Jamie Moodie did do, which was the saving of Kennart and of Moss House, was sign in a spidery hand the chits for credit and cash that Tolland put before him.

If Rudge and Scarf were not saints, no more were they fools. They understood the business of making and selling woollen goods almost as well as did their master. They saw to it that when one market closed another was promptly found to replace it; saw to it that the quality of products from Moodie's looms was not compromised by his absence; saw to it that the artisans in their employ did not become too strident and demanding and continued to toe the line that Moodie himself had drawn.

They also made sure that Mr Moodie was not cheated by anyone other than themselves. For performing this necessary service they lined their own pockets to a degree by tapping off on most cash transactions a shilling here and a pound there; compensation, so they told each other, for the additional burden of responsibility that Mr Moodie's illness had placed upon them.

Tom Tolland's virtue also had its limits. He too skimmed a few shillings from the housekeeping each week, money to put away against the dreary day when the whole uncertain edifice might collapse and he would find himself on the market at an age when each grey hair would be a mark against him.

At no great cost to the domestic purse Tolland had taken into employment a brand-new maid to replace those to whom he had given marching orders. The girl, Hazel by name, had been picked up at a hiring fair in Drymen. She was a lithe, pretty wee thing, slightly short of a full measure of intelligence. She had not yet learned to give herself airs and did all that was asked of her without a murmur of complaint – and warmed Tom Tolland's bachelor bed once or twice a week without demanding favours in return.

Twenty months trickled past without much change in Mr Moodie's condition or circumstances, except that he became withered and pale and, even in warm summer months, less and less inclined to leave the confines of his room under the staircase. Every so often Tom Tolland would scrape the master's chin, bully him into donning a clean shirt and lead him out to the gig or the cabriolet and take him for a ride in the quiet country lanes in the hope that it might awaken some interest in the world that he, Moodie, had once grasped by the pigtail and which he had all but abandoned now. But Mr Moodie did not respond. He sat hunched on the seat, staring disconsolately into space, did not answer when Tolland addressed him or when some passing acquaintance gave him a greeting. It seemed that nothing could touch him, that he would slide mute and inconsolable to his grave.

About the New Year of 1816, however, changes in the master's behaviour impressed themselves on old Tom Tolland. Brandy decanter and whisky bottle in the 'study' were no longer emptied in the course of the day. All the food that Tolland put upon the master's plate was eaten, not a scrap being left. Mr Moodie even saw fit to stir himself to lay coals upon the fire when it was cold and draw the curtains over the window when night came creeping across the moor.

After Robert Rudge's February visit it seemed to Tolland, though he could not be quite certain, that the monthly trading statement had in fact been read and the wooden chest in which past statements were stored had been taken from its shelf.

Tolland took to listening at the door; heard nothing.

The steward adopted a breezy manner, struck up conversation once more; received no reply.

For all that, Tom Tolland had the oddest feeling that sense was stirring in James Simpson Moodie, that the 'madness' that had clouded his mind was drifting away like mist from the moon. Tolland deemed it prudent to warn Mr Rudge that it would do no harm to prepare for the master's return to cognisance.

It was March, though, before James Moodie drew himself out of the slough of despair into which he had sunk and once more began to communicate.

One night, very late, Tolland found Mr Moodie in the hallway. It was as well that Tolland had not brought Hazel down from the servants' loft but had been occupied by himself in the kitchen, totting up domestic accounts and making them all shipshape. The sound was slight: the creak of a footstep on boards. Tolland was out of his chair and into his jacket and shoes on the instant. He peeped out of the kitchen, saw that the door of Mr Moodie's study stood ajar and, knocking, opened it.

The master, it seemed, was on the prowl. He had prowled no further, though, than the foot of the main staircase. He stood there, all dishevelled and shrunken, staring up at a blink of moonlight that defined the window on the landing. He was mute no more. His 'madness' had become sorrow. He wept.

"I've lost her, Tom," he said, wiping his cheeks with his fingertips.

"No, no, sir. She'll come back in time, perhaps."

"No, I have lost her." James turned. "How long is it?"

Tolland paused.

"You may tell me, Tom. How long?"

"Since last we heard word, Mr Moodie, it's been two years."

"How long since she fled?"

"Nearly thirty months."

"Thirty months?" James Moodie seemed astounded by this revelation.

He shivered. He wore only an untied shirt and trousers and his legs and feet were bare.

He said, "God, Tom, but it seems only a wink of time since I had her with me for the first. She sat up there on the window-seat, I recall, an' stared out at the moonlight on the moor."

To help dispel the awful shadows of the past Tolland removed a candle from its fixed holder and carried it closer to the stairs.

The steward wondered at this new turn of events. He did not understand the inconsistencies of mental disturbance. With Coll Cochran's wife, Etta, it had been ether addiction that had stolen away her reason. With Mother Moodie it had been the ravages of age, pure and simple. But James Moodie's illness had not, it seemed, impaired his ability to remember detail, unless this was but some devious new twist in the progress of the disease.

Tolland shivered too.

"It's cold here, Mr Moodie," he said. "Will ye not step into the kitchen where it's warm? I'll brew us both some tea."

65

Though the tears had ceased, James stroked his cheeks with his fingertips, pinching and dragging the flesh. It was a strange gesture, not manly. He wiped his fingers on the front of his shirt and continued to stare up at the landing, at the shape of the window cut out of the gloom.

"I did not love her," James said, suddenly.

Ah, Tolland thought, he's not rational after all.

"Now she is dead."

"No, Mr Moodie, no."

"And her daughter – my daughter is gone."

Tolland could not chase the man's thoughts; he had not regained his reason after all. The steward said nothing. James sighed, softly, turned and padded past the servant and into the corridor, into his room, without another word.

Tom Tolland was disconcerted. He did not take himself to bed for several hours after the incident but sat in his chair by the fire with the door to the corridor propped open, listening for any sound or cry that his master might make, ready to hasten to his aid. But James Moodie was in bed asleep, fast asleep, untormented and unashamed now that he had lost her in himself.

Shift's end on the Abbeyfield was not a signal for the immediate downing of tools and a disorderly dash for the buckets. At six o'clock precisely Snippets Smith, the paymaster, would stride from the counting-house to the top of the main shaft, would lean over the brick coping and, in that shrill, seagull voice of his, would cry out, *"Time's up, time's up. All out, all out."*

Word would pass down the ladders and along the roads and into the rooms and the pit would begin to empty from the bottom to the top. Woe betide the trapper or putter who had drifted into a trance and failed to relay the message promptly to his neighbour. A cuff on the head or a kick on the backside would be the punishment for such negligence of duty, for children were the links in the fragile chain of communication that connected all the sections of the workings.

Women and children were obliged to queue in the tunnel by the checkman's stall, for hewers, as befitted their station, had first call on the bucket. Women and children would have to wait until the men had all been cleared, spinning up, two by two, to the surface, before they could step into the bucket and be cranked up into the sweet fresh air.

For the sake of warmth rather than decency, the men dressed before leaving the seams. Some even covered their heads with scarves of coloured wool to keep their brows from cooling too quickly. The habit made them appear raffish. But even the cockiest collier had lost his crow come the end of a Saturday shift and it was all a man could do to drag himself from the bucket into the milky daylight and trudge off to his bed in one of the cottages along the road to Placket or by the Rutherford burn.

The women were in no better state than their menfolk. Pain gripped all of them in some form, and there was precious little banter on a Saturday morn, only a chorus of moans and groans, lamentations in the dark. Knees were swollen, elbows bruised, brows gashed, eyes all teary and red-rimmed. Lungs and throats were clogged with black dust. The fortunate ones would recover by Monday but some would carry their ailments back down with them and work on in pain and discomfort until their abrasions suppurated or their gullets closed or fever smote them down and laid them off completely for a spell.

Mouse and Elspeth saw Jock Bennet safe out of the tunnel before they toiled wearily up the ladders to the main road and joined the crowd around the water barrel. Mr Rance ensured that the barrel was kept full of clean, fresh water, for workers plagued by thirst might otherwise be tempted to drink from the drains, a habit that led to sickness and disease.

Mouse and Elspeth managed a ladle of water each before the flow of the queue carried them on. Down the length of the high tunnel women were retching as the liquid loosed the dust that had accumulated in their stomachs.

Elspeth looked round for sight of Davy but he was nowhere to be seen and had, most probably, sneaked a ride early in the bucket, which some of the boys managed to do if they could catch the checkman off guard.

Jock Bennet's 'discovery' was far from Elspeth's mind. She could dwell on nothing but thoughts of hot tea and blankets, sunshine and a green breeze, and her daughter's welcoming smile. As she neared the bottom of the shaft, however, she noticed that Malcolm Elginbrod, the checkman, had failed to sign through the last of the coal loads. Several tall baskets were piled by his stall to advertise his incompetence. Tired or not, hewers whose tallies showed in the baskets would have found strength enough to curse the checkman for not seeing their coal to the day's count, particularly as it was a pay-night Saturday and they would now have to wait another fourteen days for recompense for their labour on the last hard loads.

Mouse caught Elspeth's hand and dragged her forward as the empty bucket thudded to the buffer. A hefty woman in baggy pantaloons and pea-jacket punched Mouse in the small of the back and would have kneed her too if Mouse had been less agile.

Hauling Elspeth after her, the little girl clambered into the bucket.

Elginbrod yelled, "*Take away.*"

The horse-men on top drove the beasts into the collars and the bucket jerked and rose, spinning.

Elspeth, as she always did, closed her eyes.

Many pits now had squat, snorting steam-engines to ravel up the cable at a fine old rate of knots but steam power had not come to the Abbeyfield yet. Things were still done in the traditional manner and most of the hewers claimed that they preferred it that way. Cable and rope twanged. The shaft sides shot downward. The ascent was quite fast enough for Elspeth Patterson, thank you. She clung tightly to Mouse until the bucket jerked and halted, and cold, welcome air flooded about her face.

She slapped away Jim Neave's helping hand, pulled herself on to the platform and stepped down on to solid ground.

She was aware of Mr Rance and Snippets Smith standing not far from the shaft, and the acrid odour of dung from the horse-walk and the salt tang on the wind and the prickling pain of light in the eyes. She would have stumbled away in the wrong direction if Mouse had not found her hand and dragged her clear of the steps and off in the wake of the dwarf-shapes that straggled across the field.

Elspeth blinked. She rubbed her eyes and felt momentary disorientation pass. She glanced up at the sky. It was grey with cloud and the wind was strenuous. She doubted if there would be sunshine at all that day.

"Mammy, Mammy. Here am I."

From a hunch of bushes by the old field gate Mary Jean rushed to greet her mother. The child was bustling, sturdy and sure on her feet. Her arms stuck out comically and her face was radiant with pleasure.

Elspeth released Mouse's hand, knelt and caught her daughter into her arms, hugged her and fussed over her with an affection that masked her exhaustion.

"Mammy all dirty."

The joke was repeated at the end of every shift. There was a well-rehearsed response. Elspeth wetted her fingertip and dabbed a smudge of coal-dust on to the tip of Mary Jean's nose.

"See, now we're both the same," she said.

Mary Jean clapped her hands and laughed, buried her face in her mother's coat collar and waited to be lifted for a ride.

Back aching, Elspeth carried Mary Jean towards the gate where Sarah, solemn as always, waited. There was no smile of welcome on the little girl's lips. She was sober, though not surly, and Elspeth had grown used to her manner and the fact that, even at the age of nine, Sarah took her responsibilities most seriously.

Elspeth offered Sarah her hand. If there was need in Sarah Bennet she refused to let it be seen and, ignoring the hand, walked step-in-step with Elspeth, not touching.

"Did Mary Jean eat all her stew?" Elspeth asked.

Sarah nodded.

"Did you have some too?"

Sarah nodded again.

"Was it tasty?"

"Aye. It was grand."

"Did you finish what was in the pot?"

"Aye."

"I'll make more tonight."

"I'll help," said Sarah.

If Jock Bennet carried out his threat to take Sarah into the pit then Mary Jean would have to be put to the school. It was not a school like the one Elspeth and Anna had attended; no teaching was done there. But the widow who ran the establishment was reliable and did not charge much for looking after the very young children who were put into her care. Mary Jean was tall for her age and not shy. Even so, she would not take kindly to the rough-and-tumble of a minder's school.

Changes of any kind made Elspeth uneasy. She had come to prize the drab routine of life on the Abbeyfield. It was her version of security. Here, among the colliers, she had no fear of being discovered by her father. To be free of that fear was considerable compensation for the hardships of pit labour.

Mouse hurried on ahead to make tea and butter bread, the 'morning' supper. Little Mary Jean could not quite understand why Mammy had to go to bed when she was just up and ready for fun. Today, with the weather dry if not warm, Sarah would take Mary Jean outside and keep her amused while the others slept. Not until two or three o'clock in the afternoon would the Bennets begin to stir in their blankets. It would be after four before there was much liveliness about the place.

Shivering, Elspeth trotted the last few steps to the cottage door. Pushed with her shoulder, it opened and the young woman staggered in. Fatigue caught up with her, enveloped her. She put Mary Jean down at once.

Davy was already rolled in blankets in the aisle by his father's bed. Black with grime, wearing only his work shirt, Jock Bennet slouched at the table, a dish of hot tea in his hands. He had enlivened the brew with a drop of whisky from the flask he kept under his bed. His eyelids drooped. He appeared more stupefied than sleepy, as if he might slump just where he sat. He paid not the slightest attention to Elspeth or the children.

The house was clean but marvellously untidy. Sarah did her best. The crocks were all washed and dried and put away on the shelves and only the big iron stewpot remained unscoured for it was too heavy for the little girl to carry out to the backs. It was, Elspeth thought, a far cry from Moss House where there had been servants trained to do the work, and fine linen, delicate china and silver teapots, warm baths and doors that locked.

"Penny for your thoughts," Mouse murmured.

Elspeth dumped herself down on the three-legged stool by the hearth and held Mary Jean between her knees.

She glanced at Mouse, who was stirring sugar into a dish

70

of tea. Considerately she brought it to Elspeth who drank a mouthful of the hot liquid before answering.

"I was thinkin' how much we'll get paid tonight."

Behind Elspeth Jock Bennet stretched out under the blankets and groaned with the pleasure of it.

"Three o'clock, Sarah," he said. "Wake me no later."

"Aye, Daddy."

Elspeth was so tired that she was reluctant to make the effort to rise and take herself to bed.

"Will ye buy me a gingerbread?" said Mouse.

"I will. An' a ginger beer to wash it down," said Elspeth.

"Gi'ger, gi'ger for me too," said Mary Jean.

"What would you like from Mr Nicol's, Sarah?"

Sarah hovered by the table.

She shrugged her thin shoulders. "Cinnamon."

"Cinnamon it shall be," said Elspeth.

"Ci'mon for me too," Mary Jean yelled.

From the bed Jock Bennet growled warningly. He was patient enough with the young child as a rule but they were all bone-weary at that hour and tempers would fray easily.

"*Shh*, dearest," said Elspeth. "Mr Bennet's sleepin'."

Elspeth gathered her daughter and carried her behind the curtain while Mouse crawled fully-dressed into the blankets that were stuffed into the space beneath the dresser. She curled herself into a ball, shielded her eyes from the seep of light with her arms and almost instantly fell asleep.

Sarah had filled a bowl with warm water from a pan on the hob and had placed it on a chair in the corner. Elspeth washed her face and arms clean of clinging pit-dirt, dried herself on a towel and unfastened her outer garments and stepped out of her skirts, a habit that the Bennets could not comprehend. Sarah removed the bowl and towel and thoughtfully drew the curtain on its string.

Quite wide awake, Mary Jean jumped about on her mother's mattress but, when Elspeth lay down, restrained her restless spirits and uttered a tiny "*hee hee hee*" as if this was part of the game too. She stuck her bottom in the air and her face in the pillow and touched her nose to Elspeth's cheek lovingly. Her breath smelled of apples and fresh milk and her eyes were blue as a summer sky.

71

Elspeth kissed her.

"Sleep tight, darlin' girl."

"Sleep tight, Mammy."

Elspeth was comforted not disturbed by her daughter's small stirrings.

In a minute or two Sarah would silently coax Mary Jean away. They would spend the morning on the shore or along at Mrs Baxter's cottage looking at the chickens and goats that the old woman kept, or playing with the cats that were always assured of a welcome there.

Elspeth closed her eyes and let herself drift, drift like a leaf on water.

Her daughter's breath tickled her cheek.

Outside the walls of the little cottage the March wind rushed about and from the blackthorn trees came the noise of birds, birds that, in Placket's grey spring dawn, twittered but did not sing.

"Why, Mr Moodie, sir, it's grand t' see you up an' about so early in the day," Tolland said.

The steward fumbled with his waistcoat buttons, ran a hand over what was left of his hair. If he had known that James Moodie would recover his wits so swiftly he would have curled one of his wigs for the occasion.

Mr Moodie might be active but he was not wholly himself. His eyes were sunken and his flesh the colour of unbleached linen. He moved woodenly, as if his limbs resisted the dictates of his will.

"The girl? Who is the girl?" James said.

It was odd enough to see the master within the confines of the kitchen but to see him buttering a tear of bread from a corn loaf was like watching a dog do arithmetic. It reminded Tom Tolland that Mr Moodie had not been born into the gentry, like the Bontines, that once, not so long ago, he had lived in a low cottage near the Bonnywell.

James ate the bread without appetite, stuffing it into his mouth, swallowing without chewing. He no longer seemed indrawn but was possessed by a new demon, one which drove him to frantic activity. Concern swelled in Tom Tolland again.

"The girl?" said Tolland.

"A young lass, a stranger to me. In the corridor. Ran as soon as she saw me."

"Och, that's Hazel," Tolland said.

"Who – is she?"

"A servant, Mr Moodie. Do ye not remember when she came?"

"Where's Betty?"

"We dismissed Betty, sir, not long after the—"

James pushed the crust of the bread into his mouth with the palm of his hand, chewed, swallowed. The tendons of his throat stood out like grooves on oak. His eyes were dead again. It seemed, though, that he could now heed his own derangement. He waved his hand to silence the steward.

"No matter, no matter, Tolland. No matter, no matter."

"It was to save expense, Mr Moodie. What wi' so many rooms closed, it—"

"No matter."

Now that he had eaten, the energy in Moodie had no focus. He tore at the rest of the corn loaf, ripping it into four chunks which he then discarded.

Saying nothing, Tolland filled the iron kettle from the water bucket and put it on the hob. The fire was almost out. Hazel should have been down to light it but the master had obviously scared her upstairs again. Order, upon which he thrived, was gone from the day already. He had put up with Mr Moodie's sickness only because it gave him control. He must either be led or be a leader in the house; he could not hang between two bent hooks.

Still toying with the bread, James said, "Is she yours, Tolland?"

"Mine, sir?"

"The girl."

"She's—"

"Is she your daughter?"

"Oh, no, Mr Moodie. She's not that."

"Where are my – shirts?"

"I'll have them brought, Mr Moodie."

"See that you do."

"Are you venturin' out, Mr Moodie?"

"Where's my best – kerseymere?"

"I'll have it brought too, sir."

"See that you do, see that you do."

"Is there anythin' else you'll want, Mr Moodie?"

"I—"

James screwed up his eyes, elongated his features. It was grotesque, like a forester straining to lift a trunk too heavy for one man's strength.

An indrawn breath: "Rudge."

"Ah, you're goin' down to Kennart, sir?"

"Here. Fetch Rudge here."

"I'll send the lad from the stables."

"Tell him – tell Rudge to come – at once."

"I will, Mr Moodie. Will that be all?"

"Refreshment."

"Of course, sir. Will I see to it that the drawing-room's opened an' a fire lighted?"

"Yes, yes, yes."

"Mr Moodie?"

"Yes?"

"It's but half past six o' the clock. Do you wish Mr Rudge fetched from his house?"

"What day?"

"Saturday, sir."

"Kennart?"

"Aye, he'll be at Kennart, I expect. But not so early."

"Kennart."

"In the meantime, sir, shall I make you some breakfast? Cook's not in till seven."

"Is she – your daughter, Tolland? You can – you can confide in me."

"She's just a lassie, sir. From the hirin' fair."

"Look after her, Tom."

"Aye, Mr Moodie. I will."

Tolland sidled from the kitchen in dismay. He had no choice but to send for Robert Rudge, though what possible weight James Moodie hoped to bring to any discussion with his manager, what sort of convoluted plan had evolved in Moodie's brain Tolland could not imagine.

"Hazel," he shouted. "Get down here."

In the kitchen, seated now, James Simpson Moodie played

74

with the fragments of bread, moulding them back into the shape of the loaf.

The whalers had left for Greenland and the Davis Strait. The anchorages beyond the old dock were temporarily vacant, though two schooners of the Rotterdam Sailing Company were tacking towards the harbour and a brigantine from Archangel had just nosed around the beacon and was scudding fast across the wind now that the tide had turned again towards the land.

Inshore, from the Custom House to the Chain Pier, the Port of Leith was packed with luggers, 'whitesiders' and Hull barges, little boats of no particular denomination that made the quays bristle with masts and riggings, while in the vicinity of Coalhill collier brigs and keels exhaled a cloud of granular dust that the breeze whisked back over the rooftops of the town.

Keir Bolderon's sea-legs were fairly sturdy but he had no love of voyaging and was relieved to step ashore, drenched but undrowned, from the deck of the keel-boat *Czar of Perth* that had ferried him across the Forth from Placket. He wasted no time in searching for a conveyance but, to dry himself out, struck off on foot for Salamander Street and the warehouse premises of Phillans, Adams and McNeil.

There was no Phillans in the firm these days. No Adams. The original founders of the merchant trading company had long since been gobbled up by johnny-come-lately Neil McNeil.

McNeil was one of Leith's most famous citizens. The fact that he had ruined a large number of rival merchants, as well as Phillans and Adams, did not seem to matter a jot. He continued to be regarded not just with respect but with affection by all who had not fallen foul of his methods. He dressed these days in a kilt, jacket, waistcoat and sporran, and sported a splendid tartan cloak. He gripped a painted wooden sword with which he would gruffly acknowledge the greetings of all the folk that he encountered about the town's streets and wynds. He was blessed with a soft, round sort of face, cherry-red cheeks and had a halo of snow-white hair which made him appear not just paternal but positively benign. Most people assumed that Mr McNeil's rudeness was an affectation. Keir Bolderon was not deceived.

Neil McNeil claimed to be descended from the clan of that name which had its home on Barra, that lovely isle on the rim of the Atlantic. The truth was less – or, perhaps, more – romantic. He had in fact been spawned out of wedlock by a packman's daughter in Edinburgh's Cowgate and had dragged himself out of it with nothing but a basket of shoddy tied to his back and a tongue as quick as a viper's.

Keir Bolderon found it impossible not to admire a man who had made such a success of things, who, by dint of determined effort, had created a trading empire reputed to be worth in excess of twenty thousand pounds per annum. Close to the bottom of the page of McNeil's interests were the three old keel-boats that lugged coal from the Fife fields to be sold to house-dwellers in Edinburgh.

It was to Neil McNeil that Bolderon had traded away twelve per cent of his slice of the Abbeyfield's profits in exchange for a cash advance of four hundred pounds. In recompense McNeil had been granted right to purchase all the domestic coal which was dug from the Abbeyfield at a discount of five per cent on the market price. Even at the time, five years ago, Bolderon knew that he was being put to the screw but he had been desperate for working capital to knock the pit into shape and had agreed to the trader's usurious terms without much quibble.

One benefit had accrued from his relationship with Neil McNeil, however, for the old man had put Bolderon in the way of meeting with a certain Mr Melrose of Perthshire, another 'investor', and Mr Melrose had forked out three hundred pounds to become a 'sleeping' partner.

The dealing had seemed wonderful at the time. It had enabled Keir Bolderon to whip the Abbeyfield into production after years of neglect by Hector Fotheringham and the more immediate predations of manager Agnew. But it was coal not gold that came out of the ground and now, with the end of the lease period in view, Keir Bolderon had to face the fact that he had traded away just too much of his share for that initial lump of capital. He had not saved enough cash out of profits to make himself independent and was thus obliged to come once more, cap in hand, to Neil McNeil's door.

The door in question was a plain pine board in the plain

pitch-pine wall of an enormous warehouse in Leith's Salamander Street. Keir Bolderon knocked upon it and was duly confronted by a lad who carried his name within the building and left Mr Bolderon to cool his heels in the street.

Mr Bolderon was not dismayed. He had grown used to such treatment over the years, particularly from Mr McNeil who had a foible about allowing strangers to see within the confines of his store. After three or four minutes' delay, Neil McNeil appeared in the doorway.

"So it's yourself, is it, Bolderon," he said, in a dry, rasping voice.

Although the meeting had been pre-arranged by letter, McNeil glowered at Keir Bolderon as if he had slithered out of the waves like a merman.

"It is. It is, indeed, sir," said Keir Bolderon, "me."

"Well, I've had my dinner an' I'm due a breath o' air so you may walk wi' me, Bolderon. I'll give ye a mile, no more, for I have many things to concern me this afternoon."

"Most generous of you to spare me time at all, sir."

The old gentleman stepped from his doorway, brushed past Bolderon and turned to the right.

Since last Keir Bolderon had met with him, McNeil had aged considerably. In the space of three or four months, crookedness of character had become visible in his physique. His shoulders were hunched and his hairy knees were bowed and feeble. He used the sword not for waving to folk now but as a crutch and he crabbed slowly along the paving towards the road which would lead them to the links. They would not, Keir Bolderon realised, make anything like a mile. The old chap would be fortunate to reach open ground beyond the warehouse walls before his strength gave out.

It saddened Keir Bolderon to see how the years had shrivelled McNeil and he hoped that the brain had not been reduced on a similar scale.

McNeil concentrated on walking. No word passed between the pair until they had cleared the protection of the walls and the wind gave the old man something to lean upon. He braced himself, fists clasped over the handle of the sword, the point stuck into the grass verge.

"What business brings ye to see me, Bolderon?" he rasped.

Keir Bolderon explained briefly the position that Hector Fotheringham had put him in. He had no need to disguise the facts, for there was no bond between McNeil and the land-owner and the old man was too clever to deceive.

After Bolderon had finished, McNeil gazed out across the estuary in silence, the wind flicking the pleats of his kilt and billowing the tartan cloak behind him like a spinnaker. In the strong gusts of air, Bolderon thought, he looked as old and noble as a castle keep.

"So, Fotheringham would have ye finance the search for new lines o' coal but will give ye no guarantee of a partnership when the lease falls due for renewal; is that it?" Neil McNeil said at length.

"In a nutshell, Mr McNeil."

McNeil snorted. "So you canna spend much on the employment o' labour to find new coal since big expense will leave ye bare if no coal's found?"

"Quite so."

"I suppose it'll have occurred to ye that Hector Fotheringham might decide t' dispense wi' your services in any case?"

"That thought did rise in my mind, yes."

"What worries ye, Bolderon?"

"The cleft stick, Mr McNeil. If I do *not* find new lines of coal then Mr Fotheringham will certainly cut me from a new contract. If I put out my own capital to finance boring and *do* find new coal then Fotheringham might also cut me off, having had not only my effort but my money for his profit."

"Will he not negotiate now?"

"He pretends to be vague about it."

"Aye, that's the way wi' men like Fotheringham," said Neil McNeil. "*Is* there coal down there in the Abbeyfield?"

"I firmly believe that there is."

"But you need proof?" said McNeil.

"Yes."

"I'd be needin' proof too," McNeil said.

"What I need, Mr McNeil, is somebody who is willin' to share the cost of exploration with me."

"To what tune?"

"Four or five hundred pounds."

"Have you not got five hundred pounds?"

"Yes," Keir Bolderon said, "but it is almost all I have in savings. I dare not use it all."

"What would ye offer in return for five hundred?"

"The opportunity to extend our present agreement on purchase and transportation across nineteen years, the full term of the new lease."

"What interest have I in nineteen years?" said Neil McNeil. "Aye, or nine for that matter. You'll be needin' to find some other investor. If ye do secure a partnership I'll negotiate the purchase agreement wi' you, in the same or similar terms. You can tell Fotheringham that. But I'm no' inclined to plunge into exploration wi' a man who has no legal claim on the return."

"I understand, sir," said Keir Bolderon. "I trust that you do not think it forward of me to ask for your advice."

"Advice?"

"Who better to advise me on how to solve this predicament than you, Mr McNeil?"

If the old man was flattered he gave no sign of it. He did not respond to Bolderon's appeal but gathered his cloak about him and turned himself away from the river. Slowly he picked his way from the verge on to the road and set off towards the warehouse once more.

Hiding his disappointment, Keir Bolderon followed the trader, measuring his long stride with some difficulty to the old man's shuffle.

He had not, of course, expected McNeil to fall for such a nebulous proposal, which is why he had been so frank and open about it. After all, the Great McNeil had not acquired his wealth by playing long odds, and any transaction that depended upon the scruples of a landowner like Fotheringham had to be regarded as dubious. Somehow, though, Keir Bolderon had expected more from the old man, some sign that they were akin, that he, Bolderon, was a passenger on the same ship, a climber on the same ladder, that McNeil recognised in him a similar sort of energy and ambition to that which had made McNeil what he was today.

Apparently the old man saw no such qualities in Mr Bolderon. He stumped on without a word until the wooden walls of the warehouses blocked off the sea breeze and made the sun seem warm. Only a half-dozen yards from the warehouse door, McNeil stopped. He glanced over his crooked shoulder and, to Keir Bolderon's amazement, grinned.

His teeth were sparse, worn, brown, and the grin had no paternalism in it. It seemed malicious, almost evil.

"Advice, Bolderon?"

"Yes, Mr McNeil, if you care to give it."

"Ach, Bolderon, ye have the grit, man, but ye do not have the guile."

"I've not been cunning enough, do you mean?"

"Money will bring ye coal. Money will find new seams. But you canna throw money into another man's hole."

"That's the reason I need capital."

"Capital you'll have to beg for."

"I beg from no man, Mr McNeil," said Keir Bolderon, sharply.

"Admirable sentiments. But if you'll no' beg, Bolderon, what will ye do for money?"

"Negotiate favourable terms."

McNeil's grin widened. He might have laughed, except that no sound escaped his lips. "You canna offer favourable terms, though."

"Sir, I feel I've earned my share of the winnings."

"Hard work alone is not enough. Find money, Bolderon. Negotiate for it. Sell what you have to give."

"Easy to say, sir. How do I find money?"

The old man leaned his shoulders against the wooden wall. He disregarded the bubbles of pitch that the sun had coaxed from the boards. He eyed Bolderon slyly and, still without sound, laughed again.

"Obtain it as your friend Hector Fotheringham obtained it," McNeil said. "Find your fortune as others have done before you, Bolderon."

"I – I confess I do not take your meaning."

"Get it as I got it, damned be it, all those years ago."

Keir Bolderon held his breath. He felt that he was on the edge of something tremendous. He expected some complicated secret of commerce reduced to a simple maxim, to receive from the lips of the famous old trader a revelation that would change his fortunes for ever.

For once in his life Keir Bolderon was not disappointed. "How?" he whispered. "Tell me how to do it."

"Marry it, of course," said the venerable Neil McNeil.

Gradations of society had originally placed Mr Robert Rudge in the position of gentleman. His father had not been rich but he had been educated and had held several positions of trust to true aristocrats. Mr Rudge's elder brother was, even now, secretary to a Minister of the Crown. One of his sisters had married into the peerage. Mr Rudge, however, had not required so much of society and lacked that spark of vanity which might have ignited his ambition.

The truth was that Mr Rudge had become lazy. He wanted just enough in income to enjoy a modicum of security and peace to indulge the pleasures of the flesh. It was for that reason that he had never married. Since he had found employment with James Simpson Moodie he had dwelled in a small, stout house on the outskirts of Drymen, attended by a devoted female housekeeper and by a manservant who could turn his hand to most things.

Mr Rudge did not require much to hold this height of comfort. He ate well, drank good whisky and better wine, and took young women wherever he could find them willing. Half the girls in Kennart had been blessed by Mr Rudge's 'attentions' at one time or another, though he was careful never to meddle with the married ones.

Robert Rudge, however, had reached an age when the thought of giving up what he had gained ruffled his equilibrium and made him not just cynical but irate. Like Tolland, he would find it difficult, if not impossible, to secure another position which suited him as well.

For that reason, on receipt of Tom Tolland's curt note, he came at the gallop to Moss House.

Mr Moodie had summoned him? Rudge could hardly believe it. He had fancied that Moodie had sunk too far ever to be likely to summon him again. He had hoped that the weaver would peg out indefinitely in a lovelorn limbo, that status quo might be maintained until he himself had reached a stage when retirement from the concerns of business was not only financially possible but desirable.

A month ago Moodie could not have summoned a water bucket if his feet had been on fire. As he spurred his horse up the hill from Kennart to Balnesmoor, Rudge wondered if Tolland had lost his wits too and was exaggerating some garbled phrase that his master had uttered in delirium. But there he was, James Simpson Moodie, if not exactly his old self at least upright in a chair in the library, with something akin to intelligence glinting in his eyes.

No bottles, no decanters, jugs or glasses were visible in the handsome room. The table at which the weaver sat was bare, save for the sheaf of monthly accounts. Profit and loss: October 1813 to February 1816.

Rudge recognised the sheets instantly. After all, he had penned them, reducing a mass of invoices and chits, bankers' orders and debit drafts to an accurate month-by-month summary. He did not do it for Moodie. He did it for the business, for himself. He had nothing to fear from the columns of figures. Clerk McAlpin had checked his arithmetic and Scarf had verified and initialled all the external billets.

Embezzlement was not Rudge's crime. John Scarf and he had practised a less refined form of larceny. Unless Jamie was willing to saddle his cuddy and ride the roads round farms and markets from here to Perth and back again, unless he was prepared to needle carriers and knuckle shipping-clerks, he would find nothing to prove that money had been tickled from his fist by his manager and chief agent. Whole, round and crusty, the trading-records were as neat as pie.

"Tread with care. He's not yet himself," was Tolland's only admonition as he showed Rudge through the hallway and into the library.

Moodie was clean-shaven, groomed, and wore a suit of sober black and a shirt as white as a lily flower. His hair, though, had turned white. His complexion was grey and his mouth was wrenched down at the corners.

Rudge gave a little bow.

"Are you well, Mr Moodie?"

"Sit. Sit," James Moodie said.

His gestures were bizarre, all stiff, as if his joints needed oil. Rudge seated himself on the small, uncushioned chair that had been placed before the table. He was suddenly nervous; he did not know why.

"I – I see that you have been robbin' me," James Moodie said.

"Not at all, sir," said Rudge, with a calmness that was entirely superficial. "The trading-records have been accurately kept, I assure you."

"No matter, no matter."

It was on the tip of Robert Rudge's tongue to complain at the slander but he thought it more prudent to say as little as possible. It was clear that Moodie was whistling in the dark.

"No matter, no matter," said the weaver again. "If you have been robbin' me, nobody else has. Tell me how the stock stands."

"The exportation orders are being maintained, Mr Moodie," said Rudge, relieved to be asked a question that took him away from theft. "Coatings and duffields are meeting stiff competition from Holland, however, and we cannot long hope to hold against it. Messrs Johnston and Hepple, for instance, have already informed us that they will reduce the quantity of the standing order for yard lengths from September."

James did not nod his head to indicate understanding. He remained rigid in the neck and shoulders and stared at Rudge like a man who must read the movement of lips to make out words.

Rudge went quickly on. "Blanket cloth and flannel, in the mix, do well but, as you'll recall, we turned to finer weave and have not the production that we had on cheaps."

"The – the – the ten-shillin' cloths?"

"The rise in importation duty has affected Mr Moore's American trade again," said Rudge. "It's recorded, I believe, in May of the last year. But Mr Scarf has found a shipper to Germany for the made pieces."

James did not respond, and Rudge went on, rattling out all sorts of facts and figures, neglectful of the fact that his employer had grasped nothing of the affairs of the world for the past thirty months, knew nothing of war and treaties and taxes, the slump in farm prices and the drop in piece-rate which had all the weavers in the country, not just Kennart, grumbling. He,

Rudge, had undertaken that cut, not out of greed but from the need to produce cloths competitively.

The community at Kennart might be tight-knit but its weavers were not ignorant of what was taking place in other parts of Scotland. They had sense enough to accept that their lot was better by far than that of their brethren at the handlooms in Glasgow, say.

On and on went Robert Rudge, spilling out all that the master of the mill should know about changes made in changing times, all couched in the commercial jargon which, previously, James Moodie had understood as a child may read an ABC. What penetrated, what engaged, what had relevance now, though, Rudge could not be sure.

He paused, awaiting a question.

None came.

James said, "I – I – require of you an inventory."

"Stock in store, Mr Moodie, is that what you mean?"

"Total inventory."

"Value of property and of engines too?"

"Scarf will know what field holdin's we have. Ewes in lamb and the like," said James Moodie.

He had clenched his fists upon the unopened sheaves of figures on the table before him. His knuckles were bulbous as tubers and white with some sort of effort.

Did he hold physically to his sanity? Rudge wondered.

He felt pity, as well as apprehension. His employer had never required a full inventory before. He fretted over the reason for the request. Was it a madness, a folly too, or did the weaver suspect that Scarf and he had been selling the ponies and the carts and the very timber from the roofs?

"It will take some while, Mr Moodie," Robert Rudge said.

"It must – must be done within the month."

"But why, sir?" Rudge blurted out.

"No matter, no matter, no matter."

"I'm not certain it can be done thoroughly in so short a time, Mr Moodie."

"Must be, must be done, Rudge."

In the past there would have been force, an impatient authority in James Moodie's manner of delivery but now the words were uttered in a low, withered voice that seemed to make its appeal to pity. It was as if the weaver was crying, "Help me", not issuing an order which must be obeyed; a tall order too.

"End of the month, Mr Rudge. I cannot wait."

"Mr Moodie, what is the purpose of this inventory?"

"Evaluation."

"Ah!" Rudge exclaimed.

He need press the point no further. He believed that he understood. James Simpson Moodie wished to put a worth upon himself. He wished to have his value set down in ink upon paper. For the best part of his life, all the years that Rudge had known him, James Moodie had been an archetypal materialist. He had measured his days in feet of cloth, tallied his hours in pennies earned, had had vision enough to expand his mania for turning time into money into a thriving concern which used other folks' time to convert into money too.

That, Rudge supposed, was the whole principle of commerce. But with James Moodie it had become something akin to a religion in which pride and jealous passion had also had their part. Now he had lost it, had felt it dim within him. The sacrifice of the young wife and the daughter had created doubt about the whole purpose and meaning of his existence. He was groping backward into the past, seeking the feeling that had once consoled him, the assurance that he might own not only wealth but through wealth a lease upon his own small soul.

It came to Rudge as both knowledge and sensation. He felt for Jamie Moodie for a brief moment, equated the man's emptiness with his own – and flinched, literally, away from it. All he, Robert Rudge, had to protect him was his fatalism. He knew that he was worth little and would pass unrecorded from the vale of tears, from Drymen and Kennart to be exact, leaving hardly a memory of his time there.

Rudge got to his feet. He swallowed the expression of sympathy that was on the tip of his tongue.

"Will that be all you require of me, Mr Moodie?"

"Everything, everything. Miss nothing out."

It would be a miserable task. It would take many days of weighing, measuring and counting, summoning of tallies from distant farms where the only system of calculation that was really understood was sheep louping a gate to a tick on the fingers, and the sun coming up and going down again. But it must be done.

John Scarf would turn pink with annoyance at this extra burden. But he, Rudge, would convince his agent that the taking of the inventory must be done thoroughly and honestly, without sulking, without cutting a corner or guessing a count.

If poor old Jamie Moodie wanted himself scaled and weighed then he was entitled to have it done. His enterprise and industry had earned him that much. In Robert Rudge's opinion it would not solve his distress or cure the malady that afflicted him. Only the return of Gaddy Patterson's foundlng would do that – and she had vanished like snuff thrown with the wind.

Rudge bowed again.

James Moodie said not a word of farewell.

The weaver sat rigid, staring, knuckles white with tension.

Closing the door of the library behind him, Rudge crossed the hallway where he was met by Tom Tolland who had been lurking in the passage beneath the stairs.

"What did he want wi' you?" Tolland asked, without prevarication.

"He wants an inventory made. An evaluation of all that he owns."

"Dear God!" Tolland exclaimed. "For what purpose?"

Rudge kept his opinions to himself.

He said, "To keep us all busy, I expect."

He took his hat from Tolland's hand and let the steward open the front door for him.

It was still quite early in the day but it took no expert in weather to predict that there would be no sunshine to warm the ewes and promote a grass growth. Cloud lay in ribbed waves out from Balnesmoor and across the loch to the distant mountains.

Rudge adjusted his hat, buttoned his collar, turned.

"Tell me," he said to Tolland in a lowered tone, "is Moodie still mad or is this some wily game he's playing?"

Tom Tolland, having no sure answer, merely shrugged.

"Time will tell, Mr Rudge," he said.

"Of that we can be sure," Rudge said and, without another word, sauntered off to find his horse, leaving the steward and his master to their own devices.

THREE

Saturday Shifts

Until a year or two ago pay-outs had been conducted in the comfort of Mrs Figgens' drinking establishment on the Placket road. But William – Snippets – Smith would have none of that. Tailor to trade, Snippets had gravitated into clerking and the keeping of accounts because he was as meticulous numerically as he was morally. Mr Bolderon had enticed him away from a desk in the cloth-mill at Alloa and in Snippets had got rather more than he had bargained for.

Each Saturday fortnight, about three in the afternoon, Snippets began his particular 'shift'. He would install himself in the counting-house with his ledgers and strongbox. At four o'clock he would be joined by Mr Rance and a couple of muscular clerks named Henning and McCaffray. On Snippets' instruction they would erect and put in place three wooden tables and cover them with baize cloth. Henning would wheel from a corner a tall, gibbet-like desk.

At five, Snippets would unhook from his belt a gigantic bunch of keys, would kneel before the strongbox and unlock each of its four padlocks. He would lift the lid, unlock the inner bolt, lift a second lid and then extract banknotes and bags of coin that had been saved for the pay-out. These he would pass to Thomas Rance who would pour the money on to the table and begin sorting coins into slotted wooden trays that Snippets had had the carpenters make for the purpose. Colliers were a damned conservative crowd and suspicious of written money.

About a quarter past the hour of five the pitmen would begin to sidle into the yard. Lanterns would be lit, hung on nails on the building's external walls, jugs of whisky and pots of ale would circulate and a general buzz of expectation would enliven the night. Snippets, indoors, ignored the clamour.

About a quarter to the hour of six, chanting would start up, would swell rapidly into a deafening chorus of impatience.

Grimly, Snippets would tug on his grey suede gloves. He would nod to Mr Rance who would take his position on a box directly behind the counting-table. He would nod to Henning who would clamber on to the stool behind the tall desk and would open the ledgers. He would signal to McCaffray to man the door. And then he would wait, wait without conscience, until the hands of the clock on the wall crept to six exactly, and then he would say, "Gentlemen, are you all prepared?"

"Aye, Mr Smith."

"Ready, Mr Smith."

"Admit them."

Poor McCaffray would hoist the bar from the door and begin his fight to ensure that only four men at a time gained admittance, while out of sheer devilment the rabble in the yard stormed the citadel.

Snippets could not understand why pitmen refused to be orderly and well-mannered. Could they not see that the process of payment had been regularised for their convenience and would be speedier still if only they would not brawl and buffet, and harass the doorman?

"Name?" Thomas Rance shouted.

"McClure."

"McClure," Thomas Rance shouted.

"McClure, McClure." Henning would trace his finger down the list of names in the ledger. "Aye, James McClure. Sixty shillin's, less rent o' two shillin's. Pay fifty-eight shillin's, Mr Smith."

Snippets' fingers would deftly pluck coins from the tray and toss them into a huge earthenware bowl which stood in the centre of the table.

When the sum was all counted into the bowl, Snippets would say, "Take your wage, James McClure."

The hewer would scoop the money out of the bowl and pretend to count it, then would shift away from the table as the litany began again. He would make his way to the high desk where Henning would hold down a ledger and a pencil on a string and the pitman would sign his name or make his mark as a receipt.

"Name?"

"Norman Provan."

"Provan. Norman."

"Provan, Provan. Sixty-six shillin's, less rent o' two shillin's. Pay sixty-four shillin's, Mr Smith."

And so it would go on, four men in and four men out, with McCaffray fighting every admission as if he was holding a fort against an invasion by barbarians.

It was twenty minutes after six o'clock when John Bennet squeezed past McCaffray into the counting-house. He had a smug, swaggering look to him that Thomas Rance remarked at once. But the oversman put it down to a high take, for Bennet was known to be a big earner who sweated himself and his women hard.

"Name?"

"John Bennet."

"Bennet, Bennet." Henning paused. "My, my, Mr Smith! It's eighty-eight shillin's."

Jock Bennet found Rance's eye, smirked and shook his hands loosely by his sides as Snippets doled out the wage. The three other colliers in the room gave a cheer of appreciation and Jock raised his fist and punched the air before he scooped out the silver coins and, without bothering to count them, stuffed them into his pocket. He swaggered to the desk to make his mark, a bushy squiggle that he claimed was a signature. He did not, however, quit the desk at once.

He flexed his body, stretched up towards Henning and whispered, "My lad, Davy Bennet; take him off the book."

"Davy?" said Henning, in surprise. "What's wrong wi' him? Is he sick again?"

"Just take him off the book."

Henning was nonplussed. Before Jock Bennet could prevent it the clerk had called out, "Mr Smith, a word wi' you, please."

"What's amiss?"

"Mr Bennet here wants his laddie's name taken off the book."

It was suddenly quiet within the counting-house.

Snippets glanced over his shoulder at Mr Rance who, hands clasped behind his back, rocked on the balls of his feet and regarded Jock Bennet with a probing gaze.

"Is he ill again?" the oversman enquired.

"Nah, nah. Davy'll be in for his wage tonight." Jock Bennet hesitated. "But from Monday he'll be comin' down wi' me. I'll fee him from then on."

"Is it you that's sick then, Bennet?"

"I'm as fit as a bloody flea, man."

"Then why do you need the help of the boy?"

"To clear an' carry, Mr Rance. Yon tunnel's damned tight, if ye recall."

"Not so damned tight you can't pull near ninety shillings out of it," said Rance. "It's hard to believe you can rake even more out of yon hole."

"I can rake enough extra t' pay our Davy."

Some ruffian in the yard took a flying kick at the door, and McCaffray shouted, "Hold your bloody horses, eh!"

Jock Bennet said, "Mr Rance, it's my right t' take Davy down wi' me an' fee him from my earnin's, if I've a mind to."

"That's true," Thomas Rance agreed.

Davy Bennet was sufficiently mature to descend from the upper level and learn how to cut coal on his own account. As operator of a ventilator flap, just tugging a rope all day long, he earned a miserable six shillings per week. On a fat seam, even a weakling could pull down that much. But the room in which Bennet worked was not particularly rich in coal. Besides, the boy was puny and Thomas Rance found it difficult to believe that he would be of much use to his father in the stifling base level.

"Mr Rance," Snippets interrupted, "I am conductin' a pay-out, if you please."

"Take David Bennet off the book," said Mr Rance to Henning, "after he is paid tonight. Is that what you want, Bennet?"

"No more an' no less, Mr Rance. I give y' thanks."

"I wonder if Davy'll thank me," the oversman murmured, as he watched Jock Bennet cross from desk to door.

It was all most peculiar. Bennet had two good haulers in his daughter and the Patterson woman but had surely reached the maximum take that the narrow seam could feasibly yield. The Ogilvies, now that he thought of it, earned several shillings less than Jock Bennet, and Willie Ogilvie was no mean hand with pick and hammer.

"Tom Yates."

"Yates. Tom," Rance called out automatically.

He hardly heard the response. He was intent on watching Bennet until the hewer was let out of the counting-house into the yard, hopeful that the man might say something that would give a clue as to his true intention.

Thomas Rance was not satisfied with the pitman's explanation. There was more to this than met the eye. He would not rest content until he discovered why Jock Bennet, a sly devil if ever there was, needed Davy in the room with him. There was only one way to obtain an answer.

Tonight, Thomas Rance decided, he must go below.

The day had been soft for the month but wintry mist returned with evening, sifting from the hills and along the banks of the Lightwater and over the fields to envelop the castle's tower and yards.

Anna had worked quite willingly that day. She had made sure that her industry had been duly noted by her mother-in-law and even by Mistress Alicia, but had done her share of the outdoors work too without being prodded into it. With Sandy away, Anna had gone to the pasture and fetched the milking cows to the byre, a task she normally considered beneath her dignity.

Because of the chill in the air she had left Robbie in the kitchen in the care of Aileen Sinclair, who certainly did not object to having her grandson to herself for an hour or two. Anna had milked the cows and put them out into the pasture again, then had carried the pans into the dairy for the cream to separate. She had even remembered to light a lantern and peer under the shelves to make sure that none of the estate's slinky cats was hiding in the shadows to have an illicit feast in the dark.

By a quarter past five her chores were done and she was free to hurry to the coach shed to check that the gig had not returned. To her relief she found the place empty, save for the big, dusty old carriage that Mr Gilbert had purchased last November at a Falkirk auction and hoped to refurbish so that the family could ride out in style. In the meantime Mr Gilbert was driven in the gig by either Lachlan or Sandy Sinclair.

Today, Mr Gilbert had gone down the road to Ottershaw to call upon his brother. Sandy had been at the reins. Anna would have sacrificed a year's wage, such as it was, to have ridden to Ottershaw with them. But she, even she, could contrive no excuse for such a jaunt and would have to be content with the news that Sandy brought back.

When Lachlan was the driver he brought back only dull gossip about old acquaintances, comments about the farming procedures of the new grieve, an energetic young bachelor named Hornbeam who, as far as Anna could gather, seemed to be living up to his reputation for efficiency. She cared not a fig about fatstock, crop rotation and the high cost of seed corn. She cared only about Randall. Naturally she could not question Lachlan directly on this subject. She was obliged to hem-and-haw, to put her questions about the laird and his doings indirectly, otherwise Lachlan would have closed his mouth and told her nothing at all. With Sandy it was different. She could pump him for every drop of news without fear of incurring displeasure. In Sandy Sinclair's eyes she could do no wrong and she milked his infatuation to gain her own ends as she had done with all men daft enough to be attracted to her.

She had only just emerged from the coach shed when she heard a clatter of wheels on the section of paved road that led from the front drive into the yards at the rear. Gig lamps loomed out of the gloaming like two big yellow eyes. Sandy drove easily, relaxed in a manner that Matt had never been. No matter what job he was doing Matt had always seemed tense and resentful, cramped by grudges and ill will. But Sandy took pleasure in work and was more expert with horses than his brother had ever been. He steered the buxom mare, Maisie, into and around the perimeter of the yard as easily as if he had been saddled on her and did not have the width of the gig to contend with.

"Hey, lass. Hey, Maisie. Whey now."

He coaxed the mare to a halt with the gig perfectly backed to the coach shed door. Slack rein in hand, he hopped from the board and soon had the animal uncoupled, out of the shafts and into the stable for a brush down and a feed.

Sandy had spotted his sister-in-law the moment he had

entered the yard and acknowledged her wave with a wag of the head and a boyish grin.

As he led the mare away he called out, "Extinguish the gig lamps for me, Anna, then come by an' I'll tell you all the news from Ottershaw."

Anna was disgruntled at being given an order by the youngest Sinclair but she was too anxious to argue. Swiftly she unclipped the little square windows of the lamps, pinched out the candles with wetted fingers, closed the doors again and, wiping her hands on her dress, hurried into the stable.

Sandy had already stripped off Maisie's tackle, had backed her into a stall and was brushing dirt gently from her legs and flanks. When that was done he would fill her manger with a mixture of bruised beans, oats and meadow hay, a system of feeding that Lachlan had introduced for hack and road horses in spite of prejudice against it. The feed mix was stored in a slanted bin the lid of which was battened down by four big stones, as if Strachan rats were more muscular and daring than rodents elsewhere in the Lennox.

To show her willingness, and because she could not get close to Sandy while he remained in the stall, Anna opened the lid of the bin, forked out a quantity of feed into an old blanket and carried the bundle to the mouth of the stall, ready for Sandy to spread into the manger.

The young man looked up from his work.

"My, my, Anna! You're bein' uncommon helpful the night."

"You must be fair hungry?" she said.

Sandy stroked the brush down the mare's legs.

"Hungry enough," he said, "though I had a good dinner in the kitchen at Ottershaw."

"Were you taken into the house?"

"Aye."

"Did you see Randall?"

"I saw him – but not in the house."

"Did he – did he enquire about me?"

"I'm afraid he did not, Anna."

"What *did* he say?"

"He didna speak to me at all."

"How did he look?"

"Fine."

"How did he – seem?"

"He seemed as he always seems."

"What was he wearin' today?"

"Trews," said Sandy without hesitation. "Old boots an' the long jacket he's had for years."

"Did he show much of his limp?"

"Aye, it was visible, but no worse than usual."

"Where had he been?"

"With Mr Hornbeam, up in the tree plantin's."

Anna did not pursue that line of interrogation lest Sandy, like his father, be deflected into discussing estate work and not Randall. She asked several other trivial questions to which Sandy gave non-committal replies while he completed his work with the mare and put away the tackle on its hooks.

When he went out into the yard again, Anna followed. She watched him open the shed door and, unaided, run the gig into the shed. Even that effort did not seem to tax the strength of the youngest Sinclair. He emerged, unwinded, dusting his hands in satisfaction.

"There," Sandy said. "Everythin's done. I think I'm due my supper now."

"Wait, Sandy. What else have you t' tell me?"

"The rest was just chatter about aches an' pains."

"No more about what the laird's been doin'?"

"Hunter was hangin' about much o' the time an', as you know better than me, Hunter'll not entertain gossip about his master."

Anna recalled the steward of Ottershaw only too well. She had never been fond of the man, nor he of her. He had resented her for the influence she'd had over his lord and master, for the fact that he could do nothing to harm her.

"Here!" said Sandy. "Where's the wee appendage?"

"Appendage?"

"Robbie, the bairn."

"Watch your lip, Sandy Sinclair. My son's no' an appendage."

"God, he clings t' you like a growth."

"Too cold for him tonight. He's in wi' your mother."

"He's a lucky wee beggar, though," said Sandy.

"What way he is lucky?"

"He gets plenty o' cuddles from you."

"Oh, I see. So that's why ye envy him, is it?"

"I wouldna refuse a cuddle from you, Anna."

He was candid, teasing but not conniving, not as Matt had been when first he had wooed her.

"Would ye like a cuddle from me right here an' now?" said Anna.

"Aye, I would."

"Well, you're not gettin' one," said Anna, laughing. "Not now, not ever."

"Ever's a long time, Anna."

"Sandy Sinclair, you're naught but a laddie."

"Ah, but I'm growin' bigger every day."

"You'll never be man enough for me," said Anna and flounced across the yard to the kitchen door, leaving Sandy by the coach shed, looking after her with rueful longing.

Thoughtfully Sandy closed and barred the coach shed door. He had not expected Anna to give in to him and had kept his true feelings hidden behind chat. For all that, he was disappointed that she had not rewarded him with a quick, sisterly kiss upon the cheek. He had never liked any other lass half as much as he liked Anna. He did not think of her as his brother's wife, as a mother. For Sandy, she still had the fresh, daft sparkle of girlhood; and her teasing ways pleased him.

According to Matt, Anna was a witch who had led him a destructive dance. It was undeniable that she had seduced Randall Bontine and had bedded with the man. But Sandy managed to put all that to one side. Anna was so damned pretty that he could not resist falling in love with her. He was hard-pressed to smother his desire to take her in his arms, kiss her lips and squeeze her against his chest.

Of course, he kept his feelings to himself. His father, mother and sister Catriona would have fits if he so much as hinted that Anna attracted him as a woman is supposed to attract a man. But he would do anything for her – anything that would not give her too much power over him. Sandy Sinclair might be in love but he was not entirely daft.

Today, for instance, he had lied to her. He had not told the truth about his visit to Ottershaw.

He did not wish to be the one to bring news that would surely distress her and probably throw her into a black mood.

Sir Randall Bontine had not been dressed in his working clothes, nor had he come down to Ottershaw from the plantation in the company of his grieve. Sir Randall had been dressed up in his finery and had looked every lean inch a gentleman for the laird had been entertaining guests, a man and a pretty girl.

Sandy had glimpsed them out upon the terrace at the front of the mansion. The male guest was wonderfully well dressed too and seemed, like the laird, to be swaggering, arrogant and carefree. The girl who was with them was as young as Anna and equally as beautiful. She had been wearing an emerald-green riding-habit and a tiny black beaver hat that must have cost ten guineas at least. She had laughed gaily at every word the laird uttered and clung to his arm and fluttered her blue, rapacious eyes at him.

Sandy Sinclair did not have to be a sophisticate to realise what was going on. But how could he tell Anna that he had spoken with Mrs Lacy, the cook at Ottershaw, and that the conversation had confirmed the evidence of his eyes?

"Who is yon gentleman?" Sandy had asked the cook.

"Major Seaton, a friend from the laird's army days."

"How long have they been here?"

"They cam' yesterday an' are said to be stayin' for a week."

Sandy could tell by the way Mrs Lacy imparted the information that the cook knew he would carry it back to Anna and that Anna would be wounded by it. Inflicting hurt was the cook's intention for she too had hated the upstart girl from the hill.

"What about the woman? Is she Seaton's wife?" Sandy had asked, feigning innocent curiosity.

Mrs Lacy had grimaced at his apparent naivety.

"Is she figs his wife," the cook had said. "She's Major Seaton's sister. His *spinster* sister."

"She's bonnie, right enough," Sandy had remarked.

"If you ask me, that bonnie spinster has come here huntin' a husband."

Mrs Lacy had tapped the side of her nose with her forefinger and had given Sandy a knowing wink to impress the point upon him.

"A – a husband!" Sandy had said. "Surely ye canna mean the laird?"

"I can, an' I do, mean the laird."

Sandy was tempted to question Mr Gilbert during the ride home to Strachan Castle but he did not know how to go about it without seeming impertinent. It was, after all, no business of his what Sir Randall Bontine chose to do with himself. Sandy's mother had overheard Alicia and Gibbie discussing the matter of legitimate heirs for Ottershaw, saying, in effect, that it was high time Sir Randall found himself a wife.

None of this information did Sandy impart to Anna.

Let Anna find out about pretty Miss Seaton in her own good time for there, Sandy felt, was a rival that poor old Anna would not be able to defeat.

Enclosed by trees, gardens and grazing-pastures, the village of Placket occupied the face of a steep hill that climbed from the shore to the Malkin, an undistinguished knoll a half-mile inland from the river. Placket's square was small, oppressive and tilted at an angle to the south. It was fed only by a cobbled lane and a muddy track that wandered up to the cornmill.

There was nothing grand about the antiquities that flanked the square. St Austin's church was patched with lichen and streaked with gull droppings. The long, two-storey dwelling on the west side of the square, the abbot's house, had fallen gradually into a state of decay and was now used only to store straw and old fish barrels. The only lighted front in Placket's square was that of Duncan Nicol's shop. It provided a centre for the community and, on pay-nights, had all the bustling cheerfulness of a dancing-floor.

Duncan Nicol was a plump, jolly fellow without an ounce of prejudice against pit folk. He would serve colliers with the same broad grin that he bestowed upon sour-faced fisher-wives or farmers, local inhabitants who thoroughly disapproved of the hordes of godless barbarians that swept in from the Abbeyfield. Nicol was as honest as any shopkeeper could be. He did not put chalk in his flour, water his milk, adulterate his teas or tamper with his set of measures. His shop had a good reputation even among keelmen who had, of course, choice of provision merchants on both sides of the Forth. Coal workers, however, were the backbone and ribs of Mr Nicol's trade and Saturday night, especially on pay-days, brought them out in full force.

Much as Elspeth enjoyed shopping she was still a little apprehensive when she visited the village. It was here that she had severed connection with her 'old life', with Balnesmoor, and here that the two lives touched. She was mildly afraid that James might even now find her trail from Stirling and track her to this spot. When she had fled from Balnesmoor that autumn day in 1813, she had thought that her escape from her father was complete. She had not been in Glasgow a week before she had been accosted and recognised. A weaver mannie, whom she did not know by sight as much, grabbed at her arm, thrust his face into hers and demanded to be told her name.

"I – I am Elspeth Patterson."

"Ye are James Moodie's wife, are ye not?"

Shocked, she had denied it, had torn herself from his grasp and had run away along Argyle Street while the man pursued her, crying out after her as if she was a thief. If she had not had Mary Jean in her arms some honest, enterprising person in the crowd might have tackled her, tripped her and she would have been caught there and then, dragged back to Balnesmoor only days after she had left the place. She had hidden out in a vennel by the cattle market until dusk and had walked eastward out of the ring of the city and put up, very late, in a disreputable little inn on the road to the village of Stepps. Next day she had taken to the road again and had gone on walking, since the weather was fine and she had money enough for lodgings and food, and had eventually, after several days, come round to Falkirk.

There she had taken stock of her position. She had acknowledged that though she had gravitated to a town where she might be recognised, she felt more comfortable nearer home. She would most probably have gone on, gone north into the highland territories, perhaps, if she had not fallen into work in the counting-house of a cooperage and, being in need of income, had stuck there for fifteen weeks.

It was a good job, if not well paid, and Mary Jean was safe

with a minder each day. They lodged in a room of a house on the town's outskirts, and were favoured by the keeper of the house, a Mrs Inglis, because they were clean and quiet.

She might have settled in Falkirk, her nervousness might have dwindled with the passing weeks, if she had not encountered a man in the counting-house who believed that she was Elspeth Moodie and not Elspeth Patterson. He was a salt-fish merchant and had a brother in a woollen-mill in Airth who had been given a handbill on a 'Wanted Female Person' by an agent named Scarf. John Scarf. The man was inclined to link Elspeth Patterson with the missing wife and, by insinuations and enquiries, might soon reach the conclusion that he was entitled to the five guineas reward that the handbill promised.

Elspeth left the cooperage and the lodging and went back towards the town of Stirling, intending to follow the road to the west, heading for the remote ports of the seaboard where James did not do business and she might find work on farm or croft, or a place in some small community. She stopped in Stirling, however, to earn a few shillings more. The truth, she supposed, was that she was reluctant to quit the central plain, to strike far from the towns whose names she knew and from people who spoke the same dialect as she did.

The bleachfields gave her piece-work. A hovel in the vennels by Wolf Crag gave her lodging at little cost. An auld wife cared for Mary Jean while Elspeth earned their daily tithe. It was a mean, fettered sort of existence and she was possessed of the feeling that she would inevitably be recognised and this time, perhaps, caught. Perhaps, she thought, that was what she secretly longed for, to have no choice but to return to the comfort of Moss House. But when it came to it she did not surrender, did not give herself up. She fled.

The woman was enormous. She blocked Elspeth's way across the side of the Stirling bridge. The woman was much more sure than the man in Falkirk had been, though again Elspeth had no recollection of having encountered her before. The huge waddling woman clasped her without warning, a bear-hug, and cried aloud: *"Mr Moodie's wife. I have Moodie's wife."*

How did they recognise her? Did she bear some mark or brand that made her known to them on sight?

She drove her knee into the woman's belly, punched a forearm into her face and dashed away, not for the bleachfields but for the Crag and the house where Mary Jean was in care. And that same evening, in the rain, she slunk out of the town, walking through the rain with Mary Jean girning in a shawl in her arms and her bundle roped to her back.

Constantly she had to remind herself why she had fled from James Moodie. It was not just the shadow of incest that she feared but the shadow of murder. She was far enough removed from Balnesmoor to see that her father had plotted murder. Earlier, he had schemed to have her foster-father ruined. James might claim that he had done it all for her, to bring her to him and to keep her safe for evermore, but she sensed that he might be rid of her too if circumstances turned him against her. She could not admit to herself that she was James Moodie's flesh and blood, that Mary Jean was his granddaughter. It seemed inconceivable that she was linked by an indissoluble tie to that fierce, brooding and unscrupulous man, though the facts could not be denied.

She spent the night in the lee of a hedge on the river-bank, was awakened close to dawn by the voices of salmon-fishers and, hugging Mary Jean to her breast, stole away to the road again and walked on and on until she came to a posthouse where she paid sixpence for bread and milk and a warm by the day's first fire.

Later she had cadged a ride from a carrier who had lifted her eight miles along the river road to Gaines. One short ride had followed another until the thieving old carrier with the cargo of chemicals had put an end to her escape, had delivered her, unwittingly, to the Abbeyfield and to Jock Bennet.

On occasions, even now, however, she would feel the rub of anxiety along her spine, would pause by the wall of St Austin's Kirk and scan the crowd in Placket square to make sure there were no strangers there, no faces from out of her past.

Mouse would say, "What's bitin' you, Elspeth?"

Elspeth would answer, "Nothing. I'm just catchin' my breath."

And Mouse would take Mary Jean by the hand and, with

Sarah following, the girls would scamper across the square to Mr Nicol's shop and, after a moment or two, Elspeth's anxiety would wane and she would go after them.

Elspeth had made no serious enemies among the pitfolk. She was not particularly popular, however, for she kept herself to herself too much for friendships to ripen. Some of the girls were jealous of her looks and imagined that she was hoity-toity, too good to frolic with them. Elspeth cared little what they thought of her. She assumed that they assumed that she was more wife than servant to Jock Bennet but she had no reputation to protect and, if she had been challenged on the point, would not have denied that she was Mr Bennet's woman.

It mattered not to Georgie Haynes whose woman Elspeth Patterson happened to be. Georgie Haynes wanted her and intended, somehow, to have her.

There were willing girls in plenty to be found in Placket but Georgie Haynes had wearied of the kind that would go up the hill with him to roll in the grass behind the cornmill or lie on wet sand under the lading pier. Georgie was twenty-six years old, young and arrogant enough to want a woman he could not buy. And Elspeth Patterson was as pretty as any woman upon whom he had ever clapped eyes and had a certain air to her, a mysteriousness that would make her worth possessing.

Georgie did not quite know why he had become fixated on the woman from the Abbeyfield but, over the winter months, he spoke of her often to his two shipmates and bragged that he would take her before the summer was out. He fully intended to make good his boast.

On that Saturday night in March the *Matchless*, one of McNeil's three keel-boats, was moored on the mud below Placket's north lading. Skipper Hamilton had decided that wind and tide were too strong for a plunge back home to Leith, that they would load and run on the Sabbath day and risk the wrath of the Lord. The truth was that none of the three-man crew had any particular desire to return to their wives across the water and would seize any sort of excuse to stay out upon the river shore. That was the aspect of the life they enjoyed, recompense for the filthy labour of loading and unloading cargoes of coal from the shallow hold of the little beetle-black boat, for enduring cold, wet crossings of the Forth which could often be as rough as an ocean.

Keelmen were much given to drinking, scrapping and wenching and the crew of the *Matchless* were agreed that the Bunch of Grapes served ale as good as any in Alloa or Leith and that the square in Placket on a Saturday night provided a 'cattle show' better than Edinburgh's Haymarket.

Girls young, and girls old enough to know better, were attracted to keelmen. As a rule the sailors were more muscular than collier lads, and taller too. They were free-spending men whose bold, intoxicating promises gave them a glamour far removed from the dull and dirty nature of their work at the quays.

Georgie, for instance, measured six feet in height, had shoulders like an ox and a deep, weather-reddened chest matted with russet hair. His smooth manners and sly, suggestive charm had many a lass falling over herself to gain his attention, even though it was known that he had a wife and bairns stowed somewhere in Port of Leith and that he was nothing but a casual philanderer.

Skipper Hamilton was a quiet-spoken man in his forties. He had worked keels for Mr McNeil for thirty years. He was less 'romantic' than young Georgie and paid for his women in the fond belief that 'matching' for money was not a mortal sin and that he would thus remain faithful to his good lady wife, in spirit if not in ordinance.

The third member of the crew, Lewis Turner, was a gigantic, gangling chap only three or four years older than Georgie. But already the glint had been extinguished from his eyes by addiction to spirits and he was happier lying in the slops on the floor of a tavern than in the sweet grass of the Malkin with a girl. It was Turner who had fished for information on the pretty young woman whom Georgie had first noticed back in the autumn. From Turner, Georgie had learned how Elspeth Patterson had come to work on the Abbeyfield, that she had a bairn, and that she shared a cottage and probably a bed with pitman Jock Bennet.

Georgie did not have a chance to begin wooing before winter came. Short hours of daylight curtailed the activities of the river rovers. He did not dare ferret down into the cottages in search of her, of course, for pitmen distrusted strangers and would have covered him in tar and slung him in the cesspool, like as not, if they had caught him in their territory. Come March, however, Georgie was ready to begin his courtship, to impose himself upon the Patterson woman as a man who is any sort of man must do with a woman who has snared his fancy.

She was plain-dressed that evening and walked sedate as a lady, not with the bustling, swinging gait of other eligible girls; modest, Georgie thought, demure.

He stepped out of the shadow of the arch of the abbot's house and cut across by the old pump, calling out as heartily as if he was greeting an old and dear friend, "Ach, if it's not Mistress Patterson."

She stopped dead, swung round. In her eyes was something that Georgie could not name: horror, panic.

Surely he was not that unattractive to look upon, not with the coal muck sluiced from him and clean clothes fresh from his locker upon his back.

He smiled and took off his cap.

She was still staring at him, one hand raised before her as if to fend him off.

"I've been seekin' an opportunity o' makin' closer acquaintance, Mistress Patterson," Georgie Haynes said; he had practised the speech and thought it damned pretty. "You'll recall seein' me before. I nodded t' you, an' you were gracious enough t' nod back."

She did not seem to recall. She blinked, stared at him and retreated three or four quick little steps towards the shop.

Georgie went after her.

"I'm the keelman. I'm Georgie Haynes," he said, offering his hand, rolled over at the wrist the way he had seen gentlemen do when they greeted a lady.

She retreated again.

Georgie pursued.

Behind the Patterson woman, from the congregation by the shop, a child separated herself, a girl of nine or ten years. Georgie glanced at her, found himself disconcerted by the solemn intensity of her gaze. It was almost as if she could see right through him and, in spite of her youth and innocence, read what was on his mind.

"Surely this canna be your daughter, Mistress Patterson?"

"I'm not her daughter," Sarah retorted.

"Your sister, then?"

He could not for the life of him get the Patterson woman to open her mouth. It was the little girl who answered once more.

"*She* bides in *our* house."

"My – my daughter's inside," said the Patterson woman.

"An' is she as bonnie as her mother?" said Georgie.

He gave a salty little bow.

Now she had opened her mouth he would press the advantage. Candy talk was reckoned to be his strong suit and he had jawed more than one shy maiden off her feet.

Encouraged, Georgie Haynes moved in.

Elspeth's first thought was that the keelman had identified her, that somehow he had got wind of the fact that she was the runaway wife of James Simpson Moodie of Balnesmoor, and, like the salt-fish merchant in Falkirk, had accosted her and engaged her in conversation with the sole intention of proving himself right.

Heart thudding, mouth dry, Elspeth was paralysed by uncertainty. His question about her daughter did not allay her fear. On the contrary, it would seem a natural sort of question for the situation she had imagined. Inwardly she cursed Sarah for intervening.

When the man came into the light, close to the shop front, Elspeth realised that she had seen him in the square on several occasions, that he was certainly what he claimed to be – a keelman – and that his interest in her might have no connection with the past. She forced herself to make reply and when he stepped closer she instantly, and with relief, sensed the truth: he was no agent, no spy. He intended to flirt with her, not betray her.

This man, Haynes, would not be the first to insinuate that he would like to strike up a friendship with her. Elspeth was not naive. She was not shocked by the crassness of his advances, that mock-gentlemanly behaviour which colliers, as well as keelmen, thought of as a precursor to the making of improper suggestions. No doubt he had watched for an opportunity to separate her from Mouse and Sarah, to have her alone. If Mr Bennet had been in the vicinity the keelman would not have dared doff his cap.

Elspeth could not keep the relief out of her voice.

She answered his last question. "Oh, my daughter is far bonnier than I am, Mr Haynes."

"She must, then, be a bloody angel come down from Heaven."

"I give you thanks for the compliment, Mr Haynes."

"Georgie is my name, Mistress Patterson."

"Well, Georgie, it has been a pleasure t' talk with you but now I must be on my way. I have purchases to make."

"Stay for a minute."

It was only a flirtation, a clumsy attempt to woo her. Elspeth's relief increased.

She laughed. "I must do the buyin' now, Mr Haynes, before all the best cuts are sold."

"I could bring ye meat from the flesher in Leith."

"I doubt if I could afford the price, Mr Haynes."

The conversation was interrupted by half-blind Betty Pickard who burrowed through the folk in the shop doorway lugging a wooden bucket filled with steaming tripe.

The smell wafted about in the evening air and pulled after it, like pups chasing a rope, a gang of small boys who smacked their lips and yapped in exaggerated hunger. Betty trailed her daughter Ginny by the hand. Ginny was but twelve years old, yet, when she caught sight of Georgie, she turned all winsome and coy and straightened her shoulders and thrust out her budding breasts and set her head on one side and, as she brushed past the keelman, said, "Good evenin' t' you, Georgie."

Georgie Haynes ignored the child who was gripped by the forearm by her mother who, blind or not, knew what the girl's tone signified and whipped her quickly away across the square into the shelter of the lane to smack her for her brazen insolence.

The little boys followed, still dogging the tripe bucket.

Elspeth said, "I must leave you, Mr Haynes. It's Saturday night an' I've a pitman an' his family to cook for."

Haynes stepped to one side. He swept his cap out as if it

had a peacock's feather sewn to it, showed all his white teeth in a grin.

Elspeth nodded and went past him and into the shop.

She did not know Georgie Haynes well enough to be other than amused by the incident.

Mouse was pressed against the inside of the door. She too had seen the keelman. She had her tiny hands pressed tight on Mary Jean's shoulders as if to prevent the child from running out to her mother, from intruding on the romantic interlude, spoiling it.

Mouse licked her lips, then said, "That's – that man's Georgie Haynes, off the *Matchless*."

"He did introduce himself, Mouse. Do you think I'd talk so long to a stranger?"

Taking Mary Jean by the hand Elspeth led the girls into the crowded interior of the shop.

Mouse plucked at her skirt. "He's wicked, is Georgie Haynes."

"Well, I do not intend to have anythin' more to do with him, Mousie, so you can stop frettin' on that score," said Elspeth, and distracted Mouse and Mary Jean by directing them to the sweetmeat stall where, in bowls and on trays, all sorts of sugary delicacies were displayed.

It took Elspeth an hour to make all her purchases. She found all three girls at the trinket counter. They were chattering excitedly, anxious for Elspeth to admire their buys. Mouse had selected a ring, a cheap tin thing with a painted diamond at its centre, while Sarah had spent her money on a tin hair-clasp and a foot of mock-silk ribbon. Being not much interested in geegaws, Mary Jean had settled for edibles and was coated with cinnamon paste, almond crumbs and the sticky dust of a sherbet.

With the girls about her, Elspeth set off across the square, lugging her heavy basket of provisions. She had put Georgie Haynes out of mind and was in good humour, when, emerging from the end of the lane, she saw that the keelman had stationed himself at the bridge.

He leaned against the post, arms folded.

Spotting him too, Mouse reached at once for Sarah and Mary Jean and drew them against her as if Haynes was an abductor of young children and might bag them on to his boat to sell as slaves in the city. Even Mary Jean seemed to sense the threat of the man. She pressed herself against Mouse without a word.

Once more Georgie Haynes did a bit of swank with his cap.

"Well now, Mistress Patterson, is this no' an astonishin' coincidence?"

"That," said Elspeth, stiffly, "is a matter of opinion."

Indolently Georgie stretched one leg across the width of the little bridge.

"I'll carry your basket, if ye ask me nice," he said.

"I can manage perfectly well, thank ye."

"I'd prefer it," said Haynes, "if ye'd let me carry you."

Elspeth had had enough of the keelman's sauce.

"Stand out of my way."

She imagined that the keelman, for all his arrogance, had reached the limit of boldness. He would not dare assault her, not sober, and not with the Grapes only three hundred yards away down the Placket road. The colliers would skin him if he touched one of their women against her will.

"I would prefer it," said Haynes, "if you'd stand in my way. Could we not stand t'gether for a while?"

The implications would not be lost on Mouse; even Sarah had heard enough of such talk to understand what Haynes meant by it.

Angrily, Elspeth said, "Will you, sir, let me pass?"

"Do ye hear that?" Haynes cried, to nobody in particular. "She calls me 'sir'. I'll tell you what, Mistress Patterson, if you gi' me a kiss I'll lift my leg."

To Elspeth's astonishment the keelman did not await an answer. He caught her arm and endeavoured to snake his arm about her waist. The basketful of provisions fended him off but he had effectively separated her from the girls and trapped her on the narrow span of the bridge.

"Mouse," Elspeth shouted, "go an' fetch your father."

Mouse drew back, shaking her head. It was left to Sarah to act.

Hardly had the words left Elspeth's mouth than the younger girl was in motion. She ran straight for the edge of the winter-shorn gully and leapt down into it, out of sight. The burn below was shallow enough to allow her to wade across it, though, Elspeth suspected, Sarah might keep to the gully, sheltered by it, until the slope eased and she could emerge not far behind the Bunch of Grapes.

Haynes did not back away. He hardly seemed to be aware that somebody had gone for assistance, or did not care.

His tone was unctuous. "I'll do ye no harm, woman. I want but a kiss, a token that there'll be frien'ship between us in the future."

Elspeth could hear Mary Jean whimpering. She was reluctant to discard the basket in case the provisions were lost. She took her eye from the keelman and glanced downstream into the gloom to see if she could make out Sarah.

Haynes dragged her closer.

Fearing that he might dislocate her arm, Elspeth yielded.

In horror Mouse watched, uncertain now that Elspeth appeared to have given herself to the man and endured the man's rough hands upon her without protest.

"Come below the bridge wi' me," Haynes whispered, "an' you'll discover I'm twice the man your coal-hewer is."

Revolted, Elspeth could no longer contain herself.

She raked Haynes' cheek with her fingernails, drawing blood.

The basket slid from her elbow and spilled its contents upon the ground. Haynes, who did not seem at all daunted by her fire, dragged her forcibly against him. She spat into his face, shocked at herself for doing it.

"By Christ, you're a wildcat!" Haynes said, laughing. "I like a woman wi' spunk. Come now, the kiss an' I'll let ye go."

Perhaps he would have released her there and then. Even Georgie Haynes was not so insensitive as to believe that he had won her heart by such a bullying declaration of love. He could not lose face, however. He continued to hold her on the off chance that she would give him a sign that favoured his conceit. In a minute or so he would have released her with a laugh and a promise of another meeting.

Sarah, however, who had emerged from the gully not far off, had encountered her brother. Having consumed two stoups of ale to celebrate his rise in the world of men, Davy was toddling up towards the village to bring the news to his sisters. Davy was drunk enough to be fearless. He came charging to Elspeth's rescue, armed with a wooden stave torn from a broken fence.

With a man less dangerous than Georgie Haynes the scene might have been comic but Georgie was too slow, did not release Elspeth at once and thus avoid his attacker.

Davy swung the stave low and chopped the keelman across the back of the calves with it. Haynes roared in pain. Davy was no more sensible than the keelman, however, and came in again at once, swinging the stick like a sickle.

Haynes thrust Elspeth from him. With a quick snapping motion, he clasped Davy Bennet by the nape of the neck and the seat of his breeks and hoisted him from the ground. The stave swiped and swished ineffectually as Georgie Haynes held the boy out at arm's length.

Mouse had at last found her voice.

Her shrieks brought womenfolk scampering down the lane from the square. Sobbing, Mary Jean clung to Mouse's skirts while Elspeth beat her fist on the keelman's broad back and shouted, "Put him down, damn you. He's nothin' but a child."

Haynes laughed. He took a pace away from Elspeth and held Davy, kicking and flailing, over the edge of the parapet, twenty or thirty feet above the stones of the burn. Elspeth realised at once that Davy was in great danger. The keelman had no sense. If he let Davy go the boy would surely suffer broken bones and might even be killed by a blow to the head on the stones below. She did not dare strike Haynes again.

Georgie had his audience now. He was playing up to the women and girls who congregated at the bridge and who thought that the incident was fun, a joke that Georgie had contrived for their amusement.

"Come then, pretty lass, gi'e me my kiss in exchange for this fightin' scrap," the keelman said. "That's my price, your sweet red lips on mine."

The collier girls thought this a marvellous stroke and set up a chatter of delight, whistling, catcalling, applauding, all on the side of the keelman, all for the bold Georgie. At that instant Elspeth hated them for their coarseness and ignorance. Davy had become conscious of danger. He held himself still, hanging limp from the man's fists, though he continued to utter cries of impotent frustration.

"Hurry," Georgie Haynes said. "I'm gettin' tired."

Elspeth put a hand upon the keelman's shoulder and touched her mouth to his.

The women cheered and jeered; Georgie was a hero.

"Nah, lass," Haynes said. "I'll not take short measure. It's a proper stinger I'm wantin'."

Elspeth stiffened, braced herself, pressed her lips against his ready mouth. She felt his tongue, thick and curled, probe and penetrate her lips, and tore herself from him in disgust.

Georgie grinned. "You'll no' be so bloody shy next time, m' love."

"Put him down."

"Take him. He's no' worth drownin'."

As if heaving a shovelful of coal from a deck, Haynes swung from the waist and unclasped his fists, dumping Davy on to the bridge. He administered a tap with the toe of his boot and Davy, humiliated, rolled and rose and ran away across the Placket road to hide in the foreshore grasses.

The onlookers applauded. Georgie threw back his head, stuck his hands to his hips and laughed and laughed as if the whole episode had been a show put on for entertainment. But when he turned his face to Elspeth she saw no levity at all but deadly, burning seriousness.

"I'll have you 'neath me yet, lady," he murmured, then turned, raising his arms and, bowing to the watching women, cried, "Wha's next?"

"Me, Georgie. Me."

Sarah, like Davy, had vanished. Elspeth called Mouse and Mary Jean to her, while the fatuous, bullying keelman paraded for the girls.

Hastily she gathered the provisions, those that had not spoiled in the mud, flung them into the basket, then, chasing Mouse and her daughter before her, hurried away from the bridge and the keelman's triumph, sick with loathing.

It seemed that it was not just men from her past that Elspeth had to fear but this threatening bully who had entered her life without invitation or request.

She hurried on, holding the basket on one arm and Mary Jean's hand in her own.

They had gone a good quarter-mile down the road to the cottages before Mouse opened her mouth.

"Why did ye do it?" she demanded, furiously.

Elspeth was taken aback.

"Do what?"

"Kiss him like yon?"

Mouse was accusing her, berating her. She could hardly believe that the girl-child was so unobservant.

"You – you saw how it was, Mousie. I – I had to. For Davy's sake."

"He meant Davy no harm."

"Mouse, how can you –"

"You *wanted* t' kiss him. You *wanted* t' match wi' him."

"Mouse, that's enough!"

Mouse, weeping, took to her heels and ran towards the lights of the cottage rows.

Elspeth did not call after her and did not pursue. She had troubles enough of her own without having to contend with Mouse's silly misinterpretations.

Later she was to regret that she had not paid Mouse more attention in that agitated hour, had failed to detect in the tears and the rantings the first twisted stirrings of sexual jealousy.

The road that had led Keir Bolderon to Hanover Street and to – almost – nocturnal meetings with Olivia Melrose had been one full of strange meanderings, though how strange Mr Bolderon had no notion at the time.

Five years ago, when Bolderon had been seeking investors to support his venture into pit management, McNeil had put him in touch with a Perthshire gentleman by the name of Stuart Melrose. Melrose, it seemed, was interested in wetting his feet in mineral investment and, by putting up a modest piece of capital, had become Keir Bolderon's sleeping partner. Mr Melrose had even hinted that he might be disposed to do more for the upstart manager – being a bit of an upstart himself. Alas, Mr Melrose had been cut down by typhus in the mid-summer of 1812 and had taken his only daughter and younger son to the grave with him. After a prolonged period of silence and uncertainty Keir Bolderon had found himself in dealings with the widow.

Olivia Melrose, as it transpired, was not at all difficult to deal with. She made it clear at the outset that she wished to continue her husband's investment in the Abbeyfield and had no intention of withdrawing capital from the venture, as she was legally entitled to do.

Why should she? The lump sum brought in handsome dividends, and the lady saw no reason to disturb the arrangement. She requested, however, an occasional informal report on the Abbeyfield's progress since she did not understand matters of business as well as a man would do.

Keir Bolderon was vastly relieved at being relieved of the onerous burden of finding four hundred pounds with which to pay off the widow. He agreed instantly that informal reports would be regularly forthcoming. At Mrs Melrose's request a meeting was arranged between the pit manager and the widow lady.

Olivia Melrose turned out to be a woman of character. She had married rather late and was now, Bolderon reckoned, in her thirty-eighth or-ninth year. She was dark-haired, plump and tall. An astringent sense of humour lessened her severity and she spoke with just the trace of a dialect which made her seem more down-to-earth than some glass-tongued Edinburgh matrons. Keir Bolderon soon shed his inhibitions and began to enjoy their 'secret' meetings, two or three times in the year, in Mrs Melrose's town house in Hanover Street.

In spite of the fact that conversation flowed thick and fast and that Mrs Melrose was by no means guarded or aloof, Bolderon learned very little about the lady's personal history. He did not know, for example, that she had not been baptised with the name Olivia but had chosen it for herself at a point in her life when she had grown sick and tired of slaving for her brother and had set out, deliberately, to find herself a husband.

Name-changing was but a small affectation. It in no way detracted from the able determination with which the woman had helped her husband to rise in the world, to acquire, in short order, more than his share of property, stock and wealth.

Stuart Melrose's transformation to 'gentleman' was almost complete when typhus took his soul, and Mrs Melrose had no intention of letting that struggle be wasted.

Mr Bolderon would not have dreamed of 'dropping in' on Mrs Melrose. The supper-takings, arranged by letter at the lady's instigation, were discreet and decorous. Mr Bolderon might be alone in the dining-room with Olivia Melrose but he was not alone in the house. Although the widow claimed that she travelled 'light' for her Edinburgh sojourns the entourage seemed 'heavy' to Mr Bolderon. In addition to her son, Stuart, Mrs Melrose brought with her from Perthshire a housekeeper and companion, a maid and her son's tutor, Mr Hardy. The Hanover Street residence had a permanent staff of three. Mrs Melrose's reputation was, therefore, protected by no fewer than seven loyal servants and the slightest squeak from Madam would have brought them running to defend her honour.

Mr Bolderon, of course, had no intention of challenging the lady's honour. Inclination was another matter. On that Saturday in March, in particular, he had Neil McNeil's injunction very much in mind and the dark-haired and sophisticated widow had never seemed more desirable. Keir Bolderon had always had a penchant for women of full constitution and Mrs Melrose was not in the least timid and countrified about showing off just how full her constitution was. That night she wore a clinging Grecian sort of thing trimmed of all frills that might distract attention from her figure and, after the customary excellent supper of meats and fishes washed down with best imported wines, Mr Bolderon's blood, if not exactly boiling, was certainly on the simmer.

Keir Bolderon had never been a Philistine in matters of art and literature. He had kept abreast of the doings of the capital, the backbiting and bickering that passed for culture in New Edinburgh's incestuous society. Mrs Melrose, though she professed to take none of it seriously, was well up in the latest gossip about her famous neighbours, judges, advocates, ministers of the Gospel, and had even acquired a few confidential titbits about Mr Scott, the novelist, who resided nearby in Castle Street.

While Mr Bolderon simmered gently, Mrs Melrose talked.

"Have you perused the most recent issue of *Blackwood's Magazine*?" the lady enquired.

"Indeed, I have."

"What opinion did you form of its contents?"

"It seems to me," said Mr Bolderon, "that *Blackwood's* has already become a formidable influence, albeit the contributors are impudent tomahawkers intent in the main on chopping up the reputations of better men than they are."

"How well expressed. Do you object to that sort of sport, Mr Bolderon?"

"Good Lord, no! Nothin' I like better than to see a puffed-up reputation punctured."

"How refreshingly honest of you to admit it."

"Gauche, perhaps . . ."

"Oh, no," Mrs Melrose assured her visitor. "Most people, even those who proclaim themselves models of virtue, take a malicious pleasure in seein' the high and the mighty brought down."

"Provided," said Keir Bolderon, "that it's done artistically."

Mrs Melrose laughed.

Her bosom shivered visibly in the neck of her dress, causing Mr Bolderon to swallow, unchewed, a fragment of smoked pheasant. Quickly he reached for his wine glass.

In the past he had not been immune to Olivia Melrose's charms but his conversation with McNeil had, as it were, thrown everything into high relief.

"How witty you are, Mr Bolderon."

Keir Bolderon blushed. He protested that he was naught but a simple engineer. Mrs Melrose would have none of such modesty. For five delectable minutes she tried to convince him that he was a fellow of taste and discernment.

Literary discourse continued until supper was finished and the couple repaired to the parlour where Mr Bolderon, following the usual procedure, prepared to buckle down to business; trouble was, he was no longer sure what business he should buckle down to. The moment that the venerable McNeil had uttered the fateful words, "Marry it", a vision of Olivia Melrose, shimmering in candlelight, had popped into Keir Bolderon's head. Now that the vision was before him, very much in the flesh, he found that his intention was divided. He did not know how to behave, how to protect his reputation as a perfect gentleman – and still plead for money for the Abbeyfield.

Gathering his wits, he tried to ignore the sibilant sounds of Olivia's skirts as she seated herself on the divan by the fire, to blot out her silhouette, to revive images of the Abbeyfield's reeking coal piles and straining horses. He must not, he admonished himself sternly, merge money and matrimony too hastily.

Thrown off stride, Mr Bolderon's explanation of his relationship with Hector Fotheringham became long-winded and tendentious. He stammered a little, stuttered a lot, and paced distractedly on the square of carpet before the hearth.

Mrs Melrose sat calmly by the fire twirling a glass of claret in her fingers and regarding him as if he was a model of lucidity and not a tongue-tied fool.

At length, however, she felt impelled to put him out of his misery. "Mr Bolderon, what is it that you are tryin' to say?"

"Simply put, that I require several hundred pounds to explore the Abbeyfield."

"Are you askin' me to give you several hundred pounds?"

"Apart from paying for boring, the pit needs new sinks, a replacement wagonway to the ladings, a proper pumping-engine, and—"

"I accept that drawin' coal is expensive," Mrs Melrose intervened. "Tell me, however, what you offer in return."

"Five per cent."

"No share, only an unstable investment?"

"I – I—"

"How much do you require?"

"Five hundred pounds."

"For one thousand pounds, Mr Bolderon, I might buy into a company."

"What company?"

"I hear that Mr Mowbray has leased ground near Alloa and is actively searchin' for partners."

"At what guarantee?"

"At five per cent."

"Mowbray," said Keir Bolderon, "is developing new winnings. I think you'll find, dear Mrs Melrose, that the resolution of co-partnership includes provision for a sinking-fund. If the development is mismanaged you might well be pitchin' good money after bad."

"Is the Abbeyfield better managed?"

"I would not prejudice myself by saying otherwise," said Keir Bolderon. "May I point out, with due respect, that it's done fairly well by you over the years."

"I'll grant you that, Mr Bolderon. But, you see, I have no contract with the landowner, with Mr Fotheringham."

"That was how your late and lamented husband wished it."

"It was a suitable arrangement at the time," said Mrs Melrose. "The situation has changed, however. If you are discharged by Mr Fotheringham at the termination of the present lease, my capital will leave with you, will it not?"

"If I discover new coal—"

"Good money after bad, Mr Bolderon?"

Keir Bolderon did not answer. He sighed and seated himself wearily on a little tub chair. He had been through the rigmarole too often of late. He was tired of it, almost bored by it. McNeil was absolutely right. Any man who wished to make his way upward in commerce should be free from the trivialities of business, from having to balance a penny on a shilling and both on the point of his nose.

Marriage, marriage to a woman as rich as Mrs Melrose was indeed the solution. For one fleeting moment Keir Bolderon was tempted to sink to his knees there and then, take her plump hand in his and propose an immediate engagement. But courtship was unbroken ground. He flinched from it. He did not know what it meant to be in love, or how to feign the condition. He doubted if what he felt for Olivia Melrose was honest enough to stand upon for thirty or forty years.

"Well," he said, lamely. "Well, I have put my case, Mrs Melrose, and I will leave it with you." Using a trick he had learned from Fotheringham, he dug into his vest pocket and ostentatiously consulted his watch. "Ah, I see it's late. I must be on my way."

"So soon, Mr Bolderon?"

Keir Bolderon got to his feet.

The woman, too, rose. She put her glass upon a side-table. She was taller than Bolderon by an inch or so and her height seemed to add refinement.

"Am I – am I not to be persuaded?" she said, softly.

"I believe, dear Mrs Melrose, that I have made my position plain. I suggest that you ponder upon it or consult your advisers, if you wish."

She touched his arm. He sensed either sympathy or pity; he could not be sure which. God, if he could not separate such ordinary emotions how could he hope to cope with more abiding ones like love?

"Are you insulted by my caution, Mr Bolderon?"

"Not at all, madam," said Mr Bolderon. "But I confess that I cannot compete against men like Robert Mowbray. You see, I came from nothing. I stand on my own feet by what I've gained through honest industry. I've much more to lose than a Mowbray or a Fotheringham."

"I understand."

"I doubt if you do, Mrs Melrose. We were born into different worlds, you and I."

Olivia Melrose did not seem dismayed by his outburst. Instead she gave a soft little laugh and shook her head.

"Silly man," she said, "to be so easily deceived by appearances."

She kissed him upon the cheek and, before he could recover from his surprise, rang the bell for Scobie to fetch Mr Bolderon's hat and topcoat and to escort him down the ill-lit staircase and out into the street.

Davy's anger had soured into a black sulk by the time he crept home from hiding in the grasses of the foreshore. The beer he had consumed had curdled in his stomach and he was ill and wretched as well as humiliated. Elspeth, ignoring his temper, forced him to drink a spoonful of the mixture that his father used to offset the effects of alcohol and more or less ordered him to bed. Without a word to anyone the boy crawled into his blankets and cowled them over his head.

Mouse too had hidden herself in bed, burrowed away under the dresser, her head under the straw bolster. She would not come out, would not converse, and kicked away the bowl of hot gruel that Sarah brought her.

Elspeth would have preferred to follow the trend and take herself immediately to bed too but there were chores to be done and she did not feel it right to leave them all to poor Sarah. Together the woman and girl prepared vegetables and meat for the Sunday stew. Mutton-fat and flour were creamed into a thickening and added to the pot. The fire was carefully banked to maintain its heat so that the big iron pot would simmer gently throughout the night. Soon the aroma of stew stole into the air. Elspeth was comforted by its familiarity. The keelman would not bother her here, would not cross the plank bridge of the Rutherford burn, protected by its row of cottages. In Jock Bennet's cottage she was safe from the outside world.

Mary Jean was fractious. She protested when Mammy made her ready for bed, squealed at the face-wash that Mammy inflicted, wailed when Mammy carried her outside to use the earth closet in preference to her little baby pot in the corner. She settled down, however, when she was laid in Mammy's bed and, thumb in mouth, dropped off to sleep almost at once.

When Elspeth returned to the hearth after attending to her daughter she found that Sarah too had taken herself to bed without a word of goodnight. Elspeth sighed. The children should not have been subjected to the sight of the keelman's callous actions and she felt her loathing of the man increase.

Elspeth changed into a flannel shift, washed herself and brushed her hair before she snuggled under the clothes by Mary Jean's side. Tonight she would not transfer the child to the wooden cot, for she needed to feel her daughter by her. Mary Jean champed on her thumb, rolled against her mother's body but did not waken.

It was still outside. The wind had died away and the trees were motionless. From the fieldgate came the sound of men's voices. A dog barked in the distance. The fire glow painted the curtain a lovely red and the stewpot gave an occasional croak as it released its savoury steam. Tension in Elspeth slackened. She felt heavy and drowsy. She would waken, perhaps, when Jock Bennet came home from the Grapes for she did not sleep dead away like most colliers but lightly, listeningly, like a shepherd or a drover. She closed her eyes, folded her arms to her breast as if she must crawl into sleep through a tunnel. And then the whole cottage shook.

The door burst open, slamming on its hinges. Jock Bennet barged through it and crashed into the table. Crocks smashed on the floor.

Elspeth sat up.

The collier's shadow loomed on the curtain.

"What's wrong?" Elspeth cried.

Jock Bennet tore the curtain from its string and flung it behind him. He reached down unerringly, snarled Elspeth's hair in his fists and hoisted her on to her knees.

Mary Jean wakened and howled.

Elspeth had enough sense not to resist. Jock Bennet could be ugly when he had drunk too much, though usually he kept his fists to himself and struck nobody except Davy.

"What –"

"*I heard about you,*" he shouted. "*I heard how ye were matchin' wil' a bloody river tink.*"

Elspeth opened her mouth to protest but the breath was taken from her as the pitman yanked her to her feet.

Mouse, Sarah and Davy were all awake, sitting up in their beds. Mouse held the bolster before her like a shield, and Davy squirmed on to his knees ready to leap to safety lest his father's wrath turn, as it so often did, against him.

Elspeth clutched the miner's forearms. Corded muscles slid against the bones. Somewhere along the road he had discarded his jacket and was bare-armed, bare-chested, icy cold. The reek of whisky was sharp on his breath as he roared into her face, "*D'you want another bairn stuck in your belly, eh? Is one bastard no' enough?*"

In spite of his strength and the violence of his mood, Elspeth did not fear Jock Bennet as she feared the menace of the keelman. She had an understanding of the pressures that had formed him, his prejudices, his pain.

Jock Bennet had lost two wives and had never admitted to a living soul how much he had needed them, how much he had relied on them and how much their deaths had scarred him. He could not bring himself to match again for fear of more pain, pain that he could not bear. It was for this reason that he did not desire Elspeth Patterson, however much he might pretend to his work-fellows that he took his pleasure with her whenever he fancied. In Jock Bennet's book women were never innocent, but brought to a man the kind of hurts that could not be bound and healed.

"If you canna content yoursel' wi'out a man, find a decent collier for your bed, not a bloody river tink. We match only wi' our own kind, lady. Do ye hear me?"

Suddenly Elspeth realised that she had betrayed not only Jock Bennet but the community too. Those men who had cast longing glances in her direction had turned on Jock as if he was her legal-wed husband and she had deceived him in broad daylight with Georgie Haynes. With that realisation came an instinctive knowledge of how she must react to the unjust charge.

She shouted back.

She had no notion of precisely what she said; it was the garbled language of retaliation, not a defence.

Bennet let go of her hair and, catching her by the shoulder, dragged her from the protection of the corner.

Elspeth went on shouting.

She shouted, shouted, shouted until Jock Bennet slapped her to make her cease.

The blow stung, spread heat like a scald across her cheeks. She wiped her mouth, tasting blood, then, sucking a deep breath, began to shout at him once more.

Jock Bennet surrendered. He had had enough.

Haughtily, if unsteadily, he retreated towards the hearth, turning his back on Elspeth. The storm had blown itself out. He had asserted his authority, had made his point, had bawled loudly enough to be heard half-way to Placket, had told the community who was master. Mumbling, he rested, one hand braced on the chimney-face. Mouse and Davy were both alert, ready to rescue him if he should sway and fall towards the fire. If he burned himself he would not be able to hew coal come Monday morning, and that would be a tragedy to end all tragedies.

Elspeth dabbed her bruised lip with the back of her hand, silent at last. She glowered at the pitman. His small, sweating head was made bloody by the firelight. His eyes had gone dull now that he had discharged his duty. The fumes of all the whisky he had consumed were taking effect.

He went, grumbling, outside, relieved himself by the door and, grumbling, returned.

Mouse, Davy and Sarah had sunk down into their bedclothes once more and Elspeth had picked up Mary Jean to soothe her. She carried the child in her arms, pacing softly, but when she spoke directly to Jock Bennet her voice still contained a strident note.

"Do you want your supper?" she asked him.

"Nah, nah."

Bennet rested his shins against the bottom of his bed. He stared down at the neat brown blanket and the brown bolster.

"Nah, nah, lass. Nothin' for me."

Sluggishly he bent from the waist, rolled forward on to the bed and with a long, shuddering sigh twisted himself on to his back and lay still.

Elspeth continued to walk with Mary Jean, a dainty step, a soothing, crooning dance in the confined spaces of the kitchen which, in due course, coaxed the child down into sleepiness once more, though her little arms clung tight to Mammy and would not let her go.

"Elspeth?" It was Sarah who spoke.

"What?"

"Did he hurt you?"

"No. Now go to sleep, all of you."

She seated herself at the table, still holding Mary Jean, and remained there until the steady rhythm of breathing told her that the Bennets were taking their rest.

She drew a blanket over Jock and only then went back into her corner and, exhausted by the events of the day, lay down to sleep with her daughter in her arms.

At about nine o'clock on that Saturday evening Tolland knocked on the door of the study. He received no reply but, having grown used to working on his own initiative, he entered the darkened room and found his master already in bed. James paid not the slightest attention as the steward raked and coaled the fire and removed the supper dishes. He gave no answer when the steward softly enquired if he required anything for his comfort. Tolland noticed that the brandy bottle was out upon the table, however, and had sunk by a good inch. He could not decide whether it was a good thing or a bad, that his master's taste for spirits had revived. But he took a decanter, filled it with whisky from a keg in the larder and brought it back, wiped decanter, bottle and glass and set them, with an earthenware jug of fresh water, upon the stand on the table and then left again, bidding the motionless figure in the truckle bed a goodnight.

All day Tom Tolland had been unsettled. Rudge's question about Mr Moodie's sanity rattled about in his head. It galled him that he could give no answer. He would decide first one way and then the other, change his mind every half-hour or so. If he had supposed that Mr Moodie's resurrection would be swiftly completed then Tom Tolland was doomed to disappointment. Jamie Moodie had been back in his cell in manacled silence since half-past eleven in the morning. Saturday, however, was not quite over, not for the master of Moss House or his loyal, if bewildered, servant.

Tolland 'dined' with Hazel in the kitchen. The girl had lost her shyness with the steward, which was small wonder considering the intimacy of their situation. But she was nervous that night after her confrontation with the mysterious master, a meeting, Tolland supposed, that must for the lass have been akin to bumping into a ghost. The cook had made a beef pie, however, and Tolland had raided the cellar for a bottle of good wine and he plied Hazel with food and drink and treated her as if she was a lady, fussing over her and serving her with his own hands.

It was warm, even hot, in the kitchen. Young Hazel had reached a glazed state, with bodice unlaced, cheeks and bosom equally flushed and a pearl-like drop of perspiration on her brow. Tom Tolland had unbuttoned his waistcoat and discarded his collar. In three or four minutes Tom intended to invite Hazel to sit on his ample lap and enjoy a petting. He would stroke and fondle her as if she was a placid cat. Ten or twenty minutes thereafter, about midnight, steward and servant-girl would repair to the cubby, and kitchen door and cubby door would be carefully locked. Tom Tolland was looking forward to it with a lazy sensuality and not a shred of guilt; and then he heard the voice, the voice that he had not heard raised in many months, except to rave hollowly from time to time.

There was nothing hollow in the tone now.

"Tolland. Tolland."

"Blast and damn!" Tolland muttered. "Blast and damn!"

Hazel had gone whisking off into the dark cubby where, if Tolland's guess was correct, she would hide not in but under the wooden bedstead. Hastily the steward wiped his fingers, buttoned himself up and draped his jacket across his shoulders.

"TOLLAND."

"Aye, I'm comin'."

He took the candle from the mantel-holder, stuck it into a dish and hastened through the darkened corridor to the door of the study. He did not knock but entered without hesitation, the candle before him.

James Moodie had lighted an oil lamp. He had poked the coals in the grate and made a blaze of them and the room was filled with rufous light. Moodie had also dressed himself, trousers and a shirt, stockings and shoes, and had slung a dressing-robe about his shoulders, though he could hardly have been cold. He did not enquire if Tolland had been abed, did not make apology.

He said, "I canna write, Tom."

Tolland glanced at the table. Paper had been taken from a drawer, a number of sheets, and the inkwell's silver stand too. Two pens, with new nibs attached, and a blotting leaf and a little knife, and even sealing-wax, had all been unearthed and set about as if James Simpson Moodie at that inauspicious hour had been suddenly possessed by the need to begin his memoirs.

"What is it ye wish t' write, Mr Moodie?"

"Letters."

"Are they of a private nature, Mr Moodie?"

"My hand, my fingers."

Tolland glanced now at the decanter and the brandy bottle but they did not appear to have diminished in content. He scratched the back of his neck.

"Would it not do t' write the letters tomorrow, sir, since tomorrow is the Sabbath an' there will be no post for them?"

"I have a cramp, Tom. I canna grip."

To demonstrate the reason for his need of a secretary, James flexed his fingers. It was not his knuckles but his brain that could not find a grip, though, Tom Tolland knew.

"Is it your wish for me t' take down writin', Mr Moodie?"

"Trust you, Tom. Trust you."

Tolland blew out the candle, put the dish on the window-ledge and his jacket on the back of the chair. Bedclothing had been flung aside violently, he noticed, as if the impulse to commit words to paper had come upon Moodie with over-whelming suddenness.

"Verra well, sir, if my poor penmanship will suffice," Tom Tolland said, as he seated himself at the table and adjusted the paper and inspected the pen-nibs to find the better of the two, "I'll gladly record your words."

Out in the hallway the clock struck twelve jangling notes. James did not appear to hear them, though he paused out of habit until the mechanism fell quiet again. In reality Tom Tolland doubted if James Simpson Moodie had the least idea of time. Perhaps he did not even know what day it was or what month of the year.

As if to confirm the steward's suspicions, James said, "Date?"

Patiently and carefully, Tolland wrote the date in numerals on the top right-hand of the blank page.

The pen was small, one of the new-fangled kind, but the nib was smooth and ink flowed well from it. Tolland, however, was more used to a pencil or a chalk. He crouched awkwardly over the work, half turned towards his master so that he could keep an eye on the man, to gauge the sense as well as the sentences that came so haltingly from the weaver's lips.

As in all things now the formulation of words into logical phrases seemed to strain James Simpson Moodie. He who had once been capable of penning a dozen letters in an hour, each different and each concise, groped and fumbled for the simplest construction.

"To – to – Bontine."

"Is the letter t' Mr Randall Bontine or t' Mr Gilbert?" said Tom Tolland.

"One – one to each."

"Shall we be startin' wi' the letter to Mr Gilbert, then?" Tom Tolland suggested. "What is it ye wish to say, Mr Moodie?"

"Here. Bring him here."

"Aye, so ye wish Mr Gilbert Bontine t' call upon you?"

"Yes."

"When, Mr Moodie?"

"Yes."

Writing as he spoke, the steward composed the letter. He, not his master, chose the day, Wednesday, and the time, ten before noon, for the appointment and filled in the courtesies. He had already decided that he would not trust the missive to the post but would despatch Luke McWilliams with it on horseback tomorrow, Sunday or not, and instruct the young man to await a written answer.

Though he had spoken only a word or two, James Moodie watched and nodded as the steward wrote on and on, the script sliding a little unsteadily to the right-hand of the page and the letters becoming narrower as he grew used to the pen.

When it was done, Tolland charged the pen with ink, stood up and guided Moodie to the table and, with his forefinger, showed him where to make his signature.

In a jerky but legible hand, it was done.

Tolland poured a glass of brandy, added a little water, and gave it to his master before beginning the process of extracting from him the substance of the second letter, that to Sir Randall Bontine.

James, however, seemed to have caught the memory, to be connected with his intentions. He sipped brandy, held the glass in both hands and stooped over Tolland's shoulder.

Very rapidly he said, "To Sir Randall Bontine of Ottershaw. My dear sir, havin' need of the services of a gentleman versed in fine points of the law of inheritance, I would be grateful if you would recommend me to—"

Tolland tapped the end of the pen upon his lip.

"Have ye forgotten, Mr Moodie?"

"Yes. Yes."

"The Ottershaw lawyer, the one Mr Randall brought in for the settlements, is that who ye require?"

"His name – gone."

"His name is Angus Hildebrand."

"Yes."

Cautiously, Tom Tolland squinted up at his master. It was, he saw, only the name that had evaded James Moodie and not recollection of the lawyer's worth. He had heard from Hunter what the Dumbarton lawyer had done for Randall, how settlements had been made and deeds expertly interpreted and executed in Randall's favour.

Tolland said, "If I may ask, Mr Moodie, what is it ye require of Mr Hildebrand?"

"My will," James said.

"But you've already draftit a will."

"Altered."

Tolland could not help himself. "In whose favour, Mr Moodie?"

James's eyelids drooped, blanked out his pupils. His mouth closed firm and, for an instant, he looked his old, implacable, unforgiving, conniving self. And, Tom Tolland realised, however dismembered his abilities had been, however disjointed his reason had become there was intelligence enough in old Moodie yet, a protective layer of cunning that would help him keep his secrets to himself.

He put a hand on the steward's shoulder.

"Write. Write my letter, Tolland," James Moodie said.

Thomas Rance clambered on to the beam and walked along it until he was poised over the shaft. From about his body he unfurled a coil of hemp rope and, straddling the beam, knotted the rope to it and let the coil fall, whirring and slapping, away down into the darkness.

Saturday night had merged now with the small hours of Sunday morning and the workings were deserted. In progressive pits there would have been crews below ground and workers here on the surface to give them service but the Abbeyfield was not equipped for a two-shift system and the pit was allowed to breathe easy and undisturbed after the long Saturday haul.

Rance curled the rope under one arm and hitched it about his waist. Cocking his wrists, he cinched it tight, pushed himself into space and lowered himself down the shaft, down and down for a hundred and twenty feet, which was the full length of the rope. There was not a collier on the field who would have done such a trick, not for ten guineas and the promise of a fine funeral. But Thomas Rance had served on inspection gangs in the fiery pits of Ayrshire and had developed many amazing skills which he kept modestly to himself. When he reached the knot at a hundred and ten feet he swung himself from the rope to the shoring on the side of the shaft and clambered down, hand over hand, to the bottom.

Rats squeaked and scuttled away in alarm as Thomas Rance knelt and fumbled with his tinder-box, lit the candle in Elginbrod's lantern and, carrying the light, set off down the road to the ladder that would lead him down, level by level, to the room where Jock Bennet cut coal.

Accompanied by Mr Bolderon, who was by no means afraid of narrow places or of dirtying his hands, Thomas Rance had explored the length of every seam in the miles of tunnels. Tapping with hammers, manager and oversman had listened to the ring of the rock, tapped and listened, listened and tapped. But nothing but aching backs had come from the sorties. Mr Bolderon, however, would not admit defeat. He had offered a bounty of ten pounds to any pitman who broke into a bearing seam of any worthwhile size. So far the bounty had not been claimed.

Even Mr Bolderon admitted that the upper strata of coal-bearing rock had been picked clean over the years and that the small coal deposits that were being scraped from the remaining rooms would last hardly a twelvemonth at the present rate of extraction. He professed to believe that there was coal deep down, along the base tunnels. Here the strata was fragile and subject to slippage but, oddly, the existing tunnels were not unduly wet and lathery and gave up quality great coal in the odd pockets that could be reached by deter-mined hewers like Ogilvie and Bennet.

When he reached the base level Thomas Rance quickly shed his jacket, shirt and undervest. Naked to the waist he tucked the tinder-box, his fob-watch and a bundle of three extra candles into his belt, got down on all fours and peered into the 'broad' tunnel that ribboned away to the diggings. Bennet's air of smugness, though requiring investigation, was partly an excuse. In truth, Thomas Rance enjoyed being in the workings when they were free of bustle and clamour and felt most at home underground.

From the flow of water against the sump he saw that he

would need to send down an extra bucket-boy though what had caused the rise in seepage level was a puzzle since there had been no abnormal fall of rain in the hills this past fortnight. The tunnel had been burrowed out of soft rock. It followed the inch-thick, treacle-black splint closely, twisting and changing direction to the dictates of the bearing strata. Twenty feet into the 'broad' tunnel Thomas Rance was obliged to be rid of his trousers and boots, for he had put on weight about the middle since he had given up daily labour with pick, bar and hammer. He belted the candles, watch and box into a pouch made from his handkerchief and knotted it and, pushing the pouch and lantern ahead of him along the rough floor, made headway to Willie Ogilvie's room. Here the seam opened out into a long pocket, slotted behind slabs of sandstone. Only one hewer could work the room in comfort and Ogilvie had drawn claim to it some years ago. He had brought out a remarkable tonnage too, digging carefully back behind the long rock to expose a wedge-shaped coal seam over which, on a Sunday morning not many months since, Mr Bolderon had pored for a good couple of hours in search of the point where the seam might have slipped. But nothing had been found and Rance's experience told him that a year would see this pocket worked out and the base tunnel would have to be abandoned too.

Three rats were in the room. They gnawed happily at tallow splashes that the candles had left. But when Thomas Rance rattled the lantern and made the shadows dance they leapt and scampered away into the narrow tunnel, chittering angrily. Thomas Rance brushed aside their droppings and, arms about his knees, rested. He felt relaxed, at peace. Shepherds might have their meadows, drovers their broad glens and sailors the infinite vistas of the green, green seas. He preferred the warm damp confines of a coalpit in the off-shift. Here every road had character; and every road was the same. Thomas Rance felt that he knew where he was, below ground. Below ground he felt close to his sons, Peter and Gavin, who had died a dozen years ago, fifteen miles to the west of here in the pit at Slamannan.

If his lads had survived they would have been full-grown colliers with wives and children of their own by now. What a pair of scallywags they had been as youngsters, though. How they had badgered him to let them down to work by his side. Since they were strong, healthy boys for their age, he had willingly accommodated them. Sound lungs and broad backs had not protected them from the slab of burnt dolerite that had slumped, without warning, from the roof. It had been no trumpeted disaster. Only Rance's sons had been crushed. He had pulled them out of the rubble. He had seen their broken bodies winched to the surface and, in due course, he had seen them put back in the ground.

Within a month of the accident Cathy, his wife, had left him. He could not find it in his heart to blame her. She was afraid he would have the youngest lad, Colin, aye, and even the girls down too, would sacrifice them as callously as he had sacrificed the boys. He knew she was right. He could not have prevented it. He was the son of a collier, and they were his children, and the pit was their birthright and their fate.

Cathy had never been lettered and he never heard from her or of her again, not from the day she took her children, his children, and set out to return to her father's croft on the bleak moors north of Inverness, in the far highlands. He thought of her, and of his son and daughters, almost every night, lying alone in his bed in the lodge by the gates of Crove. But he did not think of her as much as he thought of the sons who were dead, of Peter and Gavin, whom he loved now more than he loved anything that lived.

After resting for several minutes Thomas Rance pushed on. He had to get down flat on his belly and make his bones feel thin to run the narrow tunnel out of which Bennet and his women extracted all of each day's haul. Jock Bennet's room was a remote and isolated pocket of dusty coal. Only an ardent collier like Bennet could be expected to work it at all. The air was scant, the heat like noon in August after rain. Thomas Rance felt as if he was being pulverised. He was relieved when the tunnel opened at the room and he could raise his head. He watched cautiously for rats, but there were none, not even under the shelf of the cutting-seam where the floor was splattered with tallow.

He would waste as little time here as possible. It was too uncomfortable a stance for 'mooning'. He left the lantern by the tunnel mouth, lit one of the candles and, creeping forward, examined the surfaces of the coal face, jabbing his fingers into the tightest corners by the roof. He held the flame out to see if it would flutter and show draught, but the room was breathless and the coal petered out into scales of rock without a hint that Jock Bennet had broken through to a thickening seam. Even so, Thomas Rance was puzzled and not quite satisfied.

He hunched himself into a sitting position of sorts and leaned his back against the marl that Bennet had flung out of the room. He scooped up a handful of the stuff and let it leak through his fingers; just plain dirt. In a way he was relieved that he had found no 'secret' catacomb of coal. It would be a job for the devil himself drawing sleds from this depth.

For a moment or two Rance stared past his feet into the tunnel. It was, he thought, like looking into the mouth of a small-bore cannon; and he had to crawl through it again. With a deliberate exhalation of breath he extinguished the candle, returned it to the pouch, flattened himself to the floor and, in that position, wriggled back to the broad tunnel and thence to the ladders and the shaft.

It was close to daybreak when Thomas Rance clambered out of the Abbeyfield. Shaft-structures, stables and outbuildings were beginning to take shape in the darkness. The oversman shivered. He felt isolated and lonely here on top. He turned towards the track that would lead him past the counting-house and on to the road to the lodge at Crove, not far away. Then he stopped, turned, stared back at the rigging.

Where, he wondered suddenly, had the rats gone? He had not seen them after they had chased off down the narrow tunnel; yet from Jock Bennet's room there was no escape, no other exit.

Thomas Rance took a pace back towards the shaft, then, with a shrug, let it go. Rats, after all, were slippery creatures and might have got past him in the dark. He turned and set off, jogging, for home. And Jock Bennet's discovery remained a secret, hidden, for a time, safe below the millstone grit.

FOUR

Deaths and Entrances

In the corner of the Lennox over which the Bontines held sway Mr Angus Hildebrand had become something of a celebrity. He was not a native of the parts and did not make the trail up the Vale of Leven from his house in Dumbarton very often but he had gained a reputation for negotiation and, as it were, the laird's seal of approval.

In the course of much legal and financial wrangling over the will and testament of the late lamented Sir Gilbert Bontine, Angus Hildebrand had first been consulted by Gibbie's wife Alicia and then, for a considerably larger fee, had been employed as a strong right arm in Randall's war against his brother. Since then he had handled many pieces of business for the new laird of Ottershaw and for several other gentlemen in the district as well.

Mr Hildebrand considered himself a master of the laws of Scotland which related to heritage and succession, wills, deeds and the settlement of moveables. His appearances of petition before the courts, and the intricate arguments put there on behalf of clients, were spoken of in awe and had obtained place in many digests and judicial journals. Never, however, had Mr Hildebrand encountered a procedure like that put to him by James Simpson Moodie of Balnesmoor.

Tall and stork-like, Angus Hildebrand had none of the usual flamboyance of advocates. He dressed in rusty black, in a style that was, to say the best of it, provincial, and usually presented himself in a manner that was dry and pedantic. But Angus Hildebrand was shrewd, too shrewd to bring to his meeting with James Moodie any tool, any weapon but clarity. From discreet enquiries here and there, including a long conversation with Sir Randall, Hildebrand had learned something of the background of the half-mad weaver. He had never met the man before, though, and had no notion of how best to approach such an enigmatic person and, being just a lawyer and not a mystic, not even he could knit the whole truth from ragged facts and threadbare rumours.

Angus Hildebrand had gleaned enough information, though, to intrigue him and he entered the library at Moss House on a drizzling afternoon in early April with a certain sense of expectancy. He was keen to meet James Moodie, who had once been so strong and powerful, keen to learn what service it was that Moodie might require of a lawyer.

It being about dinner-time, and the ride from Dumbarton having occupied the best part of the morning, Mr Hildebrand was delighted to partake of the meats and cheeses that had been laid out on a side-table, and to drink a single glass of ale. He was a little less than delighted by the fact that his host did not put in an appearance to share the repast with him and that he was entertained by a servant, even if the servant was the house steward.

In due course, when Angus Hildebrand had eaten his fill, the steward cleared away the dishes and announced that Mr Moodie would join Mr Hildebrand directly, which Mr Moodie did. He came in as the steward went out, and Angus Hildebrand was able to observe the peculiarities of the gait, the almost crippled stoop to Moodie's shoulders. He had not expected this physical malformation, the halting senile walk or the astringency of expression which marked James Moodie's features.

Moodie did not shake the lawyer's hand or offer other greeting. He was not churlish, merely distracted by his own concentration. Hildebrand, who had met all manner of queer fish in his day, had not encountered anyone who disconcerted him quite so much as the Balnesmoor weaver. He was, how-ever, professional, and assumed that it was upon a matter of business that he had been summoned. He let Moodie seat himself behind the long table and then, since he was obviously not going to be invited to do so, took the liberty of finding himself a chair.

Up to this moment he had spoken not a word. He held his tongue, waiting for the client to make the running and dictate the pace.

Moodie licked his lips.

"What can you do for me, Mr – Mr Hildebrand?"

"What do you wish me to do for you, Mr Moodie?"

"My – my will."

"Do you wish me to draft a will for you?"

"New will."

"Do you already have a will in draft, Mr Moodie?"

There was no immediate answer to this question but Mr Hildebrand waited with immaculate patience. He studied the man, his condition, very carefully. He had, he realised, seen similar manifestations in another person once, a master of the Freemasons' lodge in Dumbarton, Boyle by name. Boyle had displayed similar characteristics of illness and had died, as Hildebrand recalled, of a swelling of the fluids of the brain after a bizarre period when he reverted to the gay and carefree behaviour of a child. Not that there was anything childish or childlike about James Moodie.

At length Moodie said, "They'll take it all, my sisters, if you do not protect her."

Hildebrand said, "Ah, you have sisters who may make claim upon your property?"

"After – after I'm dead."

"How many sisters, Mr Moodie?"

"Two."

"Do you not also have a wife and child?"

"It is – it is – that, aye."

"Male relatives?" said Hildebrand.

Moodie shook his head. He pinched his forehead with his fingers as if movement made it ache. He was, however, gathering himself. Hildebrand could see it, see the effort of intellect. Shoulders lifted, breath expanded the broad chest for a moment, and the dull sullen eyes were suddenly upon him.

"My sisters are wealthy," James Moodie said. "They have no need of me an' have neglected me. Mother died, they did not come t' see her decently put to rest. My marriage, they scorned t' acknowledge."

"How long since you met with them?"

"Years, long years. Not years enough."

"Tell me, Mr Moodie, what prevents you making a simple will that leaves all to your wife and daughter? Apart from any legacies you may wish to make – to a favoured servant, say – the court will certainly apportion all residue to a wife and to a surviving child of either sex."

Hildebrand could not be sure that Moodie heard, let alone grasped what he had said. He hoped that he had not made the journey from Dumbarton just to 'swat a little fly', as it were.

"Keep their hands off it," Moodie said.

"Do you mean, sir, your sisters' hands?"

"Aye."

"The Court of Session will—"

"You must protect her."

Hildebrand folded his long legs and sat forward on the chair. "Where is your wife, Mr Moodie, that she cannot defend herself?"

"She'll come – when I'm gone."

"Gone?"

"Dead."

"Is she lost, Mr Moodie?"

"She is lost to me."

"You say that you have a child?"

"I – I do."

"What age is the child?"

"An infant."

"Two or three years old, do you mean?" said Hildebrand.

"Thereabouts."

"Do you not know where your wife and child are to be found?"

"Lost," James Moodie said. "Both lost."

Hildebrand had heard of the handbills, of the frantic and prolonged search that Moodie had instigated across the breadth of Scotland, had heard of the rewards and how the wife had fled from each discovery.

"How long has she been lost?" he asked.

"Years, long years."

"Mr Moodie," Hildebrand snapped, "answer my question."

"Two years."

"Why are you concerned, sir, that your sisters will take your estate, when you are patently both alive and *compos mentis*?" said Hildebrand, with subtle purpose.

"When I'm dead – they'll descend like crows."

"Painful though the question is, Mr Moodie, I must be informed if you have a mortal illness that prompts you to seek my counsel; if the period prior to the will becoming active, as it were, is prescribed."

Moodie shook his head; he did not understand.

Hildebrand said, "Do you know yourself to be dyin', sir?"

To the lawyer's amazement, Moodie laughed. It was a dry rustling sound like a hedgehog stirring in old leaves. Mr Hildebrand prickled with apprehension and the hairs on the nape of his neck lifted slightly.

"You have not given me reply, Mr Moodie."

"Preserve it all for her," Moodie said. "That's what I'm requirin' of you. And of the law."

"Do you mean, Mr Moodie, you wish to protect the realised value of your holdings, including moveable property?"

"I mean – as it – as it is. Intact."

For the moment Mr Hildebrand let that disturbing statement pass. He said, "To your knowledge, your spouse is not deceased?"

James Moodie shook his head.

"Or, to your knowledge, she has not bigamously remarried?"

Again James Moodie shook his head.

"Therefore the lady is your wife in law and the child recorded as your sole heir?"

Hildebrand had fallen into relentless questioning which, in other circumstances, drove sheriffs and opposing solicitors to distraction with its meticulous insistence on detail and definition.

"Aye."

"What is the lady's name?"

"Elspeth Patterson Moodie."

"And the name of the child?"

"Mary Jean. My mother."

"Quite!" said Hildebrand. "Now, Mr Moodie, let me return to your nebulous request that I contrive to 'preserve intact' your property. Exactly what do you mean by that?"

"As – as it is."

"Operating?"

James Moodie nodded.

"Operating as a going concern, the woollen-mill and its attendant enterprises, after you are deceased?" said Hildebrand.

"Aye. As it is now."

"It will be a ship without a rudder, Mr Moodie."

Petulantly, Moodie screwed up his face.

"Preserve intact," he shouted.

Hildebrand stroked his chin thoughtfully, then got to his feet and began to walk forth and back before the table at which the weaver sat. James Moodie did not follow the lawyer with his eyes but – and Hildebrand noted it – he listened with rapt attention. He, Moodie, might have been blind but he was not deaf and the matter of an opinion was crucial to him and drew his disjointed wits together.

"I take it, sir," the lawyer began, "that you wish all to be as it is now. You desire that your wife shall return to this house, intact, to inherit a manufactory that is in profit and milling money, to acquire such capital sum as you may have in deposit – assuming you are not in debt – and to assume responsibility for such other sundries as you have lien over."

"Aye."

"You will require to be drawn up, Mr Moodie, a will and a testament and other documents which will satisfy the court that there is a competent person, or persons, in the charge of operating the concerns, in paying out wages and other accruing debts, et cetera." Hildebrand paused before the table. "The functioning of the court of Chancery is not as it is with our English cousins. The Scottish court is more efficient, more decisive. It will detour special decrees in particular cases back to a sheriff or upward to a Court of Session."

"Can you do it?"

"I cannot, by any legal means, protect the will and testament against challenge by, let us say, your sisters for a period of time without limit; not, that is, if your appointed heirs, wife and child, are not *in situ* or in a position to signal their wish for the disposal of the heritable property, land as well as moveables."

"Can you not do it?"

"By dint of careful drafting of the will and the testament,

and by ensuring that you select an executor who will be both trustworthy and entirely sympathetic to your intention, I might be able to preserve your holdings, as you request, for a limited period of time. But that period must be stipulated in your address to the service of heirs."

"How long a period?"

"I would think that two years from the date of your death would be the most that one could hope for. After that time the petitions which your sisters' representatives would draw for waiving of the will and dispersal of the estate *in toto* would carry too much weight. I might defray and delay, by various means, a final decision but, in the interim, the assets would in all likelihood be frozen by court order and the traffic of trade thus brought to a halt."

"She'll come when I'm – gone."

"How will she know?" said Hildebrand.

"Can you do it?"

"I'll need an inventory of all your holdings, Mr Moodie, particularly those related to the holding of land property. If the land held is dispersed across several jurisdictions then it will make the matter more complicated and I might be able to extend that period by some months or years. To hold all in working order, as it were, for much more than two years is beyond my powers, and the powers of any draft."

"She'll come."

Hildebrand leaned his bony hands on the back of the chair.

He said, "Will you have listings of all your earning sources and of your capital drawn for me?"

Weaver Moodie pushed himself back from the table and jerked open a drawer in the facing. He extracted from it a thick kidskin wallet and pushed it, with both hands, across the table towards the lawyer.

"It's done," James Moodie said.

Hildebrand lifted the wallet, weighed it in his hand but did not untie the leather strap that held the package of papers together.

"Everything, sir?" he enquired. "Inventories too?"

"My worth," said Moodie.

"On which account, sir, I will, with your sanction, proceed to draw up a series of documents which will entail provision for the return of your heirs to claim the whole estates and holdings within a span of twenty-four months after the date of your death; which, Mr Moodie, may not be yet for many a year."

"She'll come," James said. "I'll bring her back."

"That being the case," said Hildebrand, "she will find all that you desire her to find."

"A place," said James Moodie. "A place for her."

"Two weeks from today, at the same hour, I'll return with the preliminary drafts," said Hildebrand. "If you are not prepared to receive me then I would be most grateful if you would have your steward inform me by letter."

"I'll be prepared," said James Simpson Moodie in a strange, suave murmur that once more made the hairs prickle on the wily old lawyer's neck.

Hiding the newly discovered coal source at the end of the Bennet digging was more easily accomplished than Elspeth would have believed possible.

The Ogilvies showed no interest in what was going on down the narrow tunnel and the shoring and ramping of the new seam, the knocking up of a little wooden door to screen its entrance, was done quietly and quickly, in the course of a single shift, with wood drawn legitimately from the carpenters' shop bolstered by odd planks smuggled to the road-end under sacks on the sleds.

Jock Bennet had no sense of wonder at the existence of the fissure. He regarded it not as a freak of nature but as a gift made by God to His humble servant the coal-hewer. From the outset it was clear that the yield from the new seam would make the Bennets rich by the lights of Abbeyfield colliers. But the gaining of money was an end in itself, distinct and separate from the comforts and opportunities that the money might buy. There would be more meat, more sweetmeats, more trinkets bought, more whisky consumed by the head of the house. In a month or two, when income outstripped expenditure, there would be the purchase of a new jacket, a dress for Sarah, handsome thick-soled boots for Davy, and after that ingenious ways would be found to be rid of the excess cash that flowed into the household purse. Little or none of it would be saved.

The little door, the trap, was hidden by three or four shovels of loose marl and footprints smoored over with a flat blade or slat. Beneath the trap were four short wooden steps up which Davy carried the lumps of coal which Jock clawed down from the face. Davy would manhandle the lumps into the doorway and Mouse or Elspeth would drag them through and load them on to the sleds. The coal was of high quality, all dull and dusty, not bright-black and brittle. It did not have to be cut cleverly but, when the wedges were inserted, slumped down in massive pieces off the face. It was a far cry from hewing chows and the supply of it, Jock Bennet claimed, was endless. Elspeth took the hewer's word on that. She would not set foot beyond the lips of the fissure, would not go through the trap and into the dry seam at any price, though Mouse popped in and out without a qualm.

Circulating the air in the seam was a problem and the trap could not be closed during the shift, though Jock put them all through a drill for sealing the fissure for concealment should anybody venture into the narrow tunnel unbidden.

For two weeks the Bennets and Elspeth cut and hauled the booty from the new seam; and discovered another problem in so doing.

"Bennet. One hundred an' eighteen shillin's."

Paying staff and other hewers in the counting-house were stunned.

"How much, Henning?" said Snippets Smith, though he had made and checked the calculation personally.

"One hundred an' eighteen shillin's."

The hewers muttered in disbelief.

"Your lad, Davy, must be a cutter wi'out equal," said Thomas Rance, rocking on his heels on the box behind the table.

"It is, I believe," Snippets announced, "the highest take from this pit since Mr Bolderon became our manager."

"I'll take bankers' notes, Mr Smith," Jock Bennet said.

Within an hour it was all over the Abbeyfield.

Over a hundred shillings had been dug and hauled by the Bennet family. Even young colliers, working back to back, could hardly bring down so much. By what means and method, folk wondered, had Jock Bennet utilised the services of his puny son to sail the take so high?

"How many hours did he work?"

"Sixty-two hours, like the rest o' us."

"God in Heaven! Ten like Bennet an' Mr Bolderon could pay off the levellers."

Behind the locked door of the counting-house Snippets asked Thomas Rance for a logical explanation.

"Was it the boy, just the boy?"

"It would seem so," Thomas Rance answered.

"But the coal pocket, I thought it was narrow?"

"Aye, it is."

"How did it bear so much?"

"It's deep enough," said Thomas Rance. "But if he cuts down so much extra in the week, it'll not last long."

"What of the coal?"

"Best quality."

Snippets Smith paused. "Is it possible, Mr Rance, that Bennet has found a run to the splint?"

"Possible," said Thomas Rance. "But I have been down and examined the room. There's no evidence of a swelling to the splint."

"What do you think?"

"I think he must have put his back into it."

"Did you weigh his baskets?"

"Elginbrod did not inform me that we were bein' treated to such a demonstration," said Thomas Rance. "But I'll be watchin' the baskets this fortnight, I assure you, Mr Smith."

"What of the haulers, the women?"

"What of them?"

"How in God's name did they carry out so many extra hundredweights?"

"If the coal is cut, it's hauled," said Thomas Rance, with a shrug. "The man sees that it's done."

"Such rogue labour must take its toll."

"It does," said Rance.

Snippets Smith said, "Mr Bolderon should be informed."

"I'll tell him personally tonight."

Keir Bolderon was just as astonished by the increase in Bennet's tally as everyone else; and just as inquisitive.

"Have we ever had such a take, Thomas?" he asked.

"Once or twice," said Thomas Rance. "But years ago, when the third level was first opened, and only for a month or two."

"Was Jock Bennet involved in these prodigious hauls?"

"No. Younger men."

"But the base level is very narrow, as I recall, and sparse."

"Aye, Mr Bolderon. In my opinion it's most like to be freak coal. In all probability he's struck a 'back' to the thin seam and needs the boy, puny though he is, to reach into it."

"But does it look like 'back' coal?"

"From what I've seen, no," Thomas Rance admitted.

"Do you think we should both kit up and venture down to Bennet's room for an inspection?"

"Bennet would resent it, Mr Bolderon."

"Oh, I don't give a damn about that. Should we, Thomas?"

"No, Mr Bolderon. Let's hold off till we see what Bennet comes up with durin' the course of the next fortnight. If he hauls out much over a hundred, we'll tumble in on him and take him by surprise."

"Sound idea, Thomas," Keir Bolderon agreed.

If Jock Bennet was concerned by the reaction to his mammoth earning, he gave no sign of it. He was, perhaps, a little put out by the fact that he received few pats on the back or shakes of the hand for his feat and that, by earning quite so much more than his companions underground, he caused a certain degree of indignation and envy among them. He said nothing of the pay-night's events to Elspeth but she learned enough from Davy to give her pause for reflection.

She waited until Sunday, until Mr Bennet was fed, rested and sober. The children were all out of doors, playing in pallid April sunlight.

"How many times before," Elspeth asked, "have you drawn in a hundred shillings?"

"In the Abbeyfield – twice."

"But it's rare," said Elspeth, "is it not?"

"It'll not be rare from this time forward, I promise."

"Mr Rance'll come down; you must know that."

"Let him come. We'll hide the seam, like we practised."

"If he comes with a rod an' bar an' starts pokin', he'll find the trap without bother," said Elspeth.

"If he does, he does."

"Mr Bolderon'll be furious with you for keepin' the find to yourself. Perhaps he'll even march you off the Abbeyfield."

Jock Bennet laughed. "Bolderon'll not pay off a miner who can find new coal for him. Anyhow, he'll be needin' me to work the bloody seam for him."

"It's invitin' trouble," Elspeth said.

"What is?"

"Drawin' such a high wage."

"No regulation says a man canna earn—"

"Use your head," Elspeth urged.

"Rance'll think it's Davy made the difference."

"Full thirty shillin's difference?"

"Aye, I see what you mean," Mr Bennet admitted.

"Davy might be expected to increase our haul by twelve or fourteen shillin's, but not *thirty*."

Jock Bennet was not stupid, but he was stubborn.

He said, "We'll just have t' brazen it out."

"We could work less hard for a reasonable take," Elspeth suggested.

"So that's it, lady. You want a slack an' idle time o' it?"

"Slack an' idle! I work as hard as any," Elspeth retorted. "But if you want to keep that seam hidden, you'll need to guard it with more than a wooden door. In any case, what do you need with so much extra cash?"

"I need it for protection."

"Protection?"

"I could be breakin' a leg tomorrow, could I not? Where would you all be then? Wi' money saltit away, that fear vanishes." The collier glanced at the young woman, then reluctantly continued. "It happened once before, a while ago. I fell sick wi' a terrible flux. For the life o' me I couldna cut coal. I couldna stand on my pins unaided, let alone go down the shaft. I had three children an' a wife dependin' on me."

"How long were you laid in bed?"

"A month. Three weeks more when I could but stagger. She, my wife, she'd nobody t' haul for, so she went on harness, drawin' a wagon. It's no job for a woman in her sixth month.

143

Heavy, heavy labour in the harness. When it came her time she was ill-delivered an' left this world, aye, an' the wee bairn wi' her. There was no help for it. It was bring in a wage or starve for the lot o' us. You know nothin' o' life's hardships, lady, or you'd not bait me wi' questions about money."

Elspeth suspected that Jock Bennet had not told her the whole, unvarnished truth. He would have had his wife hauling for him until the last possible moment in her pregnancy. There were women below ground now who were within a day of delivery.

Besides, every man in every community genuinely believed that he had a lease on hardship and suffering. Many a time Elspeth had listened to men who were wealthy enough to buy the Abbeyfield complain bitterly about 'poverty'. On the road she had met folk who lived in the stark shadow of penury, folk to whom the loss of one day's wage might spell the beginning of a spiral of debt that would lead to the loss of family and dignity, to the poorhouse, the charity ward or the horror of a pauper's grave.

In Balnesmoor there had been want and suffering too but the community had managed, somehow, to protect itself against the savage indifference that she had found in towns and cities and in those places where laird had given way to manager, workshop had replaced croft. She was sure that Jock Bennet was not moved by concern for his family's future. For men like him the future was measured shift by shift, basket by basket, and a man's pride was the price of his sweat, counted out in silver into his hand. Yet she was part of this world, this system, and could not ignore the changes that had occurred in her as her will had gradually shaped to the community's ends and her selfishness had thickened like a muscle.

"How long's this seam?" she asked.

"What I can see extends east for sixty feet, at the height o' my head."

"What lies at the nether end?"

"Boulder clay."

"Boulder clay? So deep?"

"It'll be a plug. More coal'll lie beyond it."

"How long will it take you an' Davy to cut it all?"

"Months, years."

"So there's enough."

"Aye, but enough's not so much, lady," Jock Bennet said, without explanation of what he meant by the statement.

"Have you thought of what will happen to us if Mr Bolderon or Mr Fotheringham find no new coal elsewhere an' the Abbeyfield is closed for want of sufficient profit?"

"It'll never happen."

"It might. There have been pits here closed before, have there not?"

"Preston Island was too wet."

"I've heard Mr Rance declare that the Abbeyfield's finished."

"Rance!" said Jock Bennet disparagingly.

"Save your strength, Mr Bennet. Let's take what the seam offers piece by piece. If it's as long as you say then we can cut an' haul a good wage without grindin' ourselves to skin an' bone doin' it," said Elspeth. "An' nobody will suspect because of a silly wage every other Saturday."

"There's some sense in what you say," Jock Bennet conceded. "But I'll not give it up, not till I've hauled my last bloody basket an' got the silver for it right here in my fist. Then, if Bolderon might founder wi'out new winnin's, I'll give it to him."

"In the meantime," said Elspeth, "what?"

"God, Patterson, ye may look like an ordinary woman under a coatin' o' dust but you're a smart one when you're washed."

"Smart enough not t' kill a layin' hen," said Elspeth.

"We can take ninety-five shillin's, easy as makin' water," said Jock Bennet, nodding. "In the rest o' the time below we can cut an' stack. I won't have t' excavate space for the crack widens further on, an' the bottom's so dry the coal will not decay."

"Won't ninety-five bring Mr Rance breathin' on you?" Elspeth said.

"No. Davy's labour will account for the extra." Jock Bennet pushed himself from the table and reached his bonnet and jacket from the peg. "But I want no more talk o' openin' this seam t' Rance or Bolderon, lady. If makin' money distresses you, you're at liberty t' pack your bundle an' seek employment

145

elsewhere. Rackin' for a keelman might suit your delicate nature better, eh?''

Jock Bennet hesitated. He was never quite sure when he had scored over her, for Elspeth seldom sulked and never retreated.

"You're no' much of a one for ale?'' he said.

"I prefer tea,'' said Elspeth.

"How would a pint of sherry wine suit your taste?''

"It would suit my taste fine.''

"I'll bring back a jug at supper time.''

Elspeth sighed. "I haven't supped sherry for –''

Jock Bennet raised an eyebrow. "How long?''

"Many years,'' said Elspeth.

"Did the drover buy it for ye?''

"No, I bought it for myself,'' said Elspeth and, flustered by the collier's questions, hurried out to the stubble field behind the cottage to fetch in sheets and shirts which had dried in the April sun.

Major Walter Seaton had not gotten to see Napoleon Bonaparte on that memorable afternoon of 18th June in 1815. He had missed the sight of *le petit caporal* with greatcoat unbuttoned and flung back to display his epaulettes and green uniform, his cocked hat askew on his head. He had passed along the ridge, had Napoleon, in full sight of the British line, surrounded by staff officers, all brilliant as peacocks but riding, Walter had heard, like jockeys and pot-boys, galloping willy-nilly towards *La Belle Alliance* until they were chased behind the French line by the fire of a few twelve-pound field-pieces.

Major Walter Seaton had not gotten to see Paris, the city of delights, had not participated in the return of the heroic battalions to Scotland, in their triumphal march from Mussel-burgh to Edinburgh where every street was packed with adu-latory crowds and even the Bailies and the Lord Provost managed to turn out to welcome them. By all accounts, the lads were in good trim and loved being lionised. But Seaton did not see them saluted and dismissed in the castle's gloomy old quadrangle, though he did attend, by invitation, the great ball that was given in the Assembly Rooms to show off, for the last time, the handsome cross of St James and his other medals and dance with his sister Suzanne to the strains of Spanish waltzes and Scotch quadrilles.

Like Randall Bontine before him, Major Seaton had been denied the pleasures of victory by a wound. He had been brought down on the Brussels road in an encounter with an outpost of stragglers who were hidden behind the hay cart of some Flemish clodpole not far from Quatre-Bras. He had been back in a sick-room in Brussels when the great battle was finally turned.

The ball had taken away the joint of his left elbow. He lost considerable quantities of blood before an assistant-surgeon sawed through the bone and removed his arm some six inches below the shoulder. It was neat enough done and, to Seaton's surprise, he had recovered swiftly from the shock and its attendant fever. He did not, however, recover from the inconvenience of having but one fin to fight with and, as soon as was decent, resigned himself to return to Scotland and abandoned all thought of a further career as a serving officer.

From Edinburgh, after the rejoicings, Seaton had returned home with his sister to the family seat in Aberdeenshire, a glad enough house set in an extensive and well-managed estate in one of the long tame valleys that lay between Dee and Don. Walter, though, would never be laird of Piperhaugh. He was the youngest of seven sons and his father, an old, old man of eighty-three, still lived, though he had sensibly abrogated all but the title to Augustus, who was himself not far off sixty and had five grown sons of his own.

The Piperhaugh Seatons were part of a great, scattered clan of Seatons who, over the decades, had sought fortune in foreign lands. Walter and Suzanne had brothers, cousins, aunts and nephews all over the globe. For a far-flung family they were remarkably free of feuds and Father Seaton and Augustus conducted a vast correspondence with all the émigrés and knew, more or less, where each was to be found and how he or she fared.

Piperhaugh was home for Walter. A place would always be found for him at the table. All the sons who bided at home – three including Augustus – and all the nephews and nieces and in-laws had a weep for the one-armed warrior and praised

God that most of him had been returned to them. None wept more than Suzanne for she had always loved her brother Walter best of all her kin.

Welcome though he was there, Walter could not rest at ease in Piperhaugh. Using the allowance which his father pressed upon him, he gathered Suzanne into a four-horse coach, stuck her maid inside and his man on the dicky and set off, at the reins no less, though he had but one hand to steer with, to visit his friend Randall Bontine and, by the by, to see what sort of career he might find for himself in the course of the tour.

If it was in Walter's mind that he might find a personable husband for Suzanne he let no hint of it slip. Nonetheless he was gratified that Randall took to Suzanne and she to Randall, and that both his fellow major and his vivacious sister confided, at various times, that the attraction between them grew stronger day by day.

No cuckoo, no leech, Walter was not a man to prey on the hospitality of friends. He had intended to stay at Ottershaw for two weeks, no longer. Randall would have none of it. Randall insisted, absolutely insisted, that Walter and Suzanne remain as his guests until fair May weather made the roads less sore. The forward journey had been cold and rough and if Walter was not moved by Randall's hospitable pleas – which he was – he was certainly persuaded by his sister's little tears and the whispered confession that she wanted to stay here in Ottershaw, for ever.

Walter correctly interpreted this to mean that Suzanne had fallen in love with Randall. Forthwith he took it upon himself to drop a discreet word in Randall's ear that his sister had lost her heart, as young girls will, and that he, Randall, must not take it too seriously. Walter also thought it wise to mention that Suzanne was not without a dowry and would bring to her marriage the revenue from a small parcel of land or, if her bridegroom preferred it, a sum of guineas. Randall feigned indifference to this information, professed that Suzanne's affectionate respect was all that he wanted, and went on to assure Walter that he would treat the young woman properly and not impose upon her temporary infatuation. Randall also claimed that he had not been so happy since the day he had ridden at the head of his first troop, an analogy that Walter Seaton understood only too well.

The true state of affairs was not quite so light and airy. Suzanne was wildly in love with Randall Bontine. She found in the laird of Ottershaw a man not unlike her beloved Walter, though less mild and charitable. She wanted to become his wife. It would be a sound match. She was nobility and not poor. He had a titled estate and a house. What was not explicable was her desire for him, her indelicate longing to be made love to by the soldier-laird of Ottershaw.

If Randall had met Suzanne Seaton in an Edinburgh salon or the drawing-room of a Glasgow hostess, he would have seduced her, loved her, and disentangled himself from a permanent relationship once he had had his way. But Suzanne Seaton was the sister of a close comrade, a friend who had attended him in his hour of need in far-off Spain, and it would be marriage or nothing for the sake of honour and decency.

Though they talked of Egypt and of Spain, of battles fought, of rumbustious drinking in the mess, of horses and brave deeds, talked endlessly and with conceit about the regiments and battalions, it had all slipped away from Randall Bontine. He was not the same man who had courted danger, flirted with death and stormed the walls of Almarez. Balnesmoor's tenants and Ottershaw's parks, the keeping of accounts and the tending of sheep, had all laid soft paws on him, had made him motionless enough for change to catch up with him. And with it, since he had sent Anna Sinclair away, had come unconscionable loneliness. He was surrounded by servants; but he had no friend.

It was not memories of his glorious past that Walter Seaton brought to Randall Bontine so much as a knowledge that his youth was over. The Seatons brought change, change within the context of the duties and traditions of Ottershaw for the Seatons came from the same sort of land-owning stock as did Randall and had never, as he had once done, scorned it. He was damned glad of their company, glad of an excuse to light the candelabra in the dining-room, build up the fires, air empty rooms where once Alicia had held sway, glad to have an excuse for not working day and night, for coming out of the library, out of his shell.

Dunn, Sir Randall's trusted valet, measured the master, took the lengths to Mr Petrie's tailor shop in Harlwood with instruction as to the material to be used. In due course Mr Petrie produced the suiting and came to Ottershaw himself to take in a tuck here and a seam there, and to display other fashionable shapes and accessory wares. Evening dress, with a striking change of coloured waistcoats, a coat with a velvet collar, new hessians for riding out, a tweed sporting coat and mated trousers, shirts, cravats and stockings of silk not wool all appeared in Sir Randall Bontine's closets. Twice each day, before breakfast and before dinner, Dunn shaved the master with scented lather, and old Hunter, blowing the dust off his memory, recalled how to use a heated scissor to plant a few masculine curls around the master's ears.

Sir Randall remembered how to laugh aloud, how to converse in French, to be charming and teasing as well as masterful and arrogant.

From the cellar he had dragged out an old spinet upon which his mother used to play, decades ago. It was dusted and polished and a tuner was brought in specially from Glasgow to adjust the wires. Suzanne played upon it after dinner. Randall and Walter sang. Randall was persuaded to find the old bagpipes that his father had owned and to puff and drone on them while Walter, his good arm held elegantly above his head, retraced the steps of a reel he had learned in dancing-school then showed off a fandango taught him by a dark-eyed whore in old Castile.

In the servants' hall, where Hunter fussed, and Mrs Lacy perspired over delicate dishes whose names she could not pronounce, the sounds of laughter echoed. The servants made eyes at each other in a knowing way and both enjoyed and resented the novel air of gaiety that the advent of guests had brought to staid old Ottershaw.

Walter Seaton, however, was a shrewd drawing-room tactician. Perhaps he had not sought Randall Bontine as a husband for his sister but with the discovery that such a match was possible his skill came into play. He realised that he would have to take Suzanne away from Ottershaw before she could be invited to return. Spring would soon give way to summer and the duties of the property would claim Randall's time. Ottershaw was not so large as Piperhaugh nor so well tended. The laird himself would here have to give the lead for cattle-sellings and tree-cuttings and the various sowings and harvest-ings. The new grieve was honest and efficient but it was not his purse that rain might turn to mush, his income that would suffer if sheep-gathering was done too late for market. God knows, farming prices were erratic enough in this turbulent time, and Randall not so skilled that he could do it all by signals of the hand.

No, Seaton decided, he must concoct an excuse to leave on a particular date and hold to it over Randall's protests and Suzanne's tears. He hoped that absence would fan a flame in Randall Bontine as well as in his sister, and would go home and prepare his father and brothers for the fact that the youngest might be on her road to the altar. He would certainly recommend the match to them in glowing terms.

"We must leave, alas, on Monday," he announced one morning at the breakfast table.

To his chagrin, Randall nodded. "I understand. It's selfish of me to lay claim to you for so long."

Suzanne's eyes were blue and round. She stretched her graceful neck so that it appeared to be on a stalk, like a flower. She was not entirely lost in the game that Walter had been playing on her behalf, however, and not impertinent enough to argue with him there and then. But she too was dismayed by Randall's abrupt agreement to the plan of departure for she did not read into it a subtle strategy.

That night, in an interval in the playing of the spinet, Randall left the drawing-room and returned bearing an old, leather-bound book in which he had marked certain pages with figs of paper.

He opened the volume and laid it on the lid of the spinet.

"Seatons, do you see this?" he said, smiling.

"What is that book, Randall?" Suzanne asked, leaning forward on the square stool and inadvertently showing her pretty bosom, half exposed, to the laird. "It appears to be very ancient."

"It is almost two hundred and fifty years since it was printed," said Randall, hands on each side of the open book.

"Can't imagine which of my ancestors might have purchased it."

Seaton put down his glass and stepped to Randall's side. "What's its title?"

"Anatomie of Abuses," Randall said.

"What, sir!" said Suzanne cheerfully. "Do you intend to abuse us before we go?"

"I would not be so churlish," Randall answered, "nor would I need a written prompt."

"What particular passage have you marked to rail us with, old scallywag?" said Walter.

"Listen." Forefinger tracing the text, Randall read aloud. *"First, all the wild heads of the parish, conventing together, elect a grand captain of mischief, and him they crown with great solemnity, and adopt for their king."*

"Hah!" said Walter Seaton. "You would be royalty for sure, Bontine, in such a society; a 'grand captain of mischief', indeed."

Randall continued to quote. *"This king anointed, chooseth for the twenty, forty, three score or an hundred lusty guts—"*

"Lusty guts!" Seaton laughed. "Oh, how I like that, Randall."

"– like to himself to wait upon his lordly majesty and to serve his person. Then every one of these his court, he investeth with liveries of green, yellow or some other light wanton colour. And were this not gaudy enough, I should say—"

"I should say so too," put in Walter Seaton, an arm about Randall's shoulder as he followed the movement of the forefinger down the dusty page.

"– they bedeck themselves with scarfs, ribbons and laces, hanged all over with gold rings, precious stones and other jewels borrowed for the most part of their pretty mopsies and loving bessies, for bussing them in the dark."

"La, la!" said Suzanne, looking at Randall's lips moving as he read, flickering her lashes just a little when he paused to glance at her.

"Thus," Randall went on, reading, *"all things set in order, then have they their hobby horses, dragons and other antiques, together with their bawdy pipers and thundering drummers, to strike up the devil's dance, withal."*

"How pagan!" said Seaton. "How deliciously pagan!"

"The devil's dance, withal?" said Suzanne.

"Aye, would kirk elders nowadays not turn purple at such a gathering?" said Seaton.

"What do they do next?" Suzanne asked.

"Many odd things," said Randall. "The account refers to Englishmen, of course; and they, as a race, have always been prone to silliness. However, they did have a purpose, these chaps, and not one I would care to mock."

"Read on, Macduff," said Walter Seaton.

Randall quoted, *"And all this done, they return to where they have their summer halls, their bowers, arbors and banqueting houses set up, wherein they feast, banquet and dance all that day and, peradventure, all that night too. And thus these terrestrial furies welcome in the May."*

"Hah!" said Seaton. "What harm can there be in welcoming the May? May is a month I warmly welcome since it presages summer."

Smiling, Randall gently closed the volume.

"I would not draw the line at being a 'terrestrial fury' for an evening, would you, Seaton, old fellow?"

"It has an appealing ring to it, certainly."

"Randall, what do you mean?" said Suzanne.

"I mean that I think I'll summon a batch of bawdy pipers and thundering drummers, send out invitations to a few of the local lusty guts, and have a ball to welcome the May. What say you, Seaton? Would you stay for that?"

"How long?"

"Two weeks should give sufficient time for invitations to be written, sent and answered. Shall we say, two weeks come Friday?"

"We had planned to be away by —" Walter Seaton began.

Suzanne was off the stool and at her brother's side, her slender fingers on his sleeve, her cheek against his side-whisker.

"Oh, Walter! We *must* stay. We *must*."

"Do you want us to 'crown' you, Randall, as this grand captain of mischief?" Walter Seaton said. "Is that it?"

"I fear I need no crown for that office," said Randall. "However, is it agreed? Will you be the honoured guests at Ottershaw's May Ball?"

"Yes," Suzanne chirped. "Yes, oh, yes."

"We'll have the big hall cleared," said Randall. "And we'll feed all the servants too, out there in the pasture under lanterns in the trees."

"What if it rains?" said Seaton.

"It would not dare," said Randall.

To forsake the soft greening dawns of spring for the black unchanging landscapes of the pit took effort of will even in men and women to whom the work was all. There was no trace of April under the ladders, except that the air seemed oddly humid and sweat broke more readily from the skin. Even when he was not toiling up and down his four-step treadmill Davy Bennet sweated. It was a peculiar infirmity for Davy had not a pick of fat on his frame and his chest was narrow and his ribs could be counted like tally sticks.

Davy also had a cough as round and brassy as a hunting-horn. The sound of it echoed out of the fissure and a good way along the narrow tunnel. The cough was so persistent that Jock had bought his son a patent remedy from Nicol's shop to try to be rid of it. The medicine came in a long brown bottle which Jock wrapped in rags and bound with twine so that Davy could carry it down below without risk of breakage. Every five or ten minutes Davy would drag the bottle from its niche, uncork it with his teeth and, like a little toper, suck a mouthful of the black liquid in the hope that it would cool the ache in his chest. The remedy offered more comfort than cure, however, and the cough, though it might abate for a while, seemed permanent.

The medicine curdled Davy's breath and he exuded the pungent odours of gum-ammoniac and poppy syrup to add to the nuisance of the noise. As the shift progressed he would grow progressively weaker. The coal lumps that he dragged from the hewer's room and carried to the steps seemed to increase in volume, to grow monstrous heavy. His fingers would turn to pith, his forearms to straw. He would drop a lump here, a lump there, sometimes gashing a knee, bruising an ankle or causing a toe to swell. He hardly seemed to notice his wounds, would cough, not cry, while he stooped and fumbled for the fallen coal, cough as he lumbered to the steps and climbed them, cough as he levered the burden up and through the trap to Mouse or Elspeth.

Elspeth was concerned about the boy. At the sight of his chalky, dirt-smeared face poking out of the trap, she would forget her own aches and pains and would try to cheer him with nonsensical conversations.

"Davy, Davy?"

"Wha'?"

"D'you know what time it is?"

Davy would consider the question, fingers gripping the edge of the trap, eyes glazed and stupid. He would cough, cough, cough, shake his head.

"Nah."

"Time you had a clock."

"Ah-hah," he would say and cough, not laugh.

"Davy?"

"Wha'?"

"Dinna fall off the step."

"Nah."

"Davy?"

"Aye."

Elspeth would chant a riddle, "*Drawers o' water an' hewers o' coal, all fell into a big black hole –*"and would wait, encouragingly, for Davy to complete the rhyme. But Davy could not think of the words, though he knew them well enough. His brain would not function when coal-dust was thicker than the particles of air and his arms were racked with carrying and his neck would hardly support his heavy, clouded head.

"*Davy, Davy?*" Elspeth would say, sharp and urgent, to wake him from enshrouding sleep. "*Davy, answer me.*"

At his own insistence he wore a little loincloth that dangled from the leather strap that circled his waist. When he grew tired he lost interest in modesty and the cloth flapped loose and Elspeth would glimpse his parts, tiny and unformed and innocently white.

"*Davy, please,*" she would beg. "*Talk t' me.*"

But if she raised her voice much above a whisper Jock Bennet would hear her and would call out, "Shut your mouth, lady, an' let him get on wi' the work."

Daddy's reprimand would steel the boy. He would scowl,

cough, scowl, say, "Aye, let me get on wi' the bloody work, for Christ's sake," and go stepping down again close to his father, source of whatever strength he still possessed.

Passing Mouse in the broad tunnel, Elspeth would voice her fear. "He's sick, your brother."

Mouse would snort and answer, "Aye, sick lazy."

Even Willie Ogilvie, however, twigged that Davy Bennet was not fit to be so far down, not fit, perhaps, to be labouring at all. Once or twice, when Davy's cough was especially raucous, Ogilvie would lean out from under the eave and shout at Elspeth as she crawled past his room, "God, what's wrong wi' that lad? T' hear the way he splutters you'd think he was gnawin' the coal off the bloody wall."

At all costs Elspeth must remain loyal to the Bennets and could not confide her anxieties to her neighbour.

"Davy's fine, Mr Ogilvie," she would say. "He just hasn't got used t' the dust yet."

"Tell him from me t' breathe through his nose, then."

"Aye, Mr Ogilvie."

If Elspeth had told Ogilvie her opinion that Davy Bennet was being worked to death, the miner would have been scandalised. It was not cruelty that made the colliers of the Abbeyfield so casual about their kin but refusal to acknowledge that frailty might exist at all in their midst. At least she had persuaded Jock Bennet not to bring Sarah down to haul for him. She had saved the young girl from that fate, for the time being.

While Elspeth dragged the recalcitrant sled through the tunnels, while she transferred the load to a creel at the ladder foot, slipped the broad straps over her shoulder, while she climbed precariously from rung to rung, while she staggered the last stretch along the broad road to Elginbrod's stall for weighing and checking, she had little enough on her mind, not even worry. The demands on her body obliterated all thought. When she was free of the dead weight of the coal, however, and returned with empty creel, unladen sled, anxiety would uncoil again and she would find herself hurrying along the tunnels to check on Davy.

It was ironic, really, that she should be more concerned about the lad's welfare than were his sister or father. She did not much like Davy Bennet. In his heart the boy believed himself to be a great baying hound of manly virtue, full of strength and conceit. If his lungs recovered and his body grew he would one day become a master far worse than his daddy. Now, however, Elspeth pitied him for his weakness and his illusions. Nothing he did or said could shake her compassion for the puny wee pup who would be lucky to see another winter let alone another spring.

She met Mouse with a laden sled; three hundredweights of dusty great coal. Elspeth pressed herself against the side of the broad tunnel, for an 'outward' hauler had right of passage. The girl-child elbowed past her without a word. When Mouse shuffled on towards the ladder Elspeth filled the tunnel that Mouse had vacated. Thirty feet further on she had to 'lie' again to let Milly Ogilvie squeeze past. Again there was no exchange of greetings. Milly's dumb, bovine features were screwed up with the effort of the haul and she hardly seemed to see Elspeth let alone wish to converse with her.

When Milly had gone, Elspeth slapped her sled down from its slanted position against the wall and went on past Mr Ogilvie's room. Peggie Ogilvie was loading from the ree that Willie had pushed behind him with his feet but Peggie gave no more sign of recognition than had her sister and Elspeth crawled out of range of the neighbour's candle and came to the mouth of the narrow tunnel.

Hunching, dipping her hips, she adjusted the sled's handle between her thighs. From up ahead she heard Davy's cough. She fitted her shoulders to the shape of the hole, then stiffened. Sound boomed from the tunnel, a crack, a rumble, a vibration against her skin. Instantly Elspeth tugged down her hood to cover her face. She tensed her spine and raised her bottom to jam against the roof as if she might have to hold the overlay in place by herself. She sucked in frightened breath.

Dust billowed in a solid wall from the tunnel, enveloped her. She closed her eyes tightly, compressed her lips, arched her back and tucked her chin to her chest. The cloud spread over her, coating her with fine grains. She did not dare open her eyes. She waited for the next drum of sound to roll up the tunnel, for the splintering that would announce a fall. There was no second wave, only foggy silence out of which, after a minute or so, came the rattle of Davy's cough.

Elspeth opened her eyes. Dust billowed into grey visibility. She peered along the narrow tunnel in search of Mr Bennet's candle. She could not bring herself to stir, however, not even when Davy coughed again.

"What the hell was that?" Willie Ogilvie shouted.

Elspeth looked back under arm. Peggie Ogilvie was crouched by the side of her father's room. Elspeth could only make out her pantaloons and one black-knuckled fist planted on the floor by the candle-cup.

"I – I canna tell," said Elspeth, stupidly.

"Was it a fall? Was it a bloody fall?" Peggie Ogilvie demanded shrilly.

Before Elspeth could contrive an answer, she heard a hoarse voice from the narrow tunnel. "*Roof's sound. All's solid, never fear.*" Jock Bennet cried the news with a seething heartiness. "*Everythin's fine here, Willie. Everythin's secure.*"

"What's that he's sayin'?" hissed Peggie Ogilvie. "Is it no' a fall?"

"No, no," Elspeth said. "It's just coal comin' down."

Davy's monotonous cough added a convincing touch to Jock's claim that nothing was amiss. But now that the dust had settled Peggie Ogilvie stooped, peered along at Elspeth and, to exorcise her fright, swore fiercely at her.

Elspeth, shaken too, was in no mood to take lip.

She shouted, "God in Heaven, Peggie! Do ye think it was my doin'? Keep your dirty tongue off me, hear?"

Willie Ogilvie chuckled. He had not even rolled off the cutting-stool, had paused in his wedging or shelling only when the remnants of the coal-dust sifted into his room. He was used to the din of coal-falls, and to squabbling women. Elspeth heard him say, "Back t' your work, Peg," and Peggie Ogilvie retreated from view.

Leaving the empty sled where it was, Elspeth thrust herself at once into the narrow tunnel and, with knees skating through a layer of fresh black dust, hastened to Mr Bennet's room and the door that led past the millstone.

Miraculously, the candle was still alight. By its halo she saw Davy. He was half-way through the trap, blacker than Elspeth had ever seen a collier, blacker than a sweep's brush. The moment that he caught sight of her, he ceased his struggles and flopped on to his side, coughing.

"Davy, what is it?"

He fought for breath, gasping, coughing, gasping again.

"Da – Da's trappit."

"But I heard his voice, his shout."

"Caught under the coal, down there," Davy wheezed.

"Is it bad?"

"I think he's finished," Davy said and, with hands to his face, burst into tears.

The day of the week was the same, the hour the same, the setting identical to that of their previous meeting. Only the weather had changed. It was a fine bright skittish April day and hedges at the bottom of the garden whisked and tossed as if shaking off winter's dust.

Though he had enjoyed the drive from Dumbarton that morning, Angus Hildebrand did not pay heed to the weather or the scene from the library window. He applied his formidable concentration upon Mr Moodie who sat, as before, behind the library table with fists squared upon its top as if waiting for a feast to be placed before him. Mr Hildebrand had brought such a feast, a banquet of legal documents, in his big battered leather box. He hoisted it on to the table and extracted from it, in the sequence in which they would be required, the testament, the will, the waiver, and the letters of liquidation.

Hildebrand studied the weaver for a long moment but could not quite evaluate the state of the man's attention or understanding. He sat, did James Moodie, like a wooden carving, all hollow and scraped and grained, and uttered not a word while the lawyer arranged the papers and put the box away below the table.

"May I proceed, Mr Moodie?"

"Proceed, sir," said James Moodie.

"I have found a way, Mr Moodie, of doing what you ask."

A twitch of the mouth was all the response that Moodie gave. He did not display pleasure or curiosity but, Hildebrand thought, he might have intended his lips to form a smile.

"The manner of it may not be orthodox. Indeed, it is a procedure that I have not used before or even heard of but—"

"Will it work?"

"Yes."

"Tell me how it'll work," said James.

He was more *compos mentis* than he had been two weeks ago. The bizarre nature of the illness that possessed him, whether it be of physical or spiritual origin, had enabled him to clear that part of his brain which had once so expertly grappled with the fine points of business finance.

With more confidence, Angus Hildebrand went on. "I have drafted a series of documents which, with your approval and the incorporation of any amendments which you wish to suggest, I will put this week into final form. The testament is the first and most important of these documents."

Hildebrand separated two sheets of foolscap paper from the summit of the pile and slid them between Moodie's motionless fists.

Moodie glanced down but made no attempt to read the screeds of copperplate script which Mr Hildebrand had, in person, penned.

Angus Hildebrand said, "I have used the testament in its strict and original sense; to wit – confined to the nomination of executors, to specifying the name of the administrator of your moveable estate. I wish you, sir, to nominate me."

James Moodie said, "Why?"

"If I hold the office under the appointment of a deceased party, as a trustee for others, I have a stronger hold upon the administration of the estate than I would have if I am merely appointed by the commissary. My legal right to deal with the wishes and bequests set forth in your will cannot be challenged by other parties."

Moodie's mouth twitched once more.

"Pray," he said, "continue."

"In competition, the executor-nominate holds a dominant position over all others, including even the widow and next-of-kin. Your sisters cannot challenge this position and must, if they wish so to do, base appeals only against unusual clauses and dispositions in the will and its directives."

"As executor can you not claim one third?"

"No, not one third," said Hildebrand, gratified that Mr

Moodie was sufficiently sane to follow the strategy and to fix upon its pitfalls. "If you nominate me as executor-trustee, and we agree the fee beforehand and state it, then I cannot make the claim for one third of the estate that remains after settlements and adjustments. Besides, I have drafted a waiver, which I will sign, and we will have witnessed. This I will leave with you, Mr Moodie, to place in the keeping of a safe person; with the parish minister or your banker."

"Yes," Moodie said.

"In essence you wish to preserve your estate as a working entity. Because it is not land-based – that is, has not a tenantry as such but is a manufactory – the court may concern itself that the estate will incur debts which will involve the *magisters* in complicated proceedings."

"Duties an' taxes," said Moodie cryptically.

"Certainly," said Hildebrand. "But other outgoings too. Payment of wages, for example."

"What can I do?"

"Liquidate those peripheral assets which it would be difficult to protect against fraud and theft," Hildebrand replied.

"My interest in the dye-works?"

"Certainly. Also the sheep which graze on pastures which you do not lease directly but only contract."

"Aye."

"Also a number of similar assets which I've catalogued separately on this page." Hildebrand placed the appropriate sheet before Moodie but the weaver did not even lower his eyes. "Liquidate your peripheral assets and accumulate the sums raised by sale into a fund distinct from your current capital accounts; in another bank, perhaps. From this fund all taxes and duties will be paid. The balance will stand as surety against claims on the estate for a period of two years or longer after your demise."

"Will the court bear with this ruse?"

"It's not a deception, Mr Moodie. It's unusual but it is perfectly within the law."

"What'll be left for Elspeth?"

"The mill at Kennart, in production, and the bulk of those assets by which the mill is maintained."

"My house?"

"Moss House is not a particular problem."

"The grazing hillside I lease from Bontine?"

"Local leases must be honoured at the terms by which they were originally negotiated, until the period of the lease expires, although such leases are not usually designated as part of the heritage. In this special case the Bontine lease will be."

"How long can you hold off my sisters?"

"Six months are allowed for the executor to do due diligence. It is my feeling that the six-month period may be incorporated into the twenty-four-month period of status quo that you state as your will."

"Will – will my sisters not—"

"Your sisters, separately or in tandem, may elect to challenge the validity of the will in the absence of widow and heir. But no right-minded member of my profession would dare make a petition for court intervention before the two-year period has terminated."

"How long after that?"

Hildebrand raised his shoulders. "As long as I can prevaricate; at the least, another full year. But the inheritor, your wife, must return as soon as possible after your – after your will comes into force."

"She'll come."

"It would be valuable to have knowledge of her whereabouts, Mr Moodie," said Angus Hildebrand.

"Elspeth will come," James said, "when there's a place for her."

The lawyer glanced over his shoulder, leaned across the table, whispered, "Mr Moodie, your gross annual revenue is close to seven thousand pounds. Your total worth, not accounting for the sale of Moss House, is near seventy thousand. You, sir, are a wealthy man. I fear that your wealth will engender much attention when it is known and that I'll not be able to stave off your sisters' claims for ever, not if they prepare their petitions thoroughly."

James ignored the warning.

"What else?" he said.

Hildebrand sank back into the chair. "I'm no younger than

162

you are, Mr Moodie. We must therefore ensure that if I, perchance, predecease you—"

"What else?"

"If your wife and child – God forbid it – are not traced before your death, how will I notify them of your wishes? The court, in time, may presume them to be dead."

"Elspeth will come back to Balnesmoor."

"But where is she now, Mr Moodie?"

"Looking for a place."

"A place?"

"Which I will provide."

Cautiously Hildebrand said, "What if she has found a place elsewhere, sir?"

James did not answer him.

After answering a few more questions James Moodie's interest in legal detail seemed to weaken and the lawyer was dismissed, sent back to his chambers in Dumbarton to finalise the drafts and, with the weaver's sanction, to prepare them for Moodie's signature.

With her forefinger she scooped dirt from the cup and tweaked the clotted tallow so that the candle would burn strongly and not splutter and expire in the thick atmosphere below.

Still weeping, Davy held out both hands to receive the cup and, urged on by Elspeth, retreated bodily through the trap and down the steps again into the crack along the seam.

It was perfectly quiet now, perfectly still.

Elspeth listened for rock creaking, the groan of the coal settling but she could hear nothing, not even a whimper or moan from the square hole in the marl. Mouse was prone to make large of things, to exaggerate events. But Davy was not given to this habit. She felt queasy with nervousness as she dragged herself up the mound and put her head and shoulders into the trap. She looked down. Everything was as before, except that atoms of dust hung in the air and gave to the candle-flame a coppery tint.

Davy coughed.

"How is he, Davy?" she whispered.

"Lady, come down," Jock Bennet answered her.

The hewer's voice sounded strong, commanding. Elspeth's

relief was instantly transmuted into an irrational fear of descent into the fissure and anger that she should be forced to undertake it.

She wriggled round, backed into the hole and lowered herself over the board at the lip. She went down into wan light, looking out for a final moment at the lineaments of the old room and the tunnel which suddenly seemed friendly and secure even in deep gloom. She gathered herself, steeled herself and stepped down to the dry, gritty bottom.

She could stand upright here. Though stippled with black dust, the wall showed the grain of the millstone. She saw that she was under a gigantic sloping slab, like a pantile roof, a slab that stretched unbroken as far as her eye could see, as far as candlelight reached. A buttress of big coal created a corner and around it was the section where Jock Bennet had begun his flensing of the seam.

Elspeth had not appreciated before just how large the seam really was, that Mouse's claim that it was higher than her head did not do it justice. Visible coal, lying nakedly exposed and not in need of clearing or preliminary excavation, was ten or eleven feet in height and did not dwindle to any degree along the length of the natural fault. Elspeth spared only a brief wondering glance at the seam for she was drawn, with returning horror, to the crouched figure of the boy and to the tumulus of fresh-fallen coal that barred passage along the cavern.

She could see the iron bar that Mr Bennet had been using, even the rutted places where he had driven wedges, his hammer lying flung to the left. She could see how the whole cut had come on him while he knelt, straining on the long bar, how he had pitched backwards from it, how it had snapped down upon him, like a trap upon a rabbit.

Jock Bennet was conscious, irascible, tormented by pain – and dying. Elspeth had no doubt of it. His body was caught below the rock and blood oozed from the flutings, mixed black as the coal itself. He bled from the side of the lips, a thin, bright red trickle that bubbled when he spoke.

"Get me bloody out of here, Patterson," he seethed.

She gaped at him, bent over, hands on her knees.

Kneeling by his father's head, looking helplessly down at him, Davy coughed, and sobbed.

"He's – he's bloody useless, crying like a damned bairn."
Jock Bennet clenched his teeth, then his tongue snaked out
and wiped away the dribble of blood, which immediately
reappeared, growing sluggishly from a single shining droplet.
"You, lady, you get me out."

"I'll – I'll fetch –" Elspeth whispered.

"Fetch nobody."

"But you're wounded sore, Mr Bennet."

Destroyed, damned, Jock Bennet would not recant. He
would not yield up the power of his authority or imperil the
hoard of coal that luck had led him to. He did not believe, did
not accept that he was finished.

Elspeth swallowed, tasting dust. She pushed Davy to one
side, disturbing his wake-like pose, and snatched the candle-
cup from his fingers. She could see Mr Bennet's eyeballs
glistening redly as she circulated the candle around him,
examining the exact nature of his wounds, those that could be
seen.

"Lift the bloody slab, damn you."

"I'm goin' for Mr Rance."

She could not believe that he had strength enough in half a
body to grip her with such ferocity. He caught her high up
under the armpit and dragged himself six or seven inches out
from under the slabby coal, brought a cry out of himself as his
flesh tore, ignored it as if it was a stranger who had uttered
the demeaning sound.

"Do that, Patterson, an' I'll flay your bloody hide," he
hissed. The blood in his mouth sprayed and freckled the
stubble on his chin, the bare and hairless skin of his chest.
"Lift the rocks. Free me. Get me out t' the old room."

"Davy?" Elspeth did not know what to do.

"Davy," Daddy snapped, "pay heed."

Elspeth thought of Mouse. The girl child would have un-
loaded by now and would in all likelihood be coming down
the ladder from first or second level, the creel bouncing on
her narrow back. In ten minutes or less she would appear
innocently at the trap, would learn what had occurred and,
Daddy notwithstanding, would set up a tremendous howling
that would have the Ogilvies along in a trice, and others soon
after.

165

Elspeth might flout his order, defy him, might go up and along the tunnel, have help here in a quarter of an hour. He, her master, could do nothing to prevent it. Davy would not. But then Jock Bennet might not die. Sheer tenacity might keep him alive and, if that happened, he would never forgive her disobedience and would make her pay for it dearly.

"Do this for me, lady, an' I'll ask nothin' else." In his throat Elspeth could hear the little resinous rub of desperation. "Please, do it for me."

"Get the bar, Davy," she said.

The boy's reaction was spontaneous. She could not be sure if he supposed that she might work some miracle which would save his daddy or if he merely obeyed out of habit. She did not have to tell him what was required. He inserted the long iron bar under the fractured slate of coal, wedged it firmly and flung his weight upon it.

The coal growled. Jock Bennet gasped and thrashed his head in agony. The bar quivered. Davy pumped on it again. Shards of coal, scalloping the edge of the slate, flaked from about the bar as the boy applied all the pressure that his strength allowed.

The slab of coal shifted, rising.

Sweat dripped from Davy's brow and coagulated on his arms and belly. Centring his effort he drove again into the bar. Jock Bennet's eyes stared hideously, his mouth sagged open into a hideous parody of laughter. The words came croaking from his throat. "Aye, Davy, that's it. That's it, Davy. Good lad."

Kneeling, Elspeth straightened her arms and braced herself on all fours. Jock Bennet gripped her shoulders, strained and dragged himself from under the slab, inch by tearing inch. In spite of his pain and the sudden welter of wet, warm blood that filled the wounds in his belly, he persisted, drawing himself out as rapidly as he dared. With a guttural cry he came free, and Elspeth dragged him sideways clear of the tumulus and along the floor towards the steps.

Davy released the bar. It sprang from the coal like a spear and clattered against the wall, while Davy danced away from it, arms over his head, and the slab settled again with a sound like teeth on bones.

Still clasping Elspeth's arms Jock Bennet pulled himself into a sitting position. He looked down at his body. Pain appeared to have eased away. He gave a wry chuckle, twisted his head and spat.

"Christ, what a mess I am," he said.

Blood oozed through the dirt, a puckered soft red rising that might have come from nothing more serious than grazing of the skin. Elspeth was not deceived. She could see the ends of bone protruding through muscles and the wounds of his crushed and punctured belly which had taken the brunt of the weight of the fall. It was astonishing that Jock Bennet had not died instantly, that he could still think rationally and rap out orders. It was as if he had somehow separated himself from the wrecked flesh below his waist, risen above his body altogether.

"Get me out o' here," he said.

Behind them Davy was racked by a spasm of coughing brought on by effort and lack of air.

"How can we safely move you, Mr Bennet?"

"Just get me out," Jock Bennet shouted, "an' see the trap sealed behind us."

Elspeth understood. She could hardly believe it. Jock Bennet was not concerned with the process of living or dying, only with protecting the coal seam, with guarding his secret. Some of the man's callous indifference to his fate infected Elspeth too. She could not be held to blame if he succumbed to shock or a loss of blood induced by violent motion.

"Lift me out, damn it."

She slipped a hand under his armpits and dragged him along the sandy bottom to the foot of the steps.

At any moment Mouse might arrive. She had not a moment to spare. What with Mouse screaming, Davy sobbing and Jock Bennet bellowing orders with his dying breath, there would be no hope of carrying out the collier's 'last wish' before the Ogilvies were roused and the secret revealed. She could do nothing to ease his pain, or staunch the bleeding. All she could do was obey him.

She manhandled him to the steps and, bent and panting, dragged him on to them. Davy appeared, candle in hand, and on Elspeth's instruction lifted his father's legs and feet. Together they raised Jock Bennet up the steps, out of the trap and on to the marl. He was still conscious, though his eyes were screwed shut and blood clung to his chin like a beard. He could no longer shout commands, however; he could barely whisper.

Feebly, he beckoned Elspeth to him.

She knelt, ear to his lips.

"Close – close – hide—"

She nodded, patted his shoulder soothingly, then drew him down the slope away from the hole to allow Davy to pull himself from the fissure and to wrestle the little wooden door into position.

"Davy, do y' know what to do?"

"Aye."

"I'm goin' to take him out, through the tunnel."

"Aye."

Turning, she slid Jock Bennet along the floor on his back, past his old room towards the narrowing. The section was thirty feet long, crawl-tight as a worm-cast and black as eternal night.

Stretched almost flat, Elspeth went in tail foremost. She wished now that she had not abandoned the sled. She could have rolled him on to it and dragged him out on the runners. Davy was tamping the door into its frame. A minute or two of work with a shovel would cover the trap so that no trace of it was visible.

She lowered her head, whispered, "It's done, Mr Bennet. It's hidden. The seam's sealed."

"Ah," he sighed. "Ah."

She pulled him, moving backwards into the narrow tunnel, and Davy, his task done, scrambled after them bearing the candle-cup.

They had made but half the distance when Davy hissed, "See, he's tryin' t' talk. Stop. Stop."

Elspeth put her ear to his mouth once more.

"Pa'son?"

"Aye, Mr Bennet."

"Are – are ye – there?"

"I'm here, Mr Bennet."

"Look ah—"

"I will. I will. Hold on. We're nearly out."

She threw caution to the winds, tugging him along after her as fast as she could, but he bled his life away somewhere in the section and was dead when she got him to the broad tunnel.

Mouse was suddenly at Elspeth's shoulder. Davy extended the candle and the light flickered over the man's face.

"Mr Bennet. Mr Bennet."

No pulse in the puddle of blood that filled his navel. His eyes, wide open, stared at Elspeth without anger.

Davy looked up, sobbing, at his sister.

"Daddy's dead," he said.

"Aye, so he is," said Mouse in wonderment and, after a moment's pause, filled the tunnel with her screams.

It was early afternoon in Strachan Castle. The men had been out in the fields all day, ploughing the long section since Mr Gibbie had at last given in to Lachlan and furnished money with which to buy a quantity of good grass seed, though he professed not to see much point as his cattle appeared to be doing well enough on the stuff provided by untrammelled nature.

Indoors Anna had put Robbie into his cot in the hope that he might take a nap, for he had been as wild as fury all morning and had flung his dinner about the kitchen until Anna, egged on by Cat, had given him a light little slap on the back of his legs and commanded him, as sternly as she dared, to behave himself and eat his vittles like a good wee lad. Robbie had wailed unremittingly for five minutes and had then scoffed every scrap in his bowl in scowling defiance.

Robert Cochran Sinclair was quiet at last. Aileen was in the kitchen dressing tripe for supper. Anna and Cat were seated at the deal table in the servants' gangway cleaning silver upon which Mistress Alicia had detected a trace of tarnish, which was not surprising since the heavy silverware was never out of its case from one year's end to the next. Cat did not speak to Anna, nor Anna to Cat. Neither of them worked with fervour. The task was not unpleasant and they would spin it out as long as possible, perhaps even until it was time to fetch the cows for milking.

Sir Gibbie had gone out as usual that morning to ride to

Falkirk where the Farmers' Bank had a small office near the market yards. Alicia had ridden over to Harlwood in the gig, returning in time to take early tea in her 'sewing-room' under the round tower. The Bontine brood had been heard but not seen and they too had been put to bed out of Mother's way for an hour or so.

It was Edith Simmons who came for Anna. She delivered Mistress Alicia's summons and waited about, timidly, to ascertain that Anna would obey the lady's command without undue delay.

Anna looked at Cat, Cat at Anna.

"What can *she* want this time o' day?" said Anna.

"The fire'll need made up," said Cat.

"That's your job," said Anna.

"It's not the fire," said Edith Simmons.

"What is it then?"

"The needle."

"The what?"

"Come quick, Anna, or I'll be for it."

Alicia Bontine had grown less gaunt since she had been ousted from Ottershaw to take refuge in Strachan Castle. With the sallow lines of responsibility smoothed away she was, in repose at least, almost handsome. She was seated in the centre of the round chamber which she had claimed as her own. A mahogany chair and a large circular table were placed on an Indian carpet as if measured and geometricised by the rule. A small coal fire burned in the grate. The tea-tray had been removed and Edith had picked up the toys and playthings that the children had scattered behind them. The slot window was open an inch or two to let in the fragrances of a fresh April afternoon.

Edith opened the door for Anna, admitted her, then stepped back, closing the door behind her.

What, Anna wondered, not without trepidation, was the purpose of this private 'interview'?

Alicia wore a day dress of mauve weave, fashioned with gigot sleeves and a low neckline. A fine old Kashmir shawl was draped about her shoulders and a mob cap of the tiniest proportions was perched upon her thick dark hair. Across her lap was a bolt of blue satin material and on the table stood the three baskets that made up her sewing-set, along with a velvet-straw ball bristling with needles and pins.

Anna had no reputation as a seamstress. Indeed the best hand at that sort of skill was nursery-maid Edith Simmons. Puzzled, Anna dropped a nonchalant curtsy which, for once, Alicia acknowledged with an inclination of the head.

"Ah, Sinclair!" Alicia called all the servants 'properly' by surname, which did lead to some confusion with five Sinclairs below stairs. "I trust that I'm not takin' you away from important occupation?"

"No, M'm."

The woman was different today, not acerbic – smug. Anna felt her stomach tighten. Mistress Alicia was just the sort of person who would take pleasure in delivering bad news, especially to her. Could it be Matt? Had Matt been taken by the Riding Officers after all these many months?

"Do you see what I have here?" said Alicia, sweetly.

"Satin, M'm."

"Satin, indeed. Do you know what it's for, Sinclair?"

"No."

"It's for making a gown, Sinclair; a ball gown."

"Very nice, M'm," said Anna, now thoroughly mystified.

Alicia was not about to shorten the interview by coming at once to the point.

Anna said, "What does satin have t' do wi' me, M'm? I'm no use with the needle."

"Much more use with the cows, hm?"

Anna's cheeks burned with temper but, in spite of her self-confidence and the security of her position in the household, she had sense enough not to show her anger at the insult. It was not the time or place, with Mr Gibbie away, to put her position on trial.

"Aye, M'm," she agreed, tight-lipped.

"No, Sinclair, I do not require you to ply the needle. I merely wanted the opinion of a younger person, shall we say, as to the fashionable shape of the bustle."

"Bustle?" Anna said.

"I am aware that servants do keep up with the fashion and, as I do not wish to seem fuddy-duddy, I thought that I might solicit your opinion, to go with Simmons's, as to whether a roll or a sausage would be 'right', shall we say, for a ball gown."

Anna had no idea. It was true that the servants of the *bon ton* knew more than their mistresses about who was wearing what and what was in and what out, but Strachan was a million miles from Edinburgh as far as Anna was concerned. Even Edith Simmons had not been far from the neighbourhood since the Bontines had left Ottershaw.

Alicia's concern for fashion, her desire to extract advice from a humble servant were false leads, opening skips in the game that the mistress was playing with her. Anna's cheeks turned crimson. She curled her fingers into her palms and hid them in the folds of her skirt. Alicia had lost interest in the bolt of material and let it slide from her lap to the floor. She gave it a careless little nudge with her foot and straightened her shoulders, showing the posture of authority, chin lifted, nose lifted, the stare coming down from on high.

"What do you say, Sinclair?"

"Where is the ball?" said Anna.

That was it, that was the question that the bitch wanted her to ask. She felt her belly tighten even more, supposing that the ball was to be held here at Strachan and that Randall would be present.

"Is that important?" said Alicia, with the ghost of a smile.

"City fashion isn't country fashion, M'm."

"How well expressed. The ball, for your information, is to be held at Ottershaw on the tenth day of May. Gilbert and I have, naturally, been invited."

Ottershaw! Anna held her breath. She experienced delirious anticipation, completely out of keeping with the tone of the conversation or with Alicia's manner. She, Anna, had been invited too. Instantly she revised the assumption; had been 'requested' by Randall. Perhaps he had made it a condition of invitation to his sister-in-law. She could imagine the injunction written upon the card: *Bring Anna*. She would need to cadge money from Lachlan to buy herself a pretty dress.

Alicia continued to stare down her nose at Anna but, as if reading the girl's silly thoughts, smiled with fatuous malice.

"Will – will I be goin'?" Anna blurted out.

"You? Why, indeed, would you be going? If I require a maid in attendance I'll take Simmons."

"Take me, M'm."

Alicia laughed, gave a little waggle of her long-boned hand. "I doubt if my brother-in-law would thank me for it."

"Did Ran—did the laird not ask—"

"Ask what?"

She realised that she had been pincered. She would not give the bitch the satisfaction of humiliating her further. Mouth closed, Anna shook her head.

"Sausage, do you think?" said the mistress of Strachan Castle.

It had had nothing to do with bustles. It had to do with the imparting of the information that she, Anna, had not been invited and that she, Alicia Bontine, would not even take her as maid in attendance.

It was, of course, totally unreasonable of Anna to expect an invitation to such a genteel affair, no matter what she had once meant to Randall. But in matters of the heart Anna had never been very rational. The image of Ottershaw all lit and gay, hall and lawns alive with the strains of music, ladies in fine gowns and gentlemen in livery, was irresistible to Anna's imagination; and the thought of Randall—

Alicia intruded. "I cannot recall the last ball at Ottershaw. When Mr Gilbert and I became engaged there was a formal supper, of course, but the old man did not care for social frivolities. I'm delighted to learn that Randall is of a different stamp. It must, I feel, be the influence of the young woman."

Alicia had turned her face away, showing her profile against the window.

"What young woman?" said Anna.

"I hope that it will be the first of many such occasions," said Alicia. "God knows, there's little enough civilised diversion in this part of the country. Society could do with a leader. After his marriage, Randall might very well provide us with one."

"His – *his marriage?*"

Alicia turned her head very slowly, the smile rapacious.

"What marriage?" Anna shrieked.

"Oh, it's not formal," the woman said. "The ball is celebratory, so Mr Gilbert says, but it's not a betrothal. Not yet."

"Who is she?"

"So you recommend sausage, do you, Sinclair?" said Alicia. "I am beholden to you for your advice."

"Who is the woman?"

"I do not care for servants who raise their voices to me. You may go now."

"I want t' know who she is."

"Do you, indeed?" Alicia hesitated. She had every intention of telling Sinclair who her rival was. No, not rival. Sinclair had never been in competition with real ladies. She had been Randall's toy, no more.

Alicia said, "She's the daughter of Augustus Seaton of Piperhaugh in Aberdeenshire. She is younger than you, I believe, and my husband informed me that she is fair of face and figure."

"How – how – did he—"

"Really, Sinclair! I cannot waste my time gossipin' with you. Be off."

Anna regained control of herself. She felt as if she had been struck a physical blow. It was all she could do not to throw herself upon Alicia Bontine and drag her to the floor, throttle her until she yielded up all that she knew of this upstart who had taken her place at Ottershaw and, probably, in Randall's bed.

Anna swung round, groping for the door knob.

She would not weep, would not shed tears before Alicia Bontine, for that was what the woman wanted, to see her swelter in misery.

"The lady in question," Alicia called out, "is Miss Suzanne Seaton, sister of Sir Randall's closest friend, a fellow officer, now retired from service."

Anna did not dare face the mistress of the house. She paused only long enough to take in the last scrap of information, then she jerked open the sewing-room door, stumbled out into the corridor and along it and down the circular stairs. Behind her, echoing, she could hear Alicia Bontine's laughter, mocking her all the way to the servants' hall.

Cat looked up from the silverware. "What did she—"

"Damn her!" shouted Anna. *"Damn all of you!"*

She swept her arm across the table and sent knives, forks

174

and big round spoons clattering to the flagstones; then rushed on, rushed through the kitchen, past Robbie's cot and out of the door into the yard.

Fear, grief and fury welled in her breast but she dammed the emotions up, running out of the yard and down the cow track and slithering through a gap in the hedge, the way she had done years ago when she was young and wild on the hill below Drumglass, before she had met Randall, before he had kissed her.

It was not until she reached the shelter of a rough stand of birch and alder on a spit of land above the river that she flung herself down on the ground and buried her face in her arms and let it flood out, a torrent of tears, fast and furious as an April storm.

When it was gone, when the weeping had stilled to sobs, Anna was not as she had been a half-hour before.

For the first time she saw herself clearly, saw the folly, the foolishness of her dreams, how unreal they had been.

Randall would never marry her.

She was nothing but a servant-girl with a bastard bairn, without power, without prospects and without hope of redemption from the humdrum toll of days that she must spend in bondage to her humble origins.

She stayed out until almost dusk and then, chastened and silent, trailed miserably back to the kitchen to feed her son and eat supper with the Sinclairs.

Five pounds was the cost of the burial, in addition to the guinea fee that Reverend Ferrie, minister of Rutherford and Placket, demanded for the 'kirk box' from families that were not members of his congregation.

It was all done with great speed. Jock Bennet's body was in the ground less than twenty-four hours after his demise. The corpse was kept overnight in the lantern hut at the back of the Abbeyfield's stables and was dressed and confined to its coffin there. The coffin, and the grave-marker, were made to pattern by pit carpenters who charged a standard fee for the items. Thomas Rance made all the arrangements and penned a cryptic report for the manager, Mr Bolderon. Snippets Smith totalled John Bennet's take to the day of his death, paid out what was owing to his son, closed the entry in the ledger with the terse comment *Died by Accident*, signed and dated.

There was no 'official' enquiry, no investigation. Davy Bennet's tearful account was taken at face value, though Mr Rance took the precaution of ordering Willie Ogilvie along the narrow tunnel to check the shoring and make sure that the slump which had killed Bennet did not presage a running fault in the overlay.

Ogilvie did not much care for the duty, particularly as there was blood smeared here and there on the floor of the tunnel and a nasty puddle of the stuff outside Bennet's room. He made his examination at the double, found no evidence of cracking and returned the message that all was tight before he crawled back under his shelf to finish off his shift.

The portion of ground allotted to colliers, though consecrated, was distinct and separate from the parish kirkyard, a sloping spur of unkempt grassland divided by a road from the last resting-place of respectable members of the community, those who were not miners. There were few stones. The markers were mainly of wood, solid and deep-dug and branded with just enough information to keep record, for a while, of the men and women who had lived and died on and under the Abbeyfield. Burned-black letters, cramped and abbreviated, on weathered wood, told no tales at all.

John Bennet's first wife was buried west of Alloa, on scrub-land by the old Crabbe pit. His second wife rested only ten yards from the slot picked out for Jock. Her grave was weedy and unflowered and the wooden cross had a tilt to it, for Jock had never visited the place from the day he put her down. Now he had joined them both, and if there was hymn-singing in Heaven at the meeting in eternal bliss of a man and his wives no whisper crept across the steel-grey waters of the Forth or drifted with the smoke from the coal pit's shafts.

Reverend Ferrie lifted the deceased's name from a hand-printed note, and mentioned it only twice. He intoned a long prayer, which he had off by heart, and read verse after verse from the Book of Numbers, all about hosts and tabernacles, which made no sense at all in the context of a burial service.

176

No psalms were sung and the old man from Rutherford kirk shuffled forward with his spade the moment the *Amen* was uttered.

It was day-shift time, mid-morning, so there were no colliers at the graveside. They were all below ground howking out their daily bread. Jock would not have expected them to sacrifice a valuable hour to pay respects to a man whose ability to earn had been reduced to zero. Present by the grave were Davy, Snippets and Mr Rance, while Sarah, Mouse and Elspeth watched from beyond the wall.

Mouse wept and wept. She had wept incessantly through most of the night and her grief grated now, a little, on Elspeth's nerves. Sarah, however, had shed no tears at all and that concerned Elspeth more than Mouse's incessant blubbing. Several times she had tried to put an arm about the girl but Sarah, even now, would have none of it and shook off 'Pet's consolations.

It was towards the end of the reading that the horseman came trotting down the road. The sound of the hoofs distracted the girls. They turned their heads and Mouse, without drying up, dug her elbow into Elspeth's hip, leaned and hissed, "It's Mr Bolderon."

Clearly Keir Bolderon had not intended to attend the hewer's funeral. He had inadvertently intruded upon it while riding from his house to the pit. At first he was nonplussed. He reined the horse, tried to back the animal but could not and, with the girls' eyes upon him, slipped from the saddle, tied the rein to a gatepost and, removing his hat, tiptoed down to join the females at the wall.

He said nothing until Reverend Ferrie had concluded his benediction and the old man had unshouldered his spade, then he came a step towards the three girls, hat held across his chest and a look of sincere condolence upon his face.

He addressed himself to Elspeth.

"You are . . . ?"

"Elspeth Patterson, Mr Bolderon."

"His wife, poor chap?"

"The – the servant, sir. But these are his children."

"Of course. It's Bennet, is it not?"

Neither Mouse nor Sarah could find voice to reply.

Elspeth answered, "Jock Bennet, Mr Bolderon. He was killed yesterday by a coal fall in the base seam."

"I believe I have the—Yes, Mr Rance did inform me."

For a moment the manager did not appear to know what to do or say. He shifted his weight uncomfortably from foot to foot and looked down at the ground, then he dug into his pocket and fished out his purse.

Mouse, her tiny face wet and swollen, stopped crying as Mr Bolderon opened the purse and took out two crowns. The coins were not common, big round objects which seemed more valuable, more real than banknotes.

He gave them to Elspeth, laying them gently on her palm and then, impulsively, lifted them again and bestowed one each on Sarah and on Mouse; then, and this was the queerest thing, he stepped forward and, hat still in hand, kissed Mouse and Sarah, each upon the brow.

Without warning, Sarah began to cry.

Mr Bolderon cleared his throat, turned, put on his hat, and to Elspeth said, "God be with the children," and hurried off to have words with Thomas Rance who was leading Davy up to the gate, a hand on the boy's shoulder.

"He gave me five shillin's," said Mouse, in awe. 'Mr Bolderon himsel' gave me five shillin's. What did he give you, Sarah?"

Sarah did not answer her sister.

Weeping inconsolably, Sarah had turned and fled.

When one thought of banks and bankers the names of the Falkirk Farmers' and Gilbert Bontine did not immediately leap to the mind. The fact was that Gibbie was no more proficient in the science of managing money than he had been in the art of managing land.

Provincial banking-houses continued to pop up – and pop down – all over the place to meet the demand for credit to oil the wheels of progress. Soreheads predicted a decline now that the war was over and it was rumoured that one of the Farmers' competitors, the Falkirk Union, was seriously over-extended and dependent upon a good harvest in the Strath to pull it through financial crisis. Gibbie paid no heed to such rumours. He had two active, on-the-spot partners to do the fretting for him and they did not seem in the slightest concerned. Gibbie was so engrossed in the 'habiliments' of banking that he was blind and deaf to its real issues.

Originally he had purchased the partnership from old Nigel Summerhays. Angus Hildebrand had made enquiries into the standing of the Farmers', had heard that it was steady if not scintillating, and had given the nod to the purchase. Gibbie had told Randall that the price of the partnership was seven thousand pounds, the bulk of his inheritance from his father. In truth the partnership had cost him twelve thousand. Alicia had come up with the extra five thousand in savings accumulated through legacies from aunts and uncles over the years, since she was an only child in a family not much given to breeding. Alicia had willingly sunk her personal fortune into banking. It seemed to be such a secure, respectable, infallible profession, ideally suited to her husband's temperament and to her social aspirations.

The partners numbered three. In addition to Gibbie there were two brothers, Francis and Alfred Pryde. They had founded the bank back in 1787 and knew the ins and outs of the local trade down to the last brown farthing. Long before it had become fashionable to do so they had financed store farmers and cattle-jobbers from booths at all the fairs and trysts and markets within a day's ride of Falkirk. They boasted to Gilbert that they had 'invented' the 50-day loan and refined the note-of-credit system and had never been cheated by a jobber or a drover in all their long years in the business. Even the gullible Gibbie took these tales with a pinch of salt.

In addition to stirring a much-needed twelve thousand pounds into the Prydes' emptying pot, Gilbert brought an illusion of stability to the company. It was assumed by depositors that Bontine lands were now 'behind' the bank, though Randall would have been spitted and roasted before he would have guaranteed Gibbie's venture on a formal basis. However, Randall did become a client of the bank, as part of his bargain with Gibbie for taking Anna off his hands. Sir Randall Bontine was the Falkirk Farmers' only landowner of any scale and he was heavily borrowed on the £1,000 line of credit that his brother allowed him. The Prydes seemed unconcerned by fraternal generosity and by the small sums that Gibbie personally borrowed to enhance his property at Strachan.

If Weaver Moodie had suspected that the Falkirk Farmers' was in a precarious position or that Gibbie did not know what he was doing, mad or not Moodie would not have chosen that little company as a depository for his all-important fund. Nobody, not Hildebrand, not Randall and certainly not Gilbert, warned Moodie off. Nobody had an inkling that the Pryde brothers were sinking gradually into debt and that one per cent interest on a 50-day loan had become, in inflationary times, a formula not for continued success but for inevitable disaster.

In the past, before Elspeth had run off, Gilbert had tried without success to persuade Moodie to bank with him. James did not trust banks very much at the best of times and preferred to divide his accounts between two rock-solid, old-established institutions, namely the Royal Bank of Scotland and the British Linen Company. But he had heeded Hildebrand's advice, felt that he could trust Young Gilbert in much the same manner as he had trusted Old Gilbert, and had plumped in the end for a convenient solution. The fund, worth eleven thousand pounds, promised a fixed return of three per cent interest per annum.

The Prydes were overwhelmed. They showered Gibbie with praise, treated him to a lavish dinner at the Market Tavern and convinced him that he was a banker born. Gibbie believed every word of it. He preened and swaggered and did not spare a thought for Moodie's intention or the weaver's reasons for selling off his investments in the first place.

Randall was no quicker off the mark. If he had not been quite so involved with Suzanne Seaton and the Ottershaw Ball he might have speculated with more attention upon Jamie Moodie's odd manoeuvres. As it was he not only neglected to discuss the implications with Gibbie but did not even raise the subject with Angus Hildebrand. He simply complied with the lawyer's polite request that he present himself at the Reverend Eshner's manse at ten o'clock on the morning of May 2nd to serve as witness to the signing by Moodie of a whole bundle of documents related to inheritance. Randall assumed that Jamie Moodie had at last lifted himself out of the slough of despond and had decided to change his will to match the change in his circumstances.

James was grim and uncommunicative during the legal proceeding which, shorn of all social frills, lasted less than a quarter of an hour. Indeed, Randall was back out of the manse and trotting home to Ottershaw almost before he knew it. Eshner had notarised, Randall witnessed and Moodie had signed each of the documents that Hildebrand had put upon the table; and that had been that.

Randall had been somewhat shocked by Jamie Moodie's appearance. The man was so torn down that he might have been suffering a leaking wound of the body and not of the soul. But Randall had too many light-hearted things to occupy him, not least the finalising of arrangements for the Ottershaw Ball, to dwell long on the strange affairs of the weaver mannie.

The May Ball, to the laird's astonishment, had become a major enterprise and a sensation in the Lennox. Every tuppenny-ha'penny tenant farmer and his wife seemed to be scheming for an invitation and tinpot traders from as far away as Duntocher took to dropping in to bid him fond greeting and to remind him that they had once done a bit of business with his father. If it had not been for Suzanne's excited amusement, and her support, Randall would have been irritated beyond measure by the pettiness of it all. But he had started it and flung himself into it in great good humour.

So Randall Bontine too spared no thought for Jamie Moodie who, after all the papers were signed and legally sealed, vanished once more behind the walls of Moss House and settled, almost impatiently, to wait for the season's first big rain to flood the Kennart lades.

FIVE

The Ottershaw Ball

When they returned from the burial Elspeth gathered the Bennets about the table for a midday meal. Mary Jean had been put into the care of benevolent Nessie Herbert and her big dozy daughter, Meg, and would be safe enough at the minders' cottage for a while. The cottage seemed peculiarly empty without Jock Bennet. His scant possessions were still evident in the kitchen, trousers on a peg, boots by the hearth, tobacco pipe lying, like a fossil, on the shelf. She had no great feeling of grief for the dead collier. She was more concerned for the welfare of his children.

Blotchy and scowling, Mouse crouched on a stool, drank tea from a bowl but refused to be tempted by slices of buttered bread or cuts of pickled ham. Sarah ate daintily, solemnly, her crying fit behind. Taking his father's chair, Davy wolfed into the food as usual.

"Have you given any thought to what you'll do now?" Elspeth began.

"What's it got to do wi' you?" Mouse demanded. "You're not our mam."

"Would you like me to leave?" said Elspeth.

Sarah answered, "No."

"Davy?" said Elspeth.

"I canna stop you if you've a mind t' take t' the bloody road again," the boy answered.

"That is the last thing I want t' do," said Elspeth. "At least I have work here."

"There's no work," said Mouse, "now Daddy's gone."

"We'll not even have a roof over our heads much longer," said Davy. "Rance'll want this house for a hewer."

"It's time to see how much money we have," said Elspeth. "I can put seventy shillin's into the purse. Mousie?"

"I've nothin'."

"Liar," Davy said. "You've the five shillin' Bolderon gave ye."

"That's mine."

"Hand it over."

Sarah slid on to the table the crown that Mr Bolderon had given her. "See, there's my share."

"Fork it out, Mousie," Davy commanded.

Quick though she was, Mouse failed to escape Davy's fist. He snared her by the neck and pushed her face down almost to the table, while she cried out, "Mine, it's mine, I tell ye."

Davy said, "Daddy's no' here t' spoil you, now. Do what Elspeth tells ye or ye'll have to answer t' me."

Mouse pushed the crown piece on to the table and Davy released her. Elspeth expected her to burst into floods of tears and rush from the cottage but the girl did not fly into a tantrum. She sat upright, scarlet-cheeked, dry-eyed, and glared at her brother.

"How bloody much can *you* put in, Davy?" Mouse cried.

"Forty-three shillin's. It's the lyin' money that Snippets costed," Davy said. "The carpenter's fee has already been took from it."

Sarah said, "Daddy kept money under the bed."

"What?" said Davy.

"Where?" said Mouse.

"Hid under the long board," said Sarah.

On his knees, Davy butted the wooden bedstead to one side. He prised up the loose board and dug out a greasy buckram parcel tied with twine. He unwrapped it to reveal ten guinea pieces. Davy handed them to Elspeth who put them on the table.

"How much is that all told?" said Mousie.

"Sixteen pounds an' twelve shillings," said Elspeth.

"That's less than five weeks' take," said Davy.

"Will Mr Rance let us stay here if we pay the rent?" said Elspeth.

"Nah, he'll want the cottage for a hewer," said Davy. "But never mind. He'll have his hewer. I'll cut the damned stuff."

"Davy, you canna," said Elspeth.

Hands on hips, Davy declared, "I can cut from the hidden seam."

His sisters, it seemed, were struck dumb. Their father had died in the fissure and, so Elspeth imagined, they were frightened of it.

"I'll cut an' you pair can haul," Davy said. "I'll not draw as much as Daddy in a shift but it'll bring us twice the wage all four o' us can earn labourin' upstairs."

Mouse stared at Davy with a shining look of admiration, animosity forgotten.

Davy went on, "When I get my full growth I'll bring in bigger hauls. Meantime there's a fair stack o' great coal cut already."

Elspeth could see that Davy revelled in the prospect of being the family's breadwinner. She did not doubt that he had skill enough to take coal from the millstone seam but she questioned if he had the stamina to last out a shift.

"Tell me, Davy," she said, "how much we might make from fixed-rate employments, the four of us."

"At most," said Davy, "forty-two shillin's."

"Why should we scrape when yon seam's drippin' wi' fat coal?" said Mouse.

"Because the millstone seam's dangerous," said Elspeth.

"Nah, yon seam's safe as a feather bed," said Davy.

"Did it not kill your daddy?" said Elspeth.

"Daddy kilt himself," Davy declared.

"But the roof fell –" Elspeth began.

"It wasn't the bloody roof; it was the wall."

"What difference—"

"Daddy chalked too heavy a cut," Davy stated. "Daddy made a mistake – an' paid the price."

"Davy, how can you slander him so?" said Elspeth.

"It's true, it's true," put in Mouse, taking her brother's part.

"Listen," said Davy. "Coal's hangin' from yon bloody wall; if we don't take it down some other lucky bugger will."

Barely a day ago Elspeth had regarded Davy Bennet as a victim of a system which made no allowance for weakness. But Davy – Mouse too – had always known what she had not –

that the system had been shaped for them and by them and that misfortune would not alter it a jot.

Sensing her indecision, Davy said, "Look, it's our seam. We found it. I'm the man in this household an' it's my say what we do wi' it. You labour for me, Patterson, or ye toddle."

Elspeth said, "I'll support you, Davy, if you're set on this course. But I'll not go alone to put the case to Thomas Rance."

Davy cocked his head, squinted at her without boyishness. His eyes were pale and fierce. "Christ, woman, it's not what I want. It's what has t' be."

"Go tonight," Mouse urged. "See Mr Rance tonight. We can all be down below tomorrow."

"Aye, why waste a workin' day?" said Davy.

Elspeth recalled the sideling seam beneath the trap. She thought of the great slab of fallen coal beneath which Jock Bennet had been pinned and realised that Davy would tackle it first. Bloodied though it was, Davy would break it up and Mouse and she would haul it to the surface piece by piece; and be paid for it, blood and all.

"Very well," said Elspeth.

Mouse laughed. "Can I have my crown back?"

Magnanimously Davy said, "Why not, Mouse, why not?"

At five that evening Thomas Rance met the delegation from the collier's cottage. He listened to their plea to upgrade Davy to hewer and stoically agreed to put him on trial for two months. The following morning the Bennets went back to work. Elspeth accompanied them, obedient not to reason but to tradition, and its destiny.

Sandy Sinclair was the one person at Strachan who suspected that Anna's passivity might bode mischief. Everybody else seemed delighted that she had been humbled and wasted no opportunity of reminding her of her precarious position at the castle now that Randall was on the verge of taking himself a wife.

As it was high season for farming, Sandy, out in fields and gardens from dawn until dusk, could not defend Anna against taunts. Besides, he had a new acquisition to attend to, a fine, five-year-old Clydesdale that Sandy had named Absalom. More by accident than design Mr Gibbie had got a bargain in the young plough-horse. Though its colour was bad and its coat uneven, Absalom had a good head, a light carcase and deep legs. Once Sandy had broken him to the plough he pulled true and strong. What little pockets of time Sandy had left after the long day's labour, however, he devoted to a study of Anna's plight, puzzled by her responses. Not once did she spit back at Catriona or Edith Simmons when they jeered her; nor did she complain when, of an evening, Mistress Alicia summoned her to the sewing-room to 'approve' of the ball gown that was being created stitch by stitch or to admire all other feminine appurtenances that were gathered to equip the lady for a voyage about the halls of Ottershaw on the night of the May Ball. Sandy watched and listened. He did not believe that Anna had bowed to the inevitable. The 'glaze' in her eye was like that of a pony before it stamped and lashed out at you with its sharp wee hoof.

One night, towards the middle of the month, Sandy was wakened from sleep by the snickering of horses in the stable. Experience told him it would be nothing more threatening than a rat on the manger but, mindful of his charges, he sighed, rolled out of his blankets and, wrapped in his nightshirt, stole out of the house and across the yard. Absalom, sleepy too, blinked at the young man's lantern with drooping lids and gave a stamp with his rear hoof to show that he was well enough. Sandy glanced about the stall, found no sharp object in the straw, no smoulder. He dabbed the Clydesdale's nose with his brow. Absalom responded with a *wuffle* and a nod. After checking the carriage horse and trap pony, Sandy blew out the lantern and returned, shivering, to the house. He was on his way to his cubby when he caught the whisper of Anna's voice from the corridor.

Robbie had been fretful all day with a rheumy sort of cold that would not ripen. Though it was dark in the servants' hall Sandy padded to the kitchen and poured warm water from the day's kettle into a glass. He added a single spoonful of whisky from the stone jar under the pot rack, a touch of brown sugar from the tub, and carried the glass back along the corridor. As he approached the wall-press that formed the angle of her bed place, he heard Anna croon to her bairn. He hesitated.

186

"So they'll not let us go, will they not?" Anna said in a purring whisper. "Well, never fear, m' wee mannie, Mam'll go without permission. It's your place Mammy'll save for you, Robbie."

Hardly daring to breathe, Sandy stood stock still.

"I'll be there for Randall, for your dear daddy," Anna went on, "an' none o' them will stop me."

Deliberately Sandy coughed.

"Who's that?"

"Sandy."

"What d'you want?"

"I brought the bairn a drink."

"Oh! Fetch it here then."

Sandy went forward to the bed. "Can he not find sleep?"

"It's just a cold," said Anna.

Whispering made it intimate, though Sandy was chilled and longed for a candle to give an impression of warmth. He groped and found the bed end.

"Where are ye, Anna?"

"Here." Her hand touched his arm.

Sandy flinched.

"Will I light the—" he began.

"No," Anna said. "I can see well enough."

Her warm plump hand clasped his fingers and carefully removed the glass.

"What is it?" she asked.

"Whisky in warm water. My sister Morven used t' make it for me when I was small," Sandy answered.

Robbie was more than half asleep. Sandy listened to the creak of bed slats, the rustle of the mattress, smelled Anna's warmth, like musk.

"See what Sandy brought for you," she crooned. "Come on, m' wee mannie, drink it up."

Robbie gave a splutter and a cough. Sandy heard the child gulp, sigh when the glass was taken from his lips.

"Is he all right, Anna?"

"Aye. He'll cuddle down wi' me in a minute."

"I'll go back t' bed then."

"Aye."

"Anna?"

187

"What?"

"Concernin' Ottershaw—"

She was suddenly tense, Sandy sensed.

He said, "I'd take you t' the ball if I could. But I'm t' drive Mr Gibbie and Mistress Alicia in the gig."

"I know."

"Anna?"

"What is it?"

"I'll – I'll tell ye all about it when I come home."

Her hand brushed his thigh. He stepped back at once. She found his hand, gave it a tug and brought him down to her. He could not understand why she could see so clearly in the darkness while he was almost blind. Robbie's knees, Anna's breast, the hard rim of the drinking-glass; Sandy bent, guided down. Her lips touched his cheek and then his mouth. She kissed him briefly, rewarded him for his kindness.

"There!" she said. "Now, off t'your bed, Sandy Sinclair."

For an hour thereafter Sandy tossed and twisted under his blanket and tried vainly to find a position in which his excitement and apprehension would settle and let him find sleep. He had heard her confession, learned of her strategy. He acknowledged with sorrow that Anna was possessed beyond reason by love of the laird.

Come Friday night, the night of the ball, shame might scrape the Sinclairs again – unless Anna could be dissuaded from her intention, unless, somehow, he could stop her reaching her goal.

All day long the sun blazed out of a cloudless sky. It westered reluctantly without losing much of its warmth. All across the shires leaves unfurled and grass grew and, in the park of Ottershaw, stretched green and springy as a carpet new-bought for the great occasion.

Horses in the shafts of delivery carts were lathered with foam on their arrival and champed impatiently while kegs and sacks were off-loaded and goods dispersed on Mr Hunter's instructions. Clad in his second-best 'browns', sleeves rolled up and apron billowing, the steward spent the best part of the morning in the yards, pointing this way and that, like a weathercock gone mad, running indoors every now and again to stir the servants into a frenzy of confusion. Nobody could remember old Henry ever being in such a state of 'decomposition'. It was feared he might not last the pace, might keel over and have to be dragged away like a side of beef and hung to cool in the long larder. By mid-afternoon, however, old Henry had found his second wind. In donning the brand-new red coat, with its big gilt buttons and gold-cord frogging, snow-white breeks and black pumps with silver buckles, he donned again his dignity. When Mrs Lacy set the powdered wig upon the steward's head an almost lordly calm descended with it, and Hunter was ready to sally forth to greet the conveyances that would soon trundle down from the gates.

Dunn too had a new uniform, fancy enough to swell his bantam arrogance and drive him, strutting, in and out of everywhere when he should have been upstairs ready to answer his master's call. Cornered in the stillroom, where girls fetched in from Balnesmoor were being instructed in the art of washing glassware, Dunn had his lugs cuffed by Mrs Lacy and, crimson with humiliation, was sent packing to annoy Sir Randall in preference to the industrious citizens of the servants' hall.

Immediately after luncheon Suzanne Seaton had retired behind locked doors to bathe and primp and pirouette, to revel in indecisions about 'finishing touches' to her ball gown which, in keeping with the tone of the occasion, was decked across the skirt with a stitching of tiny green leaves and had a hem-line that, in Suzanne's opinion, swagged too close to the ground to show her four-guinea slippers to best advantage. Walter enjoyed every minute of the day's frantic preparations. With a cheroot stuck in his mouth, thumbs hooked into his vest pockets, he sauntered about the halls and yards scattering 'suggestions' as he went. Eventually he gravitated to the long trestles in the ground-floor drawing-room and gave vital assistance in tapping casks and uncorking bottles.

The sun was still well above the trees when the first guests arrived, in a four-wheeled, nondescript carriage. The well-to-do wool grower from Gartmore was accompanied by his wife, sister and two trembling daughters. By six o'clock the patch of grassland reserved for conveyances was packed with open carriages, closed coaches, disguised carts, the Reverend Eshner's 'scriptural chariot', and six or seven aristocratic heavyweights fitted out with plush squabs and flutes of emerald hammer-cloth. When the carriages were staked and horses uncoupled, watered and fed, drivers and footboys congregated outside the old pig rows, and ate meat pies, supped good ale and prattled and gossiped like rooks. On the old drying-lawn, between the mansion and the grieve's house, trestles had been erected and lanterns poled and, later in the evening, there would be games and dancing for servants too.

Ottershaw's staircases turned into waterfalls of silk and satin as women and girls ascended to and descended from the cloak-rooms which Randall had set aside for their use. Fussy little ladies'-maids buzzed among the throng while husbands gathered in the long hall to keep a weather eye upon the staircases in case they failed to recognise their dames after transformation.

There had been no social event at Ottershaw for more than thirty years and it appeared that Sir Randall was bent on making good the deficit in the course of a single night. Claret Cup and Negus shimmered in four huge silver chalices so deep and broad that, in the opinion of experts, you might drown a bullock in any one of them. Champagne fizzed to delight young misses and provincial bucks, to whom the very foam tasted of romance. Fiery spirits were dispensed in the gunroom, from which all the guns had been removed, of course. Here hard-bitten men to whom drink was the only worthwhile entertainment congregated out of harm's way to tipple and roar and patronisingly mock their host.

In an alcove at the nether end of the hall an orchestra of bewigged musicians, imported at fabulous cost from Glasgow, played sweetly in tempo while another group, less couth, strummed and chirruped in a tented booth under the elms of the park. One might take one's pick, indulge in a little 'scandalous' waltzing or a breathless *alfresco* strathspey. Some did one thing, some another – it was surprising who chose to do what – and some guests just sat about and basked in the roseate glow of being in Ottershaw at all.

Randall did not greet his guests upon their arrival. He waited nervously in his chamber, kitted in the latest solid cloth, in breeches that clung without a wrinkle to his calves and thighs. He heard the hubbub grow, the larksong of girls on the landings, the strains of the orchestra from the hall below, and he held himself from his guests by sheer effort of will. Dunn poured him whisky and water. He sipped it slowly, watching the clock tick away the minutes until it was exactly half past six, then he rose, tweaked down his lapel, and sent Dunn along to enquire of Mistress Seaton's maid and Mr Seaton's man if they supposed that mistress and master might be ready to join him on an assault on Fort Society. One minute later Walter appeared in the doorway to inform Randall that his sister would be but another ten minutes or so as eight hours had not proved sufficient time to put a polish on perfection.

In due course Suzanne too was ready. The laird and the Seatons descended the main stairs. Guests flocked from everywhere to cast an eye over the laird's woman, flabbergasted at how regal a pair they made, arm in arm, the brother bringing up the rear like a grand vizier. Bowing to ladies, Randall escorted Miss Seaton into the dining-room where folk expanded to make an arena for them, and folk outside bustled into the hall in expectation of words of welcome from the provider of the feast. Randall did not disappoint them.

Naturally he made no mention of the pagan nature of a festivity of mischiefs and Anglo-Saxon rites. Randall Bontine was a Scot and canny. He knew that he was 'on show', that his reputation, and his 'calling price', would rise if he did well. Consequently his speech was short and pithy. He introduced his guests to his friends and neighbours, fulsomely praised the honest families of the Lennox, noted their douceness and generosity, mentioned his father in passing, threw in a couple of French phrases to appeal to the nobility and concluded by spreading his hands as if to show that there were no blind cards up his sleeve.

"Tonight let us revel together, like the good friends we are," he declared. "My house is your house."

There was applause, even cries of, "Aye, you're a grand lad, Bontine," from someone who had been at the brandy.

Randall signalled the orchestra to strike up and swirled Suzanne on his hand around and away into the hall. He was followed by couples of similar disposition and the ball was at last under way.

* * *

Alicia squinted at her brother-in-law and his partner venomously. She felt slighted by the fact that she had not been singled out for an introduction to the Seatons.

"She's a child, Gilbert," she hissed, "a mere child."

"Hardly, my dear," Gibbie answered. "To my way of thinkin', Miss Seaton is very much a woman."

Before Alicia could demand an explanation and fulminate a quarrel, Walter Seaton appeared and with considerable diplomacy begged Gibbie to introduce his beautiful lady wife. Appeased, Alicia simpered and was duly invited to perform a Highland Lilt with the honoured guest.

Proficient in all fashionable steps Walter did not twirl Alicia like a drover's rope nor prance about her as if she was a maypole. He *danced* with her. No man, not even her husband, had danced with Alicia Bontine in many a moon. Alicia was transported back to her days as the belle of the assembly rooms where Mr Clissack, her dancing-master, had called her his 'ethereal sprite' and stolen a kiss from her maidenly cheek. With but one hand to guide her, Walter Seaton led Alicia back in time. He made her feel young again, a feat without equal in the history of the two-step.

Gibbie watched his wife and Seaton for a while then wandered away to find a bite to eat. Travelling in warm May sunshine had sharpened his appetite and at the supper tables he loaded a platter with succulent viands and dipped a glass in the silver bowl. He was about to tuck in when a dry voice behind him said, "Well, Mr Gilbert, I trust Mistress Seaton has dowry enough to pay for such a splendid affair."

Robert Rudge had been invited in his employer's stead to represent Kennart. Though Gibbie had never had much time for Rudge he had to admit that the remark showed perspicacity.

Rudge added, "Or is Ottershaw doin' so well out of cattle and timber that Randall must lavish it away on parties?"

In fact Gibbie had been taken aback at the scale of the affair and had been trying to calculate the cost of it. Randall had already drawn close to the limit of his credit at the Farmers' Bank; Gibbie prayed that he was not going to ask for more. How had Rudge guessed it?

Rudge winked. "I would take the delightful Miss Seaton

without a farthing to her name, though, or a stitch to her back."

Anxious to disengage himself from the manager Gibbie put a question of his own. "How is your master?"

"Gone in the head."

"I heard he was somewhat recovered of late."

"He toys with business, aye. But I would hardly say that he's himself again," Rudge answered. "I doubt if we'll see him at Kennart again."

"A sad condition." Gibbie inched towards the door, platter in one hand, glass in the other.

"Why do you put the question to me, Mr Gilbert, when you have been transactin' business face-to-face with Mr Moodie?" said Robert Rudge.

So that was it. There were no secrets in the small world of Balnesmoor. Obviously Rudge had got wind of the private visit to Moss House. Naturally the manager was concerned about what James Moodie was up to, yet he, Gilbert, resented the manager's assumption that he would be indiscreet enough to discuss confidential transactions.

"I've nothing to say, Mr Rudge."

"Give me an opinion, Mr Gilbert. Do *you* believe that Jamie's mended in the head?"

"I see no reason to assume that Mr Moodie has permanently lost his capabilities," said Gibbie cautiously.

"Lawyers, bankers, inventories," said Rudge. "It has occurred to my agent, John Scarf, and to myself that Jamie might be on the verge of sellin' out."

"I doubt it."

"Is it not that kind of transaction?"

"Ah!" Gibbie exclaimed. "I do believe I spy my wife by the door. You must excuse me, Mr Rudge."

Alicia had indeed appeared in the doorway of the supper room. Still bearing his platter of cold cuts and his glass, Gibbie hurried to join her.

"For me, Gilbert?" Alicia said.

Gibbie glanced at plate and glass. "What? Yes, of course."

"Put them on that little table. I will partake in due course."

"Are you not hungry, Alicia?"

"Dance with me, Gilbert."

"Dance?"

"A quadrille."

"Do we not require three couples for a quadrille?"

"I have assembled them in the hall." Alicia seemed flushed and strange. "Give me your arm, my dearest."

Gibbie craved food and drink, not involvement in the complicated sections of a dance which he had dismally failed to master in his youth. Alicia would not be denied. Resignedly Gibbie presented his arm and Alicia dragged him into the hall. Gibbie was baffled by his wife's eagerness to join the fray. Alicia, however, wanted to dance, to dance and dance the night away. She had been infected by music and candlelight, by Walter Seaton's charm. She longed to feel as light and lithe and free as she had done before; but with Gilbert as partner the feeling was not the same, not the same at all. She felt as she usually felt these days – frumpish and matronly.

In the course of the quadrille much of Alicia's bitterness returned. The gaiety of the other dancers seemed to mock her loss of Ottershaw and with it her youth.

She twined her arm clumsily with her husband's waist and as they came together, hissed, "Gilbert, I want to go home."

"What? Now?"

"Yes, now."

But even Gibbie had his baulking point. He would not risk giving rise to rumours of a rift in the Bontine family by sweeping out of the ball before it had properly begun.

Husband and wife parted; met again.

"No, Alicia," he whispered.

"I want—"

"Alicia," Gibbie snapped. "Be still."

To his surprise, Alicia obeyed him and said no more about leaving for some hours.

The beef pie was filled with a jelly flavoured with onions and black pepper. When Sandy bit into it the crust flaked away and gravy ran down his chin. He ate with relish in spite of his vow not to become entangled in servants' revels but to remain watchful in case Anna came early.

He pushed the remainder of the pie into his mouth, wiped

his chin and lifted his tankard of ale from the bench under the boughs of the big chestnut tree.

A freckled coach-boy from Duntreath, who had not returned to the stables with the Edmonstones' carriage but had stayed behind to enjoy himself, also polished off a pie. He squinted at Sandy.

"Ahoy, Sinclair! What did Gibbie come in?" he asked.

"Gig," Sandy replied.

"I thought Gibbie was rich. Has he no' got a proper carriage?"

"The gig has a hood," said Sandy.

The footman to Mr William Deare of Finster joined the pair. He sniggered. "It must've been a tight squeeze wi' the three o' you in a gig."

"Aye," said the coach-boy. "Were ye sittin' on Alicia's lap, Sinclair?"

Sandy had known them for years. They had schooled together at Balfron. Unruffled by their remarks he grinned. "It would be a bold lad who'd sit on the Mistress Alicia, I'll tell ye, Billy."

"Where's yon brother o' yours?" Colin, the footman, demanded.

"I've no notion," said Sandy.

"Have they no' strung him up yet?"

Sandy's fingers tightened on the tankard. He had had little contact with the lads from the village since the Sinclairs had moved to Strachan Castle, since Matt had fled from the Riding Officers on the night of the Kennart murders. The 'wonder' of that event was not so far into the past, however, that it had been forgotten in Balnesmoor and Ottershaw.

"Aye," put in freckled Billy, "I'm fair amazed the rogue's left free t' roam about the country, slittin' throats as the fancy takes him."

"I heard," said Colin, "it was the laird let him off the hook an' handed him the stallion."

"I know nothin' about it," said Sandy gruffly.

"I heard," said Colin, "the laird let Matt go because he was puttin' it t' Anna Sinclair but never wantit t' get saddled wi' her.

"Shut your mouth," Sandy recommended.

"Who's puttin' it to her now, Sandy, eh?"

"Aye, who's got the leg o'er the lairdie's mare these days?"

Sandy did not appear to move. He flicked his wrist, that was all. A sheet of ale splashed full into Colin's leering visage and tailed across Billy's chest.

"Well, well! That's careless o' me," Sandy said, the empty tankard swinging in his fist.

"Bastard!" Colin cried. "See what you've done t' my tunic."

They could have taken him in tandem, footman and coach-boy, but something in Sandy's manner dissuaded them. Besides, other male servants, gathered by the ale keg, thought it a great joke.

"Miss your mouth, did ye, Colin?"

"How could ye miss such a wide mark?"

"Aye, Mr Deare should have clothed him in oilcloth."

A general air of good humour smothered the possibility of a brawl. Sandy dropped the tankard to the grass and, not hurrying, walked off into the trees.

Freckled Billy shouted, "Dinna touch him, man. He's Matt Sinclair's brother; he'll shove a blade in your guts quick as wink."

Sandy felt no loyalty to Matt. He had no need to protect the honour of such a black sheep. He stooped under the boughs of the chestnut tree on to the path that led to Pine Cottage. In that place in the dank wood Matt and Anna had lived as man and wife. It was occupied again. Sandy did not approach too close. Sheltered by brushy pines he looked at the dwelling's pale walls and the chimney's scut of smoke and wondered what it would be like to live here with Anna, wedded to Anna. After a minute of contemplation he returned to the paddock by the north gate to keep watch for her. At all costs he must prevent Anna reaching the ballroom and making a fool of herself before the laird.

As evening gave way to night the air became cool and sweet. Stars pricked the darkness. A piece of moon shed more light than it should have done, as if the heavens too predicted bounty for the laird and his love. Hospitable duty done Randall danced with Suzanne Seaton in the warmth of the hall and stole moments alone with her in garden corners.

In the trees around the parkland much flirting and kissing was going on, more serious wooing too.

In the gunroom boozers had sunk into roaring carousal, with coats discarded and vests unbuttoned.

In the drawing-room Alicia was complaining about the heat and insisting that Gibbie accompany her on to the terrace and do a bit of fetch-and-carry, bringing her wine and her lace shawl, her reticule and fan from the hall and, finally, because she was hungry now, a dish of pickled lambs' tongues.

Fiddlers had been coaxed from the park to the drying-lawn where a servants' jig was in full swing. Most of the lovers had come indoors, giving over the park and the terrace to couples who, oblivious to the chill, were 'lost in each other's eyes'.

Randall and Suzanne stood by the balustrade sipping wine from crystal glasses. The moment at last arrived when the soldier-laird must play the role of suitor and do what was expected of him.

"Now that you have seen them gathered," Randall said, "do you care for the folk of Ottershaw?"

"They have shown me their friendship in a thousand ways."

"Do you suppose that you might find life here agreeable?"

"That would depend," said Suzanne Seaton.

"Upon what?"

"Upon the nature of the person with whom I would share that life."

"If that person were not too old, not too spoiled, not too ugly—"

"Not too conceited," put in Suzanne.

"Yes, a very modest fellow indeed; what then?"

"I would expect him to put modesty aside, to show bold-ness."

"Pray go on," said Randall.

"I would expect him to—"

Suzanne's attention was diverted from the word game. She stared from the terrace into the lantern-dappled parkland. Randall released her hand, stepped close to the balustrade, leaned upon it and peered to the tree line.

"God in Heaven!" he exclaimed.

Suzanne moved to be close to him. "What is it, Randall? Who is that person?"

"I – I cannot be sure."

Suzanne knew that he was lying. Bewildered, she stepped back as if the hurrying figure on the pasture threatened her.

The woman hurried on, past lovers among the trees who seemed to shrink away from her, came on towards the terrace in an undeviating line like a creature drawn from the forest by the attraction of the lights.

"Randall, who is she?"

"She – she served here. Years ago."

"Is she mad?"

"No, she is not mad. She attends my brother at Strachan now."

"What is her name?"

"Anna. Anna Sinclair."

"Does she intend mischief, do you suppose?"

Randall put his arm about Suzanne's shoulder, turned her away from the balustrade and steered her towards the french doors.

"I think it would be as well if you went indoors for a little while, Suzanne."

"But why?"

"The girl – the girl is subject to – to fits."

Randall was lying again, lying without conviction. He left Suzanne within the doors, whirled and strode out. She lingered by the open door and started when a hand closed upon her arm.

"What's amiss, dearest?" Walter enquired.

"There's a person outside, some sort of servant."

"Been at the grog, has he?"

"It's a girl, a woman. Randall says she served here once."

Walter hesitated, said, "I'm confident Randall can cope with such trivial crises without our aid. Come inside. Let me close the doors."

"She – she's young."

"Suzanne, come inside."

"Yes, Walter."

Suzanne turned away. Whatever the appearance of the girl signified, whatever secrets she carried, Suzanne did not wish to be informed of them. She heard Walter close the tall doors and tap the iron bolt into place.

"Suzanne, will you favour me with a dance?"

"I would be delighted, dear brother," Suzanne answered, and sensibly moved away from sight of the terrace and the young, dark-haired intruder named Anna.

The park did not seem like the one she had ridden through on Sabre's back, clinging to Randall, one bright May morning three years ago. Ottershaw did not seem like Ottershaw. It was all garish and swollen and strange, alien, not enchanted. Its glamour was like a new fortification which Randall had built to exclude her. She was thirty yards from the steps when Randall emerged from the french doors. When he came down the steps on to the grass Anna experienced the joy and fear that had marked her connections with him in the past. She did not run to him, maintaining instead her brisk, efficient pace. Skirts held on her left hand, head up, the lace shawl she had stolen from Edith Simmons floated about her. Her kidskin pumps, carried from Strachan in her hand, were soaked with Ottershaw dew. It did not matter how she looked; she could not compete with the fine ladies that thronged the mansion. All that mattered was that Randall would be forced to acknowledge her in front of the gentlefolk of the Lennox, under the very nose of the lady from Piperhaugh. Randall must be taught that, powerful though he was, he could not be free of her, no matter how many lanterns he lighted in the trees.

Randall did not look the same. He was elegant and aristocratic in silks and faced cloth. His features were set hard. The scar on his lip created a deceiving smile, wry, not welcoming, as he waited by the bottom step, arms folded, for her to come to him, flushed, dishevelled and breathless. Doors to the hall were closed. Couples drifted from the terraces like wraiths. The laird, Anna realised, had put himself above scandal, above reproach. She had erred in coming here to Ottershaw in the hope of shaming him. Now Randall was not merely honourable; he was honoured.

Short of the steps, she halted. She opened her mouth to address Randall, to plead and berate him for his neglect.

A hand closed on her arm. She glanced to the side. Saw Sandy. Gave a tug. Felt Sandy's grip tighten unyieldingly.

"Anna," Randall said, "why have you come?"

"Why did you not invite me?"

"Because this is no place for you."

If there was anger in Randall Bontine he hid it well. He was not amused by her naivety, however, and his tone was hard and calm and polished.

"Young man, who are you?" he asked.

"Sinclair, sir."

"One of Lachlan's lot?"

"Aye, sir."

"Did you bring her here?"

"No, he did not," Anna cried. "I came on my own two feet."

She longed for Randall to command Sandy to release her, for the laird to lay hands upon her even if it was only to drag her from the terrace like a spoiled child. She hated Randall for his maddening calm.

"Ah! Drove the gig for my brother, did you?" said Randall.

"I did, sir."

Randall was ignoring her, had seen through her ruse; she had never been able to deceive him. She was suddenly in awe of the laird of Ottershaw, more in awe of him than she had been of any man. She recognised his power. Folk would remember Randall Bontine as they remembered his father and grandfather, back for many a century. Nobody would remember Anna Sinclair. No matter how outrageously she behaved only the plain, neglected scribble of her birth – and her death, when it came – would witness that she had ever existed. In a moment of terrible clarity Anna saw that it mattered not who had fathered Robbie. Robbie would not be permitted to aspire to Ottershaw. Robbie would be forever exiled from this world of candelabra and champagne, the birthright of the children of the woman from Piperhaugh.

Without calculation, Anna began to cry.

"Take the gig, Sinclair," said Randall. "Drive her home to Strachan at once."

"Will I come back for Mr Gilbert, sir?"

"No. I'll provide my brother with a carriage."

Sandy nodded; he approved of the laird's practicality.

"Come on, Anna," Sandy said. "Come away wi' me."

She leaned against the young man, not resentful of the fact

that he had been put in charge of her, as if he was a sheriff's agent and she his prisoner. Tears bleared the lights of the mansion, made rainbows about the lanterns in the trees.

"Tell me, Randall," she said, huskily. "Tell me t' my face, will you marry this woman from Piperhaugh?"

"Yes, Anna. I expect I will."

"How – how soon?"

"In September."

Rage, bitterness, covetous longing drained from her. Debilitated by the lack of such real, red emotions she rested her head on Sandy's shoulder.

"Goodbye, Randall," she whispered.

Randall Bontine did not answer her and she did not see the longing in his sad grey eyes as Sandy drew her away.

Unexpected, unpredicted, rain fell effortlessly out of thin night cloud. Wakened from sleep by the sound of droplets pattering against the window, James Moodie experienced a pang of dismay at the swift change in the weather. He lay on his back, arms stiff by his sides, a sleeping position he had adopted about Christmas-time. Rain came again with increased force like pebbles tossed against the glass.

"So soon," James Moodie whispered.

In another time he would have risen, would have swept aside the curtain and peered across the moor to see what the weather-change might mean to wool crops and the state of the roads. But he had seen too much weather, too many changes, and was patient now, patient as stone waiting for frost to break it down to dust and for wind to smoor it into the fabric of the earth.

"It's not like May," he murmured aloud. "I wonder if it's rainin' in the Fintry hills?"

If it rained for half a day in Balnesmoor his purpose would be served. Three hours of steady downpour in the high ground to the east, though, would bring water seeping to the burns and the burns crowding to the river. The wheel in the lade at Kennart would begin to turn faster, and brown water to boil in the pots below the brig. "I hear you," he said.

James's vision of an afterlife was fashioned from memory, was a paradise without angels, the Balnesmoor of old, a cottage in the Bonnywell, his papa living still and his sisters in the chimney corner, his mama handing him a cog of hot broth with a smile, her hand touching his hair, loving and tender and eternal. He longed for it passionately. He would not flinch now from that soft embrace, man grown into child. When it was done, his daughter would return and bring her daughter home. The bairn would grow and thrive in the shelter he had built. He, washed clean of disaffection, might look down on them and be content that he had done better in the leaving of his life than in the living of it.

Rain lashed the glass, hard and unremitting. Three hours would see the water rise. He would be gone before the Kennart folk trudged out to their looms.

James Simpson Moodie smiled, threw aside the blanket and set his feet firmly upon the floor.

The first spots of rain that came out of the darkness over the shoulder of Drumglass hissed on the hot glass of the lanterns and scattered the very last of the lovers from terraces and the oaks.

The Ottershaw ball had burned down to its embers. Randall had had the long tables cleared, silver washed and locked away, had dismissed exhausted servants to their beds. The very last carriage rolled off. The coach that had taken Gibbie and Alicia to Strachan Castle returned, rain-soaked. As he made his tour of the premises, an inexplicable depression came over the laird. He felt like two men, separate and distinct, joined in uneasy alliance. On nights like this he yearned for barracks and bivouacs and the high-handed selfishness of men at war. He did not want to be a Scottish gentleman, the lord of Ottershaw's peaceful parklands. If he had still been a soldier he would have taken Anna to his bed without a qualm.

"Gilbert," he had said. "I want no punishment meted out to her."

"Come now, Randall, she's done a mischief and Alicia will not let the matter lie."

"Give her a wigging if you must, but that's all."

"I cannot understand why she came here," Gilbert had said.

"No," Randall had said. "But we are not, thank God, females, Gibbie, and we'll never understand the female heart."

"Did – did Mistress Seaton—"

"Suzanne's no innocent. She has many brothers and knows what men are like. She will not, I'm sure, hold my past against me."

Randall toured the ground-floor rooms. The house seemed exhausted by revelry. He was glad when the rain came sweeping over the hill for it seemed cleansing and refreshing. Dunn, his valet, was fast asleep in his cubby off the library. The boy still wore his gay uniform but he had been tippling wine and had been a little sick and snored uncomfortably on his back. Randall drew the blanket over the boy's shoulders, then went along the corridor to his bedchamber. There was no fire in the grate, no lamp lighted. Dunn had not even turned down the bedclothes. The room seemed bleak. All trace of soft May warmth had gone with the coming of the rain.

Seated on the side of the bed, with only a wax candle to give light, Randall unhooked and unbuttoned his clothes and discarded them carelessly. He was not in the least sleepy. He poured himself whisky from the decanter and carried a glass to the window. It was very dark now. All trace of stars and moon was wiped out by gusting rain. Scotch weather, unpredictable, full of contrasts and character. Sipping whisky, he thought of Anna. He had never stopped wanting her but never again would he yield to the weakness that craved her fire. The affair was over. To revive it would only bring heart-ache and disrepute. He was not 'trade' like James Moodie. He could not take a wife off the hillside and turn her into a lady, or risk maintaining such a notorious mistress. Thinking of Anna stirred his desire. He needed a wife. He must marry and marry soon. If not, he might yet make a fool of himself, summon Anna back to Ottershaw, lose all that he had gained, lose years of contentment with Suzanne.

Suddenly Randall put down the glass and went out of the room. He stole along the corridor, wearing nothing but his tight trousers and an open shirt. Damned if he would not take her; now, tonight. If Suzanne would not be taken, he would bring Anna back to Ottershaw, would breed a string of bastards, would become a blackguard and an outcast. To put it all to one act of impulsive love in the small hours of a damp spring night was a gesture that warmed Randall's blood.

He found his way into that part of the house once inhabited by Gibbie and Alicia and now given over to his female guest. Where Suzanne's maid slept, he did not know nor care. He groped for the handle, thrust open the door, stepped inside and closed the door behind him.

"Who is it? Who is there? Walter, is it you?"

"Randall," he said thickly. "It's Randall."

She sat up in bed, pale and ethereal, a silly muslin cap covering her golden locks, her nightgown clinging to her breasts.

"Where's your maid?"

"Randall, what do you—"

"You know what I want, Suzanne," he said. "Tell me to leave, if you will."

"No. Stay."

"The maid . . . ?"

"Next door. She will be fast asleep."

He untied the cord of his trousers, stripped himself in a trice. Suzanne watched without sign that she feared the heat and the lawlessness of his seduction. He had no doubt that she was virginal. He marvelled at the quality of her trust and at the fact that such a pretty, pampered girl might harbour an ardent desire.

Naked, he stepped to the bed, reached out and drew her against him. He could feel the delicate bones of her spine through the slippery muslin. The weight of her breasts pressed against his chest. He clasped her tighter, as if to break her, crush her. He lowered his mouth to her lips and inserted his tongue between her teeth in the manner he had learned in France. She gasped, flailed her hand until she found his hair and tugged him from her. He thought that she would split the silence with a scream but she did not. Instead, she tore off the silly cap and flung it from her. She let her hair fall unribboned about her shoulders. In the furtive flicker of firelight, she was beautiful and abandoned. The real fever of desire started in Randall and he yielded to it. Making a fist about the neck of her nightgown he broke the ribbons and exposed her breasts. He dropped his mouth hungrily to her nipple, while Suzanne

204

Seaton, the modest daughter of Piperhaugh, arched her back against the bolsters and cunningly surrendered to the man she loved.

PART TWO

SIX

The Doctrine of the Law

Whistling cheerfully, Keir Bolderon strode along Hanover Street. He reached the door of Mrs Melrose's house, rang the bell and waited, heart fluttering with excitement and apprehension. He had made sure by letter that Mrs Melrose would be in residence but he had not arranged a date or time for the appointment; he felt that it would be to the benefit of his cause if he caught her just a mite off guard. He gave the iron hook a manly tug a second time and heard, to his relief, the tap of a servant's shoes upon the steps within.

It was broad daylight still. The skyline of the city was cut against a stainless blue. There was nothing clandestine in Mr Bolderon's call upon Mrs Melrose. He had come with honourable intention, to put a proposal of marriage. He was fairly confident that he would not be refused, not out of hand. His confidence waned a little when the door was jerked open and Miss Scobie confronted him. Normally he had no fear of servants, even those as highly placed in the domestic hierarchy as housekeeper and companion. But Miss Scobie was not herself. She was all flustered and feathery and, for a moment or two, at a loss for words.

"I have come to call on your mistress," said Keir Bolderon. "I trust that it is not inconvenient."

"You – you – you're not expected," said Miss Scobie.

She was one of those odd spinsterish women who had passed directly from puberty into middle age; Keir Bolderon had no notion what her age might be. She blinked grey lashes over grey eyes, her cheeks red.

"Mistress Melrose is – is verra busy, sir," she stammered.

"Ah! But she *is* at home?"

"She's wi' her sister, Mr Bolderon."

Much, if not quite all, of Bolderon's confidence drained

away. There was something materially wrong here. It was not his unexpected appearance on the stoup that had caused consternation. His arrival was but a drop in a bucket of larger concerns. Bolderon hesitated. It would do no harm, surely, to meet Olivia's sister. After all, he might soon be a member of the family and should endear himself to his relatives.

"Pop upstairs, Miss Scobie, an' inform Mrs Melrose that I'd be grateful for the favour of a word with her."

The housekeeper did not jump to do his bidding.

Bolderon said, "Is there illness in the house?"

"No. No, sir."

"I'll not keep Mrs Melrose from her guest for long."

"Come up, then, Mr Bolderon," the housekeeper said and, turning, led him up the narrow staircase and into the apartments. "I'll see what she says."

Hat in hand Keir Bolderon waited in the corridor at the top landing while Scobie buzzed into the drawing-room. He heard raised voices, female and shrill, indignation and dismay in the tone and wondered what event might have occurred to so disrupt the placid running of the household. He was more curious than amorous now and was relieved when Scobie thrust her head from the drawing-room door and beckoned him to enter.

Light from the west slanted over the roofs of the houses and speared through the windows. There was dust in the air. No fire in the grate and no candles were lighted yet. No pretty tea-things on the tables, only a stone bottle – gin – and a water jug and two pewter tankards, small in size but hardly dainty. It came home to Keir Bolderon that he had never seen Olivia Melrose in full daylight. He was surprised to note that she was not quite so youthful or so fresh as he had supposed her to be. The other woman in the drawing-room, clearly 'the sister', was not fresh at all. She was tall, bony, pinch-cheeked, with eyes as hard as acorns under plucked brows. Both women, standing, stared at him as if he had stepped naked into their company.

"We had no appointment that I recall, Mr Bolderon," Olivia Melrose began, without preliminary.

"That's true, madam," said Bolderon with a bow. He had somehow committed a dreadful gaffe but did not know how to extricate himself gracefully. "I – I see you're busy, Mrs Melrose. I shall not intrude."

"Wait." Olivia sighed deeply. Her bosom swelled with resignation. "May I introduce my sister? Mrs Janet McNaught."

"I'm delighted to meet—"

"I've spoken of Mr Bolderon, Janet, if you remember."

"The pit person?"

"Yes."

"I'm pleased t' make your acquaintance, Mr Bolderon."

There was to be no sitting down. The sisters were poised, not for flight since there was no evidence of outdoor apparel, but to return to whatever topic had engaged them prior to his intrusion, a subject of considerable weight, he reckoned, if it required raw gin to make it lighter.

"And I yours, Mistress McNaught." Keir Bolderon bowed once more.

In spite of his discomfiture he was beginning to make a modicum of sense from his observations. It seemed Mrs Melrose was not quite the thoroughbred he had imagined her to be. On the evidence of her sister there was more blue-stocking than blue-blood in her background. Mrs McNaught had a distinctive accent, a twang that she had not managed to soften. She was more direct too. He could not imagine himself engaged in 'literary badinage' with Janet. What was more, Mrs McNaught was clad from head to toe in black.

"Now, Mr Bolderon," said Olivia Melrose, "may I enquire as to the nature of your business?"

"It's – it's no business at all," said Keir Bolderon lamely. "Indeed, I see you are busy and I'll take my leave in the hope that perhaps we may meet again before your return to Perthshire."

"I shall not, I fear, be returning to Aberfeldy for some weeks. I have pressin' business here in Edinburgh."

"Business?" said Keir Bolderon. "Is it – if you will pardon me – perhaps some sort of business upon which I might offer my advice?"

Janet McNaught swung away with an almost, but not quite, inaudible snort. She was patently unimpressed by his charm. Olivia, however, gave another sigh and seated herself upon the couch. She folded her hands into her lap and shook her head. "We have suffered an unexpected bereavement."

"Oh, dear me!" Keir Bolderon muttered.

"We have, in fact, returned only this morning from my brother's interment."

"Your brother?" Keir Bolderon found the cushion of a little chair with his thighs and seated himself, all without taking his eyes from Olivia Melrose. "I did not even know you had a brother."

"It's many years since –" Olivia began, only to be interrupted by her sister.

"I question if this gentleman's interested in our domestic affairs, Olivia," said Mrs McNaught. "I canna see what a pit person would have t' do with matters of law."

"Law?" Keir Bolderon drew his chair closer. "Was your brother – rest his soul – a lawyer?"

"My brother was a man of considerable property."

"Does he leave family?" Bolderon asked. "I mean, a wife?"

"Oh, aye, he has a wife," put in Mrs McNaught.

In spite of her reluctance to involve a stranger in the discussion Janet McNaught could not resist the opportunity to vent her spleen upon the departed. Hatred, not grief, was the emotion that made her throat tighten and her voice shrill.

The romantic purpose of his visit put aside, Keir Bolderon inched his chair forward still further. He placed a consoling hand upon Olivia's wrist. She did not draw away.

"The wife, however, cannot be found," said Olivia.

"She abandoned him," put in Janet. "Ran off."

"I do not understand, quite."

"Took her child, a babe, and departed his house," said Olivia.

"Who can blame her for that?" said Janet.

Keir Bolderon chose his words with care. "So what happens to the inheritance?"

He had no reason to suppose that the brother had left property or wealth yet he could see no other valid reason for the sisters' upset. His immediate grasp of the situation seemed to bring him closer to Olivia Melrose. Even the acerbic Janet darted him a glance of admiration.

"The inheritance is to be held in trust," said Olivia.

"Is there – I mean, is the portion considerable?"

"My brother was a mill owner," said Olivia.

"Does the mill function?"

"Coins money like the Royal Mint," said Janet. "Jamie was a Midas when it came to makin' money." She poured gin from the stone bottle into a tankard and swilled it over her throat in a most unladylike manner. "He workit himself – an' us – near t' death."

Keir Bolderon relaxed. These women were not so different from himself. Airs and graces, the evidence of money, had blinded him to their virtues. Now he saw them for what they were: sisters of a weaver man who had somehow hit the mark. Questions formed in Keir's mind. He sorted them into logical order.

"Where, if I may ask, is the mill?"

"Kennart, in the Lennox," Olivia answered.

"And your brother's name?"

"Moodie, James Moodie."

The name – that name – meant nothing to Keir Bolderon. He put another cautious question – and another. Soon the sisters were tumbling over themselves to give him information. This rapport would, he was certain, stand him in fine stead when it came time to press his suit with the handsome Olivia.

It seemed that the women had risen from a humble cottage in the Lennox where they had been trapped by the ferocious ambition and tyrannical energy of their brother. They had done well enough in the marriage stakes. Once quit of Balnesmoor they had severed connection with their brother and had had no communication for several years. To Keir it did not seem callous, this shucking off of the burden of kinship. He had done much the same sort of thing, though for different reasons. He also learned that Janet McNaught was wed to a sea captain who was gone on trading voyages for many, many months at a time. She lived – in some style apparently – in Dundee. She had two grown sons, also sailors, and a daughter-in-law who kept her company in the long, lonely months of separation. She was of different stamp to Olivia whose name was not really Olivia but Lizzie. The conversation was enlightening to Keir Bolderon. It brought him closer to Olivia Melrose and her money. He might have stayed all night long, playing the confidant, wheedling stories from the women.

He was brought up short in his pursuit of information, however, by one fact, a fact so startling that he could not grasp it at first.

It emerged during a rambling sequence of questions and answers.

"He was given a Christian burial, of course," said Olivia, "but it would seem that – perhaps – Jamie took his own life."

"Drowned himself deliberately, do you mean?"

"In the river by the mill. His horse was found loose and wandering by one of the mill-hands. Jamie's corpse was dragged from the mill lade about an hour later."

"On what evidence was—" Keir began.

"I ha'e my doubts if Jamie would take his own life," Janet interrupted. "He was no horseman. He'll have fell off while crossin' the bridge."

"But he made plans, did he not?" said Olivia. "Intricate and clever plans in collusion with that lawyer."

"He was sick."

"Distracted by the runaway wife."

"The steward let it slip, remember," said Janet to Olivia. "He was wi'out the faculty o' reason."

"Was it a lunatic who shaped that will?" asked Olivia of Janet.

"Leavin' it all tied an' packaged for the young wife," said Janet. "Aye, perhaps you're right, Lizzie."

"Do not, I beg you, call me by that name."

"You'll always be Lizzie to me, dearest."

Keir Bolderon nudged them back from sisterly squabble.

"Am I to understand that the wife cannot be found?" he asked.

"She's been gone near three years. Jamie fetched in word o' her by offerin' cash for information. But that dried up," said Janet McNaught. "It's clear he was infatuated wi' this slattern off the hill."

"Off the hill?"

"She was a foundlin'," said Janet. "Reared by a drover's whore. It was a fair scandal when we were young. Am I not right, Liz – Olivia?"

214

"Yes. Now the brat's worth fifty or sixty thousand pounds."

"I beg your pardon?" said Keir Bolderon.

"Sixty thousand pounds. Even more," said Janet. "But the brat doesn't know it."

"The lawyer may find her," said Olivia.

"Is the lawyer making efforts in that direction?" said Keir Bolderon.

"Strenuous efforts," said Olivia.

"Intendit t' keep us from our rightful portion," said Janet.

"I see," said Keir Bolderon. "You cannot inherit under the law while the wife is presumed to be alive?"

"Or until we challenge the will in a law court."

"Perhaps the wife is dead. Or lost. Gone off into England. Shipped to America," Keir Bolderon suggested.

He was thinking of what it would mean to him to have access to sixty thousand pounds. What fine leases it would purchase. He did not think of the money in the abstract as the Moodie sisters seemed to do but in specific terms, in terms of power. He could feel his palms grow moist at the prospect. God knows, an inheritance of even half that sum would make Olivia Melrose doubly desirable.

"If she is just hidin'," said Janet, "she'll come out when she hears Jamie's dead an' buried."

"How will she learn of it?"

"She may read this, for instance."

Olivia, turning, brought a copy of the *Glasgow Herald* from the table behind the couch. Janet stepped from the window and stood by Keir Bolderon as he took the newspaper, folded into a rectangle to display a notice printed within an engraved box. It was a request for information on the whereabouts of a woman of twenty-four years, fair of complexion, who might pass by the name of Elspeth Patterson or Cochran and have in her care a child of three years, by name Mary Jean.

Keir Bolderon lifted his gaze from the page and stared into the dust motes. He remained thus for three or four seconds then read on.

Parties with knowledge of the woman were invited to communicate with A. B. S. Hildebrand, Esquire, of the Freemasons' Loan, Dumbarton.

No mention was made of a reward.

The Moodie sisters chittered, chattered and speculated on whether the advertisement would produce a response when all Jamie's efforts with handbills and promises of money had failed so to do. Keir Bolderon heard hardly a word. He held the folded newspaper in his fist and read the text again.

Elspeth Patterson.

A blonde mother and a blonde child.

Mary Jean.

He gave a little shiver as if an insect had brushed the nape of his neck and made the hairs rise.

"Mr Bolderon?" said Olivia Melrose.

"Uh? Yes, Mrs Melrose?"

"We have been discourteous in not offerin' you refreshment."

"No," said Keir Bolderon, rising. "I've intruded enough upon your deliberations. I'm delighted to have made your acquaintance, Mistress McNaught. I trust that we might meet again in less solemn circumstances."

He mouthed the phrases automatically, the newspaper clutched in his right hand like a baton.

Olivia Melrose got to her feet, placed a hand on his sleeve.

"Why did you call this evening, Mr Bolderon? Was it on a matter of importance?"

"No. Oh, no," said Keir. "nothin' that cannot wait."

"Will you call upon me again?"

"If you can endure my company."

Olivia escorted him to the door. "Once this matter is settled, we'll sup together."

"I'll look forward to it."

"Mr Bolderon?"

"Yes, Mrs Melrose?"

"Our newspaper."

"Ah! How silly of me."

Reluctantly he returned the copy of the *Glasgow Herald* which had somehow adhered to his fingers; then he went on his way out into the streets of Edinburgh, his head full of questions, not unmingled with doubts.

Davy did not last long as a coal-hewer. No matter how desperately the boy desired to become a man, to earn a man's

216

wage, health denied him an opportunity. It was Elspeth's opinion – though she kept it to herself – that Davy Bennet would never go below ground again. He collapsed at the face in the hidden seam in the wee small hours of a Saturday shift. He had made little progress into the seam, a few scrapings, no more, though the stock of cut coal that Jock had piled against the rock had been shifted through the trap, hauled to the tally baskets and had brought the family one good pay-day. There was less cut coal than Davy had estimated, however, and he was obliged to take hammer and wedges to the great black curtain of coal much sooner than he had anticipated. The task was, quite simply, too strenuous for him. He stuck to it for eleven days then swooned clean away and was brought out, limp and wheezing, by Elspeth while Mouse stayed at the tunnel's end to seal the secret seam once more.

The mercy of it was that it was summer. The days were warm, the nights balmy. The river was blue as a pigeon's wing which, in the long easy evenings, became feathered with gold. Colliers revelled in the weather. They took their wives for walks by the green shore after their shift was done. Men drank on the sward outside the Grapes, lay on green grass and smoked their pipes, and their voices seemed less harsh and tempers less explosive now that the winter was well and truly over.

For Davy Bennet it was a bed by the wall, out of the breeze that drifted up river and carried grit from the shafts across the cottages. He wore a clean shirt, open at the throat, and was washed clean of the ingrained grime of his occupation. The bed was lifted on three bricks to hold his head up and make breathing more comfortable. He lay there for a week, obedient and chastened. He sipped broth that Elspeth made for him, drank cups of sweet fresh milk that Mouse walked to the farm to fetch. He even let Sarah put cool compresses on his head when little waves of fever – fever without sweat – dithered over his body. Lying there, Davy Bennet looked like an angel, at least when his lips were closed and his hoarse seeping struggle for breath temporarily eased.

Thomas Rance came down to see the lad. He frowned, consoled Davy without much conviction and advised Elspeth to purchase the services of a doctor. This she did. She sent Mouse to the post in Placket with a letter to a physician that

Mr Rance recommended, a certain Mr Kidson who lived in Alloa and had made a special study of diseases of the lungs.

Mr Kidson arrived in a pony-cart about dinner-time on Thursday. He was a small dapper gentleman of forty, fastidious in dress and manner, with an accent and intonation that made him sound, Elspeth thought, like a willow-warbler. Certainly there was a liquid note in his voice when he requested payment of a fee in advance and explained, at great length, that while he was activated by a certain degree of philanthropy and would manifest a benevolent spirit in truly needy cases he did not regard himself as a totally charitable institution and must therefore request the standard rate for a four-hour journey – three guineas, please.

Elspeth paid him out of sight of Davy, then led him round to the front of the cottage where the boy lay, face to the sky, eyes closed.

Kidson was nothing if not thorough. He asked questions regarding appetite, sweating and evacuations. He took his answers from Elspeth who, with Mouse and Sarah by her side, stood back a piece from the open-air ward. He bent Davy this way and that, pressed a copper listening-trumpet against his chest, ribs and spine, asked questions about vomiting, then collected spit on a piece of cotton and studied it under a glass for a moment or two.

"Phthisis," he said, at length.

The word meant nothing to Elspeth. She thought of Michael Blaven, how he had died of a condition of the lungs, how she had not known of it until he was within days of death. She thought too, as she watched the doctor work, of Janet Blaven's herbal potions and wondered what the woman would do for Davy if he had been under her care.

Round-eyed, sullen and scared, Davy stared at the doctor who, for all the consideration he gave to his patient, might have been treating a dumb animal.

"Incurable," Kidson declared.

Sarah crept close enough to touch Elspeth's skirt with her fingers but Mouse gave no sign of having understood the import of the doctor's diagnosis. Mouse was in awe of him, struck stupid by his presence. Elspeth had no fear of men like

Kidson. She had met dozens like him; not physicians, of course, but professional gentlemen puffed with their own importance. She stepped forward and made a beckoning gesture which took Kidson by surprise.

"If you will step in here, sir." Elspeth gestured to the door of the cottage.

"For what reason, young woman?"

"For reason of discretion, sir."

Tutting quietly, Kidson followed Elspeth across the threshold into the gloom of the kitchen.

Elspeth said, "I've paid you three guineas, Mr Kidson, for which you've given me a name I do not understand."

"Are you a relative? You're not his sister, that I can see."

Elspeth did not answer. Instead she said, "You've also given an opinion, sir, which you make sound infallible."

"What do you require of me, young woman?"

"Information."

Kidson cocked his head. "The boy has a chronic inflammation of the upper and lower bronchial system. Is that comprehensible to you?"

"Aye," said Elspeth. "How far gone is he?"

Kidson stared at Elspeth out of clever little eyes. "He is basically weak, by constitution. I cannot 'cure' him."

"But will he die?" Elspeth lowered her voice to a whisper for Mouse was eavesdropping just outside the door.

"I see," said Kidson. "You do not expect me to provide him with a wonderful elixir which will have him back at the coal seam before next pay-day?"

"He's a boy, Mr Kidson, not a breadwinner."

"Where's his father?"

"His father was recently killed."

Kidson nodded again. "The boy grieves; that's not beneficial to his condition."

"He hasn't the strength to grieve," said Elspeth. "What must I do t' keep him alive and put him on the road to recovery?"

"He must never be sent to work below ground," said Kidson. "Never again. Nor must he be given any sort of labour which will tax him. In other words, he'll be a burden to you for evermore."

"But will he survive?"

"Oh, he's constitutionally capable of survival, I daresay. He was probably sent below at too early an age. The pink tissues within the body collect hostile susbstances much more readily in a child than in an adult. His blood's thick with charcoal particles. It must be systematically cleansed."

"How is that done?"

"I'll dispense a remedy," said Kidson. "Also he must be given fresh milk daily, laced with a little warm linseed. When he has been purged of some of the saturation, I will bleed him."

"What can he eat?"

"Plain food. Never to excess. Lemons will be beneficial. Some ale. No spirits. No scrag meat, either. Its digestion causes acids."

Elspeth listened carefully. Much of what Kidson told her she might have deduced for herself: the sound common sense of nursing. But the physician, if he had given her nothing else, had imparted hope. If Davy's illness could not be cured, it might at least be arrested. He might be kept alive. She knew why Kidson had termed the illness 'incurable'; the conditions of healing were such that a majority of pit families would have regarded them as impossible to fulfil, would have tacitly accepted the expert's opinion and let the lad slide away from them. But that was not Elspeth's way.

She thanked Kidson, went out with him and across the plank bridge to his cart. He had two large wooden cases there. From one he extracted a jar of white powder, half-pint size, which he gave to Elspeth with instructions as to mixing and dosage.

He climbed into the cart and took the reins in his hands, then paused and looked down at her.

"You've not told me yet who you are."

"I was the servant here," said Elspeth.

"The father's woman?"

"Yes."

"You're no pit wife, however?"

"I've been on the Abbeyfield for years," said Elspeth.

The doctor's eyes were too searching, too clever by half. She felt a chill of apprehension and was thankful that Mary Jean was down at the minder's school and not by her side. Could it be possible, she wondered, that James was still in active search for her, that a person like Doctor Kidson of Alloa might have heard of the runaway wife of Balnesmoor?

The events of the past months, and confinement on the Abbeyfield, had dulled Elspeth's fears to a dream-like indifference to her past and the threat that the past held; yet a man like Kidson, a man who might have 'connections' across the country, served to remind her that she was not, and never would be, wholly safe from discovery.

Kidson gave her a small salute.

"Write to me – you do write, I suppose? – in four weeks and report on the boy's progress. If necessary I'll come back."

"To bleed him, sir?"

"He should be ready for it by then," said Kidson, and flicked the reins.

Elspeth watched the pony-cart bounce across the field and find the path to the gate.

Unless Davy's condition worsened she would not send for Doctor Kidson again. Apart from the fact that she did not believe in indiscriminate bleeding, she doubted if, in a month's time, she would be able to muster three guineas, for, without a hewer to cut for them, Mouse and she would be forced to go on day wage and the family to live on the bone.

It was an hour before nightfall. Thomas Rance was in the garden of his lodge, giving attention to his celery plants. He was not possessed of green fingers, and the plots of turned ground were sown randomly. He had been moved to experiment with the lightest of the vegetables only because he was fond of it stewed, braised or put in soup. But the experiment was proving unsuccessful. Somehow he had let the plants run to seed. He had dug the trenches for transplanting, one foot in depth and about the same across; yet the blessed vegetables hardly seemed worth the labour, being thin as writing-quills and limp as tallow tapers.

He had come to a stop in his work, was bent forward to scowl at the things, as if he might intimidate them into growing healthy and strong, when a soft voice called his name. Looking up, he saw that Elspeth Patterson had come to the gate without his being aware of her approach. He wiped loam from his hands on the back of his breeks, unfurled his shirt sleeves over his scarred forearms and went to the gate to greet her.

He did not invite her to enter the garden. He was wary of the reputation that some oversmen had for misusing their position to bring young women to their beds. He would have none of that, not in thought and not in deed.

Brusquely he said, "What do you want here at this hour?"

"I've had the Alloa doctor to Davy," said Elspeth.

Thomas Rance grunted, waited.

Elspeth went on, "He'll not work below ground again."

"Is this sickness mortal, then?"

"Only if he works in black air."

"What do you want of me, lass?"

"A promise on the cottage."

"What sort of promise?" said Thomas Rance warily.

He folded his arms and confronted her across the wicket gate. The night air was sweet with the perfumes of flowering summer and the young woman had a lover's shyness which brought into the man's mind the breathless delights of his courtship and the first long season of his marriage.

"If I pay rent for a six month, will you let us stay there?" said Elspeth.

"Do you have such a sum put aside?"

"Aye. Mr Bennet had saved a few pounds."

"What if Mr Bolderon decides he needs to recruit a new hewer; an' the hewer has a family in need of a dwellin' place?" said Thomas Rance.

"Is there no other house vacant?"

"No, there's not."

"Please, Mr Rance, I beg you to give us a quarter. Two months, at least."

She was different from the run of collier women. They would have demanded it, claimed it as their right.

"I'll need t' make sure all the coal is gotten from Jock Bennet's room," said Thomas Rance. "That'll mean employing a hewer. I cannot give over a good house to a family without a man in it."

"There are houses occupied by widows," said Elspeth.

"Hardly more than sheds. Besides, would you have me throw a widow woman out just to accommodate you?"

"You know I would not," said Elspeth.

"If you pay rent in advance, what will you live on?"

"Our earnings from wage work."

"Och, so you want me to find you wage work too?"

"Until Davy's better."

"Do not con me, lass. I've seen what the black spit does to full-grown men. Your Davy'll not recover."

"The girls an' I can bring in enough—"

"As harness wives?"

"If that's all there is, aye."

"The harness is not for you, Mrs Patterson," said Thomas Rance.

"Why not, may I ask?"

"You haven't the bones for it."

"I'm no weaklin'," Elspeth protested.

"The best I could do for the girl-child would be a ventilator."

"Give me a harness, an' Mouse a rope; that's all I ask."

"You'd be better findin' a man," said Thomas Rance.

"I want no man. I need no man."

"Perhaps not," said Thomas Rance. "I can find you the work. For a wee while I can permit you the cottage. But I can do no more, Mrs Patterson. If you fall sick or if I decide I must have coal taken from the base level then I'll have to put you out."

"I couldn't find a hewer here, could I?"

"Even at high money it's not a job many men will jump at," Thomas Rance answered. "Besides, coal men are hard to find in these parts."

"If," said Elspeth, "it did become necessary . . . ?"

The oversman shrugged. "Leith is the best place. There are sometimes men there who have pit work in their past."

"I think," said Elspeth, "it'd be a bold man who would take on the Bennets. Saddle himself with a cripple an' a bairn."

"Aye, but if you'll excuse my forwardness, there's many a man would take you on, lass," said Thomas Rance.

She did not, he noticed, simper and protest. She had a sound sense of her own worth and little enough vanity to pollute it.

The oversman said, "What's it to be?"

"I'll take the harness an' Mouse will tug a rope."

"Very well. I'll see to it you're both booked for the shift tomorrow."

"An' the house?"

"You may have it until it's needed." Thomas Rance sighed. "I'll not throw you out. We'll find you somethin', never fear."

"Thank you, Mr Rance."

"Aye, well! I doubt if you'll be thankin' me come dusk tomorrow," the oversman said.

But all he got for his warning was a pleasant smile and a little gesture that might have been a curtsy.

It would not have been seemly for Keir Bolderon to wander about the dwelling fields in search of Elspeth Patterson. Colliers were jealous of their privacy and, though the houses and cots might belong to the pit-owner, they regarded their lives as their own and resented intervention or supervision.

It seemed highly improbable that the wife of a wealthy mill-owner from the Lennox would wind up slaving in a Fifeshire coal pit, that chance would draw a line between her husband and her employer. Opportunity and random chance, though, were birds of a feather. Bolderon had stumbled over even more outrageous examples of coincidence in the course of his existence. But his approach must be very discreet.

"Thomas, just the man I'm looking for," Keir Bolderon said.

He had put his horse to the stable to be given a good brushing and had come down, as if on a normal tour of inspection, to the counting-house where Thomas Rance was supervising the uncoiling of new hemp rope from the works at Milnathort.

"Ah, Mr Bolderon. See this," said the oversman. "It's the new improvement for a winding-cable. Hemp with wire twist."

Keir Bolderon was still an engineer and, for a moment or two, the great undulating hanks of rope caught and held his attention.

It had been delivered not on the back of a cart, like a worm-cast, but in a special straw bale, unpacked as if it was a piece of treasure from an Etruscan tomb. The rope was of novel design and manufacture. He examined it, hands on knees and head bent, foot by foot, diligently searching for imperfections that might cause it to wear out in a month instead of four. It certainly looked odd, with dark metal embedded in the flock-grey hairs of treated hemp.

"What about rust?" he asked.

"Denniston has used one at Deep Water," Thomas Rance said. "He tells me it discolours but does not decay. There's a chemical washed into the fibres t' prevent it."

"What chemical?"

"That's a secret o' the rope-makers," said Thomas Rance.

"When will you install it?" Keir Bolderon asked.

"On Sunday," said Rance.

Keir Bolderon nodded. "Good. It certainly has a different and intriguin' appearance. Let me know if it's tractable."

The oversman signalled to two young boys who trotted from the door of the counting-house and began to roll the rope into two 'spectacles', from which shape it would be put on to a winding-drum and cranked into place over the main shaft. Bolderon watched the boys at work. When he and Thomas Rance had gone, of course, their enthusiasm for the task would wane considerably and they would become less alert and energetic. He smiled. He remembered his days as a youth, how much effort he had put into doing as little as possible when out of the employer's eye.

Casually, he said, "Is that not the Bennet lad?"

Thomas Rance glanced at the boy on the rope's end. "No, Mr Bolderon."

"Bennet's below ground, I suppose."

"No, Bennet's sick. Very sick. Black spit, by the sound of it."

"Bless me," said Keir Bolderon, still casually. "That family have had a time of misfortune, have they not?"

"She asked for time in the house."

"Who did?"

"The woman who looked after them."

"The servant woman?"

"Aye, Mr Bolderon. You saw her at the kirkyard, if I recall."

"Pretty lass," said Keir Bolderon, watching the boys furl the rope. "Did you find work for her?"

"Pullin'," said Thomas Rance.

In spite of himself Keir Bolderon whipped round and stared at his oversman. "Pulling? On the ventilators?"

"Harness."

"Good God!"

"Is somethin' wrong, Mr Bolderon?"

"What? No, no. It just seems – how can I put it – dismal work for such a handsome girl."

"It's all there is. The family needs the wage."

"What about the coal, the room?"

"I've been down. There's eight or nine weeks left in the take. We can bring it out with Ogilvie after he's burnt through his room."

"Yes, that sounds sensible."

"Or we might employ another hewer," Thomas Rance suggested.

Bolderon appeared to give the matter some thought.

He asked. "Would it be worth it?"

"I doubt it, sir."

"I'll tell you what, Thomas. I'll go down myself. Tomorrow or the next day."

"I'll accompany you, sir."

"No, Thomas," Keir Bolderon said. "That will not be necessary."

Olivia Melrose, *née* Lizzie Moodie, had been more upset by the trip back to Balnesmoor than she dared admit to her sister. She had suffered pangs of regret at her neglect of her brother, at the realisation that Jamie had been alone and friendless during the last, trying months of his life. She was not altogether surprised that he had drowned himself. There had always been a dark, brooding streak in him which the events of the past years had obviously brought to the fore. Janet Mary, of course, would have none of such sentimentality. During the final stages of the carriage ride Janet had done nothing but complain. Bitterness had come trickling back as the coach rolled through Buchlyvie, Harlwood, Balfron and along the last miles to Balnesmoor.

The Moodie girls had known this part of the country intimately. Jamie had driven them across it in search of cloth orders, had forced them out with demonic zeal day after day, week in and week out in all shades of weather. Olivia recalled the pain of chapped hands and chilblains, biting winds off the moor cold enough to turn your blood to ice, days of incessant rain when Jamie was only concerned that the cloth parcels be kept dry and spared not a thought for the health of his sisters. She also remembered – cruellest of all recollections – how her mother had turned more and more to Jamie after Daddy's death, had drawn away from her girls as if she found in her son a quality of salvation that daughters could never provide. Girlhood was lost in a black fog of drudgery. It was as if the weaving-loom had become an instrument of penance upon which her brother punished himself for some secret crime. It was, Olivia assumed, that obsession that had earned him the mill, the mansion, wealth untold, that had led him into marriage with Elspeth Patterson. But what sort of woman, even a rough hill tyke, could long endure her brother's dry passion and live with the demon that possessed his heart?

She understood why Janet was so implacably bitter; would not attend the kirkyard to lay a flower on the grave; would not even stay in Jamie's house, though rooms had been prepared for them by Tolland the steward. They had lodged in the inn at Harlwood and had not attended the kirk service or gone to stand by the wall while Jamie was put into the ground. By all accounts there was a multitude of men there, including the laird and his brother, but Janet sneered at that news too and delivered her own pointed epitaph: *"Good riddance."*

Janet had come back to Balnesmoor for one purpose, and it was not to mourn her deceased brother or to see him put to his eternal rest. She had come to find out how much he had left her in plain, material terms.

The lawyer was from Dumbarton, a stork-like man named Angus Hildebrand. He had entertained them, if that was the word, in the drawing-room of Moss House only hours after the funeral and, wasting no time, read out Jamie's will and testament. Olivia was still upset and did not at first take in the significance of the legal rigmarole.

Janet, though, had quickly twigged its meaning.

In outrage, she had cried, *"The devil left us nothin'."*

The lawyer had clearly anticipated some such reaction. He had prepared copies of the documents for them to take away but had assured them, with a fishy little smile, that James Simpson Moodie's fortune, and a whale of a fortune it was, could not be wrested from trust and that he, like a sentry, would stand guard over it until the legitimate heirs were traced, however long that took.

The more she learned of Jamie's history the less Olivia understood it. She found it difficult to imagine that Gaddy Patterson's brat had grown into a beautiful woman, not at all bluff and uncultured like her mother; nor could she understand why Jamie had not cut her off without a penny to punish her for deserting him.

"Blood's thicker than water, Lizzie," Janet had said, as they drove back to the inn at Harlwood. "Jamie set it up for the benefit o' the child an' not the wife."

"I agree, dear. But I think he might have left us something."

"Something. It should *all* fall to us, should it not? We're his sisters; sisters that slaved for him for years an' years. Have ye forgotten?"

"Oh, no, I've not forgotten. He does, however, have a wife."

"What sort o' wife would drive him mad wi' her faithless behaviour an' then abandon him to die alone?"

"Janet, do you believe Jamie really did—"

"Drown himself? I neither know nor care. On balance, though, I believe he did."

"I don't care to think of it," Olivia had said.

"Could we challenge his sanity?" Janet had said.

"I'm not sure I would want to."

"By rights, Lizzie, all his property belongs to us."

"Mr Hildebrand seemed very confident that he would eventually trace the missing wife."

"It must be stopped."

"I do not see how."

"By law, of course," Janet Mary had said.

"I really don't know that much about the law."

"We must employ lawyers, experts, to challenge the will."

"Lawyers can be dreadfully expensive, dear."

"You can afford it, can y'not?"

"It would depend on the cost. I'm not poor, Janet, but my coffers are not bottomless."

"I want my full share, Lizzie. We deserve it."

"I suppose we do."

"Will you stand wi' me, then?"

"Yes. Yes, of course I will."

"Stand up an' fight Jamie's iniquity through the courts?"

"Janet, I—"

"Justice is on our side, Lizzie."

"Don't call me by that name," Olivia had said.

"Will you fight?"

"Yes."

Whatever disdainful opinion hewers held of the upper levels of the Abbeyfield and of the folk who laboured there, Elspeth soon realised that the malls that undulated away from the shaft bottom were the true roads to hell. There was more air to breathe than in the depths, more space too; but the picture she had formed by listening to man-talk was badly distorted.

Before a single shift was over, Elspeth knew that she would not long survive as a harness wife. Mr Rance was right: brute labour would prove too severe for her. Grit and determination would not harden her to its strains. She would rapidly buckle and eventually break. The security of fixed wages must be set against the surety that 'strapping' for long would cripple her and bring her to an early grave.

A woman named Turner showed her the ropes. In the woman's eyes glinted a fearful malevolence as if she derived satisfaction from the prospect that such a pretty-mannered lass would soon become as coarse and ugly as herself. Instruction was by demonstration, a dumb-show accompanied by smirks and winks. Elspeth was shown how to fit the harness, how to hook it to the wagon's chain, how the upper body must be thrust forward, the thighs braced to mobilise the 'hutchie', how the arms were used to balance it on wooden rails. The harness was of old, hard leather and brass-studded straps. Uncoupled, the hook hung down between the legs like a monkey's tail. But the thing that Elspeth hated even more than the bindings was the wagon itself. The hutchie was always with her, cramming the tunnel from wall to wall, from floor to ceiling, animate and looming and inescapable.

To a deep-seam man the upper tunnels might appear spacious but they were too low and narrow to take a pony, let alone a horse. No money had been spent on making them larger. In consequence, animals could not be used below the Abbeyfield. What need was there of beasts when human resources came cheap and every sort of economy was necessary to turn quantities of small coal into owners' profits? Old, gnarled men and young boys did most of the digging. They crouched in long rooms at the tunnel ends, chapping down the brittle chows. Shovels scraped it into heaps and scooped it into the hutchies which were dragged down to the blind and, two at a time, recoupled. Every hutch was packed with seven hundredweights of small coal and, even without a load, the vehicles weighed a hundredweight or more. Their wooden wheels sank on sagging wooden rails and the quiver of the rails turned the floor to black slush in those places where the slope ran downhill from dry top.

In this ant-hill of industry there was no room for friendships. The loneliness of the base tunnels had become isolation. Elspeth missed Mouse, Davy, even the sour-faced Ogilvies. Here no one had identity; the work was too monotonous, too racking hard. She did not even have the consolation of counting tally sticks to give a false lift of anticipation of a grand old pay-day, for the hutches were tipped on to a great communal ree that never seemed to grow smaller no matter how the bucket ducked and ate away at it.

It took no time at all for Elspeth to become indistinguishable from all the other strappers, except that she still wore flannel and not just a kilt of hempen sacking which chafed less and absorbed less water. Women went bare to the waist, breasts hanging, as they craned against the weight of coal, for the rub of any sort of fabric under the straps peeled away the skin in a matter of hours. By noon on the first day Elspeth too had shed her dress. Her shoulders and back were raw, scalded by trickles of sweat. By one o'clock or half past she hardly noticed such superficial discomforts for her muscles were jerked and her bones ached with a deep and unremitting pain that every jab of the wheels on the rails drilled deeper still. Mouth agape, eyes popping, hair straggled over her face, she struggled up and down the long mall from the main road. In flat sections, where nobody could see, she wept as she stabbed forward. Helpers, young boys, were stationed in niches on the slopes to give shoulder to the hutchies or to 'rod' them back, reining each one as if it was a thrawn bull that might charge off of its own accord and trample the strapper into the ground. Elspeth longed for her little sled, obstinate but lively. She longed for Mousie's sharp complaints in the confinement of the narrow tunnel, for the sound of Ogilvie's pick and Davy's cough, the wick of her own wan candle flickering in the dark. But all that was gone. She had become one of the herd. Below her nose was only black slush and the sight of her breasts smeared with grime, swaying against the bite of the old leather girth. When, at shift's end, she came out into the warm summer sun, part of her stayed below, attached to the hutchie; part of her was dead. That evening she ate little and fell down into her bed, unwashed.

Three days down and Elspeth knew it was hopeless. She tried to think of Gaddy, what Gaddy would say to encourage her, to bring her mother's cheerful voice to mind. But Gaddy could not be summoned into the dark of the pit. Gaddy belonged in open air, to wind, rain and sunshine, to the moor and the glen. She was silent in the vaulted tunnels where wagons rumbled and women toiled like beasts.

"You," said a voice. "I say, you."

Head down, bands of pain extended across her shoulders into the roots of her spine, bare feet slipping in the mush, the hutchie pressing insistently, Elspeth heard the voice only dimly. She did not at once lift her gaze from the scribble of light on the floor.

"Patterson, is it you?"

She closed her mouth and swallowed. She brushed rats'-tails of hair from her eyes, looked up.

He had a lamp in his hand, brown leather boots upon his feet and tweeds, even though it was summer. Tweed breeks were tucked into ribbed wool stockings of the sort that came from James's looms. She did not recognise him in the gloom, with the flutter of the lamplight between her and his face.

If he had called her Elspeth she would have dropped in fear where she stood. But it was 'Patterson', her collier name. She straightened, squinted and, even before she recognised him, modestly covered her breasts with her arms.

He did not give his name. He had no need. He was Mr

Bolderon and everybody knew him by sight. Lowering the lantern, he came forward. Elspeth saw on his face a strange look of bewilderment.

"*Are* you Elspeth Patterson?"

"Aye, sir."

"Why are you strappin'?"

"For my bread, sir."

Her tongue, like her brain, felt thick. She had hauled seven loads in the shift and, from that calculation, reckoned it was about two o'clock in the afternoon. Far down the mall behind her she heard the shrill moist shriek of a trailing hutchie as a helper applied the rod on the downhill slope. It would be here in two or three minutes, the woman plodding into the harness, snarling at her, perhaps, to push on, push on.

"I – I must make ground, Mr Bolderon."

"No. Wait."

She was almost weeping. He looked so unlike a collier, so unlike anything or anyone that she might encounter below ground. She associated him with James, with Balnesmoor, Moss House, and the commercial gentlemen that, when James required it, she had entertained to tea in the drawing-room. She was swept by shame.

Weeping, she cried, "I must make ground. I must."

She slipped, struggling, lost her footing and was held in a half-kneeling position by tension on the straps. He came to her at once, putting down the lantern. He did not touch her, did not endeavour to fondle her. He knelt by her side and, very gently, lifted the rats'-tails of hair from off her face with his fingertips.

"Are you sore?"

"Aye, sir."

"This is not work for you," Mr Bolderon said.

"Work is work. I must—"

"You need to be bred into strappin'," he said.

He leaned a little, staring into her face. She wiped away tears with her knuckle, sat back to slacken the straps and rose, staggering.

"Hear the hutchie?" she said. "I canna delay, Mr Bolderon. I'm not finished."

He shook his head. He squatted on his heels. He was

clean-shaven, his hair with a curl to it, but had collected a dab of coal dirt on one cheek and his hands were stained with slush. Dirt did not seem to bother him and he did not shy away from helping her.

"May I help?"

Elspeth did not answer. Taking it as sanction, Keir Bolderon cautiously placed an arm about her and supported her while she found position.

"Where's the girl, the wee girl?"

"Mouse – Allison – she's on a rope in the north section."

"No, I mean your child."

"Sarah looks after her."

"What's her name; your child?"

She was surprised but not alarmed. She supposed that it was part of his success as a pit manager to feign an interest in his work force. She had heard of such things, read indictments of such intimacy in journals.

She answered, "Mary Jean."

Keir Bolderon sighed and, to Elspeth's amazement, chuckled as if, somehow, she had given him good news.

It seemed incredible to Keir Bolderon that a woman in his employ might be worth sufficient sum to buy the Abbeyfield, lock, stock and barrel, from under Fotheringham's nose. Fotheringham would sneer at the source of the capital, deride it as 'trade money', but money was money, new or old, earned or inherited. Any sort of money had purchasing power on an open market. The sight of such a blonde, blue-eyed and pretty young woman strapped to a hutchie daunted even the pragmatic manager. He could not clinch his belief that he had discovered the Moodie heiress. He dawdled for a couple of days, mulling over unanswerable questions and then, because he was a cautious man, decided to seek confirmation of his 'find' before proceeding.

From Olivia Melrose he had discovered that the Balnesmoor weaver had set aside a fund of unspecified amount, put into trust with the Farmers' Bank of Falkirk. Further discreet enquiry brought the information that the Farmers' Bank was partnered by Gilbert Bontine, whose brother was the laird of Balnesmoor and Ottershaw. It required no leap of the imagination to suppose that Gilbert Bontine would be in league with the lawyer in the case, Angus Hildebrand, that Gilbert Bontine would be *au fait*, as the French say, with the ins and the outs of the Moodie affair and would, if properly approached, disperse a few crumbs of the sort of information that he, Keir Bolderon, could not otherwise come by.

Nine days after his encounter with Elspeth in the upper level of the Abbeyfield, Keir Bolderon was seated before a large oak table in a very small office in Calderow Street, in the snug provincial burgh of Falkirk. Naturally, Keir Bolderon did not barge into Bontine's chambers and throw down the gauntlet. He did not mention the name Moodie, did not slip in a question about the errant wife, the legacy or anything at all that might put Bontine on his guard. He came under the guise of supplicant to sell to Gilbert Bontine the proposition that investment in a coalfield might benefit the Farmers' Bank of Falkirk and make profits for all concerned.

Keir Bolderon had become expert at putting his pitch. God knows he had had practice enough these past months. Once it became clear that Bontine knew nothing at all about mineral matters, and precious little about finance, Keir Bolderon laid the Moodie affair gently to one side for a while and concentrated his attention on selling the idea of 'sound investment' to the amateur banker.

Damn it all, Gilbert Bontine bit.

By the time the banker got around to asking salient questions, Keir Bolderon had the answers on the tip of his tongue.

"Ah – how much – ah – would be needed to participate in the expansion of the – ah – mine?" said Gilbert Bontine.

"One thousand pounds, sir."

"Oh!" said Gilbert. "I had thought it would be more."

Keir Bolderon groaned inwardly at the man's awful naivety. It was like stealing from a blind man's tray.

"One thousand pounds will, of course, purchase only a percentage of my share of the total income derived over the period of the new lease agreement."

Gilbert pursed his lips. "What sort of percentage?"

"Eight percentage," said Keir Bolderon.

"I do not understand why you have not found an investor already," said Gilbert.

234

"Advancement money is required. Certain short-sighted people are reluctant to make short-term loans," said Keir Bolderon.

"Advancement money?"

"To open the new seams."

"Ah!" said Gilbert. "Do you mean that you need to develop a new seam before the owner of the land will incorporate you in the sharing of the new lease on the – ah – the Abbeyfield?"

"The new seam will be developed regardless," said Keir Bolderon.

"Regardless of what?"

"Of my participation."

"I thought you were the engineer?"

"I am, of course. But it is incumbent upon me to employ a team of borers to sink discovery shafts. For that I require investment capital."

"How did you come to think of the Falkirk Farmers' Bank in this connection?" said Gilbert.

"On the recommendation of Mrs Melrose."

"Mistress Melrose! Oh!"

"Is something amiss, Mr Bontine?"

"On the contrary. It's just that I'm – ah – involved in a peripheral way in a financial matter that may lead to litigation. I'm surprised at Mrs Melrose raising my name at all."

The threads of the conversation were becoming too tangled. Keir Bolderon decided to give a sharp little tug to one of the strands to see what might be unravelled.

"The Moodie trust fund," he said. "Yes, Mrs Melrose did make mention of it."

"There's no confliction of interest, that I can see," said Gilbert uncertainly.

"Is the heiress still missing?"

"In my opinion she's gone to America and might never be traced."

"In that case what will happen to the fund?"

"In the fullness of time it will be restored to the secondary heirs, one of whom, of course, is the estimable Mrs Melrose."

"From the little I know of law," said Keir Bolderon, "that process will take an age."

"Indeed, an eternity," Gilbert Bontine agreed. "The more

235

so as the lawyer who drafted the testament is very shrewd and experienced."

"Is he – the lawyer – also your adviser?"

"No. He's adviser to my brother Randall."

Keir Bolderon suppressed a sigh of relief. "What if the heiress is discovered?"

"Naturally the fund will be restored to her at once – an occurrence that will not take place too soon, I hope."

"Why so?" asked Keir Bolderon. "Have you invested it?"

"It's become part of the bank's capital stock."

"It's certainly an intriguing affair," said Keir Bolderon, "what little I have gleaned of it."

"Her sister, the heiress's sister, is also in my employment," Gibbie confessed.

"Is she indeed? In what capacity?"

"Domestic ser – housekeeper."

"Has she no clue as to where her sister may be found?"

"None whatsoever," said Gilbert. "However, Mr Bolderon, you did not come to Falkirk to exchange village gossip, I'm sure. Tell me more about the Abbeyfield and what sort of yield an investor might expect from it?"

This Mr Bolderon was only too delighted to do, give or take an ounce of truth.

The man who capped it all, as far as Elspeth was concerned, was keelman Georgie Haynes. Even without his unwelcome reappearance into her life, it is probable that she would not have allowed herself to sink into the hopeless oblivion of brute labour for her quick mind, and her experience of the world outside the environs of a coal pit, gave her choices and the reason to make choices, a privilege denied to other women who slaved along the tunnels, harnessed to hutchies.

Mouse had sunk into a depression, but it was boredom and a feeling that she had slipped in status that galled the younger girl. 'Trapping' was for children. She was not a child. She had pulled for the best collier in all Scotland. She had earned cake, not bread. Now she was back on that spot from which the children of the poor began their climb – and she blamed Elspeth for it. Elspeth could not cope with Mouse's girning. She ignored the girl, concentrated what strength she could muster in attending to Davy and to her daughter. She could not see that Mouse had much to complain about. Mouse was comfortable enough on a little stool under the vent of the old Dead Man shaft and had naught to do but tug upon a rope. The trap, a wooden square hinged to a frame, was certainly heavy but Mouse was wiry-strong and the weight of it was well within her coping. Comparison, rivalry, bitterness crept in and tainted whatever protective feelings there had been in Elspeth for the spoiled young girl.

Mary Jean, sensing her mammy's distraction, also fretted for more attention than Elspeth could give, and roasted Sarah Bennet during daylight hours. Sarah even dared to suggest that she might be better down below. The extra shillings could be used to pay minder-fee so that Mary Jean might go to school. Elspeth would not have it. There was Davy to consider. For the present, Davy required a nurse; who better than Sarah to fill that role?

It was on a hot still night that Georgie Haynes found Dutch courage and, made aware by tittle-tattle of the Bennets' situation, left Lewis and the Skipper on the *Matchless* and set out for the cottage across the Rutherford burn.

Trade was slack on the keels. Domestic coals were not in great demand in warming weather and the boats plied the river, picking up bits of cargo here and there on instructions from one of McNeil's agents, taking only what coal the market would bear from the alpine heap by the lading quay.

Since it was Wednesday, and the *Matchless* had not made shore until seven, Placket was no place for a keelman to find pleasure. The crew had scoffed a supper of tough beef and neat gin, the latter in such quantity that Lewis and the Skipper were flat on the after deck even before the sun slid down above the Kincardine crossings. Georgie, thus, was left alone. He was not nearly drunk enough to be incapable of brooding or for the hot night air to fan his ardour for the belle of the Forth, the princess of the pit villages, for Elspeth Patterson who, he had learned, was 'widowed' and alone.

Mellowed into stupidity by gin, Georgie told himself that he would go to offer condolences, play the gentleman without candy talk or ill design. He nodded to affirm the role he had chosen, while in his belly lust flickered and he suffered instinctual need to take a woman. Georgie was incapable of understanding how it was with the Bennets and Elspeth Patterson; a death to him was a thing of the moment. He was of the type that could bury a brother at eleven and be carousing in a tavern at noon, unaware that he was dumb and callous and, by the lights of more civilised men, a case beyond redemption. Georgie Haynes believed that he was only being a man, which in his way he was.

He came not by the shore track but via the by-lane that crossed to the turnpike, and by a plank bridge over the Rutherford burn. He had never ventured here before and would not have dared to do so now if he had not convinced himself that he had no intent but kindness in his heart. He expected any colliers that he might chance to meet to accept his word at face value, to see the change within. Composed and outwardly calm, he came to the door of the Bennets' cottage and, glancing this way and that like a dog shaking a shackle, lifted his fist, knocked once and entered.

The boy in the bed was clad in a white cotton shirt and might have been dead. It took Georgie Haynes a moment to realise that this was the fierce wee tyke who had swung at him with a stave not so many weeks ago. But the boy, propped against a bolster, arms by his sides, gave not one stir or murmur and his eyes remained closed.

Georgie uttered a soft grunt of surprise. He thought that he had entered into a laying-out, one in which the watchers had abandoned their charge for, on first glance, the kitchen room was otherwise empty; then he saw her. She was hunkered down, a blanket drawn about her, a rough and dirty towel pressed against the fold where her breasts would be if she had been mature. Her eyes were on him, scowling, awed.

"I – I heard the old 'un was dead," Georgie whispered. "Is the young 'un dead too?"

There was no candle to light the place. The fire in the hearth was low. The girl-child had been washing, a bowl at her knee. She was naked, or nearly so. As Georgie closed the door behind him with the flat of his hand she jerked and quailed and he saw the blanket slip and expose bare legs and thighs. He darted a glance at the boy, let his gaze linger until he detected the rise and fall of his little pigeon chest; then he took another step and looked over the table and into the corner where the girl had found privacy.

"Which're you, sweetheart?" he asked.

"I'm – I'm Mouse."

"Mouse in your corner, by your hole, eh?"

"She's out," Mouse managed.

"Where? Wi' a collier lad?"

"Takin' the air wi' Mary Jean an' our Sarah."

Georgie Haynes had a vague recollection of the infant and the younger girl but was distracted from his pursuit of Elspeth Patterson by a growing feeling of aggression that shifted his immediate interest from the pretty blonde woman to the vulnerable girl-child.

"An' what were you doin'?"

"Wa – washin'."

"What age are you?"

"Six – sixteen."

"Sixteen, eh! Why, you're near growed up."

"Aye."

Though she feared him she did not seek to avoid him. Of all men Georgie Haynes knew what that signified. He shifted closer. He lifted and laid aside a stool, making a minimum of noise. Now that she was clean he saw in Mouse new and unnoticed features. His purpose, which had not been focused, altered and became specific. It was not tenderness, nor anything as daft as love, that had brought him here in the first place, but a desire to impose. He might do that as well, or better, with the quivering young thing in the corner than with a woman who could compare him with other men.

"Come here t'me, lass," he cajoled, holding out a hand.

"I – I canna."

"Do ye not know who I am?"

"Aye, you're Georgie Haynes."

"What d' the lassies say about me?"

She blushed and looked away.

Georgie brought the stool into a new position. Blocking her in the corner by the dresser, he seated himself, knees spread. Seated thus, he appeared solid and steady, the threat of him reduced.

"Come on, I'll no' eat you, Mouse."

She was frightened. They were always frightened. But she was eager too. He knew all about the state, with fear pushing and need pulling.

"Here," he said. "Sit on my knee."

She shook her head.

Georgie Haynes laughed. He put his fingers into his pocket and brought out a coin, a shilling. He held it up.

"I'll gi'e ye this; a present. Sit on my knee, be nice t'me."

"She'll be back soon."

"Nah, nah."

"She will."

"She's not your bloody mammy, is she?"

The girl's brown eyes fastened on the shilling. He extended it in finger and thumb, then brought it towards him. She followed it as meek as a pet lamb on a string.

"Come on, m' sweetheart," he murmured. "Come an' see what Georgie's got for ye."

When she reached for the shilling he put his arm about her. She was of a height with him, him sitting. His face and the girl's face squared to each other. Her little tongue darted out and wetted her lips. There was a gleam in her expression that Georgie took for yielding. He had a sudden urge to drag her to the floor there and then for he was excited by her knowingness as much as her innocence. Her tiny body, his hand told him, was not that of a child at all. Mouse was a woman, with all a woman's attributes in miniature. He found the opening in the blanket and insinuated his fingers through it. He turned his hand and cupped her little round bottom. She sighed. She shivered. She sank against him. Her hand closed over his fist, over the shilling. Her grasp on the blanket slackened. It fell from her. He could see white flesh in the gloom, the girl's body as fine and filigree as something carved out of whalebone. He put a hand to her breast. He put his mouth upon her lips. She rubbed herself against him like a cat. He did not have to coax her now, just make sure that he did not send her into a panic with his ardour or his haste to connect. He was pleased with himself, with the venture. Here was a clean sweet virgin worth more than the prettiest woman on any shore. He liked to be first, to leave the memory of his manliness with daft girls, spoil them for what came after.

"Do ye like that, Mouse?" he whispered huskily.

"Aye."

"Sit," he said. "Sit just here."

She closed her eyes, modestly. She let him guide her down on to his lap. She had just enough weight to tell. He shifted himself back a little on the stool, drawing her closer, tighter.

"Do ye like that too?" he murmured into her ear.

She opened her eyes quick, flaringly. She twisted her head in fright. Georgie Haynes gripped her forcefully with his left arm and went for his mark. It was not panic that had caused the girl's reaction. Georgie, distracted by the clang behind him, glanced away from her.

The base of the heavy iron cooking-pot struck him on the temple. He glimpsed hatred in the boy's face, the stick-thin arm, the scoring of his cotton shirt. He felt the girl drop from him. Then there was only a red vibrating pain that swelled within his head, changed into black sand and, before he could cry out, swamped his consciousness completely. Georgie Haynes fell from the stool on to the floor. His legs twitched, toppling the stool, jarring the table. Blood oozed from his bruised temple, trickled like a thread from one ear. He gagged; then was still.

Barefoot and weak, Davy kicked him, ineffectually. All Davy's strength had gone into lifting and swinging the cooking-pot. Now he was flushed with fury. He danced over Georgie Haynes, rounded on Mouse who, big-eyed, stood by the keelman's feet staring down at him.

Davy spat out a filthy name, slapped his sister across the cheek. She hardly seemed to notice the stinging blow. She was riven by the felling of a man so large and handsome, so much in command of her, as Georgie Haynes had been. She slipped to her knees, touched her fingers to Georgie's brow, then, in amazement, hissed, "Davy, you've kilt him. You've kilt the keelman dead."

It was no unusual sight to encounter colliers on that part of the strand. The Abbeyfield was behind them and the curve of the bay tricked the eye into seeing only the rural prospect of Mr Fotheringham's parks and gardens with a glimpse of the house far off in the painted trees. In June, at that hour, the sun was reluctant to leave the sky and the vista of the river was calmly beautiful.

Ripening crops in the fields on the further shore reminded Elspeth rather too painfully of those hot, immortal evenings on the hills above Balnesmoor when she and Anna mooned over boys and marriage and the infinite possibilities of a future full of summers. She was sore, though. The stiffness in her hips and the small of her back had not eased with walking. She could not lift Mary Jean and carry her for the grip became too much to bear after a step or two. The child had to be content to hold on to Mammy's hand and, with Sarah on the other side, to swing her little legs from the ground now and then until Elspeth, aching in arms and shoulders too, would quietly say, "Enough."

A posy of wild flowers, picked by Mary Jean, was tucked into the buttons of Elspeth's dress. Their faint, subtle fragrance overlaid the warm salty tang of high-tide weed. In spite of her aches and pains she was pleased to be out and about on a night so fine and reluctant to turn for home.

Also enjoying the fine spell of weather, young husbands and young wives strolled hand in hand, renewing romance. A group of friends, women and men, shared a jug of ale on a knoll by the end of the old Preston Island wagon-way. Elderly widows, modestly wrapped in shawls and mutches, sauntered arm in arm along the little path by the unspoiled strand, the westering sun ruddy on their wrinkled cheeks. On dry tussocks, here and there, hewers collected to pass a bottle about, puff their clays and laugh in contented peaceful tones.

Elspeth, Sarah and Mary Jean had just turned into the stretch that overlooked Mr Fotheringham's land. Rooks were settling their squabbles in the massive elms and the shadow of the head-high bank fell long to the rippling river. Walking by the side of a grey pony, hand upon its rein, the man came casually around the curve of the path. He did not falter when he caught sight of the three but he did not at first pay them any particular attention. His head was raised, admiring the view, a pleasant smile upon his lips, topper tipped back. Though he did not ride – the pony was hardly of a size for a full-grown man to saddle – he was clad in a neat unostentatious frock-coat and hessian boots and carried a peeled willow branch as a switch.

"See who it is?" said Sarah under her breath.

Mary Jean stopped in her tracks. To the little girl the pony must have seemed as large as an elephant and the man, in such gentlemanly garb, almost as rare.

"Good evening to you, ladies. My! Is it not a grand night?" Mr Bolderon paused. The pony checked obediently and shook its head as if in greeting too. Mr Bolderon tipped the top hat and gave a bow. It might have been Princes Street or the Calton Hill and they dames of New Edinburgh for the sort of courtesy he displayed. Elspeth was surprised to find the manager here upon a common walk, more surprised when he gave them such a generous greeting. More, however, was to come.

"Mistress Patterson, is it not?"

"Yes, Mr Bolderon."

"The wee one's yours if I'm not mistaken." He cocked his head and winked at Mary Jean who, sensing no threat, did her coy little act and peeped out at him from behind Mammy's skirts. Mr Bolderon stooped, hands on knees, and addressed himself to her. "And what, pray, is your name?"

"Go on," Sarah urged. "Tell the gentleman."

"Mary Jean."

"Mary Jean," said Mr Bolderon as if it was an amazing revelation. "My! But that is a pretty name."

Mary Jean giggled. Already she recognised flattery when she heard it. She took a step from behind Elspeth and then stepped back.

Keir Bolderon raised himself and addressed Elspeth.

"It's a far cry this from the levels," he said.

Elspeth felt a certain shame at his mention of the underground tunnels. It was as if he was reminding her of the moment of their last encounter, that he had seen her half-naked, black with dirt and sweat. She murmured agreement. She had not really taken notice of Mr Bolderon's appearance before. He belonged to a different class from the rest of the men of the Abbeyfield, or so she supposed. Now she saw that he was not at all refined but had a pock-marked coarseness lurking there, a quality that the frock-coat and oratory could not quite cover up. She became, in that instant, less wary of her employer.

She said, "If I may ask, Mr Bolderon, is the pony a pet?"

He grinned. "A fair supposition, Mrs Patterson. It's an old beast I brought with me from – from my last position. It lives in a stable behind my house an' every so often I take it, as now, for a gentle lope."

"Pony," said Mary Jean.

Elspeth and Keir Bolderon looked down at the little girl.

"Her name's Thistle," Keir Bolderon said. "She's very fond of givin' rides to wee lassies, provided they know how to sit still upon her back."

There was something wrong; Elspeth sensed it. She felt drawn to Mr Bolderon. It was of his doing, a deliberate manoeuvre. The pony had been brought for just this purpose, to amuse Mary Jean. The meeting here on the common path had not been by accident. Elspeth's caution returned. But Keir Bolderon with his frank brown eyes and candid expression did not seem to be wolfish, not in that manner; not like Randall Bontine who had so enthralled her sister Anna as to make her his mistress.

Keir Bolderon said, "If your mam'll give permission, perhaps you'd like a ride on Thistle's back, Mary Jean?"

With eyes like saucers Mary Jean stared up at her mother, putting Elspeth into a situation which she could not now avoid.

Sarah said, "It's a nice quiet cuddy, Elspeth."

To Sarah, Keir Bolderon said, "Would you like to ride too?"

"Aye."

"Thistle's got a spine like iron. I'm sure she could manage two wee slips at the same time," Keir Bolderon said. "Mrs Patterson, what do you say?"

"The girls would – would enjoy it."

Elspeth wondered what the colliers would have to say to it when she was seen in such close communion with the manager of the Abbeyfield, what sort of malice the tongues would weave out of the innocent encounter. Perhaps the gossips had some justification for their tales. It was a weird thing, this amiable meeting, planned in advance and prolonged far beyond mere politeness. Manager and strapper should not mix. She boxed for a reason in vain.

"Hup then."

Without hesitation, Keir Bolderon put his strong hands about Sarah's waist, lifted and set her upon the soft saddle that was strapped over the pony's back.

Sarah gasped, her soberness swept aside by the magic of it. She clung to Thistle's mane with both fists. Mary Jean was put in front of her and the reins were given to the elder girl. Keeping a close eye on the passengers, while appearing not so to do, Mr Bolderon hooked a finger into the bar of Thistle's bridle and led the docile old animal forward along the path. Elspeth walked, rather anxiously, by the flank, trying not to coddle the girls with overmuch fuss.

Keir Bolderon glanced across at her. "You'll have ridden many a pony in your day, I suppose?"

Elspeth said, "Aye, one or two."

"Horses too?"

"Och nó, Mr Bolderon. I'm no gentlewoman."

"I meant in your drovin' days."

He had enquired about her. He had taken on the half-lie she had told to Jock Bennet, the 'history' that was accepted all about the Abbeyfield. Why had the manager expressed such interest in her? She began to fret again and to curse herself for her suspicious nature and for spoiling the pleasure of the evening. And a pleasure it was to hear Mary Jean giggle at the rolling gait of the fat old pony, to hear, for the first time, Sarah Bennet laugh aloud as Thistle plodded on along the path. Elspeth had almost forgotten how the simple, unexpected things in life could surprise the heart and open it to joy, particularly in childhood. She saw just how much Sarah Bennet had sacrificed to a regime of duty and responsibility.

"It was a drover you were married to, was it not?"

Elspeth came out of her reverie. "Yes, sir."

"I had an aunt who married a drover," Keir Bolderon confessed. "It was a great scandal in our family at the time."

"One need not ask why," said Elspeth.

"Ah, no. Not for the ordinary reason."

She was tempted to press for the extraordinary reason but thought better of it. It was not right for her to slip into familiarity. However, she had met many like Keir Bolderon among James's associates, eager, urgent men who strove for advancement, power and wealth but were not entirely devoid of scruples in gaining their ends.

Keir Bolderon said, "Are you a born Highlander? You do not speak like one."

"I was born in – in – by Glasgow."

"Met your husband at a tryst, no doubt."

"Yes."

"What drew you to the Abbeyfield, Mrs Patterson? It's a far piece from Glasgow and opposed to the open life of a drover."

"It was – as it happened. I was in need of work."

"Would your parents not take you in?"

"They are dead, sir."

"I see," said Keir Bolderon.

He let it rest and did not return to the subject.

As they came past the strand and on to the path by the open shore they encountered other colliers. Now there was no nod of greeting, no cheerful remark about the weather. In silence they stepped swiftly aside, tripping, some of the older women, over the tussocks and falling and lying there as if the sight of one of theirs with one of them had wounded them mortally. Hewers too, caught at leisure, stood when Mr Bolderon appeared and doffed their caps as if the pony led a funeral procession. Elspeth, they ignored.

When Sarah called out to Mr Ogilvie, "See me, Mr Ogilvie. I'm ridin' a cuddy," the amiable hewer averted his gaze as if she had come naked before him like a young Godiva.

Sarah was too excited to be aware of hostility. She called out to other colliers and was mimicked by Mary Jean. Only Elspeth felt the flush of an unjustified shame creep across her cheek. She dropped back a pace as if to disassociate herself from the unusual parade.

It was over in a quarter of an hour. It ended where the wagon track, rotting into sour grasses, cut away towards the Placket road.

"Well, ladies, it's time I was away," said Keir Bolderon. He plucked Mary Jean from the saddle and put her on the ground. "I've to see Mr Rance before bedtime an' he puts his head down early, you know." Sarah Bennet gave a long sigh as the manager swung her from Thistle's back and held her, just for a moment, with her toes an inch above the path. "It's been a pleasure to meet with you. Thistle has not had such an adventure for many a long day. Is that not correct, cuddy?"

Thistle spluttered assent and the manager stroked the pony's muzzle fondly. He made no particular thing of parting. He touched the topper, bowed, and was gone almost before Elspeth remembered her manners.

"Thank you, Mr Bolderon. It was a kind of thing t' do for the girls."

"Goodnight, Mrs Patterson."

"Goodnight to you, sir," Elspeth said.

None of them moved. The girls and the young woman remained fixed at the junction of the paths, watching the manager lead his old pony away into the russet grasses.

"Well," Elspeth said, "was it fun, Mary Jean?"

"Cuddy. Nice cuddy. Fistle's her name so the mannie said."

Before Elspeth could put the question to Sarah Bennet, however, Sarah was away. All her pent-up energy seemed at once released and, skipping and leaping, Sarah rushed home to tell her sister, Mouse, what an event she had missed by loitering indoors that special summer night.

Whatever myth there was about keelmen having skulls as thick as rock had, in the case of Georgie Haynes, proved horribly wrong.

He was still sprawled where he had fallen when Elspeth came into the Bennets' cottage a quarter of an hour later. She found Mouse, Sarah and Davy in varying states of numbness at the enormity of the crime.

"Davy done it. Davy hit him wi' a pot. Davy, not me," Mouse shouted, the instant Elspeth appeared.

The girl had dressed herself. She sat on a stool with a blanket about her, though the air in the kitchen was stifling, wringing her hands and lamenting in a low, drawling voice. Sarah, who had intruded into this scene only minutes before, had done what Sarah did best: she had filled a kettle from the bucket and put it on the chain, had poked up the coals in the hearth and fed in fresh kindling. Licks of flame were already eating into the wood raising shadows in the depths of the room.

Wheezing like a leather bellows, Davy sat on the side of the bed in his new-washed nightshirt, staring into space, shaking his head from time to time.

Elspeth felt Mary Jean crowd against her legs. Not wishing her daughter to see the dead man, she found her voice. "Sarah, take Mary Jean out for a quarter of an hour. Don't go far away. I'll call for you shortly."

"Aye." Off Sarah went, dragging the reluctant child by the hand. It was late now. Mary Jean was fractious. Elspeth could hear her crying petulantly as Sarah led her away.

Elspeth did not offer Mouse comfort. Mouse did not seem in need of it. It was from Davy that she elicited an account of the keelman's intrusion, his attempt to seduce Mouse and, Davy hinted, Mouse's acquiescence.

"Was it just a pot you hit him with?" Elspeth asked.

"Aye."

"Hard?"

"Hard as I could."

Davy wept. Not Mouse. She was hard-eyed and furious with resentment at her brother.

"What'll we do, Elspeth?" Davy cried. "They'll hang me for sure."

While she had been comforting Davy, however, Elspeth had been studying the keelman's body. She had seen more than enough to realise that George Haynes was very far from dead. She got down on her knees beside him, untied his shirt, touched the flat of her hand to his chest. The thud-thump of his heart was as strong as the pump of a donkey engine. His breathing was shallow, however, and he remained insensible to all that was going on about him.

"How long ago did it happen?"

"About – about twenty minutes ago," said Davy. "He's dead, is he no'?"

"He's no more dead than I am," said Elspeth.

"Oh, Christ Jesus!" Scrambling, Davy got himself on to the bed and, legs tucked under him, pressed himself against the wooden board as if he expected Haynes to leap out of stupefaction and be at his throat with bare hands.

"You gave him a fair crack, Davy," said Elspeth.

"He wanted me," said Mouse. "He wanted me t' kiss—"

"Hold quiet, Allison," Elspeth said. "Look outside. Tell me how dark it is an' if anybody's about."

"Do what ye're told, ye wee bitch," Davy shouted, holding a hand to his chest as if to squeeze breath enough to make the command. "It's all your bloody fault."

Mouse snapped the blanket about her like a ceremonial robe and stalked out of the door into the twilight.

"Davy," said Elspeth in a whisper, "did Haynes – you know, did he harm her?"

"She wanted it. She could've woke me easy. For all I know she egged him on."

"But he didn't—"

"She was on his knee. He was – was touchin' her."

"Very well," said Elspeth. "Are you strong enough to take his legs an' help me drag him outside?"

"I'm strong enough," said Davy, though he did not seem so. "But should we no' send for Mr Rance? The keelman beggar shouldna be here at all."

"I'll not involve Mr Rance or any other. It's our business an' we'll have to sort it out for ourselves."

"Because Mouse egged him on?"

"Yes," said Elspeth impatiently, though that was not her motive for wanting Georgie Haynes clear of the cottage before he recovered his wits. She had noticed the blood trickling from his ear, the contusion on his temple and knew that, within seconds of his coming to his senses, Georgie Haynes would be in pain and roaring for revenge. She feared the keelman more than anything. If Haynes returned tomorrow breathing fire and smoke then, of course, she would set up a clatter that would rouse the neighbours and they would defend the patch from the keelman as they would have, in days of old, from an attack by a bear or boar. But she did not want to be dependent upon the community, to demonstrate the vulnerability of her position. She certainly did not want to have to summon Thomas Rance for protection. Being rid of Haynes was all she could think of to do.

Mouse returned. "It's no' dark yet," she said. "But it's quiet enough. There's folk comin' up from the river path but they're behind the house, over the burn."

"Grasp his foot," said Elspeth.

"What—"

"Bloody do as you're told, Mouse," Davy wheezed.

It took all their combined strength to move the keelman, to drag him across the floor and over the threshold and, even as he began to groan and wag his right arm limply, to pull him over the dusty foreyard towards the plank bridge.

Hand in hand, Sarah and Mary Jean hovered not far off, watching. For them it had been a strange, strange evening: a pony ride and a meeting with Mr Bolderon and now Mammy dragging a keelman across the ground, with Davy in his nightshirt and Mouse in a blanket helping her.

When they reached the plank over the burn, Elspeth paused. She straightened, glanced this way and that. Mouse's report had been accurate. Colliers and wives were all on the river side. The high, rising bank of alders and little birch trees was deserted. She thought of pulling Georgie Haynes into them, leaving him hidden there, but the man was recovering quickly, too quickly. He thrashed his head from side to side. His lids fluttered and his fists balled, clenching and slackening. She wondered if he had been in drink when he had arrived and if spirits still clouded his brain.

"Push," said Elspeth.

"What?"

"Push him into the burn."

"We canna do that t' Georgie," Mouse cried. "He'll drown."

"In two foot o' water?" Davy drove his heel into Georgie Haynes' side, rolling him forward to the edge. "A keelman'll no' drown in that, more's the bloody pity. Heave, Mouse, or I'll skelp your ear."

Georgie Haynes went into the lentic waters of the burn with all the grace of a pike with a gaff through its gills. He struck the scummy surface with shoulders, torso and legs. His tormentors, Elspeth included, stood for a moment on the bank as his head went under. One, two, three seconds passed. Georgie rose again. Heaving upward, retching and spluttering, slime dripping from his hair, he roared and fell back with a huge blanketing splash.

Herding the Bennets before her Elspeth ran for the cottage. Once they were all inside she dropped the bar across the door, rammed a chair against it and waited, the children about her, watching the cottage door, like little things in a grisly fairytale. But Georgie Haynes did not come to blow it down. Georgie Haynes had had enough, for the time being.

SEVEN

Welcome to the Babylon

For weeks now Anna had been meekness itself. Gone were the tempers and tantrums, gone too her effervescent cheerfulness. She was not merely sulking. There were no scowls upon her brow, no darting black looks. In the wake of the Ottershaw ball she had become hang-dog and submissive, cowed by Randall's dismissal rather than the horrid dressing-down she had received from Alicia Bontine and the sarcasm of Cat Sinclair. To everyone, Sandy included, it seemed that Anna had at last learned her place. She obeyed every order. She plied the hoe in the pea-rigs and greening barley, trod blankets, scoured pots, even dusted the long hall without a mutter of protest or a pretence of incompetence. She gave attention only to Robbie, but she no longer shared the boy. She did not go out of her way to show him off, was guarded and selfish in caring for him.

The news that rumbled down from Balnesmoor of Jamie Moodie's drowning and the reappearance of long-lost sisters, of a war over the contents of the will, did not seem to impinge upon Anna's melancholy state. She listened to supper-table conversations without a word, asked no questions, offered no opinions when Elspeth's name was raised and speculation was rife about her sister's hiding-place, the reason why she had fled from marriage to the weaver mannie.

Anna, however, was not so indrawn and detached as she seemed. She was, after all, Gaddy Patterson's daughter and a natural schemer. She was not so wounded by Randall Bontine's rejection that she could not see in this latest turn of events certain interesting possibilities that might restore the benefits that she had lost to the winsome bitch from Piperhaugh.

Anna did not know enough of law to calculate the portion of Moodie's fortune that might fall to Elspeth. She felt sure, though, that Elspeth would hear of it. Even now, 'Pet might be bundling up her belongings, wrapping Mary Jean in a travelling-shawl preparatory to coming back to Balnesmoor to claim her dues. Tales of the appearance of Moodie's sisters worried Anna. She had a peasant's instinctive fear of 'society women', which she believed the pair to be. She could imagine them wheedling the whole of the Moodie fortune away from the Pattersons by devious stratagems. While she hoed in the barley field, swept out old straw from the stable or lugged piles of wet wash from basket to tub, her brain was highly active. She concentrated on the practical business of protecting Elspeth against the predations of the 'Edinburgh' ladies and wove fanciful plots of her own. Of course she could not storm into Mr Hildebrand's chambers in Dumbarton, even if she could steal a day to make the long ride; nor dared she write him a letter begging information. Such a missive would certainly be shown to Randall or Mr Gibbie and she would find herself on the carpet for meddling. Nonetheless Anna needed facts, hard facts from somebody 'in the know'. After much careful thought she came to the conclusion that the only person who might be able to help her, and who would not sneak to the Bontines, was Robert Rudge, manager of the Kennart mill and a man with an eye for the ladies.

Once decided, Anna patiently prepared herself to beard Mr Rudge in his lair. She did not know him at all well, though Elspeth had once told her, with a disapproving 'tut', that Mr Rudge had made a remark about her figure and had enquired once or twice, in a sly manner, after Anna's welfare. Admiration from men of discernment Anna considered no more than her due. After all, she had attracted not just the eye but the love of the laird of Ottershaw and, by comparison, Robert Rudge was naught but the hireling of a common weaver.

To make contact with Mr Rudge was not so easy. His home was in Drymen, his office above the mill at Kennart. He was not the sort of bachelor who did much dining out these days. It was a fair few miles to Drymen from Strachan but Anna could devise no other means of encountering the manager and, after three or four days of puzzling over the problem, she elected to confront him directly at his house.

It would have to be done on the Sabbath. She would have

to dodge the family visit to the kirk and, though she would have preferred it otherwise, would have to carry little Robbie with her since she could not leave him alone in the empty castle. She feigned a cramp and was duly left behind when the procession went off, master, mistress, servants and children dutifully tramping into the hot June sunshine in their hot sombre clothes.

"Will I not stay wi' you?" Sandy asked.

Anna said, "For what reason?"

"In case you've need of—"

She claimed female intimacy in the nature of the pain and Sandy, blushing to the tips of his ears, retreated after his family without more ado.

With Robbie in a light cotton dress and sun-bonnet, armed with a flask of small beer tapped from the house barrel, Anna set off across the Lightwater as soon as the Bontines' retainers had cleared the front gate. She calculated that she would make the distance in three hours, even on such a hot, cloudless day. If Mr Rudge was the sort to occupy a pew in Drymen parish, which Anna doubted, she would reach his house about the same time as he returned from kirk.

Mr Robert Rudge had long ago given up the pretence of being a devoted Christian. He considered the length and hellfire nature of sermons to be most un-Christian, to show no consideration for the congregation and no charity at all. He had not crossed the kirk door in many years. He was 'respectable' enough, however, to pass Sunday discreetly out of sight of the good folk of Drymen and was comfortably sprawled in the shade of an old yew tree in the garden at the rear of the house when Anna discovered him.

Anna was sticky and flushed. Robbie had had to be carried most of the way to add to her discomfort and ten miles had seemed like forty. Tentatively she came into the garden. The front door of the house was open to keep the place cool but Anna did not knock upon the brass fist since she did not know what sort of servants Mr Rudge kept or what their attitude to strangers might be.

To Robert Rudge Anna Sinclair did not appear in the least flustered. At first he thought it might be a mirage of the heat for he had cast an expert eye in Anna's direction from a distance and had watched her bud and blossom and had thought what a waste it was that she had married a coarse lout like Matt Sinclair when, in a more perfect world, she might have been employed to serve him comfortably upstairs as well as down. It had not surprised Robert Rudge when the hot-blooded and autocratic Randall Bontine had snipped her up for his pleasure. He admired the laird for exercising his 'rights' without hypocrisy. What Rudge saw then, coming around the corner of the gable, was an opportunity.

What Anna saw was a haggard handsome man snoozing after a good noon dinner, all unbuttoned and cool and, in that private bower, depleted of authority.

"Mr Rudge?"

He rose to welcome her. He acknowledged Robbie, said what a fine wee chap he was, brought a bench from behind the yew and put it adjacent to the wooden seat upon which he had been reclining. He would have sent for wine, for beef, for fresh milk for the boy, for anything that Anna had requested, though he did not mention just yet that his servants had been dismissed for the afternoon and had gone off to call upon relatives and that the house stood empty and tempting.

Anna found his affability disconcerting. The setting did not seem right for the exercise of feminine wiles nor for Robert Rudge's style of approach to pretty young women. But good looks were Anna's stock in trade, that and a mind sharper than she was ever given credit for.

Rudge said, "I can guess why you have come here, Mrs Sinclair."

"Tell me an' I'll tell you if you're right, Mr Rudge."

"For information."

"Of what sort?" said Anna teasingly.

"Information about Jamie Moodie's money," Robert Rudge stated.

Smiling, Anna nodded. She slipped Robbie from her lap and let him toddle off to explore a pyramid of earthenware pots by the flowerbeds, watching him, though, out of the corner of her eye. She settled herself on the bench, fluttered out her bodice, and fanned herself with her bonnet.

Robert Rudge relaxed, legs crossed.

Anna did not feel out of place. The house was not particularly imposing and Robert Rudge's reputation was, she had to admit, no worse than her own.

Brown bees hummed in the flower gardens, snouting for blooms. There were dainty butterflies for Robbie to chase along the rows of cabbage plantings. Floating up from the Endrick a breeze stirred the yew leaves and brought pleasant coolness to the shade.

"It's not for you, Anna Sinclair; Jamie's money," Rudge said. "I believe under the circumstances I might be permitted to call you Anna. I deplore formality out-of-doors, do you not?"

Anna said, "Why do you say I canna have share of the weaver's wealth? It never crossed my mind I'd have a claim on it."

"I'm sure it crossed your mind, Anna."

"My sister has claim on it, though, from what I know of law."

"The intricacies of the law are far beyond your understanding. Far beyond mine too," said Rudge. "Oh, I can cobble up a contract for wool wares, make a handclasp as bindin' as an iron band, and I am versed in what's called 'commercial procedures'. But the *real* laws, the laws of courts and settlements, those, alas, I must leave to experts."

"Experts like Mr Hildebrand?" said Anna.

"No doubt you encountered him at Ottershaw."

"Aye. He worked for Ran—for the laird."

"Hildebrand's no villain, Anna. He's on our side."

"Side?"

"Hildebrand's dedicated to keeping Moodie's greedy sisters at bay. James Simpson Moodie, God rest his soul, did not intend his years of toil to be squandered on ribbons an' bobs for jumped-up relatives."

"What're they like, the sisters?"

"Much like us, I suppose."

"There's a fair world o' difference between you an' me, Mr Rudge."

"Is there? I wonder." Rudge gave a laugh. "You're almost as talkative and perceptive as your sister, Anna."

"Elspeth an' I are not sisters."

"Ah, yes. Elspeth's a foundling. I forgot."

It was months since Anna had felt so much at ease. She had heard all the stories concerning Robert Rudge, though not so many of late, and she could see in the lined visage and sly eye that most of them were true. He was a man who had found his place, was content in it and would fight to retain it. It had not occurred to Anna before that Robert Rudge might be threatened by the closure of the Kennart mill and just as interested in Mr Hildebrand's doings as she was.

She embarked at once on a more direct line of questioning and found Mr Rudge surprisingly co-operative. He had questions of his own, of course, an exchange that she could not deny. His pointedness was disconcerting at the first but she squared to him and told him the truth, mostly, while Robbie played about the garden. Robert Rudge asked her about Matt, about her liaison with Randall Bontine, her standing at Strachan Castle. She could see that he was deeply curious, a true collector of gossip. She did not grudge him satisfaction.

In turn the manager of Kennart told her all that he had learned of James Moodie's mysterious death – suicide, without doubt – and the ingenious documents that Moodie had had drawn up and signed to protect the mill and preserve it for his wife and child.

"I'll never understand why she ran away," said Rudge.

Anna shook her head. "Right after the murder at Kennart, too."

"I've heard talk it had to do with your husband?" said Robert Rudge.

"No truth in that," said Anna.

"Can you be sure?"

"Sure as eggs," said Anna. "It was Moodie she ran from. She never went chasin' after Matt. Elspeth could not abide Matt. Small wonder."

"Did he treat you badly, Anna?" asked Robert Rudge, looking at the butterflies. "Did he – beat you?"

"Aye, he beat me."

"Did you not bring the beatings upon yourself?"

"He beat me long before I—" Anna paused. "There're certain things should not be mentioned in polite conversation, Mr Rudge. I'd like it better if we change the subject."

"Will you sue for a divorcement, Anna?"

Anna said, "I canna sue a man who's vanished."

"Desertion." Rudge shrugged.

"I've no reason to seek a divorcement."

"Do you want him back, is that it?"

"God Almighty, Mr Rudge! That's the last thing I want."

"Angus Hildebrand would, I'm sure, instruct you in the law."

"I canna afford a fancy lawyer's fee."

"I can."

Taken by surprise, Anna sat up and stopped fanning herself with her bonnet. "Why should you—"

"It would make you available, would it not? It would put you back upon the marriage market."

"I'm no heifer t' be bought an' sold."

"What of your son?" Robert Rudge gestured at Robbie. "Would it not be better for him to have a father?"

"Robbie's been baptised. He's legitimate issue," said Anna, who had picked up the term from Randall in another, less personal connection. "He has a father."

"Sinclair?" said Robert Rudge.

"My husband—"

"You know, Anna, that Randall Bontine's beyond your reach."

Anna had not anticipated this turn. She pouted, would not give a direct reply.

Rudge went on, "Our dear laird has picked himself a wife. He's made a wise, if not original, choice. There's no place for you or the laddie at Ottershaw, Anna. If you imagine that you might purchase the laird's interest by using your sister's new-found – or should I say un-found – fortune, then you're more of a fool than I took you for."

Robert Rudge spoke gently, without patronage or preaching. He did not pause when little Robbie toddled to his mother, climbed upon her knee and, with a weary sigh, settled his head upon her breast.

"I think, Anna, that you must make more of your life than you have done. Is it love turns you dizzy?"

"That's none o' your business, Mr Rudge."

"If you were free I'd marry you."

A sudden flash of fear came into Anna. She saw the equation

258

with Elspeth, saw Rudge as Moodie; then the fear was gone.

"Aye," said Anna, with an insincere laugh, "I think you mean you'd bed me, Mr Rudge. Marriage is another matter."

"Oh, I'd bed you all right, Anna. It would not be a platonic relationship, whatever sort old Jamie Moodie forged. You see, I can read your mind. No, no, I'd not have you away in another room. I'd want you beside me to warm my bones, and other parts of me too."

Anna did not even blush. She had half expected Robert Rudge to seduce her, or try to, but she had not thought him imprudent enough to mention marriage.

"Why make this offer o' marriage when you might have me for a servant's wage, Mr Rudge?" said Anna. "You know I'm unhappy at Strachan Castle an', as you've pointed out, I'm not goin' to be welcomed back to Ottershaw. If you invited me to become your housekeeper I might be more inclined to accept."

"Marriage, Anna," said Robert Rudge. "I have a house-keeper. I do not have a wife."

Robbie had nodded off. Anna eased the child from the crook of her arm and laid him gently on the wooden bench, head on her shawl, her bonnet balanced on the seat's arm to shelter his face. She got to her feet and walked a short distance towards the brown earth rows where the cabbage plants were.

It was quiet here in the backwater of Drymen early on a Sabbath afternoon, quiet and peaceful.

Within the house she was sure she would find solid comforts. Warm fires would line the grates in winter, clean linen would adorn the beds, wholesome well-cooked meats would be served piping hot to the table. Mr Rudge would have money put away. He would not be penniless, and when his time came he would leave her secure. She turned and glanced at her son where he slept innocent and peaceful upon the bench in the shade of the great yew tree, glanced at Robert Rudge, legs crossed, one foot wagging slightly as he observed her every movement, admiring her, no doubt, and speculating on her hidden charms.

She said, "What if I do separate myself from Matt?"

"Then there will be no obstacle to marriage."

"Marriage is what you promise?"

"I said as much, Anna."

She came back towards him. "I canna understand it, Mr Rudge. I came here today out o' concern for my sister and her welfare, an' you spring a proposal on me as if you'd courted me for years. I hardly know you, Mr Rudge."

"I hardly know you, Anna. But that's no hindrance. Marriage would be beneficial to us both, would it not?"

"My sister married—"

"I'm *not* Jamie Moodie," said Robert Rudge. "I've blood in my veins for one thing. I would ask from you all the things a man expects from a wife."

"What things?"

"Tenderness, loving, a modicum of loyalty to me in my old age."

"Tell me, Mr Rudge, did you just see me today an' fancy I would suit your purpose or have I been on your mind?"

"You've been on my mind."

"Why did you not approach me, then?"

"How could I?"

"By letter. By arrangement."

Robert Rudge laughed cynically. "And have you mock me for a fool or a lecher. Show my letter to everyone."

"I would not."

"In any case, you came to me, Anna. I'm not so 'respectable' that I can't take you out of a servants' hall. It matters not to me that you were wife to an outlaw an' mistress of the laird of Ottershaw."

"Take me inside your house," Anna said, hands upon her hips. "Take me in there now. Robbie'll sleep for an hour or more. We'll not be disturbed."

Robert Rudge closed his eyes, bridged his fingers over his nose and gave a stifled groan as if inwardly pinched by habits of indulgence and capitulation. His foot wagged wildly then he opened his eyes, planted both heels on the ground and got up from the bench.

"Marriage," he said. "Marriage, Anna, is what I want."

"Do y' not want me?"

"Damn it, of course I want you. But are bachelors not entitled to have moral scruples too?"

"Tell me the true reason."

"I cannot trust myself not to become fond of you."

"Are you not – not fond of me now?"

"Of course I am. But I might change my mind. I do not wish to compromise you, Anna."

"Change your mind about me?"

"About marriage," Rudge said. "Now, come, lift the boy an' I'll find us a rig to run you back to Strachan Castle."

"Mr Rudge, have I or have I not been proposed to?" said Anna, frowning.

Rudge grinned. "Not yet."

"After my divorce?"

"And not a moment before," said Robert Rudge.

It was early afternoon when Elspeth embarked on the cattle-boat that would carry her from the Fife shore to the Port of Leith. She had planned to cross the river at the Queen's ferry but the carter who had picked her up on the Placket turnpike had been a friendly, helpful fellow and had suggested that it would be cheaper to make the trip from Dalgetty where passengers might mill in with cattle and sheep at a charge of a penny per head. Besides, the Dalgetty barge would land her in the heart of the old town and save her a long walk from the ferry landing. Elspeth heeded the carter's advice and, since he did not charge her for the extra miles, ran on with him to Dalgetty.

The stone ramps of the quays which dipped from paddocks above the bay were thronged with shaggy spring cattle and mutton culled out after lambing. It was hard for Elspeth to realise that this was no special day for boatmen and drovers who were obviously used to such chaos. The boatman's name was McEwan but for some unexplained reason he was known to all as Deadlie. The ports of the Forth were full of such characters but Elspeth was wary, equating the bargeman, unjustly, with strutting Georgie Haynes. Deadlie McEwan, though, was a harmless little whelk of a man, burned black by salt air and sunshine. He seemed to command the respect of everyone on the quays and to have a cheery greeting for all. Elspeth was surprised when, on taking her penny, he closed his sinewy fingers over her wrist and held her for a moment.

"Aye, you're a strange face, lassie. Is it Leith for you?"

"It is, sir."

"You'll no' have crossed wi' me before."

"No, I have not."

"Stand awa' up yonder then, out o' the ropes an' the slitter an' you'll see the finest sight in all Scotland: the Port o' Leith comin' o'er the Forth on a bonnie summer's day."

Deadlie directed Elspeth towards the prow, saw that she was settled before he let a second batch of cattle be driven off the ramp into the bed of the transport barge.

Elspeth found a wooden post to cling to while the boat waddled with the weight of live cargo. Sheep were jumped on board to fill vacant pens and drovers and Fifeshire fishers who had business in the city huddled on the stern deck, surrounded by bundles and travelling props. Smells mingled ripely in Elspeth's nostrils. She started when the big spritsail unfurled, seemingly of its own accord, to be followed by topsail and staysail. The bulk of canvas made the beasts afraid and they created a great roaring and kicking that brought a lurch of water swilling over the gunwale. On a rough day, Elspeth thought, the passage would be a drenching affair. She was glad that the weather was fair and glassy. Invisible breezes filled the canvases. Two lads adroitly hoisted and lowered long-pole oars and, with a twirl, the *Gaberdine*, the barge's name, parted from the sand by the quay and tacked out towards the roadsteads and the German Sea.

It was Elspeth's first real voyage, her first sight of the wide, wide sea. It took her breath away. Like the cattle on the step below she was amazed by it and stood transfixed, gripping the rail post tightly, drinking in the scene and feeling the slap of the sea-wind upon her cheeks and the tousle of it in her hair. She did not, at first, look at all to the land. The long horizon held her in thrall. She could envisage the rim of the earth, its mountains of blue ice and salt-white snow. It seemed far and yet, from the deck of the *Gaberdine*, attainably near. She noticed how the cattle rolled their eyes to that infinity and save for a shake of the head or a stamp of the hoof now and then were soothed by the sight and made still.

Ships stood out against the haze, listless in the bay, quick against the skyline. Brigantines and schooners, Elspeth assumed, laden with rice and cotton, sugar and tobacco and other exotic cargoes which were a thousand miles removed from coal and fish and cattle and mundane coastal loads. The barge seemed tiny on the estuary amid flocks of tall ships, cutters and smacks. As the Lothian coast came near she could read the names of trader ships moored to anchors in wait for the tide – *Daedalus, Fox, Arcturus, Culloden*, the *Isabella Jaynes*. How fine it would be to have a schooner painted with your name, Elspeth thought, to have your name sailed to the tropics and the poles.

Moving like a monkey Deadlie McEwan hoisted his way round the gunwales, avoiding the sails, and gave her a hail.

"Is it no' a grand sight, lassie?"

"Aye, sir, it is."

"I've never been south o' St Ebba's head or north o' Kirkcaldy but for a' that I've seen the Americas an' the Indies inside my head. Aye, when I was sober too."

Elspeth laughed. She did not resent it when Deadlie put an arm about her shoulders and held her for a moment or two as the old barge swung again and tacked towards the town.

"What does a colliery lass seek in Leith?" said Deadlie.

"How can you tell I'm a collier?"

"I can tell all the trades." Deadlie tapped his nose with his forefinger. "Every job o' work leaves its mark. But you're o'er bonnie t' have been at the diggin' for long. Is it a husband you'll be meetin' at the pier?"

Curiosity was the bargeman's vice. He would trawl for gossip as others of his kin trawled for cod. She would be his day's best catch.

Elspeth said, "No husband. I'm going to the Babylon."

If Deadlie McEwan thought he had heard everything, he was wrong; her answer caught him by surprise. "The Babylon! My, my, lassie! I wouldna have put you down as one o' that sort."

"I'm told men without work congregate there."

"So they do, so they do. But it's a damned ill place for a visit. Have ye no work then?"

"I have work. I have need to employ a coal-cutter."

"Ach, aye." Deadlie nodded. "Kilt, was he?"

"A month since."

"How many mouths?"

263

"Four, an' my own."

"Well, there's coal men there too, I suppose. God, but there's a' sorts in the Babylon. Mostly sailors an' ships' tradesmen but a' sorts, a' sorts."

"Where is the Babylon?"

Deadlie glanced to the shore. The shapes of the houses were made indistinct by traffic along the harbour and quays but the skyline was clear, church spires and turrets, the cones of the glasshouses, crow-stepped roofs and the chimney towers of tenements.

He pointed. "See yonder under the shape o' Arthur's Seat, the tall steeple? Yon's out towards the Coalhill an' the Brigend. Between Constitution Street an' the steeple lie the Yardheads. The Babylon creeps awa' from its nether end. You'll find your way in wi'out difficulty, lass. I pray ye can find your way out again."

As they closed on the harbour Elspeth lost the company of the friendly skipper of the cattle-barge for he was required to pilot the vessel, yapping commands to his young crew, dancing hither and thither among the drovers, while the cattle, scenting the hot, heavy odours of the docks, became restless and thrawn once more and had to be held down by the horns by the herders or tethered tight by muzzle ropes.

Rafts of Baltic timber heaved on the swell. Even at this hour of an afternoon lighters were loading by the quays of the old stone harbour and, Elspeth noticed, the only part of the range of the shore that seemed quiet was the distant dump of the Coalhill for warm weather had killed the domestic trade. Smudged by the haze the façades of the town – cottages, kirks, warehouses, tenements and taverns – looked dusty and precarious, like roan-bound volumes leaning on a shelf. She felt a stab of apprehension at the thought of what had brought her here, the search for a man, a fit, trustworthy man. Even so, after a week living in fear that Georgie Haynes would return in search of revenge, fear of what he might do to Sarah and Davy if he caught them alone, Elspeth had taken the only course of action open to her. She had come to Leith to track down a collier, any decent chap who was willing to tackle the deep seams of the Abbeyfield and scour out the coal-heavy cave. When she stepped on to the stones of Leith, however, her pessimism increased. She saw how silly she had been in contemplating such an undertaking. What man would be mad enough to saddle himself with three young girls, an ailing boy and a woman with hardly a penny to her name? She almost turned and stepped back on to the deck of the *Gaberdine*. But the sheep were being driven off and cattle would be on their heels and not even the jovial McEwan had a second to spare to encourage her, or offer a wave of farewell.

She drifted back, turned and looked along the curve of the harbour to the tall, tall steeple that Deadlie had given her as a landmark and, squaring her shoulders, set out to find the stand of raddled tenements known by repute as the Babylon.

It was not the height of summer yet – country folk considered August to be the real summer month – but for June it was glorious and hot with grain growing lush in Lachlan's new-tilled patches and the clover lays thick as wool.

The cattle were down by the river, lying in the shade of the willow trees, flicking their tails and ears and lowing, in a moony kind of way, as if summoning Sandy to come down and scrub their itching hides and swat away the black flies with a wicker whisk. Sandy, though, had gone to Fintry with his father to purchase bolts of burlap to be stitched into sacks. Cat was out in the garden with Edith, the children and Mistress Alicia, lolling about under an awning improvised from old carpeting and drinking barley water from a stone jug. Robert had deigned to take a nap in his grandmother's bed, while Aileen kept cool in the cubby by polishing a dented old brass warming-pan that Lachlan had unearthed from a cellar.

It was the sort of opportunity that Anna had been waiting for. She slipped along the corridor and ascended the narrow spiral staircase that would take her to the Bontines' quarters. As usual Mr Gibbie was off on business. The library was deserted. It was seldom other than deserted. There were no scholars in Strachan. The windows of the old room were slack and admitted draughts and the chimney smoked and the woodwork, even the leaded glass cases which held 'the library', had an odour of gall that made no appeal to anyone in the household.

Anna had been considerably upset by her visit to Robert

Rudge's house. She had behaved with admirable coolness at the time but it bothered her that she had failed to tempt such a notorious old rake as Robert Rudge, that he had been able to resist her. Why had he insisted on chastity before marriage? Marriage was the weirdest turn of all. It amazed Anna that Robert Rudge had ventured a proposal and, as the days went past, her astonishment and her bewilderment increased instead of diminishing.

It was high time, Anna had decided, that she armed herself with knowledge. Taking a page, as it were, from Elspeth's book, she would seek free advice from the volumes in Mr Gibbie's library.

Stealthily Anna opened one of the cases. Grey dust lay thick within. The glass itself was greasy and unpleasant to touch. The books too had a damp, nasty feel to them and the binding left traces on the fingertips, like rust or dried blood. Anna wrinkled her nose and, peering, scanned the labels on the spines.

Sermons of Rev. James Black – Heaven and Hell – Instruction for the Ignorant.

She began to doubt that Mr Gibbie had bought the books at all. They were all about kirk matters, the strain of religion that demanded that you sell your soul to God from the moment you were born with all love and merriment traded away in tears and lamentation for the hope of a better world to come. In spite of the warmth of the afternoon air Anna shivered involuntarily, closed that section of the long case and opened another. It contained more of the same material.

To show her nonchalance Anna picked one at random, opened it and read: "*Therefore the Lord reaping the Manifestation of His Grace on the Elect and Gospel Wrath and Vengeance on Reprobates—*" Anna closed the book with a snap and hastily slotted it back into place.

She glimpsed her face in the bottle-glass pane, seemed to see the face of Robert Rudge by it, a trick of sunlight in the whorls. She wondered who, if not he, was damned; if she was damned with him. She shivered again, closed that case too and continued bravely with her search, trying to concentrate on finding what she came for and making away with it to a safer, less sepulchral place.

The book looked small and unthreatening. It lay on top of seven or eight great learned slabs in a sleek grey cloth. Yellowing labels indicated that they contained the Law. *The Pocket Lawyer*, however, was a lightweight thing and, as advertised, slipped into Anna's frock pocket very neatly.

She escaped down to the servants' hall and out into the yard, sought privacy in the musty hay loft above the stables. Sunlight streamed through the half-door and illuminated the motes and particles that drifted in the hot summer air. Cushioned on hay, Anna unbuttoned her bodice and sleeves, hitched up her skirt, kicked off her shoes then settled back and opened the little volume.

"Law," Anna read, "having thus for its object the constant and perpetual will to give every one his own, teaches us to cultivate this will by living honestly, injuring no one and giving every one his own." She nodded approval, read on: "Such is law according to the authorities, but law is not accustomed to figure on such lofty ground as this; for man is by nature the absolute master of his own will and the sort of will of which it is in general his pleasure is not that constant and perpetual will to give every man his own but rather a constant and perpetual will to the contrary – that is, to keep all that he can for himself."

Not unaware of irony, Anna gave a dry chuckle and flicked over the pages of introductory matter.

Diligence: Master and Servant: Sequestration. There it was – *Marriage and Dissolution by Divorce.*

She sank a little deeper into the hay and crossed her knees. In two or three minutes she would know all that she needed to know without paying a lawyer a penny. She felt herself no end clever.

Forefinger tracing the words Anna read of Divorce and its two particular grounds – Adultery and Wilful Desertion. She skipped through the paragraphs on adultery – for they made her slightly uneasy – and focused her attention on desertion.

There was little enough, nothing that she could not understand except some sentences about an oath of calumny and inheritance of property. Matt had left nothing of value. He had fled suddenly, Revenue Officers baying at his heels and a price on his head.

It seemed very simple as set down in the passage: "Divorce on ground of wilful desertion may be obtained after a desertion of four years, but not by collusion between the spouses."

She was not quite sure what 'collusion' meant. She was, however, certain that it did not apply to her and would be no bar to obtaining her will of the law. In fifteen months' time she would be free to marry again, to take as husband Robert Rudge or anyone else who caught her fancy and might bring her advantage.

Anna turned the page. She found no more on divorce to interest her. She sighed. She lay back, eyes open, and contemplated the atoms that hung in the still, blonde air. She gave a smug little snort; the law was not as she had supposed it to be, craggy and incomprehensible. Clearly, she might exercise her will through it and be divorced and remarried before next season's harvest was in the barn. Matt had deserted her. He would not dare return to stake a husband's claim on her again.

Anna dreamed for a bit, dreamed of Robert Rudge, who might prove an ideal suitor now she had grown used to the notion. She dreamed of Randall Bontine, whose selfishness rankled. She dreamed, almost unwittingly, of Sandy Sinclair who had been tucked away in a corner of her calculating mind and in a small soft corner of her heart this last five or six months, and who would be easy to take if ever she felt impelled to settle for love alone.

Against the slope of her knee the pages of *The Pocket Lawyer* turned under their own weight. Idly Anna glanced down at them.

Marriage.

Marriage, indeed! It was all she had to offer now, her person, her body. She must not be tempted into a valueless trade as she had been before. There was no mam now to rule her, to try to turn her into something old-fashioned. She, Anna, saw the world as it was, the real world in all its nakedness. It did not frighten her one bit.

Her eyes traced the columns of print: "Marriage is the society formed by a man and a woman when they agree to take each other, and live together as man and wife, during their joint lives." Not a word there about love. She read on. "Who may marry."

And then she sat up, fingers gripping the binding of the book, legs shooting out, spine straightening.

"What?" she said aloud. "What?"

Exceptions.

It was there under exceptions, as clear and unequivocal as the laws governing divorce. *"For instance, a man may not marry the sister of his deceased wife, nor a widow the brother of her husband."*

Anna's mouth shaped the words as she read them aloud, read them again and again.

She had known, of course, in a vague sort of way that Sandy could not marry her while Matt was alive. But she had somehow assumed that Matt would eventually be taken for dead, that once she was free of him he would pass off into a clouded land and that if she chose Sandy she might have him, might persuade folk to call her widow, to give her all her own way.

In her ignorance she had flirted with Sandy to no avail. She had teased and tempted him, made him fall in love with her in ignorance of the fact that he might never have her.

Widow, not wife, said *The Pocket Lawyer*; though Matt were to fall dead on the doorstep of Strachan Castle, though officers of the court were to have his body presented for viewing, it still could not be. She could not marry. The law forbade it. The law was not made for poor folk after all but for men and women who had property. They were the governors and guardians of the law. Nobody could sway them, not in the name of love or need or anything.

Scrambling to her feet Anna raised her hand to throw the book out of the half-door into the yard. Only sense stayed her. She closed the volume and pressed it against her breast. She must keep it hidden away, keep it secretly, covetously, as if it was a book of amorous stories and not the story of how the rich ruled the poor. She looked down from the loft and saw, in the sunlight, Sandy's field-blouse hanging on a nail on the door of the byre. She felt a sudden strong pang within her at the thought of the fair-haired young man and how he loved her and wanted her and how she – now and suddenly – loved him desperately in return.

*   *   *

Mongrels roamed sniffing about the gates of the meat-mulchers' yard and scraggy cats perched on top of the board fence that protected the place from human scavengers. A pack of small boys milled about the lane's end. A ragged girl-child, trapped in a fish barrel, had become their victim. In spite of her screams of woe, she seemed to make no effort to escape the role that linked her with her peers.

If the smells of Leith were strong by the harbour and quays at least they had freshness and variety. Here, away from the sea-walls in the hinterland of the port, the air was stale and thick. Smell became stench and, by the dripping spouts of the tenement drains, caught at the lining of Elspeth's throat and made her want to retch. She had been in squalid streets before and was no exquisite lady without experience of poverty. Even so, the narrow straggling lane of pitted cottages and four-storey tenements, the infamous Babylon, daunted and disgusted her more than she could have imagined.

She was sorry that she had eaten. The sea trip had given her an appetite, however, and she had purchased a cog of boiled cod and a tankard of small beer from a stall on the Shore. She had felt better for refreshment, encouraged in a quest that had begun to seem not only hazardous but foolish.

Leith folk seemed so content, so engaged in affairs of the port that Elspeth could not believe that there were men here without occupation. Even the sailors appeared to have a purpose that gave the lie to all she had heard about Leith as a source of labour. She had no lighter in need of a pilot, no brig to fit, not even a creel of herring to be salted or a board of crabs to be boiled. She did not belong in the thriving tarry town and doubted if she would find a pitman here, not even by the Coalhill piers where men were paid by the load and would not leave that site of employment even when the June sun dried up the trade and brought them hand-to-mouth.

She had eaten her supper at a bench outside a tavern and had stared at the traffic of the Shore and kept an eye on the steeple that Deadlie McEwan had given her as a landmark, as if she was afraid that it would grow legs and swagger away and be lost in the crowd too. After she had finished her beer, wiped her mouth and tidied her hair she went along towards the steeple and found the route to the old Brigend and swung left away from the quays. When she came to the meat-mulchers' yard she knew that she was near her destination. She did not have to ask the boys to point out the Babylon. It was here, all here, occupying the length of the short street, a lane really, which jutted into a vertical of dusty sunlight that rose like a plinth from a mound of dry dirt.

She pressed her hand to her nostrils and, keeping to the gutter in the centre of the street, walked between lowering tenements and crouched decaying cottages. She kept her head down for fear that she would somehow give offence to the blowsy women who hung from the open windows or to the men that moped about the close-mouths and wynds. Wherever might be her place Elspeth knew that it was not the Babylon. She vowed to continue, vowed also that she would not linger one moment longer than was necessary to justify the trip and to satisfy herself that no man who dwelled in this slough would be ready and willing to earn his price in a decent family.

"Ahoy, dearie. Lookin' for a crib, are ye?" Elspeth ignored the question. She darted a glance anxiously at the figure in the window, a grey-haired woman in a filthy shift open at the neck to display her mottled breasts. "I'll fin' ye a cot, sweetheart. Free lodgin' for a fresh wee smoot like you."

Elspeth was almost tempted to make a polite refusal but kept her lips squeezed shut. She knew exactly what the offer implied.

"Cam' awa' in here, hen." The woman who addressed her craned from a ground-level window, reached out a hand as if to catch her arm as well as her attention. She was young, with greasy black hair and sharp black eyes that seemed to pierce and prick at Elspeth like fish-hooks. "Ne'er heed yon fat trull. I'll gi'e ye wark a-plenty. I get a' the bonny sailor laddies comin' ben ma hoose."

The language itself was alien, not guttural but slurred in a way that made it sound sinister and depraved.

Elspeth walked faster. She had found the Babylon but she did not know what to do now. Where were the labourers, the unemployed hands that might listen to her proposal? She peeped apprehensively at a group of males ahead of her. Five or six of them lounged about a barrel, puffing on clays and swigging from a glass bottle. They were not old and yet they were burned out, scraped raw by indulgence and idleness.

One was tall, lily-skinned and wore the canvases of a carpenter. He held out the bottle to her. "Ha'e a wee nip, ma love."

"Aye," said a pot-bellied dwarf with a soiled wool cap dragged down over one eye. "Nip for a nip, eh-heh?"

A third fellow, stimulated by seeing a stranger in the unlovely street, stepped forward, not to accost her, but to show off his skill as a dancer. He hopped and kicked his bare brown feet for three or four seconds and then, exhausted and coughing, fell back against his companions who simply let him slide down to the paving as if he belonged on his back and not on his feet.

Elspeth glanced back at the group. They did not pursue her. She had left the women behind too. She had come to a section of the street where three or four hoardings gave a false impression of rising respectability.

Tenements tottered to the skyline, closing off the evening light. A peeling board caught her attention. She paused. She had a faint recollection of Thomas Rance mentioning the place. What had Mr Rance said? Heat, smells and tensions dulled her wits. Only thoughts of the family, of the threat of Georgie Haynes, of the impossibility of sustaining herself as a harness wife for long drove her on now.

THE BABYLON – BEDS FOR SAILORS – ALES & WINES

This was the lodging-house. Here casual labour was sure to be found, workers who did not have a bill to post in a craft house or a trade meeting-place.

At least no harlots flaunted themselves in the grimy windows and no loungers, stewed on bad whisky, hung about the door. The door itself was of unvarnished wood and stood an inch ajar. Beyond it was darkness, silence, and an odour of burnt potatoes.

Elspeth glanced down the street. The men by the barrel had lost interest in her and were throwing the legless dancer about between them as if he was a hobby-horse. She squared herself and pushed upon the door which swung reluctantly before her with a choked creak. She stepped over the worn step and went inside.

It was not Heaven's heartland. It was not, by the lights of Balnesmoor, say, 'respectable'. For all that, it was not a crib-shop nor a drinking-den. The dark woodwork of the hall led into a plain dark-wood corridor with several doors set into the panelling. At one time, long, long ago, perhaps it had been a mansion for a sea-captain, a comfortable dwelling filled with welcomes. There was no dirt, no litter in the hall, only a film of dust on everything as if it had been weeks or months since anybody had passed in or out of the portals.

Another board, a slate with whitewashed letters, was cocked on a horse nail by the corridor's end.

STAIRS – COME DOWN

At first Elspeth could not see the top of the stairs. They were tucked into a pitch-dark corner, flush with the wall almost, narrow as a gangplank and very steep. There was a corner on them too. It was not until she turned it that she found any sign of life. Light, and the strong odour of charred potatoes, drew her down on to the floor of the cellar where, she saw at once, the residents of The Babylon had hidden themselves away.

There were women in the broad room as well as men, two or three young children bundled in rags and at least one infant, which she could hear puling but could not separate from the shadows. The cellar was vaulted with brick pillars, and a huge hearth like a cave occupied the faraway wall. Though there had been no rain for days shirts and hose were hung on sagging ropes about it. In the hearth, amid a collection of blackened pots and pans, smoke reeked from a pile of dross and driftwood. Kneeling there was a tiny man with a coppery complexion and a brass earring in his ear. He wore baggy cotton trousers and a sleeveless vest the colour of seaweed. He was stirring a pot with a wooden spoon and, turning, saw Elspeth and winked at her. From what tropical country he came Elspeth had no notion but when he grinned she saw that his teeth had been filed to points as sharp as needles, saw too the long purple scars that marred – or decorated – each cheek.

"Mem," he said. "Mem a ted?"

She did not understand his question but when he lifted the dripping spurtle from the soup, held it to his mouth and waggled his tongue, Elspeth caught the gist of the invitation and, forcing a smile, shook her head.

"Mem ate?"

"No," Elspeth said. "I've had my supper, thank you."

In the rear portion of the room were two tables. A family occupied one of them, a man, woman and three young children. They were not taking supper, however, but used the table's surface to sort out pins. A mass of the cheap metal things littered a green cloth arranged for insertion into little mushrooms of cloth spread over twists of straw which were tied with strands of red wool. The children made the mushrooms, dexterous and fast, concentrating so thoroughly upon their work that they did not even notice Elspeth. With wetted fingers the woman dabbed up a bristle of the pins, pressed a dozen or so into each of the holders and, with a stretch of her arm, pushed it towards the man who transferred it as carefully as if it was a bubble of spun glass into a fish creel by his feet.

Opposite the industrious pin-sellers, his back to Elspeth, a scarred, blond-haired man, with a matted beard, was slumped over the table. A bottle was before him – whisky – and a tiny thimble-shaped vessel of silvery metal which he filled and flicked to his mouth. He put the vessel down, contemplated it, refilled it and tossed the contents into his mouth once more. He was strong-shouldered and wore trousers that had once been oiled, a shirt of heavy canvas material that, for coolness, he had loosed about his waist and chest.

He ignored Elspeth. Eight or ten men in the room regarded her from listless positions with only passing interest and no visible spark of curiosity. She did not know what to do. Something told her that it would be imprudent to announce to all and sundry that she could offer one man employment and a wage. What quality of man, what sort of grotesque, would put himself forward? How could she refuse him without giving offence? In the cellar of The Babylon there was no feeling of resentment or of angry frustration. Despair, a lowness of spirit, was the mood that Elspeth experienced. She advanced towards the pin-sellers only because they showed evidence of energy and industry.

The man looked up at her approach. His cheeks were stubbled, his complexion pale as fungus. The woman, not much older than Elspeth, was puffy, not fat. She had a pitted rash about her mouth and swollen knuckles. Tiny work, it seemed, told on the body too, took its toll as much as hauling or strapping and brought in less to spend on nourishment. The children had the build of whittle sticks; all girls, all younger than Sarah Bennet. The work did not cease when Elspeth approached. Only the man and the oldest girl even turned their eyes to her.

Elspeth said, "Who's the – the keeper of The Babylon?"

"He's ga'ed out," said the man.

"When will he be back?"

The man took a mushroom from his wife and laid it on to the others in the creel. Tomorrow they would tour the streets of Leith or Edinburgh and offer the little pin-rolls at a half-penny each. How much could be made by such miniature trade? Precious little, Elspeth realised.

The man said, "When it's time."

Without looking up the woman said, "Are ye seekin' lodgin'?"

"No," said Elspeth. "I – I have need for a workman."

She spoke without emphasis, almost a whisper. Even so, in the main chamber three or four lethargic heads lifted.

At the table opposite the pin-sellers, the fair-haired sailor gave a sigh, slid out his arms and laid his face between them as if the very hint of employment wearied him beyond endurance.

"What kind o' work?" said the man.

"Will ye have need o' family work?" said the woman.

"Only a man, for – for coal diggin'."

"Nah, nah." The man shook his head and popped another pin-cushion into the basket by his leg. "Nah, nah, nah."

"It pays good silver," said Elspeth.

"Not all the siller in a duke's coffers wad get me down yonder," the man said. "Nah, nah."

"Do ye know of anybody here—"

"They'll be in late."

"How many?" said Elspeth.

"Thirty or forty," said the woman. "It's cheap here. There's no drink sold on the premises, though some can find it. It's a family lodgin'. Clean enough, if chill in winter."

"How long have you been here?"

"These three year," the man answered.

Elspeth said, "Do ye think I'll find a coal-digger among the others?"

The man and woman shrugged in unison.

Elspeth seated herself on the end of the bench out of the way of that rhythmic industry. She noticed that the girls' fingers, pricked by the pins, were speckled with tiny gnat-bites of blood. When some seamstress, secure in her post, plucked a pin from the cushion and saw the tip of it stained with blood, would she think of how it had got there, and feel herself sustained by the thought of those scaled beneath her, those who must bleed, as well as sweat, for their porridge?

The airless cellar had affected Elspeth already. She felt weary, bleary with lack of light and sifting smoke from the fire. Since the pin-sellers did not object, she put an elbow on the table and rested her head on her hand. It was hopeless. Tomorrow she would return to Placket and its mess of problems, to Davy and Mouse and the threat of retaliation from the keelman, to grinding days in the black dust, dragging wagons to the shaft. But at the end of it there was money and here in the heart of the Babylon she could almost believe that it was worth it just to have a place and a penny in her pocket.

Tonight, though, she would buy a bed here. She had slept in worse places during her days on the road.

"What's the price of a night's lodging?" Elspeth asked.

"Down here on the straw it's one penny. Upstairs wi' a blanket it's three pence," the woman replied. "But you're no' the sort t' tarry long in the Babylon."

"No," said Elspeth. "I'll be goin' home tomorrow."

"Home." The woman shook her head wistfully. "What's your name, lass?"

"Elspeth Patterson."

She heard a grunt. She swung round and saw that the sailor had come round. He thrust himself up on his elbows and raised his head, stared at her out of icy blue eyes, wide with shock. His hair, as tangled as his beard, veiled half his face.

"'Pet?" He spoke in a hoarse whisper. "God an' Jesus! Is it yoursel', 'Pet?"

Knocking away the stool behind him, he shot to his feet, swayed and then, with a gesture that she remembered of old, swept the hair from his brow with the back of his hand.

"Do ye not know me, 'Pet?" he whispered.

"No, I—"

"It's Matt. Your brother-in-law, Matt Sinclair."

Perhaps it was the ale that he had consumed in the yard of the inn at Fintry after the buying of the buckram was done that had restored to Lachlan Sinclair some vestige of uprightness. He was not used to strong drink. Only the heat of the day and the fact that he had sweated heavily had persuaded him to indulge. He was far from drunk, however, and sat up very straight on the board of the cart with the reins firmly in his hands. He had rebuffed Sandy's offer to drive. He had taken charge of Maisie with much of his old authority.

Sandy was both amused and puzzled by his father's stiff attitude but he was no longer a boy who could be awed by it. He had grown into his own man and, while he would obey his father, he would not back down from a quarrel if he thought the old chap was wrong.

There was no quarrel in the air, however. Maisie jogged the light-loaded cart along, heading by a string road for the bridge at Honeywell which would carry them over the Endrick and west to the Lightwater.

It was as fine a day as there had been that summer, blue and hot, with the broom bright yellow on the banks. Sandy had drunk his share of Wilson's brew but he was younger and more used to it and it did no more than refresh him. He felt fine and easy as he swayed on the board by his father's side. It did not occur to him that it was aught else but the ale that had stiffened Lachlan so.

They were half-way home to Strachan before Lachlan cleared his throat – and cleared it again. Sandy hardly noticed. He put it down to the dust that Maisie's hoofs kicked up now that the ruts had finally dried out. Sandy leaned elbows on knees, gently swaying.

Lachlan Sinclair cleared his throat once more.

"Son." He began in the sort of tone that he had once reserved for reading Scripture in the kirk. "Son, it has not escaped my attention that you're attracted to your sister-in-law."

Sandy squinted in surprise at his father who was watching the mare's ears flick and tail whisk.

"Anna! She's—" Sandy could not find words.

"She's the legal wife of your brother."

"I know that fine."

"I'll confess that she's bonnie."

"She's all that," Sandy agreed.

"But she can never be right for you."

"I'm no' daft, Father. I know the law."

"Until her dyin' day – may that be far hence – Anna Cochran will be forbid t'you, son."

"Aye, aye." Sandy tried to make light of it.

He had known all along that marriage with Anna was impossible. Alive or dead Matt had full claim on her. The odd thing was that he could not stop wanting her, not just to bed with her but to make her his own. Yet he bridled at his father's tone, resented the fact that his father was forcing him to admit the futility of being in love with Anna.

"Do not dismiss my advice," said Lachlan sternly.

"Even if it was possible," said Sandy, "do ye think for a minute Anna'd have the likes o' me for a husband?"

"I'm sure she would."

Sandy darted a glance at his father but the man stared at the leafy hedges and sweep of the fields.

"Has she – has she told ye as much?"

"Sandy," his father warned.

Sandy nodded. "It's hard, Daddy, wi' her livin' so close."

"Resist her," said Lachlan Sinclair. "Resist wi' all your might. I've had enough with Matt, with the trouble he brought to us. I could not stand by to see you ruin yourself o'er the same girl."

Resentment came again in Sandy. Could his father not see that he would do nothing dishonourable, that he had resisted so far and would resist into infinity? He might be drawn to Anna but he was not blind to the dangers of loving her. There was too much of the grieve in him, too much of his father's moral dignity, for him to take her against her will. It was love not loving that he wanted from Anna Cochran.

"It matters not a toss," said Sandy, with a sigh. "Anna's still yearnin' for Randall Bontine."

"The laird's had his fling with her, Sandy. She was a fool to be taken by him, but it was understandable."

"Understandable?"

"She was flattered by the laird's attentions. I canna hold it against her, try though I might."

"Aye, but what about Sir Randall? Surely it was wicked o' him to take her when she was married t'your son?"

"Anna – Anna is—" Lachlan Sinclair could not confess that he too had felt the attraction of the dark-haired girl. He had made his defence of the laird of Ottershaw, of the whole Bontine tradition. He trusted his son not to push him too far lest the edifice on which he had constructed his existence slumped still further. "Anna is – Anna."

"Matt's wife," said Sandy.

"It's time that Anna thought of releasin' him."

"That's a queer way o' puttin' it," said Sandy, "since it's our Matt who did the desertin'."

"High time she married," said Lachlan Sinclair. "Aye, and you too, Sandy."

"I've no mind to marry."

"You need to marry. You're of an age to marry."

"Father, I'm barely twenty."

"There's Edith."

"Edith?" said Sandy. "God in Heaven!"

"She'd make ye a good obedient wife."

"An' would continue to serve the Bontines, I suppose?"

"Your mother an' I will not live for ever," said Lachlan. "If Edith's not to your likin', take one of Davidson's daughters. Fine girls they are, always with a laugh on their lips."

"I'm not denyin' it," said Sandy. "But I hardly know them."

"Come now, you're no shy laddie. You've been boastin' to me, not a minute since, that—"

Sandy interrupted. "Leave the findin' o' a wife to me, if you please."

"Put Anna Cochran out of your mind, Sandy, that's all I ask."

"Aye, aye," said Sandy, angry now.

"Swear to me."

"I told you I wouldn't—"

"Swear."

"Very well," said Sandy truculently. "I swear."

Physically Matt was so much changed that he seemed like a stranger; yet the questions that tumbled from his lips carried Elspeth back to that dreadful time when she too had been faced with decisions, to the night when she had found incontrovertible proof that James was her father. Matt, of course, had no knowledge of that discovery. For Matt the life of the good folk of Ottershaw and Balnesmoor had become frozen at the night he had ridden off on Sabre, Randall Bontine's stallion, to escape the officers of the law and evade a hangman's noose.

"I told the truth, 'Pet. I never killed yon mannie. Well, I did, I suppose, but it was not done in cold blood. He killed the shopkeepers an' was lurkin' in the store to do me harm."

"I believe you, Matt."

"What of the others? Do they believe me?"

"I canna say. I left Balnesmoor only days after you."

"Because o' me?"

"Because of what you told me about my – my husband."

"He had it done. Moodie ordered the murder."

"Yes," said Elspeth. "I think it's true. He did."

"Can I go back?"

"How can you? I doubt if there's proof that another hand fired the shop at Kennart or that you killed only to defend yourself. Proof will always lie against you, Matt."

Matt had embraced her across the table, much to the astonishment of the pin-seller's family; then he had drawn her away to the privacy of a small table in an alcove. Furtive and possessive, he had trapped her there with questions and with talk of his 'adventures' while the poor residents of the Babylon trailed in from their pursuit of employment and set about preparing a pick of fish or dish of gruel, gathered about the smoking fire.

"Tell me, have you heard from Anna?"

"Matt, I've heard from nobody. I know no more of the village than you do."

"Is she still wi' Randall Bontine?"

"I just do not know."

"How did ye find out I was here?"

"I didn't. It was chance; a wild coincidence."

"Did ye not come for me?"

"No, Matt. How could I possibly know where you were?"

"Aye." He nodded. "If Anna found out I was here she'd spiff me to the King's officers. It was my fault, though. I never loved her enough. I wanted money. I wanted money t' spend on her, to woo her away from Bontine."

Elspeth let him talk. He had not asked obvious questions, had not sought to find out what purpose had really brought her here or where she lived or what she did or how her daughter thrived. For the time being, Matt was his selfish old in-centred self; yet he was changed too. The arrogance had gone. Uncertainty was manifest in his quick nervous movements and the tension with which he clung, now and then, to Elspeth's hand as if he feared that she was a figment of some drunken dream and would vanish if he did not hold her to him. Not for the first time Elspeth found that she pitied Matt Sinclair more than she despised him.

He poured out a thimble of whisky and tipped it into his mouth. "Christ, do ye know, I *had* money. I earned a walletful o' money on the whalers. Two voyages I made, each one successful."

"Whalers?" said Elspeth. "Is that where you went, to sea?"

"One week after I horsed out o' the Lennox I was stuck in this port. I'd no notion o' what to do wi' myself. I harboured a daft idea I might find passage on a ship to the Americas. Then an agent approached me. I thought he was a bloody sheriff at first but he was just an agent for a whaling line, crewin' for a voyage."

"In winter?" said Elspeth.

"Nah, nah," said Matt. "He wanted a crew signed before the spring. He had a square-rigger set up for a whale-oil run."

"I've not heard o' a 'whale-oil run', Matt."

"A man named McNeil owns three whalers here in Leith. He owns the blubber works too. When the catch is returned and the blubber rendered down, he ships it o'er to the Low Countries an' into parts o' France, even Spain. Whale-ships carry the cargo through the heavy winter seas. They have

281

double hulls, strengthened against the ice, y'see, an' furnish oil at a time when the sea trade's low. Sound business, 'Pet.''

"But you aren't a sailor."

"I learned right quick on the cargo voyages," said Matt. "I was better than a green hand by the time we returned t' Leith. While the *Argo* was fittin' for the whaling season we were paid a small daily fee on the promise we'd not sign on wi' somebody else. The ship was all crewed, y' see, an' ready for a sprint t' the whalin' grounds the instant the weather cleared. It was a race t' reach the Arctic regions before the boats from Whitby or Hull. Mr McNeil's captains are always fast away."

Matt talked on and on as if he had bottled up the story of his travels and the privations he had suffered for months, with no sympathetic ear to listen to it. Elspeth listened in fascination while Matt told her how the cold ate into the body so that your heart and lungs seemed made of ice. He spoke of foul, weevil-ridden food and the cramped, heaving confines of the fo'c'sle, of climbing the shrouds in sheets of icy rain, of rowing a whale boat after great leviathans of the deep day after day until your hands bled and your spine was bent like a sheepshank. He did not make the whaling seem glamorous or brag of his achievements. The gambler in Matt had been reduced by hardships that the sailor born takes for granted. Money had not compensated for suffering. The son of the grieve of Ottershaw found that he could not bring himself to sign for a third voyage.

Matt stroked his beard. "Scurvy, sailors call it," he said. "I thought I was like t' die of it. Frost hides Greenland. Frost so sharp it strips the flesh off your bones. See." He offered his cheek as if for a kiss. "Without hair on my face I'm a sight t' make dogs bark an' bairns cry out." He grinned. "It's a fine disguise for an outlaw, is it not?"

"I – I would not have known you, Matt."

"I call m'self Shearer now. Matthew Shearer. I signed that name on my articles. I've grown used to it. I made up stories about where I came from, about my family. From Ayrshire, I say I am."

Outlaws; they were both outlaws, Elspeth realised. She was also in hiding, not from officers of the Crown but from her husband. They talked on. Matt paused now and then to listen to his sister-in-law or to sup the whisky which, he claimed, had been bought with the last of his savings.

"I live here," he said at length. "Here in this hole wi' strangers."

"Have you no friends, Matt?"

"Only companions in starvation," Matt answered. "I scrounge a day's work here an' there down at the coal dumps, scooping dross."

"Coal, perhaps, that I dug out o' the Abbeyfield."

"It could be so," said Matt. "Is money t' be made in the diggin'?"

"Fair money."

"Have you money in your purse now, 'Pet?"

"I have some, aye."

"We should celebrate our reunion in a more comfortable establishment than the Babylon," said Matt. "I know an inn by the Shore that has good beds."

"Matt, I'm here for a special purpose."

Matt blinked. It had not yet occurred to him that Elspeth had not deliberately followed his tracks.

"What purpose could you have in this hole?"

"I'm seekin' a man t' dig for us," Elspeth explained. "I was told I might find one here."

"So you might." Matt cocked his head and squinted at her. "How does a hewer get paid?"

"By the quantity o' coal he digs out."

"No truck?"

"Cash in his hand on the Abbeyfield."

"Cash in hand, eh! Must be a rare sort o' place."

"Jock Bennet, the hewer I worked for, was killed by a fall in the seam. Since then his girls an' I have not been able to earn what we're worth as daughters to a hewer."

"I'll dig for ye," said Matt without hesitation.

"I'm not sure it's for you, Matt."

"Am I not handsome enough for ye, 'Pet?"

"It's not that. Deep seam work needs skill."

"I can learn."

It was not Matt's ability to learn that made Elspeth hesitate. She did not doubt that he had strength and she had no more than a passing qualm about his influence upon the Bennets. Matt was no longer a boy. Much of his stubborn temper had been wrung out of him. But he was big, perhaps too big for the cramping spaces of a base-level seam. He had not been reared in narrow places, might not be able to endure them.

"I'm not afeared o' tight places, Elspeth, if that's what you're thinkin'," he said. "I can learn quick how t' cut coal off a wall. It canna be that difficult. God, if I can learn how to clamber up shrouds in a snowstorm an' tie a knot wi' my teeth, I can learn how t' lie on my belly an' put a nail into a coal seam."

"What plans had you made on your own account, Matt?"

"Plans?" He laughed and shook his head. "I had plans t' finish this bottle, eat a cog o' stew then doss in the straw till tomorrow."

"And tomorrow?"

Once more he shook his head, spread his hands, shrugged.

"Another day," Matt said. "Just like t'day."

Elspeth glanced over her shoulder.

The cellar had filled now for evening had laid melancholy shadows over the streets of Leith. The weary and irresolute felt the coming of night as keenly as any shepherd with a croft light winking in the vale or a ploughman with chimney smoke to guide him past the day's last furrow. Perhaps the folk of the Babylon felt it even more; they congregated meekly, making no great chatter or clatter of noise, going about their chores with charitable regard for their neighbours, bundled cheek by jowl into this house for the homeless.

Matt might have changed his name and his appearance, but he was still kin to the community of Balnesmoor. Elspeth felt obligated to rescue him from the company of these apathetic strangers.

She said, "We're paid only what we earn, Matt."

"You haul the coal out, is that it?"

"Two of us. There's a Bennet girl."

"Is this pit, this Abbeyfield, rich in coal pickin's?"

"We've a secret seam, very deep underground. We found it by chance an' have kept it hidden."

"So that's it," Matt said.

"There's a year's good wage in it. An' it's all ours."

284

"An' no man knows who you are, Elspeth?"

"I tell them I'm the widow o' a drover."

"An' no man will know me?"

"No, or care who you are," Elspeth said.

Whether she would have chosen Matt or not was of no moment. She had chanced on him and chance had bound her to him. She could not reject him. He was eager, roused, keen for the adventure or the money he might make – or to take what he might from her in other ways.

"We'll not stay here," Matt said. "I've had enough o' the Babylon."

He rose suddenly and grabbed Elspeth's hand.

"Come on," he said. "We'll bide tonight in the Shore Inn, ready for a crossin' first thing tomorrow. Have you chink enough for that, 'Pet?"

"Matt, I—"

His face clouded in sudden anxiety, fear of rebuff. "Do ye not want me, 'Pet?"

Elspeth's heart gave a tumble at the pathos in his voice.

"Of course, Matt. Of course I want you."

"Come then," he said.

He drew her by the hand out of the cellar and along the corridor, shouting out to some unseen person, the owner of the Babylon, that he had no more need of dry straw and that his day's bill for a seat in the dark was paid.

In the street the harlots packed the windows and whale-oil lanterns smoked outside the dismal taverns, flocked with men. The loungers did not jeer at her now, however, and the women in the windows merely stared, for Matt had taken her arm possessively and held her close as they hurried the length of the Babylon towards the Shore.

Elspeth no longer knew what it meant.

But she did not let him go.

EIGHT

Marriage Four Square

It was the gaunt Alicia who brought ruin to the Bontines. She did it adamantly but in innocence. Alicia was sure that she knew more of money matters than the brothers Pryde who, so Gilbert informed her, would have nothing whatsoever to do with mineral investments.

"Has this fellow Bolderon not put an excellent proposal?"

Gibbie was fatigued after a long day in his chambers in Falkirk and a long hot ride back home. All he wanted was a glass of claret and his supper, not a lecture on commerce from his wife.

"Yes, it's a sound venture," said Gilbert.

"What is its essence?"

"The coal pit of which Bolderon's manager requires a modest influx of capital for exploration and development work."

"Which Mr Bolderon wishes you to supply?"

"Indeed."

"And his terms?"

"Bolderon proposes to sell a share of *his* share in the profits for the term of the lease; nineteen years."

"Bolderon is not the owner of the land, is he?"

"No, only a share-holding manager. The landowner retains majority." Gibbie unloosed his necktie, slipped off his shoes, sat back on the little divan. The parlour was misty with the sunset and, apart from the clacking of Alicia's tongue, quite peaceful. "Alicia, may I have a glass of claret?"

Alicia ignored his request. "Why is capital so urgently required?"

"To break into new coal seams. Lines must be expertly charted in advance to save time and money in tunnelling."

"Is the landowner so impoverished that he cannot find

money for such essential work?" said Alicia. "Who *is* the landowner?"

"Hector Fotheringham of Placket."

"I have heard of Mr Fotheringham. He married on to the Mitchells, did he not?"

"I really could not say, Alicia."

"What did the Prydes say when you put Bolderon's proposition to them?" said Alicia. "What reason did they give for refusing to consider granting, at least, a loan?"

"Too risky."

"Do you think it's risky, Gilbert?"

"I really do not know, Alicia. Mr Bolderon seems to believe that there's coal in quantity upon the present field, that it requires only a modest investment to make it available to his miners."

"What is a modest investment?"

"Four or five thousand pounds."

"I see," said Alicia. "Mr Bolderon, however, is only the manager."

"With a guaranteed share in the profits."

"Does he *own* property?"

"Alicia, how would—"

"Hector Fotheringham's the person with whom you must make your arrangement, Gilbert," Alicia said. "Fotheringham owns the land. Is it not a fact that reputable bankers will lend money to most landed gentlemen?"

"With some exceptions, yes."

"Write to Mr Fotheringham, Gilbert."

"Alicia, I cannot simply make a loan like – like that."

"The bank would benefit from owning a share of a coal pit, would it not?" said Alicia and, without awaiting an answer, went on. "Clearly, Gilbert, purchase of a share in a coal pit would be very rewarding. It would take the bank out of pennyweight trading with scrofulous cattle dealers and niggardly farmers."

"I would have to peruse the pit's trading account to answer your—"

"If the Prydes will not show a spirit of adventure, Gilbert, perhaps you should lead the way."

"Alicia, I'm hungry and weary, and—"

"Will you write to Fotheringham?"

"Yes, if you wish. But, I warn you, I cannot extract capital from the Farmers' Bank on my own cognisance; at least, not to buy share."

"Use Moodie's money."

"Alicia! Moodie's money lies in trust."

"Does it not earn interest?"

"Well, yes, but it's invested piecemeal; and very securely."

"Are you not responsible for it?"

"The bank is—"

"Take a portion in share; outright," said Alicia. "Make a loan of the residue, up to Fotheringham's needs, at one per cent above rate interest—"

"I'm the banker, Alicia. Please do not intervene in—"

"How much is Moodie's allotment?"

"Twelve thousand pounds."

"Twelve thousand pounds wasted."

"What if she – if Elspeth Moodie should return?" said Gilbert.

"Hildebrand has not traced hilt nor hair of the woman, has he?"

"No, not so far. But—"

"It might lie for years, that twelve thousand pounds."

"On the other hand, Alicia, it might be required next week or next month."

"Where is *your* spirit of enterprise, Gilbert?"

"Well, I suppose it would do no harm to communicate with Fotheringham. I do take your point; he is the landowner and, as such, is the person with whom I should be dealing."

"At last, Gilbert, you're showing some sense."

"Now, Alicia, may I have a glass and my supper?"

"Certainly, dearest," Alicia said and, rising, rang a bell to summon one of the Sinclairs from the servants' hall.

In spite of his best efforts Angus Hildebrand had raised not one scrap of information concerning the whereabouts of the heiress of Moss House. To a degree he was concerned about his lack of progress. On the other hand he relished the challenge of contest with the Moodie sisters. He had all but abandoned his other legal clients to give his undivided attention to the management of the affairs of the late James Simpson Moodie. Hildebrand was an honest man. Even so he would feather his nest quite nicely from extractions made under the terms of the will.

Both he and Tolland were aware that Moodie had taken his own life, had thrown himself into the rushing waters of the Lightwater with the deliberate intention of removing himself from the scene and making the way clear for his wife and daughter to return. It was an act of folly, of madness, of course; yet it had about it just a touch of noble self-sacrifice. It would seem even more 'decent' to Hildebrand and Tolland if only the blessed woman could be found and the martyr's cause given fulfilment in a happy ending.

There was nothing in the wide world that the lawyer could do to expedite that conclusion, however, except exercise his patience and fend off the sisters who had now enlisted the services of professionals to prepare their case for an appeal to the courts. Without doubt, it would take years for a decision to be reached on the matter. Even if it should eventually go against the absent heiress Angus Hildebrand was confident that management of the Moodie case would see him comfortably into old age. He spent a great deal of time as a 'guest' in Moss House, checking each and every item of expenditure that in any way affected the Moodie estates. There was a 'domestic account' upon which Tom Tolland was empowered to draw to upkeep the mansion and to feed himself and his maid-servant.

There was also a much more complex system of accounting related to Kennart mill. To understand the language of the wool-stapler and the manufacturer Angus Hildebrand summoned Robert Rudge to a regular weekly meeting in Moss House. It took Mr Hildebrand several weeks to master the jargon of the woollen industry and several weeks more to pick his way down to those unexplained items in the accounting that seemed to cause Mr Rudge such embarrassment. Mr Hildebrand did not challenge Mr Rudge nor did he pursue his enquiries to the point where he might accuse Mr Rudge of embezzlement or theft. He simply made it very clear that nothing would escape his scrutiny and that in future Mr Rudge had better not be 'embarrassed' by anything.

Among those clients whose affairs Angus Hildebrand did

continue to administer the laird of Ottershaw came top of the list. Randall Bontine was involved not only in consolidating the earning power of Bontine lands but in preparing for his forthcoming marriage to the lady from Piperhaugh. To formalise his proposal and make the necessary arrangements in respect of the dowry it had been necessary for Randall to travel north and to put on, for a week of gracious hospitality, his most gentlemanly aspect. When he returned he presented Hildebrand with several contracts that would give him income from the rentals of a nice little parcel of Seaton land to add to that from Ottershaw.

If Randall Bontine was top of Angus Hildebrand's list of important clients June brought him one to add to the bottom – a female of no rank and with hardly a penny to call her own. Nonetheless Hildebrand did not disregard the letter he received from Anna Sinclair. On the contrary, he had reply delivered by special rider within a day of receipt. He was only too well aware that Anna Sinclair's rank might quickly change when her sister returned to claim her inheritance. In due course a meeting was arranged at Moss House. Mrs Sinclair arrived in a gig driven by a fresh-faced handsome young fellow whom Tolland identified as the girl's brother-in-law, Alexander. Anna entered Moss House alone, however, and with a haughty nod to Tolland took herself straight into the drawing-room.

Angus Hildebrand assumed that Anna Cochran Sinclair was concerned with separating herself from her outlawed husband. To the lawyer's surprise, however, Anna's first question was, "Have you heard any word on my sister, Mr Hildebrand?"

Hildebrand said that he had not.

Anna asked then a pointed question about the disposition of Moodie's wealth which Hildebrand coolly answered.

She was a pretty girl, very pretty, with dark hair and eyes. Hildebrand was wary of such beauty. He had not always been a dry old stick and had had his encounters with 'heartbreakers' in the past, usually to his detriment. Offhand he could think of a dozen gentlemen who would have snapped up Anna Sinclair as wife or mistress. She was wasted here in Balnesmoor, lost in Strachan.

Angus Hildebrand cleared his throat. "I believe," he said, "that you wish to discuss the dissolution of your marriage to Matthew Sinclair?"

"Aye, I do," said Anna.

"On grounds of desertion?"

"Aye. Not the other one."

"Other one?"

"Adultery." Modestly she averted her glance.

"As your husband is sought by the law for a crime in which you were not involved, and in which you took only innocent part," said Hildebrand, winding himself up, "there would appear to be no impediment whatsoever to the said dissolution. I take it that you are not currently entangled, shall we say, with another male person?"

"What does that mean?"

"Living as wife to another man."

"I am not."

"No, Mrs Sinclair, I did not believe you were. I merely address to you the sort of questions that a court officer will wish answered before sanctioning your bill of divorcement."

"Matt's a murderer. He's gone for good."

"I must correct you on that score," said Hildebrand. "Your husband, Matthew Sinclair, is *not* a murderer. He may be *suspected* of having committed the crime of murder and, thus, be a person sought by the law but he is *not*, I repeat, a murderer until he is so proven."

"Very well." Anna primped her hair in annoyance. "But he's a – a fugitive, is he not?"

"He is. And you may seek a divorce. And that divorce will almost certainly be granted to you," said Angus Hildebrand. "If you wish it I will represent your petition when the time comes."

"When will the time come?"

"How long is it since you last co-habited with your husband?"

"Thirty-four months."

"Have you not heard from your husband in that time?"

"No, not a word."

"In fourteen months' time you may, therefore, petition the court to free you by divorce from your marriage to this man."

"Will you act as my—"

"If you can afford my fee, Mrs Sinclair."

"What will it cost?"

"Ground of wilful desertion requires an oath of calumny as well as evidence of desertion, even if the accused does not appear to tender objection. In the region of seven pounds would be my charge."

"I'll pay it."

"Seven pounds, Mrs Sinclair? Do you have as much?"

"I can get it."

"May I enquire if you wish to be divorced from your husband in order that you may marry again?"

"I may marry again, aye."

"Will the gentleman pay my fee, is that the intention?"

"Aye, he might."

"It would not be advisable to tell the officer that."

"Why not?" said Anna.

"Heed my advice. Keep the source of payment to yourself."

"I may decide not t' marry, of course."

"Have you been made a proposal of marriage?"

"Aye, I have."

"Have you given indication that you will accept, after you become free so to do?"

"I've said I'll consider it."

"I trust that the gentleman in question is not the young man who brought you here in the gig?"

Hildebrand noted how her lips pursed and a soft flush spread across her cheeks. The polished black eyes were brittle. He had heard that she had a temper and was wilful and, seeing her now, Hildebrand could well believe it.

"I canna marry Sandy Sinclair. He's my husband's brother."

"In that case you certainly may not marry him. It is forbidden by the Scottish laws."

"Even if Matt dies?" she asked.

Hildebrand sighed through his nose. She cared for the handsome young Sinclair, of that he was sure. It might even be that the appointment had been for no other purpose than to have him confirm that she could not, under any circumstance, become wife to another Sinclair, trading the older for the younger.

Angus Hildebrand said, "Even if your husband dies and can be proved to be dead, you cannot marry his brother."

"I thought as much," said Anna. "Aye."

She lifted her shoulders high, let them sink and, in the same motion, flung out her hands, palms uppermost. For all his experience in reading the mannerisms of witnesses and would-be clients, the lawyer could not interpret Anna's gesture. Was she shrugging off her brother-in-law or, God forbid, was she shrugging off the law?

"I cannot recommend that you ignore this point of law," said Hildebrand. "It would be against Christian teaching. Also, in latter years, it will lead to confusion about the status of your child."

"How will it concern Robbie?"

"Take me at my word," said Hildebrand, who did not wish to offer the young woman even the slender hope that she might find happiness out of wedlock in the arms of Sandy Sinclair. "It would not be at all to your son's benefit."

"Robbie has no inheritance."

"Be that as it may, marriage four-square is the only sort of marriage that operates to the benefit of all parties and for the good of our society."

Anna tossed her head arrogantly as if to indicate that she thought herself above society's laws.

She said, "It's of no consequence, Mr Hildebrand. I want nothin' more to do wi' Sinclairs, any Sinclairs, once I'm divorced from Matt. I wouldna have Sandy for a husband even if the law was lax enough for it t' be possible an' he crawled o'er coals o' fire to get me."

"Yet you do have a suitor?"

"Aye. No stable-hand. He's a gentleman, a real fine gentleman."

If the girl had been the victim of an errant rogue who had grown weary of hearthside and a husband's duties, if she had not been Anna Sinclair and a shade notorious, Hildebrand would not have given her the satisfaction of rising to the bait. But he was curious as to the nature of the man who would take on such a firebrand.

He said, "May I ask, who is this gentleman?"

"None other than Mr Rudge," said Anna. "Mr Rudge o' Kennart."

For once, Angus Hildebrand was struck speechless by the *coup de théâtre* that Anna Sinclair had impulsively pulled off and by the little smile of triumph and despair that settled on her lips.

Matt was hard at work within a day of his arrival on the Abbeyfield. Thomas Rance was not wholly taken in by the tale that Matthew Shearer, backed by Elspeth, told to him and suspected that the woman had found Shearer on the dumps of the Coalhill and had lured him away from there as much by her looks as by the promise of fat money. But Thomas Rance, who had a fondness for Mrs Patterson, turned a blind eye on his suspicions. He told Snippets to write Mr Shearer's name upon the books and was surprised as well as gratified when, within an hour of Matt Shearer's descent to the base seam, coal came out to the tally basket.

Matt Shearer did not look like a collier; he was far too large. He had no softness about him, though, and his scarred hands indicated that he was no stranger to hard work. Beard and long locks set him apart from his fellow hewers and he was known, in response to rumour, as 'the sailorman'.

What astonished Elspeth was the eagerness with which Matt fell into the work of coal cutting. He learned quickly, worked tirelessly and did not seem in the least cramped in the tiny seam.

Elspeth remembered her brother-in-law as an idler and shirker. She wondered what had caused the change in him. Was it the events of that night in September when the storekeepers at Kennart were murdered or was it his experiences on whalers? Was it, perhaps, the months spent sucking on a whisky bottle in the stagnant backwater of the Babylon? Whatever had caused the change it was much for the better. At last Matt seemed to have realised that there was hope and satisfaction in honest application, however monotonous and uncomfortable the job.

Each morning Matt was first to the top of the shaft. Each shift's end he clambered from the bucket exhausted and sore but quite undeterred, demanding to be told the weight of his day's cut and how much he had earned on the tally. In the evenings Matt too showed evidence of a sea-change in character. He was no longer the surly boy, sulking and complaining, but immediately took on the role of man of the house with an authority that even Davy came to respect.

Sarah was in awe of the incomer. Mary Jean in her outgoing way soon made friends with him and would run to greet Matt as well as Elspeth each evening and would beg for a ride on his shoulders, to be carried home in high style. Only Mouse did not take to the stranger. She would not speak to him at all. She snapped at Elspeth when the woman tried to foster harmony, would turn pointedly away when Matt made friendly advances, even ignored his peace offerings of gingerbread and almonds. Matt could not replace her father. He was not family, not even a coal-hewer. Mouse could not forgive him for being capable of cutting coal at all.

Elspeth was careful not to reveal details of her past connection with Matt Shearer. By agreement they never spoke of Balnesmoor within earshot of the Bennets, especially Mouse. What Matt did talk of, though, were his days at sea. Burgeoning pride and a desire to consolidate his position made him into a story-teller of no mean imagination. He did not dwell on suffering or reveal the wounds caused by loneliness and hardship. He made tales out of reality, tales worth telling, tales to fascinate Davy, Sarah and Mary Jean.

Matt talked of great ships, jagged mountains of green ice, of a sea frozen hard and thick as a coal seam, of whales blowing jets of steam from holes in their heads. He spoke of the courage of the mighty sea-beasts who would haul a ship for miles, with blood pouring out of them and harpoons bristling in their sides. He made Mary Jean cry out of pity for the big fishies and instantly changed tack to tell of an Irish cook who could play the fiddle while standing on his head and dance a jig in the air. But later, when Mary Jean was snuggled in bed, Davy would draw Matt back to speak of the life of a whale-catching man and would click his tongue and cough, shake his head and say in a tone of wistful annoyance, "B'God, though, I wisht I could have been with you, Matt. I wisht I had the stomach t' be a sailor."

"Aye, it's too hard a drag for you right now, Davy," Matt would say. "But when you're fit an' well again, if the mood's still on ye, I'll see if I can find a kindly captain who'll sign you on for a season or two."

"I'll never be fit," Davy would say.

Matt would punch him softly on the chin and wink. "Best keep well, lad. I'll be needin' a man beside me when we break deeper into yon coal cave."

But it was simpler for Davy Bennet to yearn for the unattainable than to torture himself with thoughts of a goal that he could not quite reach.

In Matt, Davy had found a hero. He wished that Georgie Haynes would come back to plague his sisters. He would tell Sarah, during the long sunny mornings, what Matt would do to the keelman, describe in bloody detail the punishment that Matt would mete out to Haynes, until Sarah would wrinkle her nose and beg him to stop since it was making her sick just to think of it. Georgie Haynes, however, did not appear in Placket in that season.

The colliers did not make Matt Shearer welcome. Like Mouse they resented his intrusion. They vowed that when his giant frame got stuck in some tight hole they would not sweat to fetch him out with a rope round the ankles. He was too large a man for them, too open, too secret, a mystery, a paradox, and not wise in the ways of the coalman's trade. When, on pay-night, he came into the Grapes to buy drink they turned their backs on him and would not reply to his greeting. If Shearer wanted their friendship he would damned-well have to earn it – and that could take years.

"I expected no more, 'Pet," Matt confided stoically. "It would be the same if a wee black-breeked collier appeared in Balnesmoor for the reapin'."

Later on that first pay-night, when Matt lay on the new palliasse he had bought at Nicol's and had unrolled beneath the kitchen table, arms folded behind his head, he had whispered into the darkness, "You're not sorry ye found me, Elspeth, are you?"

From behind the curtain in the corner, Elspeth answered, "I'm anythin' but sorry, Matt."

He laughed. "I feel that I've found my place. Even if it is

shut off from light an' air there's no taint o' Sinclair here, 'Pet. No Randall Bontine t' call the tune. It's a proper place this for a blackguard like me an' I'll hold it as long as I can."

Elspeth heard the new straw rustle. She stiffened a little on her mattress in the corner. She half expected him to come to her in the darkness, to show that he wanted more from her than a place on the floor now that he had proved his worth. But Matt did not come near. She wondered at it. She did not realise that Matt had no more desire for her than she had for him, that they were tied by decent needs and cleansed by the sharing of sins and sorrows that had chased them both from home out into the world. She would never be common wife to Matt Sinclair Shearer. The Abbeyfield women could think what they liked. Colliers could snigger over the rolled palliasse and imagine that the sailor was doing a hornpipe of a different sort but what passed between a woman and a man was private and subtle, shaped by the heart to accommodate particular needs and, if nature so elected, might not be a thing of matching and mating but of affection and respect.

Besides, within a three-month, Matt Shearer would find another girl, one who knew him only for what he was and not what he had been before his term in the Babylon.

Randall would have seen through the Fotheringhams in a trice but Gibbie, a simple soul, was completely taken in by the ambiance of Monksfoot Priory. Unlike Keir Bolderon, Gibbie did not find Margaret in the least bloodless. She seemed to him to represent a perfect type of Scottish gentlewoman, beautiful, modest, gracious and touched with piety, a perfect match for her husband, Hector, whose elegance and noble bearing stamped every word with sincerity. Wined and dined on the best that the Priory had to offer, Gibbie was taken to walk about the grounds in the company of the landowner. He was not, however, offered a tour of the Abbeyfield, was not introduced to Mr Thomas Rance or any other person who might spoil the illusion that mining coal was akin to mining gold and as steady as the Bank of England. He was held at a distance by Hector Fotheringham's suavity, but, before he retired to bed in the beautifully appointed guest-room on the second floor of the Priory, was given a folder of emerald-green morocco leather within which, in immaculate copperplate handwriting, were the Abbeyfield's trading figures for the preceding five-year period. The copperplate handwriting was Hector Fotheringham's. The figures would not have been recognisable to Snippets Smith or to the agent in the Bank of Scotland with whom Mr Fotheringham had previously done business. That inveterate reader of *Blackwood's*, Keir Bolderon, would have identified the accounts at once as pure fiction.

When Gibbie dared to mention Keir Bolderon's name, Mr Fotheringham gave a tinkle of laughter and waved away the manager's authority as he might have dismissed a daft gardener, spoke in the sort of indulgent tone he might have reserved for discussing the misdeeds of a scallywag son.

"Quite!" said Gibbie, a shade embarrassed at bringing up the topic. "Quite, quite!"

"So, do you see, sir, how it is with Mr Bolderon? I do not question, you understand, his *intention*. Oh, certainly not. He intends only to do well by me and by the Abbeyfield. But it was *mischievous* of him to pretend to you that he had *authority*. Out of the goodness of my heart and because I value his service I allowed him a share in profits for a limited term; the residual period of the lease, in effect. One must encourage trust, do you not think, Mr Bontine?"

"Indeed, indeed!" said Gibbie.

"It's one's duty to demonstrate to the servant that he is valued, do you not think?"

"Quite!" said Gibbie. Lachlan Sinclair popped into his mind as corroboration. "But is it not within Mr Bolderon's power to promise return on circulating capital?"

"Circulating capital?" said Fotheringham in an odd sort of tone that had Gibbie wondering if he had misused the term. "Oh, yes, I see what you mean, sir. Yes, Mr Bolderon can offer nothing."

"He seemed to think—"

"Nothing."

"Oh!"

"On the other hand Mr Bolderon has done us both a considerable service by bringing us each into the other's ken, has he not?"

"I would say so, yes," Gibbie answered.

Before them lay the silvery Forth, dotted with sails, a plume of smoke from some burning or other lying far off on the nether shore, the hills calm in the approaching dusk. Fotheringham's hand was on his sleeve. Gibbie was flattered by the gentleman's touch, grateful to Alicia for pressing him to this connection with nobility. Even though Mr Fotheringham had no title to speak of, he had a beautiful wife and a priory, owned much land, quality land, not hill acres and bog as on Ottershaw. No doubt he grazed a few cows, perhaps the odd flock of mutton, a hog or two in a sty well away from the gardens but this was land in use, land diligently exploited.

"Let us put Mr Bolderon from our minds." Fotheringham led Gilbert on along a flagged path that snaked through tall clean pines. "If there is to be expansion on the Abbeyfield it will be my doing. Mr Bolderon will not, however, suffer punishment for his zeal, his enthusiasm. He will have what he wants."

"What does he want?"

"A new contract of employment."

"Of course," said Gibbie.

Looking back on it, sadder and wiser, from the vantage point of experience Gibbie saw how Fotheringham had fastened like a lamprey upon his ignorance. He was appalled to realise just how naive he had been and how he had been led without a whimper of protest, figuratively as well as literally, along the garden path. It was inconceivable to him that a gentleman as well set up and as pretty as Hector Fotheringham could be such a blackguard as to take advantage of a simple rustic squire.

Fotheringham said, "Now, sir, what you want, I believe, is to share in the earning potential of the coal pit that stands on and under my land?"

"My bank does," said Gibbie.

"Oh!" said Fotheringham. "I received an impression from – from somewhere – that your partners, the Pryde brothers, were not disposed to invest in minerals."

"They – the brothers are not – they are – reluctant, yes."

"I see," said Fotheringham, "that the Prydes are not men of vision. They lack the spirit of enterprise that moves you so, Mr Bontine."

"They know cattle."

"We all know cattle. There is nothing to know about cattle."

"Quite, quite!" said Gibbie.

"But we – you and I, sir – do we not know *opportunity*? I have already sunk into my coalfield a considerable portion of money. I am not averse, of course, to putting more out to bring more in. On the other hand I do have other enterprises and I have no wish to bind all of my capital to my coalfield, however lucrative."

"You wish, I believe, to finance exploration."

"Opening new seams is somewhat expensive," said Fotheringham. "I seek, therefore, a partner."

"My bank would not, I fear, care to—"

"*You*, Mr Bontine. I am offering this opportunity to you *not* to the Falkirk Farmers' Bank, *not* to the company. Bless me, if the Prydes are so constricted in their view of what will make money why should you include them in our transaction?"

"How – how much money are we talkin' about?" said Gibbie.

"Eight thousand pounds; ten thousand, perhaps."

"Profit?"

"Stake." Fotheringham thought better of the word. "Initial investment."

"On what guarantee?"

"Half."

"Half of what, Mr Fotheringham?"

"Half of all net profits."

"What are the current profits?"

"I have them at the Priory for your perusal and study. Take my word on it, Mr Bontine, they are not inconsiderable."

"Fifty per cent?"

"Broadly speaking, in round figures, it would generally amount to approximately three thousand pounds in the year. That, sir, as I have no need to tell you, is equivalent to a return of thirty per cent on an investment of ten thousand pounds."

"Would you – yes, of course you would – would you guarantee the security of the invested sum?"

"I would put it against the value of the land."

"Monksfoot?"

300

There was the slightest hesitation, then Hector Fotheringham said, "The Abbeyfield. The pit. As you will no doubt be swift to inform me, sir, the value of the Abbeyfield as a lot does not reach to ten thousand pounds. It is, nonetheless, a working pit and far from exhaustion. Indeed, when the new seams are open and yielding it will increase not only its profit but its worth as security."

"I see," said Gibbie. "It's your intention to pledge the lands of the Abbeyfield as security against—"

"Yes," Fotheringham interrupted. "I will pledge the pit to match any sum that you may care to invest."

Gibbie did not understand the hair-splitting niceties of the amendment. He took it at face value. He believed that he would be protected. Other risks did not occur to him. For instance, he could not imagine that Mr Hector Fotheringham might lose all in another direction and that he would be obliged, as a creditor, to queue with other claimants upon the estate. He could not imagine how death might alter the conditions of the investment and did not precisely define in his own mind the difference between making a long-term loan and purchasing a share of the field. Any competent man of business would have laughed at Fotheringham but the heir of Placket had not reached his exalted position in life without being a shrewd judge of character and, specifically, of discerning weakness, want of bottom and of brain.

The rope was looped, knotted and drawn in a matter of seconds.

The following evening, in the parlour of Strachan Castle, Alicia pulled it tight.

Alicia said, "Am I to understand, Gilbert, that Mr Fotheringham is offering you a partnership in his mining company for ten thousand pounds?"

"Yes."

"Have you perused these figures?" Alicia turned the foolscap leaves of the contents of the leather folder.

"Yes."

"Do you see what the yearly profit comes to?"

"Yes."

"More than double what we accrue from Strachan."

"Yes."

"Twice what you earn from the bank."

"Yes."

"Gilbert, will you kindly stop saying *yes*? Answer me."

"I don't know what to say, Alicia."

"Is Mr Fotheringham a gentleman?"

"Oh, yes," said Gilbert. "But, Alicia, I do not have ten thousand pounds."

"Borrow it."

"What?"

"Is it not a fact that coal-owners become bankers?"

"Well, yes. There are several—"

"Borrow ten thousand from the bank."

"It would eat into our capital assets. In addition, the Prydes would—"

"Borrow from Moodie's fund."

"What if Elspeth Moodie returns?"

"In one year we will have put aside three thousand pounds. In two years—"

"That, Alicia, is beside the point. I cannot use the Moodie fund for my personal ends. Do you not see that it would be against the law?"

"What does the fund currently earn for her?"

"Four per cent in interest."

"Twenty-six per cent; two thousand and six—"

"Alicia, I *can* count," said Gilbert. "Really, you know, I should consult with Randall on this matter."

"Randall is not concerned with our affairs. His head is too full of that child from Piperhaugh. Would Randall consult you on a matter of business?"

"No, but—Hildebrand, then."

"You fool, Gilbert. Angus Hildebrand is *Moodie's* lawyer. He must never learn of our intention."

"Oh, Alicia, it's so dreadfully risky."

"Nonsense! Do you honestly believe that Moodie's sisters will be able to break the will in a court of law within, say, five years?"

"I doubt if they—"

"By then," said Alicia, "we will have earned by our investment the sum of nine thousand pounds, or more."

"We must save the earning, though, as a protection."

"I think not," said Alicia. "If the brat returns, we have a valuable asset to sell."

"Asset?"

"Half-share in a coal pit."

"I hadn't thought of that," said Gibbie. "Of course. The contract of partnership would of itself become a realisable asset. That does rather take the sting out of the gamble."

"Mr Fotheringham would hardly put up his land as security if he did not feel entirely safe in doing so."

"No," Gibbie admitted, "that's true."

"Gilbert, borrow the money discreetly from the trust."

"How much?"

"All of it."

"Alicia, I am—"

Once more his wife put the question: "Is Mr Fotheringham not a gentleman?"

"Yes, yes."

"Gilbert, do you not see that this is our golden opportunity? In five or six years Randall will covet our fortune. Indeed, if that girl from Piperhaugh is the spendthrift I mark her for then it's possible that you might be asked to bid for Ottershaw."

"I think, Alicia, that will not happen."

Alicia wagged the leather folder. "Figures do not lie."

"Well—"

"Gentlemen like Mr Fotheringham do not lie."

"Alicia, let's not be hasty."

"Borrow the money, Gilbert."

"All right. All right. I will."

Summer, in that year of 1817, had a broken back. On the first day of July the long spell of sunny weather broke in rain and gales which did not much abate throughout the month and brought the misery of mud to the cattlemen of Ottershaw and tenants of farms all along the strath.

At Strachan the Sinclairs were treated to rare fits of temper from Lachlan who was frustrated by the condition of the fields and could not reap the crops that he had sowed. Day after day the grieve mooched about the yards, glowering, while rivulets of water ran downhill to the river and tugged away new-turned soil and weakened the roots of growing plants. When Lachlan sought out Mr Gibbie, who was not often to be seen in or out of the castle that month, groused and sought the master's sympathy he was rebuffed by an almost lunatic cheerfulness and the assurance that every cloud had a silver lining.

"What does he know about farmin'?" Lachlan was prone to enquire of anyone in the vicinity. "Does he think the market'll pay money for black potatoes or cereals scooped up like mush? God! But he has no interest in his land. Old Gilbert would turn in his grave at the very thought o' it."

"If this wet keeps up another month, Dad, it'll be a right poor tryst come September," said Sandy, who was no happier than his father at the souring of the summer season.

"Aye, if Mr Gilbert thinks his bank income'll save him he has a shock awaitin' him. The drovers'll not be able to pay their debts on the price these poor drowned beasts will fetch."

"Och, some'll put on weight."

"The late calves'll not thrive."

"We've a full month an' two weeks until harvest," said Sandy. "Perhaps we'll be fortunate an' have a late blink to stiffen the stalks."

Lachlan would grunt at such optimism and tramp away, disgruntled, with a canvas sack held over his head.

As if his father's mood was not enough to contend with Sandy had no consolation from Anna. She was as shy of him, suddenly, as if he had become a leper. He told himself, ruefully, that Anna would never have given him a tumble in any case, and that he was better heeding his father's advice and going out and about in search of a more suitable lass to court and to marry.

Anna's intentions towards Sandy were even less clear. Perhaps it had been in her mind, when she blurted out that she was almost betrothed to Mr Rudge, to goad Sandy into an impulsive gesture, to cause him to sweep her up and carry her far from Strachan Castle. If so she was doomed to disappointment. Mr Hildebrand breathed not a word of her confession, except to confirm the truth of it with Robert Rudge. Mr Rudge had not denied that he was 'matrimonially' interested in Anna Sinclair and enquired rhetorically what harm there was in a bachelor of good standing entertaining intentions towards a young woman who had been wronged and abandoned and who would soon be divorced from her brutish husband and at liberty to marry again. Hildebrand did not reply and kept his opinion of the romance between Rudge and the servant to himself.

In the wake of her strange interview with Robert Rudge, however, Anna shaped new dreams. She began to find the prospect of being pampered by a man rich in experience as well as material possessions rather attractive. She did not doubt that Robert Rudge would love her, and she would not want for matching. He was not handsome as Randall was handsome and did not have Sandy Sinclair's form but it would be a triumph of sorts to be courted by such a man. To be wife to the manager of Kennart would release her from the byre and the servants' hall and bleach out the stain of being Matt Sinclair's wife.

She waited throughout the month for Mr Rudge to make further advances, to press his cause with a letter or a visit, but he did not. She received no word from him in any form and began to wonder if she had dreamed the whole incident. When the rain came and field work was impossible she hung about the hall and brooded. Keeping herself withdrawn, she speculated on why Mr Rudge had teased her with a false promise. The more he neglected her, the more she wished for him – and that was Mr Rudge's strategy, his intention.

Sandy would come to her, seek her out casually, as if by accident.

"What's wrong wi' you then, Anna? Why the long face?"

"None o' your business, Sandy Sinclair."

"Are ye ailin'?"

"No, I'm not ailin'."

"Are ye pinin' then?"

He would try to put an arm about her in the old familiar fraternal gesture but now she would have none of it.

"Leave me alone, Sandy. Damn you, leave me alone."

Nodding, Sandy would step back.

"Aye, it's comin' near September," he would say.

"September?"

"The laird's weddin' day."

"God in Heaven! Do y' think that grieves me?"

"I think it does, Anna."

"I've better things t' concern me than the doin's o' the laird."

"Can ye put him out o' your mind so easy?"

"He's made his choice," Anna would say, haughtily, as if Randall had rejected her for some tinker and had lost a fine chance to better himself in marriage. "Let him stew wi' it."

"Do ye not like it here, Anna?"

She would laugh, false and shrill. "What a question! Och, aye, I just love it here. At everybody's beck an' call. Wi' your sister an' mother turnin' up their noses at me as if I was a brat and not a relative. *I* never killed a man. *I* never burned down a shop. *I* never stole a stallion an' rode away, abandonin' wife an' bairn."

"What if Matt came back?"

"I would turn him over to the officers."

"Do ye say that?" Sandy would ask. "Do ye mean it?"

"Aye, I mean it. I want no more from your brother except t' be parted from him."

"If you were parted from him . . . ?"

"I would find another husband of better stuff than any damned Sinclair."

"Not just – not just run off, Anna?"

"I have Robbie t' think of. I don't want him t' sleep under hedges an' drink from the burn."

"It would be marriage then or nothin'?"

"Aye, Sandy," Anna would say, her tone softening a touch. "Aye, it would be marriage. Indeed, it will be marriage."

"Nothin' less?"

"Nothin' less."

Sandy's conversations, well-meant and kindly, triggered in her a realisation that it would soon be too late to mourn for Randall, that she must be firm with herself and put the laird out of her mind completely. It would be easy to coax Sandy into her arms. She might find satisfaction in it, in deceiving Aileen and Cat Sinclair; it would serve the bitches right for forcing her into a marriage with Matt. But she was reluctant to hurt old Lachlan, who had been kind to her. Besides, now that she had an option in Mr Rudge she could not bring herself to ruin Sandy; she had too much affection for him to leave him with a broken heart when she went away from this place to the house in Drymen.

She wrote to Mr Rudge. She took the letter to the coach office at Mallock, three miles' walk on a dismal day. She paid the due for delivery and waited and, in five days, received a reply.

Edith brought the letter down to her. It had come with the Bontines' packet. Edith and Aileen hovered about while she examined seal and tape and then, with a smile, tucked it unopened into her bodice and refused to tell the women who it was from.

Later that afternoon she stole off to the hay-loft to read what Mr Rudge had to say.

> *My Dear Sweet Anna,*
> *With what delight did I receive a missive penned by your fair hand. I had supposed that I had offended you with premature talk of marriage. Many times since that Sabbath have I taken up my pen to express the regard I nurture for you. I was stayed by temerity. I dare not let myself believe that you would think of me as a new-found friend and suitor for your hand. I cannot properly express my feelings for you. I long for the day when you will be free, when I might take your hand and kiss it – and kiss your lips too.*
>
> *Nonetheless, it is to crave your indulgence that is my purpose in this letter. I am separated from you by years as well as miles. My longing is not lessened by the distance between us but I cannot court you candidly as I would wish and shout my love for you from the hilltop for all to hear of it. I will not be so reticent when the happy day arrives when you are no longer wife to another.*

A second page of compliments and assurances followed and the letter was signed with a great flourish – *Your Respectful and Affectionate Servant, Robert Rudge, Esquire.*

It was the first love-letter that Anna had ever received. Randall had never written to her. Matt had never had need. She cherished the letter, admired its floweriness, was warmed by its sentiments. Most of all she valued it as evidence, a promise that, in course of time, she might cash like a banknote for its weight in gold if Mr Rudge should try to leave her in the lurch.

* * *

Marriage was not on the mind of Keir Bolderon in that high-summer season. From Fotheringham he had learned that a financier had been found to develop the Abbeyfield, that the financier was none other than Gilbert Bontine of the Farmers' Bank. He was not overjoyed at the news. Indeed, it was all he could do to hide his anger at being deceived. The future of the Abbeyfield might now be secure but Keir Bolderon needed no fortune-teller to inform him that his days as a manager were numbered. In a stroke, he had become a man without prospects.

Flooding in the upper levels, the collapse of a vent near the Dead Man and other minor disasters required his attention. He could not shirk responsibility to the safety of the colliers no matter how shabbily he had been treated by the landowner. A pit was more than shafts and tunnels. It had character of its own, even a sort of soul. Keir Bolderon had poured his sweat and his savings into it and would not see it drowned by summer floods no matter what became of the place when his contract expired and he was given the boot.

Elspeth spared no thought for managers or landowners. Matt, Mouse and she went down in rain, came up in rain. Droplets shot from the rim of the shaft to greet them and it was almost as wet in the bucket as in a keel-boat on the Forth. Davy had made a recovery from the spring sickness. In spite of the dampness, he did not cough so fiercely now. He was still weak and fearfully thin, of course, and his nature had not sweetened. He was more assertive and voluble than ever. Only Matt could silence him with a sharp reprimand when his insolence became too much to bear.

Matt did not seem to mind the rain. Matt did not seem to mind the slog to the shaft, slippery ladders, the stench of wet flannel. His 'room' on the base level remained dry and warm. It was, he said, more comfortable than the fo'c'sle of a whaler. Meat-fed and muscled, Matt appeared to thrive on the hard and narrow life of a collier. He had 'Pet to talk to and Mouse to tease.

When Mouse wriggled into the trap to assist with loading, Matt would give her a white grin, mop his beard with his wrist, cry out in a collier's whisper, "Hey, lassie, you're damned slow today. Yon gingerbread ye scoffed last night at supper must ha'e been made o' lead.''

Mouse would not rise to the bait. She would mutter and curse under her breath and shoot darts of dislike at the interloper. She would not be drawn into trading insults with Matt Shearer; that was too friendly a relationship for a modest pit girl. Matt was patient with her. Elspeth supposed that he had learned to endure the foibles of womankind from Anna, a professor of tantrums. By comparison Mouse Bennet was a mere apprentice. It would have surprised Elspeth to learn that Matt felt tender concern for Mouse. She reminded him a little of his pet monkey, Jacko. Beneath her scowls and snarlings she too was feckless, helpless and much in need of care and cuddles.

Days mounted into weeks, weeks into months. Pay-nights came and went. Matt's haul increased. With increased earning, though, suspicion and dislike of the bearded sailorman grew. The other hewers were jealous and made no bones about it. They did not know, of course, that Matt Shearer had a tall cave to work in and coal that was dense and easy to carve. If he had had to fit his bulk into a thirty-inch seam he would not have taken a quarter of the weight that he did in the millstone cavern.

Matt kept himself to himself and ignored remarks made to provoke him. He had fashioned a life that did not depend upon being his father's son. When the long day's haul was over he had no need for male company, to whistle away to the Grapes for cups of whisky. If the colliers thought he was bedding Elspeth, let them. What did it matter? He was happy. He had learned at last that there was pride in work and in being settled.

Like other folk with less dramatic histories, Matt ate and worked and slept, gave attention to Elspeth and the children and was unaware that a long ground-swell of circumstance was about to lift him once more and carry him, with Elspeth, towards disaster.

Keir Bolderon had kept Mrs Patterson in view, as it were, through the long harassing days of July and August. He had learned from Snippets that there was a new hewer on the books and that Mrs Patterson had had the gall to go out to Leith and find the fellow and lure him back to cut for the family. Snippets was not without admiration for the woman's self-reliance. Even Thomas Rance expressed guarded approval.

"Have you met the man?" Keir Bolderon asked.

"Aye, Mr Bolderon," Thomas Rance answered. "I would not employ a hewer I had not met."

"Quite so. Is he – is he youthful?"

"Some twenty-four or -five years old I would guess."

"Fair or dark?"

"Fair as a Viking."

"Well set, I suppose?"

"Tall. Too tall. He has shoulders on him like an ox."

"She knew him in the past, do y' think?"

"She tells me they had met in Ayrshire, when she was with her drover husband."

"Ah, yes, the drover husband."

"Have I done wrong, Mr Bolderon, in permittin' her to bring an outsider to the field?" said Thomas Rance.

"Can he cut coal?"

"He cuts his share, aye."

"If he can cut, Thomas, he can stay. It's not up to us to question Mrs Patterson's morals."

Keir Bolderon was not overly pleased at the arrival of the male stranger who had stepped mysteriously into the heiress's life and might have knowledge of her past. He must soon make his move.

In the middle of August, on pay-night, Keir Bolderon went to the counting-house to have a squint at Matthew Shearer. He was not a little dismayed at the size of the man and at his bearded individualism. Shearer's drawing was respectable if not spectacular. He took his money with a grin and a swagger that indicated indifference to the colliers' murmurous hostility.

It would be even more difficult than before to reach Elspeth Patterson now that she had this rough, arrogant young man to protect her. Keir Bolderon could work out no feasible means of reaching across the gulf that separated him from the heiress and pulling her from the family circle. All that weekend he puzzled and fretted while grey rain lashed the windows of his house and his servants bickered out of boredom and depression. The gods were with Keir Bolderon's cause, however. If the manager could not weave a fine pattern to save himself the gods were more devious and less fastidious.

It happened in the middle of Tuesday night in some tiny, unmentionable cavity within the body of Mr Snippets Smith; a small thing which, like so many small things, engendered enormous quantities of pain. Snippets' screams awakened his wife. She was greatly distressed by her husband's condition. She imagined that he was dying before her eyes. Writhing and thrashing on the bed, he clutched his back and belly with his fists as if to tear the burning pain out of him. He had a fever too and was not sensible. Mrs Smith sent her youngest girl to run to Mr Rance's house. In haste, Mr Rance ran to the pit, borrowed a horse and rode all the way to Alloa to fetch back Mr Kidson. Such was the state of the weather and the roads that the doctor insisted on half his fee in advance and would not budge until he had received a note of promise for the sum signed by the oversman and witnessed by a servant. It was almost dawn before Mr Kidson reached his patient but the condition had not changed and Snippets continued to howl like a fox with its brush on fire.

By the start of the shift the news was all over the Abbeyfield. Snippets had an inflammation of the kidneys. He was seriously ill and would not be at the tally for months, if he survived Kidson's treatment at all.

Little sympathy was spared for poor Snippets. There was more concern for the accuracy of the tally. Snippets was the fellow they all trusted. He was prim and sharp and correct and as honest as a kirk elder. Now, it seemed, Snippets would be on the flat of his back with a hot brick on his belly and leeches stuck to his flank for a long while to come. There was speculation about who would replace him and if that man would keep the tally exact and count the cash as well as Snippets had done.

When Keir Bolderon heard the news his first thought was that he must assume the chore of acccounting himself. He knew of no other man on the field who had a good enough fist to fill the ledger columns, coupled with an arithmetical brain.

But then, out of the blue, came inspiration. Had he not originally culled Snippets from a weaver's factory? Clerks to weavers were famously accurate in calculations. Did he not have the wife of a weaver – and what a weaver – in his employment?

Mr Bolderon could see no reason why a female could not compile the tally just as well as a man, once you put aside the prejudices and traditions. In a matter of minutes after the thought had entered his head Keir Bolderon was determined. He would give the post temporarily to Mrs Elspeth Patterson. He would bring her out of the pit and into the counting-house. He would have her, in consequence, within easy reach.

Keir Bolderon realised that he was risking the wrath of his colliers by taking such an innovative step. But for the time being he was still manager of the Abbeyfield and might do what he willed with the workers. Damn them! Let them shout and stamp and groan all they liked. He would have the heiress at Snippets' desk whether they approved or not. He could woo a clerk as he could never woo a hauler. He wasted no time in putting his scheme into action.

Elspeth was brought to the counting-house before the shift the following morning. Her hewer and her tiny companion were left to descend to the seam, to speculate on what was happening to Elspeth and what the manager could possibly want with her.

Keir Bolderon had had the stove lighted for, though it was still only August, the dampness had an autumnal edge that made you shiver. Flames crackled cheerfully in the brick cavity and the extra lanterns he had taken down from the shelf made the long wooden room seem almost festive. He had put on his best tweeds. He had had his servant polish his boots. He had even been twice shaved.

Mrs Elspeth Patterson was neat and clean. Though garbed no differently from her fellow haulers, with her hair pulled back and pinned under the cap, the lines of her face showed not just a prettiness but beauty. Her pores had not become coarse yet and she did not squint with the failing vision that was common in blue-eyed colliers.

Keir Bolderon leaned against the counting-table while Thomas Rance, who had been invited to the interview to keep it above the board, hovered by the high desk. On the counting-table were those items – ink and pen and paper –

with which Mr Bolderon would test the young woman's fitness to tackle the task he had in mind.

"I'm sure she can do it, Thomas," he had told Rance.

"Aye, perhaps she can, Mr Bolderon. But *should* she?"

"That's my decision."

"Henning or Elginbrod are more obvious choices."

"Elginbrod is careless and slow; and Henning—" Keir Bolderon had shrugged.

Thomas Rance had made no more argument. Perhaps he assumed that the manager merely hungered for the Patterson wife as a man might hunger for any pretty woman over whom he had a modicum of power.

Elspeth came uncertainly into the counting-house.

"You sent for me, Mr Bolderon."

"I did, Mrs Patterson."

She was nervous but showed none of the squirming petulance with which some of the other young women would have greeted him. She waited, hands clasped, eyes scanning his face for some sign of his purpose in pulling her from the line, in singling her out.

Keir Bolderon said, "I hear that you have improved your lot, Mrs Patterson; that you are no longer in harness."

"I have a hewer, yes."

"I'm pleased to learn of it. You were never cut from the cloth that makes a harness wife."

She took a long breath, released it softly. She was very tense indeed.

Keir Bolderon said, "In your days with the drover, did you learn to read and write?"

"I learned at school."

"School?"

"Aye, in – in Ayr."

"Did you also learn to count?"

"I did, Mr Bolderon. May I enquire what—"

"In other words, Mrs Patterson, you have an education."

"Of sorts, sir."

"Show me your hand. I mean, your handwriting."

She glanced at Thomas Rance but the oversman remained inscrutable. She stared at the sheet of yellowish paper that the manager had put upon the table, at the ink-pot and the pen.

"First you must tell me the reason, sir," Elspeth said.

"Very well. As you'll have heard, poor Mr Smith is sick. He will not be fit to take up employment again until October or later, no matter how he struggles. I do not wish to employ another clerk in the interim, yet I must have the ledgers attended and paying-out done thoroughly."

She closed her eyes, lids fluttering, and pursed her lips and let out a long breath, indicating relief. To Thomas Rance it would seem natural enough in the context but to Keir Bolderon with his knowledge of her past and her present circumstances it said much more. It told him, that gesture, that she had come in fear of discovery, that the mere request for her writing on a paper seemed to threaten her. She did not, Keir Bolderon realised, know that her husband was dead. He felt a surge of gratitude and an odd kind of warmth towards her.

"Is it the job of clerk you're offerin' me?" Elspeth said.

"If you are capable. Will you show me your hand, please?"

She nodded. She came to the table and took the pen, licked the new metal nib and dipped it into the pot, stroked off the excess fluid and, without more than a moment's hesitation, wrote down upon the paper: *"Nobody on the Abbeyfield will like having a woman behind the counting-house table. Mistress Elspeth Patterson."*

Keir Bolderon, watching over her shoulder, laughed. He had an urge to put an arm about her and give her a companionable hug but Thomas Rance had come over too, curious to see what she had written with such swiftness and authority. Rance did not smile. He did not raise an eyebrow at the wit she had displayed.

Elspeth leaned forward, blew gently over the paper to dry the ink and wrote: *"I cannot accept the position so generously offered as it will mean that my hewer, Mr Matthew Shearer, will not have two hands to haul coal for him."*

Keir Bolderon found himself touching her lightly, a hand upon her arm. "Enough."

He shuffled away the paper with its manuscript and brought forward a ledger sheet which he had personally prepared. The sample was exact, eight names, eight entries, but with sums untotalled, the rightward column left empty.

She did not even ask what was required. She turned a little

to exclude him and concentrated, did not move her lips much but, in seconds, put down a total against the first name and, a second later, filled in the next and the next.

"You have done this before, Mrs Patterson?"

"For my husband."

"I did not know that drovers kept such records."

"Do you wish me to finish, sir?"

"By all means, do."

Snippets himself was hardly faster and, when he checked off her results against the real page, Keir Bolderon found no error. He felt as elated as if she had signed away her fortune. He could not help himself from giving her a little friendly pat of praise and encouragement.

She said, "I meant what I wrote, sir. I canna take on the clerkship. Your men would never stand for it."

"If you pay them properly, they'll stand for it."

"I've no experience of this sort of accounting."

"I'll keep you right, Mrs Patterson, never fear. In a week or two you'll find your feet and be more assured."

"No, Mr Bolderon. No."

"Because of opinion against you?"

"I have coal to haul."

"Is there not another hand in the family?"

"Davy's too sick to go below ground."

"Bennet's son, do you mean? Yes, I've heard of his trouble. What of the other girl?"

"Sarah?"

"Is she not old enough to pull a sled?"

"Old enough. But—"

"Why are you here?" Keir Bolderon said bluntly.

"What?" The question alarmed her.

"For what purpose do you work?"

"To earn money."

"In that case I'm offerin' you more money for less arduous work. You have more of a talent for desk work than you do for sleddin' or puttin'. Come now, Mrs Patterson, why do you insist on wasting such a clever skill?"

She saw the sort of a trap he had set for her.

"How much will it pay?" she asked.

"Twenty shillings."

315

"The fortnight?"

"The week."

"What!"

Keir Bolderon was aware of Thomas Rance's grunt of astonishment. Snippets himself was not paid so grandly. Keir Bolderon did not turn around or give any sign that he had heard the oversman.

"Forty shillings in the fortnight. Clean work too. What do you say?"

She could not possibly refuse such an opportunity. She had admitted, if admission to such an obvious point was necessary, that the wage and its earning were all that mattered. She could not and did not revert to her previous argument concerning the need to find some young person to pull the sled that she would abandon for a desk.

"There are procedures, systems," said Keir Bolderon. "But I have no doubt that you will master them with alacrity. Forty shillings is good money, Mrs Patterson. Why, from that sum you could hire a child to take the sled from you and still be in sound profit, could you not?"

"But to pay a woman—"

"What you are paid will be a secret."

"I must tell Matt."

"Your – your man?"

"He hews for all of us, Mr Bolderon. He is not my man."

"Did you not know him from the past?"

"In a slight way. We were acquainted, that's all. It is not what you might suppose. We do not live familiarly."

"It was a lucky accident that led you to him," Keir Bolderon said.

"It was."

"If he came here to work for wages he will be pleased with this opportunity to add to the family income."

She hesitated still. She made a little grimace which did not seem ugly at all, Keir Bolderon thought. Nothing that she did was ugly.

"I must speak to him, to them all," she said. "I'll go below now an' do it, for you'll be in need of an immediate answer."

"By noon," said Keir Bolderon. "I'll accompany you below, to the room to—"

316

"No."

Alarm again; the reason for it less obvious now.

"No," Elspeth said, shaking her head. "Let me put the matter to them in my own way, Mr Bolderon."

"Will they believe you?"

"I hardly believe it myself."

"It's only until Mr Smith is well again, you understand."

"Aye, sir, but in two months I can earn a half-year's wages."

It was an irony beyond Keir Bolderon's comprehension that she should place such an accent on the earning of a living wage when she had deserted a husband who had left her a fortune.

"Will you go down now?" Keir Bolderon said.

"I will, Mr Bolderon."

"It is, need I add, a golden opportunity for you and for the Bennets."

"While it lasts, Mr Bolderon."

"An answer by noon?"

"Aye, sir."

She left, hurrying away towards the shaft. Only in the haste with which she crossed the yard from the counting-house did her excitement display itself. Keir Bolderon watched her from the open doorway. It was smirring with light rain and dawn had only just managed to struggle up from the east through the cloud. He liked the cheerfulness of the counting-house and, as soon as Elspeth had disappeared, stepped back into it.

"She'll accept I reckon, Thomas."

"She would be a great fool if she did not."

"And Mrs Patterson is nobody's fool, is she?"

"Mr Bolderon, if you'll pardon my impertinence – why are you doin' this thing?"

"Because I need a clerk."

"If she takes the post, sir, it'll mean trouble."

"Trouble? Ah, yes, Thomas. Trouble from the colliers. I think we might brave that, don't you?"

"Trouble for her, Mr Bolderon."

"Mrs Patterson can, I'm sure, cope."

"For forty shillin's the fortnight?"

"Cheap at the price, wouldn't you say?"

"No, sir, I'd say that Mrs Patterson's service will cost us all very dear."

"I cannot share your view," said Keir Bolderon. "Now, if you'll fish out Snippets' keys I'll make ready the ledgers and the cash receipt book. This afternoon, with any luck, I'll have to play the teacher to Elspeth Patterson."

"Unless her man's too proud t' let her take the job."

"A sailor from Leith?" said Keir Bolderon. "He's bound to put money before pride."

"Aye, Mr Bolderon, I'm afraid he will."

Elspeth waited until Mouse had gone into the tunnel, the sled chittering behind her, before she slid through the trap and entered the millstone cave. It surprised her that their secret had remained undetected for so many months. She still hated the high curving slit beneath the millstone slab. Not even the sight of Matt happily breaking up a cut with his hammer could rid her of a sense of oppression.

She had brought a fresh can of water. He paused long enough to take a swallow then squatted, naked save for his drawers, by the cut coal again.

Elspeth said, "Mr Bolderon wants me to act as the paymaster clerk till Mr Smith's well again."

Matt did not seem particularly surprised.

He said, "How long'll that be, 'Pet?"

"Six weeks or eight."

"How does it pay?"

"Twenty shillings in the week."

"Take it."

"Is that all you have t' say? Have you no thought for how your coal will be hauled?"

"It'll be hauled by wee Sarah. She's old enough for the work, Elspeth, as well you know. If you hadn't come to Placket when you did Sarah'd have been down by her daddy's side two years since."

"It's no life for—"

"For any decent person," Matt interrupted. "But it's the buyin' o' bread an' the payin' o' rent. Take the clerk's job, 'Pet."

"The colliers'll hate me for it."

"They hate us now."

"Aye, but—"

"You didn't used t' be so shy, Mrs Patterson. What's wrong wi' ye?"

"I canna understand why Mr Bolderon asked me."

"Because he recognises a lady when he sees one."

"Does he know who I am?"

"God, no! How could he?" said Matt. "He knows only that you've got somethin' the others lack. He wants a cheap hand for his countin' an' he canna find a man who can do the job."

Elspeth could not deny the attraction of a job in the counting-house. She had always been comfortable with books, with pens and ink. Though she was no snob and no idler she knew that the work was suited to her even if she was a female brought out of the ranks. She thought of Mr Bolderon and his kindnesses, never overdone, never effusive. She wondered if he had offered her the surface appointment as a manager or as a man. She found she liked the notion of being close to him, and of having a place of power. Responsibility attracted her. Mr Bolderon would not have given her the chance if he did not think she could cope with it. She could not, in conscience, refuse Mr Bolderon. Could she?

"Aye, 'Pet, I can see in your face how you want out o' this hole," said Matt. "The truth, now."

"Sarah; I—"

"Sarah's not your bairn. Think o' yourself for once."

"Davy's still so weak an' frail."

"But I'm not." Matt grinned suddenly and flexed his muscular arm. "Leave the rest o' it t' me, Mrs Patterson."

"But—"

"Damn it all, 'Pet Patterson. Take the bloody job."

She nodded, relieved and excited by the prospect of working upstairs, close to Mr Bolderon.

She spent the afternoon and part of the evening in the counting-house in Mr Bolderon's exclusive company. She found him patient and attentive. He led her through the procedures and taught her how to translate weight-of-coal into hard cash. He introduced her to the male clerks, Henning and McCaffray. Henning was friendly towards her. He had no desire to take over Snippets' job and its responsibilities; but McCaffray, who was hardly more than a doorman and messenger, was full of prejudice and treated Elspeth with patronising disdain. She had expected as much and did not let it rile her. There would be worse to come when word leaked out that a woman had been appointed to such an important job as paymaster.

The majority of colliers could add and subtract, make the price of three cans of ale or cups of whisky, cost a slither of fresh herring or a bole of oatmeal but they were lost in sums involving hundredweights and pounds sterling. It would be an easy thing for a paymaster to cheat a hewer of a shilling or two on the count, a fact which made the job important and powerful. Elspeth realised now why Snippets was such a martinet and so addicted to ritual. It was his method of demonstrating his firmness and precision. She could never acquire such a character. In Elspeth, however, was a perverse sense of justice. It made her determined to ignore the colliers' taunts, to sit tight on her stool in the counting-house and brave the storms of disapproval that her presence would engender.

Nonetheless it was with considerable trepidation that she embarked upon her first pay-out on a rain-lashed Saturday night in the last week of August. She could not be sure that the sight of a female seated primly behind Snippets' sacred table might not be too much for some men to swallow.

In a nervous voice she called out to McCaffray to open the door and admit the first hewers.

Keir Bolderon placed a hand comfortingly upon her shoulder. She glanced round, saw the manager wink, and looked quickly back towards the door in anticipation of the customary charge.

"Is she there? Is it her right enough?"

"Bloody knock me down! It *is* her."

"What's she *doin'*, Willie?"

"Just – just *sittin'*."

"Is Bolderon there an' all?"

"Aye. He's there."

"Who's doin' the cash?"

"*She* is, damn me if she's not."

"Get in then. The rain's pourin' down my neck, man."

"I'm no' goin' first."

"Here, step aside. *I'm* no' frightened o' any bloody woman."

In he came, bold and pugnacious: McClure, James. He swaggered to the table, not meeting anybody's eye, thumped his fist upon the counter and made the coins jingle.

"Jim McClure," he shouted.

Elspeth licked her lips and lifted her gaze. She dared him to look her straight in the eye. Her stomach was knotted with apprehension and resentment.

The hewer gave the table another rap with his fist.

"I'm not deaf, Mr McClure," Elspeth snapped. "Take your hand off this table at once."

"*What?*"

"I think you heard me well enough."

"*I'll be—*"

"If you tell Mr Rance your name once more, Mr McClure, you'll be *paid*."

Nostrils flared, cheeks flushed crimson, little hairs bristled about the man's tight collar. In the doorway a dozen colliers crowded, piled against each other under streaming eaves while McCaffray barred the way with one arm. There was still no press to enter. It was as if McClure had been appointed champion for all.

McClure snorted. He huffed and puffed, while Elspeth, Thomas Rance and Keir Bolderon waited. Neither oversman nor manager said a word. A single word from either of them would have given McClure the excuse he seemed to need to obey the perfectly polite and reasonable request from the blue-eyed bitch at the cash table.

Elspeth swallowed, forced a smile.

"Come along, Mr McClure, before the Grapes runs out o' ale."

The collier made a queer little sound in his throat, a whimper almost. "McClure, James," he said in a quiet little voice.

"McCLURE," Thomas Rance bellowed.

Young Henning had already found the entry. He called out, "James McClure. Seventy-two shillin's, less rent o' two shillin's. Pay seventy shillin's exact, Mr—I mean, *Mrs* Patterson."

Deftly Elspeth plucked the coins from the trays and put them into the big earthenware bowl.

"There you are, Mr McClure. Count it, if you please."

James McClure did not count it. He scooped out the money and stuck it into his pocket and as if stunned by the fact that he had taken payment from a woman and that it was just as plain and painless as if old Snippets had been at the table he blundered towards the doorway and would have reeled out into the rain if McCaffray had not nudged him back to make his mark in the ledger at Henning's high desk.

Stifled laughter caused Elspeth to swivel on her stool. Behind her, half turned away, Keir Bolderon had a hand over his mouth. As she caught his eye he altered his laughter into a fit of coughing.

McClure crossed the floor and went out into the yard.

"Dear, oh dear!" Keir Bolderon whispered. "Did you see the look on his biscuit? He doesn't know whether to hit you or hug you, Elspeth."

Elspeth found no humour in Mr McClure's confusion, no triumph either. She was doing a job that should not – even she believed – have been allocated to a female. But she would do it to the very best of her ability. She too was confused, and not entirely out of sympathy with her male companions.

"NEXT MAN," boomed Thomas Rance.

McCaffray reached out and yanked in another man before he could retreat.

"Napier, William."

"William Napier."

Henning read out the wage.

Elspeth paid the hewer who, pleased with his take, gave her a grudging nod before he advanced to the desk and made way for William Todd and others.

Now that the ice had been broken the colliers soon lost their awe if not their ire and came barging into the counting-house to claim their wages, woman or no woman.

It was all over by eight o'clock.

McCaffray chased out the last wee laddie with a shilling in his fist, put the bar on the door, turned and leaned against it with a sigh. Henning ran his thick forefinger down the pages of the ledger, to check that every man, woman and child had left a sign that they had received their due and closed the book with a snap.

Elspeth was more exhausted, though in a different way, than

at the end of a night-shift. Stretching her arms above her head she sat back and, from the tops of her eyes, saw Keir Bolderon behind her like a guardian angel.

"Well done, Mrs Patterson," the manager said. "Even Snippets could not have found a flaw in your auditing."

"Aye, Mr Bolderon, but they'll find fault wi' something else, I'm sure."

"Henning, McCaffray, come an' be paid," said Keir Bolderon. "You too, Thomas."

Elspeth would be last. He would give her the wages out of his own hand, as she, an hour ago, had paid Matt out of hers. There was something wrong in this exchange. It made Elspeth uneasy, though she was satisfied that the job had been well done.

Once Mr Rance had received his hatful of cash he was dismissed, though it was usual for him to wait until Snippets had counted the residue of banknotes and coins and stowed them safe in the strongbox bolted to the floor. Elspeth caught the little nod that Mr Bolderon gave to Thomas Rance, the nod of understanding given in return. Mr Rance left before she could bid him a good night.

Keir Bolderon rubbed his hands in cheerful appreciation.

"Good, good," he said. "Now we'll tidy here and get home to supper." As if the idea had just struck him, he said, "Will you take a bite of supper with me, Mrs Patterson? It's not far to my house an' my servants will have prepared something hot to put upon the table."

Flustered, Elspeth answered, "I thank you, Mr Bolderon, but I have a family waitin' to be fed."

"Of course you have." Keir Bolderon paused, stirred his palm over the coins on the table-top. "There's precious little left after our brethren have had their dues, is there?"

"Where does it come from?" said Elspeth. "The money, I mean."

"From the bank in Alloa. It's earned from coal sales, mainly in Leith – where you found your hewer."

Elspeth had already begun to count the coins. Her fingers were soiled, different to the dirt that coal made. She felt hot now. Rain had ceased and moths and other insects had found their way into the counting-house, drawn by the light of the oil lamps. There was spit upon the floor, plugs of burnt

323

tobacco, mud, and damp maps of rain water. She felt her satisfaction wane.

She counted quickly. Mr Bolderon put the cash into the metal box and the metal box into the strongbox and locked the padlocks with his keys. Elspeth rose from the stool at last, stiff and aching.

"Shall I put out the lights, Mr Bolderon?"

"Aye, do."

She went round lidding ink-pots, drying nibs on a canvas pad and, as she passed, turned out the lamps and lanterns, save for the one that Mr Bolderon required to make fast the counting-house door.

She wanted out of the house, clear of the odour of money, and the gloom. She did not know why it should be, yet she felt again that same threat she had felt all those many months ago when first she entered Placket from the road, not knowing what lay there and what the village offered.

When Mr Bolderon put his hand upon her arm she had to resist an urge to lean on him.

"Mrs Patterson."

"Yes?"

"Your money."

"What?"

"Your wage. You've left it lyin' neglected on the table."

He put the four crowns into her palm. His fingers brushed lightly. He was close to her, a hand still gently upon her elbow. She could smell from him that manly scent of spirits and tobacco but it was not strong and not repugnant. It reminded her, for an instant, of her father. She closed her eyes and experienced a faint astonishing longing to be home again, home with him in Moss House.

In a flash she realised that she had never feared her father's intention towards her, only the manner of the love he bore her, its indecent possessiveness.

Keir Bolderon said, "What's wrong with you, Mrs Patterson? Do twenty shillings mean so little that you can discard them?"

"No, I—"

He took the lantern from its peg and brought it to the door. "I do believe you're blushing."

324

"No, Mr Bolderon. It's the warmth of the air now the rain's ceased."

She went across the threshold. The ground of the yard glistened with black mud. She could hear a gurgle of water in runnels and ruts, drawing down to the Rutherford burn and via the burn to the river and the sea. She held the lantern while Keir Bolderon locked the door to the counting-house. He turned and, swinging the keys on his forefinger, scanned the workings and the sky with strange affection.

"See, there's the moon, on the edge of the trees."

It was swollen and yellow as a candle flame and streaked by the flying clouds of the rain-storm but the sight of it and the sweet clean smell of the night air and the quietness and the nearness of the man softened Elspeth's fatigue, brought in her again a wistful longing for Balnesmoor, for home.

"Tread carefully, Mrs Patterson."

"Aye, sir."

"Goodnight to you."

"Goodnight."

She picked her way across the yard to the stone path that straggled away from the workings. She paused at the field gate and looked back, hoping to see the lantern, to have a last glimpse of Keir Bolderon as he saddled his mount for the ride home. But the light had been extinguished and Keir Bolderon had gone.

Clutching the four crowns in her palm, Elspeth swung towards the bridge over the burn, towards the smoke-reek of the cottage where Matt and the children waited, hungry for supper before bed.

Changes were in the air in Strachan Castle. The Bontine boys were bound for school in Edinburgh. Their little boxes had been packed bit by bit with clean linen and flannel and Alicia had entered one of her frantic states. Her voice could be heard belling along corridors and through windows and seemed at times to emerge from the very chimney heads as she told the world of her troubles not only in making her offspring ready to be educated but in preparing for the great journey north to attend the wedding of her brother-in-law.

Compared to the heirs in other big houses in the Lennox

Gibbie's sons were not harshly treated. They all knew that mother's bark was marginally worse than her bite and that father, when he was forced to beat them for misbehaviour, could not bring himself to lay on more than half a dozen strokes of the switch. Now, however, they were suffering torments of uncertainty, fired by threats of such vividness and proportion that they wept in corners and cowered quivering under the sheets, haunted by the prospect of an encounter with the dreaded Doctor Creech.

"Wait," Alicia would cry, "until Doctor Creech lays hands on you, my fine fellow. He'll not put up with your wickedness as I have done. There's no charity in Doctor Creech's heart for small boys who do not do what they are told."

Gibbie could offer his sons no comfort. Memories of Doctor Creech still disturbed his dreams. Almost all of the things that Alicia, in her ignorance, said about the great educator were true. Creech had added new refinements to discipline and his severity and strictness had become legend throughout Scotland.

"Latin and Greek," Alicia would shout. "Latin and Greek will give you respect for your dear mother, my lad. Mark my words; you will wish yourself back here before a day of Latin and Greek has gone by."

Latin, Greek and Creech had become entwined in the minds of the young Bontines and they were so mortal afraid of that trinity of demons that they concocted plans to wrap their belongings in a sack and run off to be cabin boys on a clipper ship and, if they had had more gumption, might have done so too.

Only Uncle Randall, in the few brief minutes he could spare for his nephews, offered a modicum of reassurance.

"Oh, school is not so bad," he told them. "I survived it, as did your father. It did not do us much lasting harm."

But Latin – gulp – and Greek?

"Dull stuff," Randall would say. "But not beyond the grasp and mastery of the Bontine brain. Remember, chaps, I beg you, that you are Bontines. Buckle down to your studies with a will and you will prosper well enough."

But – another gulp – what of Doctor Creech?

"Creech is unpleasant, aye; yet he knows where to draw the

line. If you do as you are bidden and do not sauce him, he'll leave you pretty much alone. It's only wilful, rebellious boys that he beats regularly."

Uncle Randall's consolations were lost, however, in Mama's awful torrent of threats. Alicia made full use of the device to keep the children cowed while she fretted over her wardrobe for the journey and speculated on how she would be received by the Seaton family. She had sense enough not to burden Gibbie with her uncertainties, for he was absent, in mind as well as body, for much of the August month.

Gibbie had a slippery fish in his fingers – Fotheringham – and was intent on holding it while he teased ten thousand pounds from James Moodie's trust and transferred it, two thousand pounds at a signature, through an intermediary account in the Farmers' Bank to Mr Fotheringham's account in the Bank of Scotland. It was not a scheme that required much ingenuity. Gibbie effected it by the simple ploy of hiding from the Prydes the documents by which transfers were made. The brothers were far too busy setting up for the autumn trysts to spare much thought for what Gilbert might be up to.

If Gilbert had doubts about the wisdom of what he was about, he kept his doubts from Alicia who was already behaving as if he had increased their income fivefold. Alicia was spending money with an indifference to debt that Gibbie found faintly awe-inspiring yet he too felt that it was incumbent upon them to make a show of prosperity before the Piperhaugh Seatons. He did not want to let down his brother, and the good name of Ottershaw.

No common mail-stage for the Bontines; a hired coach from Falkirk with teams, driver and footman would be needed to carry the entourage to the wilds of Aberdeenshire and back again. Lachlan would go along as Gibbie's 'man'. Alicia would be attended by Edith. The hire fee, not to mention wardrobe expenses, would cost Gilbert a hatful of guineas but he could not find it in his heart to refuse Alicia her wish to do it in style.

Accompanied by Dunn and faithful Henry Hunter, Randall left Ottershaw early in the month. He was unwilling to risk flood, accident and upset, delays that might retard his arrival. Of course, Randall left Ottershaw ticking like a German watch and in the very best of hands. In contrast, Strachan was put into the care of young Sandy Sinclair, with new grass plantings wallowing in water, many cattle sick with bloat and a general tinpot air of disrepair about the place.

Lachlan was reluctant to leave home. He declared that he was too old for such adventures and had far too much to do at Strachan but when he finally climbed on to the seat on top of the big, polished coach his sullen expression vanished and he managed a wave of his new cocked hat and gave a grin that showed his excitement at the prospect of seeeing the Grampian mountains and the great lush valleys of the north. Aileen Sinclair shed buckets of tears. She might have been waving Lachlan off to a campaign in India or to exile in Australia. But at last the coach rolled off through the gate and climbed on to the Fintry road. With Robbie by her side, his hand in hers, Anna watched the conveyance out of sight.

Anna remained on the path staring at the still trees under calm grey cloud. She was waiting for some overwhelming emotion to claim her; none did. All her despair and pain had been expended long since. Little was left of her love for Randall Bontine save a certain featherweight rancour at how he had abandoned and betrayed her for a lesser love.

Robbie looked up at his mother. She smiled, swept him into her arms and turned to face the castle.

Strachan's façade seemed friendly with possibilities for diversion, as if, with the Bontines gone, she had come into possession of it. She tapped her son on the nose with her forefinger, made him chuckle and carried him around the edge of the ragged lawn, avoiding cow droppings and scatterings of horse manure. She did not know why, of a sudden, she felt so light and relieved. Perhaps it was because she had been freed of the supervision of her master and mistress and the authority of her father-in-law. She had no fear of Aileen Sinclair or of Cat and could twine poor Sandy around her finger if it suited her. For the time that the Bontines were gone, Strachan Castle was her domain and she would have fun. She would begin by playing hide-and-seek with Robbie for a quarter of an hour.

She put the little boy down.

"A kiss an' a cuddle if I can find you," she said.

Robbie, who had often played the game before, scampered off on sturdy legs to hide in the rhododendron shrubs.

Crouching, Anna prowled about the bushes.

"I spy a wee mannie." Robbie held his breath. "I spy him there." Robbie broke and, with Anna in pursuit, ran to another bush, trailing laughter behind him like a ribbon. "If I find him, it'll be kisses an' cuddles for me."

Leaves rustled on the path side. Anna stepped softly, touched aside the moist leaves with her elbow.

Robbie was on the edge of the path, staring towards the gate.

By the castle, cattle grazed peacefully. There was no sign of Sandy, Aileen, Cat, or any of the day-labourers. But riding down the path from the gate came a man on a handsome black horse.

At first Anna did not recognise him. She went quickly to Robbie and folded her arms about the little boy. No matter how much time passed she still feared the unexpected return of her husband, of Matt.

It was not Matt, however, who had come calling that morning.

"Anna," the man called out. She recognised his voice at once. "Mistress Sinclair, how kind of you to welcome me."

She felt her cheeks glow and did not move forward to greet Mr Rudge immediately. She did not understand her own confusion. She wanted him there, to talk with him, to be with him, to listen to honeyed compliments come from his lips instead of a pen nib, to be reassured that none of his promises were being retracted and that he would remain 'devoted' until such time as she chose to accept him in marriage; yet she did not want him at Strachan Castle, put against Sandy. She was afraid of the effect of that contrast.

"Am I not welcome, then?"

Robert Rudge slid down from the horse. He was not so stiff in the shanks as she had feared he might be, though the ride from Drymen or Kennart had been lengthy. He wore no fancy coat. His shoes were plain and grubby, without buckles. His plainness confused Anna further.

"Aye – aye, Mr Rudge, you are very welcome."

"I have come for conversation with your master, with Gibbie."

"Och, but they've gone."

"Gone? To the wedding, do you mean?"

"Aye, only ten minutes since, Mr Rudge. You must have missed them at the gate by a hair."

He nodded without any sign of annoyance. She knew that he had missed the parting coach quite deliberately. He had probably lurked in the woods across the road, well hidden, until it had gone out of sight.

Robert Rudge came to her and took her arm. She could not predict what he would do, how he could act. From the instant of their first 'real' meeting in his garden in Drymen, he had kept her on the hop. It was part and parcel of his wooing. Anna frowned but did not seek to evade his touch.

"Robbie," said Anna, "run on an' tell Grandma there's a visitor."

Her son hesitated, displeased at being cheated of his mother's attention, yet in awe of the tall man with the pale haggard features and the dubious eye.

"Go on, Robbie, do as you are told," said Robert Rudge, without severity but with that firmness which a child respects in a man, be it parent or stranger.

Robbie went off running, arms akimbo.

Anna said, "You did not come to see Mr Gibbie, did you?"

"I came to see you."

"Hah!" said Anna. "Timed t' perfection, Mr Rudge."

"How would you have done it, Anna?"

"The same," said Anna. "Quite the same."

"We're a devious couple, are we not?"

"I – I've told them nothin' of your proposal, Mr Rudge."

"I would have been disappointed in you if you had."

"I told only Mr Hildebrand."

"Seekin' information?"

"Aye."

"For the sake of appearance I had better let you go now, Anna, though fain would I cling to you for the rest of the day; in faith, for the rest of my life."

Mr Rudge's sentiments sounded so sincere that Anna clenched her elbow to her side to retain contact with him for a split second longer. He patted her hand, disengaged and, with the horse following as obedient as a collie dog, moved on with Anna by his side towards the kitchen archway.

Anna's heart was pounding. Mr Rudge's arrival had been so unexpected. Now she must confront the inevitable moment of comparison; Sandy and Robert Rudge would meet, would each sense that the other was a rival. Men were no less sensitive than women when it came to sniffing competition.

Hands on hips, his shirt smeared with glaur from the stable and a smith's short apron flapping at his loins, Sandy called out, "What can we do for you, Mr Rudge?"

"I've business with Mr Gibbie who, I hear, has already gone off to his brother's wedding."

"Did ye not know of it?" Sandy took the reins of the agent's mount and hitched them to the post within the yard. "I thought it was common knowledge that today was leavin'-day."

"I'm not *au fait* with Mr Gibbie's itinerary," said Robert Rudge, a little haughtily.

He sized Sandy up and down. They had met seldom in the past, only now and then at Ottershaw when Sandy had been no more than a stripling and of no interest to the manager of the Kennart mill. Anna watched the men parade for her benefit. Robbie came to her, skirting the horse, and Aileen and Cat Sinclair fell, at that moment, out of the kitchen door, disturbing the hens that clucked and strutted about the inner yard and sending them into a squawk.

Mr Rudge picked a feather from the breast of his coat.

"I'll not stay then," he said.

Sandy said, "It may be that I can help you, Mr Rudge, since I'm put in charge here."

Mr Rudge smiled flatly. "I fear not. It's not a load of hay I require but Mr Gibbie's payment on purchase of several bolts of cloth."

"It'll have t' wait then."

For a moment it seemed that Sandy was about to dismiss Mr Rudge, to hand him back the rein and slap the horse around until it was nosed towards the archway and the road out of Strachan, but Aileen Sinclair intervened.

"It's a long drive you've had, Mr Rudge. Will you no' be takin' a dish o' tea wi' us before you ride back?"

Robert Rudge seemed relieved to be given the invitation.

"I would be delighted, Mrs Sinclair."

Sandy darted displeasure at his mother. How had he divined that Robert Rudge was here because of Anna and for no other purpose? Anna realised that Sandy was even more intuitive than she had supposed him to be. Laughter rose within her, pressing like a cluster of tiny bubbles at the base of her throat. She put a finger to her lips to suppress the sound and watched Sandy, his face coloured and his hair inexplicably spiky, as he sullenly led the horse away.

In contrast Mr Rudge seemed much at ease. He strolled to the kitchen door and doffed his hat, dunted mud from his shoes on the iron and, with Aileen and Cat unctuously urging him on, stooped and entered the kitchen door.

Anna summoned Robbie, lifted him into her arms, hugged him and, with that excuse, let out a little of her laughter. She enjoyed being a centre of male conflict, even if the contest was patently unequal. She was relieved that Sandy was forbidden to her. She did not want love, she told herself. She wanted only that which Mr Rudge had to offer, flattery, attention and security. She was not going to be silly about him. The silly days were far behind her. She had been silly about Randall Bontine and it had cost her dear in the long run.

Marriage to Sandy Sinclair, after the first season of passion had been expended, would be dull, dull, dull. As if he had caught the thought Sandy emerged from the stable and glared at her. He spun on his heel without a word and stalked into the anvil room where, half-shod, his precious plough-horse waited.

Anna stuck out her tongue at Sandy's back, then, with Robbie in her arms, stepped into the kitchen to join the ladies, to take tea and listen to the pearls of wit and wisdom that Robert, her Robert, would drop into the Sinclairs' unappreciative ears.

It was almost two o'clock before the tea-taking was over and Mr Rudge bid farewells to the Sinclair ladies and suggested, quite candidly now, that Anna might walk with him to the gate to ensure that he was not set upon by the heathen tribes from the hamlet of Strachan. Mr Rudge had apparently succeeded in charming the kinfolk of his intended, and even this little parting joke sent Cat into another peal of laughter for, being a native of Balnesmoor, she felt superior to other provincials and was delighted to endorse any insult towards them.

There was no sign of Sandy. He had not come in for his midday bite and Mr Rudge's horse had been left, fed, watered and rubbed down, tethered to a post in the shade. A thin haze of late-summer sunlight had struggled at last through the cloud.

"You did well, Mr Rudge," said Anna.

"Perhaps you had better call me Robert. When we are alone."

"Robert."

"Is he my rival, Anna?"

"I beg your pardon?"

"Sinclair, the smith."

"He's my husband's brother."

"I did not ask if you could wed him; I know that you can't. I asked if he was my rival."

"Mr Rudge, Robert, you have no rival."

"Does he not come t'your bed?"

"What sort of question is that, Mr Rudge? It's indelicate, an'—"

"The sort of question a man like me can put to you, Anna, without offence. Come now, we're not star-crossed and dewy, are we?"

She did not like this strain of conversation. She preferred oratory, arabesques, pretty compliments, even if, at heart, she knew them to be superficial. She *hoped* that they might contain some grain of truth, some sort of reality. She did not wish to marry a man who was so uncannily aware of her vices and her calculations.

"*Does* he come t'your bed, Anna?"

"No. No, he does not."

"Never?"

"Never."

"I would not want him to," said Robert Rudge.

She looked up at him, faltering.

"I'm not yours yet, Mr Rudge," she said, pleading with him inwardly to say more, to give her a reason for virtue. "Besides, is it different for me than for you?"

"Oh, yes, Anna, of course it is."

She accepted that fact. She had been reared with it. A man might be wild and profligate and receive no more than a certain superficial censure for his behaviour but a woman, even a servant or a field-hand, was supposed to be chaste and modest and without impure thoughts or carnal desires. Randall had told her as much many a time, making a joke of it, but she had been cuddled in the laird's bed and had thought of the meaning not at all.

Anna said, "When I come down t' Kennart mill how many lassies can I look in the eye with the sureness they've not enjoyed your attentions?"

"A few," Robert Rudge said. "But only a few."

He did not preen himself on his ability to seduce women. He looked down at Anna with a sober and sincere expression. "But none, none at all, since that afternoon in the garden."

"Did y' mean everythin' you wrote to me?"

If he had come out with an answer immediately she would have been suspicious and still on her guard. But Robert Rudge was honest enough to hesitate. He gave a faint purse of the lips, a restrained smile. "*Most* of what I wrote."

"Dear God!" said Anna. "I never thought—"

"Is the rake, the lecher, the man of bad reputation not entitled to fall in love, Anna?"

"Not without a reason."

"Love is the reason."

"I – I canna believe it."

"Don't," said Robert Rudge. "If you believe it too soon, without a true proving, then you are as doomed as I am."

"What do ye say?"

"One fool in the household will be quite enough."

They had not stopped walking along the curve of the gravel path that bounded the ragged lawn.

Cattle grazed about the gate where tasty weeds sprouted along the wall and blueflies buzzed and dung smelled strong in the unaccustomed warmth. High above the trees, pinned over the moorland, two buzzards circled, uttering that high, *kee-kee-kee*-ing cry that was at once both plaintive and barbarous, a lost and liquid sound that was beaked and barbed only to small cowering creatures in the bracken below.

Robert Rudge halted. He looked down at Anna.

"I think that if you kiss me now, Anna, I shall be your slave for ever."

Her lips were dry, her heart pounding again. Deliberately she raised herself on her toes and pressed her breasts against his chest, placed her lips to his. Robert did not grab her, did not display eagerness in response to her touch. Anna did not want it of him, not there, not then. Lightly she held herself against him for a moment or so and then let go.

She tried to think of a jocular remark but could not.

Robert looked so serious, so distinctly unhappy, and not in the least superior.

"Does my kiss not please you after all, Robert?" Anna said, at length.

He swallowed, Adam's apple bobbing. "It pleases me too much."

"Too much?"

"Now I'm truly doomed."

She could not decide whether he was being pretentious or intended it as a joke.

Robert gave her no clue as to his feelings. He took off his hat, presented her with an old-fashioned bow, stuck the hat on the back of his head and swung himself up into the saddle.

Puzzled, Anna watched him ride away through the gate. She frowned and scampered after the departing figure, out on to the Fintry road.

"Mr Rudge? Mr Rudge? Robert?" she cried.

He reined the horse, turned in the saddle.

"Will – will you write me more letters?" Anna called out.

At last he smiled, appeared to shed ten years.

"As many as you like. Provided you reply in kind."

"I will. I will. I promise," Anna said.

Robert Rudge snatched off his hat, spurred the horse and, pretending that he was still a wild young buck, galloped rapidly off along the road and vanished out of sight round the bend.

It was Elspeth's second pay-out Saturday before Davy plucked up courage to ask Matt to take him to the Grapes and buy him a tankard of brown beer from the big barrel that was roped to the trestle in the inn's main room.

The idle monotonous life of an invalid was hard for Davy to bear, particularly now that he was alone all day without Sarah for company and Mary Jean's chatter to divert him. He was aware, by instinct, that quietness helped the soft processes of healing and he had sufficient sense not to strain his strength or squander it. He did odd chores about the house. Now that Sarah had become a pit-hand, all black and exhausted like her kin, a certain guilt overrode Davy's innate manliness and, behind a barred door, he scrubbed and chopped vegetables, steeped barley for broth, cut and seasoned meat for stews and even tried his hand at baking bread – a disaster – one lonely boring afternoon.

For the most part, though, Davy brooded. He had long ago rejected self-pity and did not whine much or complain. He had seen young children die, too many of them to cherish a belief in immortality. He had heard travelling preachers cry out that death was payment for wickedness and that the child would burn in the fires of hell, visited by the sins of the fathers. Davy did not understand what the preachers meant. When he thought of his father, which he did often, it was without rage. He thought of his father as the ghost of the man he, Davy, had never become as if he too had died in the seam. But he had not died. He had lived, would live – though what would become of him when Elspeth and Matt grew weary of the Abbeyfield and sick of Mouse and Sarah – aye, and crippled Davy too – and took the bairn and went away, he could not imagine.

Billy Mackenzie had been found dead in a seam. Billy Gibbon had taken a fit of the vomit and choked before his father could find him at shift's end. Gordon Lewis died of a fever, Janet Lewis of the same fever. And Long Jack Lowe of a wasting fever that had rotted his lungs. Long Jack had been fifteen, old enough to fight his way down the shaft each shift and hew coal from the wall until the day he breathed his last, slouched in the bucket, the rope creaking, while his wee brother, Hugh, held his head and cried, "See, Jack, see the light," as if light alone could heal him, like a miracle done by Good Lord Jesus long, long ago.

Davy had come out of the real world into a world of doubt and speculation. His thoughts moved about the question of whether this sort of life was better than no life at all; and if there was a Hereafter would he meet his father there and would Daddy take him to coal and would they be able to cut side by side, whole and strong and tireless, the pair of them. Davy found it impossible to imagine that all angels were white. He could grasp a vision of toil without pain, effort without exhaustion and even in the midst of childish uncertainties he was sure that Good Lord Jesus would not condemn a boy to eternal idleness, no matter how bad he had been.

Davy clung to Matt Shearer. He could no longer command the respect of his sisters since they were earning wages and he was not. He no longer trusted Elspeth. She had gone to the desk and the counting-table, had joined Mr Rance and Mr Bolderon, men put up as enemies of his class. Davy felt that only Matt understood him. Matt had been low too, before he had become a brave whaling-man. Matt would not pamper him just because Elspeth said it was wise to have him rest.

Davy would ask his sister, "What's wrong wi' you, Mousie? Why will ye no' talk to Matt?"

"I *hate* him," Mouse would answer, still.

It would be better for them all, Davy decided, if he could go below, be in the seam with Matt. He would snap Mouse out of it, would see that she worked hard, that she did not overload Sarah's sled, since Sarah was thin and not used to the tunnels yet. But he could not con Matt here at home, not with the tousled sick-bed behind him, not in his damned nightshirt, with his sisters sticking their noses in.

Davy was all dressed, spruce and eager, when Matt came trudging in from the counting-house that Saturday night. It was not quite dark yet, though the nights were drawing in and there was a nip of frost in the dampness of the mornings.

"Well, will ye be headin' into Placket, Matt?"

"Nah, nah. We've provisions enough for tonight. The lassies can go if they're keen for a sweetmeat or a new ribbon."

"I – I could do wi' a taste o' ale, Matt," said Davy.

Matt had slept until three o'clock that afternoon and was rested and fresh and not wholly inclined to spend another evening shuttered in the cottage. He resisted, nonetheless.

"It's too far for ye t' walk, Davy. I'm damned if I'm carryin' you on my back."

337

"I can walk fine, for God's sake."

"I'm more in need o' food than drink."

"Sarah'll have the supper ready by the time we get back."

"Sarah's fair done," said Matt.

"Mouse can help her. Come on, come on, Matt. I'm dry as a husk for beer."

"I'll fetch ye a can, then."

"I'll go m'self, if you'll lend me fourpence."

Matt shook his head. "Well, since you're all shiny an' keen, lad, I'll wander that way wi' ye. Will I leave a message on the slat for the girls?"

"They'll know where we've gone. Come on."

If Elspeth had been there she would have forbidden him the adventure. It would be the first occasion since the spring that he had crossed the Rutherford burn and on to the road, that he had walked further than the near shore. But he had no crippled feeling on him now. His chest did not hurt and the cough was only an occasional irritation. He wanted out of the prison of the cottage, wanted Matt's company, his attention, and the colour of the Grapes in his eyes, its chatter in his ears.

Matt did not walk quick enough for Davy who hurried the man along as if he was the stronger of the two.

"Steady, Davy, steady. I'm weary still."

"She sells pies, does Mrs Figgens, if you're starved."

"Aye, I've seen her pies, an' they're terrible."

"Salty, aye, but that just spices the beer."

"Did ye go often t' the inn wi' your father?"

"Every other Saturday," said Davy, lying.

"Is that so, now?" said Matt without a trace of scepticism.

If Davy was shaky after the walk he gave no sign of it and managed to march boldly along the final stretch to the inn.

Ahead there was Placket, its blunt tower, its fish smell, the glow of lights from the square dabbed on the sky. It seemed like years since he had been here last.

Matt had been paid early, given his wage not from Elspeth but from Mr Bolderon, to assure the other colliers that there was no deception or favouritism. There were women on the road, though, and a handful of colliers wending back over the bridge towards the inn.

The wooden doors of the Grapes stood open. It was too soon

338

into the evening for the fiddler to have turned up and there was no hubbub from the inn room. But the light itself was the colour of good ale and you could catch a whiff of whisky, sharp as a herb on the wafting breeze. Davy gave a great sigh of pleasure. He clamped his hands to his thighs to stop them trembling and swaggered into the inn ahead of Matt Shearer.

Georgie Haynes was the first thing that Davy saw.

Haynes was standing by the long trestle, a tankard of beer in his fist. The skipper and the other one off the *Matchless* flanked him. Georgie Haynes was caught in laughter, head back, teeth and tongue showing. The braying sound cut off when he caught sight of Davy Bennet and the man behind him.

"Aye, aye. An' what have we here now?" Georgie Haynes demanded. "It must be the night the fairy folk ride out."

Matt had heard a version, three versions come to think of it, of Georgie Haynes' assault upon the privacy of the Bennet family, of his lustful interest in Elspeth. Matt recognised the keelman without introduction. He put his hand at once on Davy's bony shoulder and held the boy still.

At the long table were three or four colliers. They were all sober and not at all inclined, Davy guessed, to cross the keelmen. It had not occurred to him that Georgie Haynes might still call in at this particular port, for, stupidly, Davy had imagined that the keelman would be too ashamed to show his face near Placket.

Legs trembling uncontrollably now, his face suddenly on fire, Davy leaned back against Matt and hissed, "That's him. That's Georgie Haynes."

"Aye," Matt murmured. "So I can see."

Haynes said, "So you're the mannie they brung from the whalers, eh? Blubber left over, eh? You're the mannie that sticks it –"

"I want no trouble here," Matt interrupted.

Davy glanced round. Matt's blue eyes were hooded. In the hair of his beard his lips seemed pink, not red, pressed into a thin, angry line.

The old keelman, the skipper, had detached himself from the table and had his fingers on a big wooden cog that contained hard-boiled eggs pickled in oil and vinegar. The man called Lewis was smiling, shaking his head a little bit as Georgie Haynes went on, "Or is it the boy here? Is he what y' fancy, whaler, eh?"

Davy said, "Matt?"

Perhaps he had guessed that Haynes would be here. Perhaps he had hoped that Haynes would challenge Matt, knowing that Matt would whip the bullying keelman even with odds against him.

Davy's heart flittered against his ribs. He was entitled to retreat and nobody would hold it against him; he had been sick and could not fight. But he had brought his champion, Matt Shearer, in his stead. Matt would beat Georgie Haynes so sore that the keelman would not dare show his face in Placket again.

"Go on, Matt. Go on. Hit him."

With a glance at his companions Georgie Haynes casually dropped the tankard to the floor.

Mrs Figgens was behind the trestle along with her elder son, William. They would not interfere. They knew that colliers and keelmen could afford to pay for damages to the premises and that it was too early for a brawl to harm the drinking-trade.

"I know ye ducked me." Georgie Haynes addressed himself to Davy. "Since your mottes aren't here I'm goin' t' gut you in their stead."

The knife had a handle of cork and twine, a short thin little blade with a curve to it, the kind that fishwives used to gut herring. It appeared in Georgie Haynes' fingers as if by magic.

"Take him, Matt. Take him quick."

Smirking, Georgie Haynes stepped forward, the knife lightly cradled in his palm.

Davy had never seen steel drawn in a quarrel before. Fights between colliers were with fists, knees, sometimes feet, but never with a weapon, never dangerous to life. He huddled involuntarily against Matt and then was lifted and flung towards the inn door.

Sprawling, he twisted his head, expecting Matt to tackle and disarm the keelman. Matt did nothing of the kind. Though Matt's fists were clenched so hard that his knuckles were white and his shoulders quivered with rage, he did not advance on Georgie Haynes.

The keelman taunted him again, calling him a yellow-belly, insulting Elspeth, Mouse, even their daddy, though he was dead and could not protect himself.

"*Matt,*" Davy cried.

Matt would not be urged or tempted. Saying nothing at all, Matt stepped back. He groped for Davy's arm, hoisted the boy to his feet and dragged him out of the door and across the sward to the road. Matt had retreated before the bully, before the threat of a little knife.

Davy was thunderstruck, mortified and ashamed, sick at the realisation that Matt Shearer was no hero but a craven coward. If Matt had been beaten in a fight then Davy would have admired him all the more. *But not to fight at all*; how could that be? How could a man do that? How could Matt so let him down?

They were scuffling along the road away from the inn now, Matt still dragging Davy by the arm, Davy shouting, "Matt, go back. Go back an' fight the bloody keelman," and Matt saying, "You canna understand, Davy. I dare not fight him. I dare not."

Breathless and gagging, Davy tore his hand from Matt's grasp, rounded on him.

"Matt Shearer, I thought—"

"It's no' what it seems, Davy."

"Bastard! I wanted you t' take me down wi' you. I'll never work wi' you now, y' coward."

He spat saliva with a little furious motion of the head. He saw spit adhere to Matt's jacket, then, before he could be felled by the exhaustion that such a large emotion might bring, Davy set off at the double along the road to the Abbeyfield.

Matt did not pursue.

Matt stood disconsolately in the dusk while women and girls coming up from the field to the village passed him and stared at him, giving him a wide berth.

After a time, though, Matt too went – hurting – homeward, because he had no place else to go.

"Is Mouse sleepin'?"

"Aye, they all are."

Pretending to be fast asleep, Mouse lay very still. Elspeth

341

had come to the side of the dresser, stooped and peered in at her. She had kept her breath flowing, her mouth open and had somehow prevented her eyelids from flickering until the candle had gone away and she had heard Elspeth tell Matt in a soft, soft voice that Mouse had dropped off too and that it was safe for them to talk.

It had been a strange, diverting evening. Mouse could not decide whether she had enjoyed it. She understood, of course, what had happened and why Davy was so mad.

It had been Georgie and Georgie had met Matt and Georgie had stood up to Matt because Georgie was jealous of Matt living with her and thought that Matt had the run of the house and the women in it, and was jealous of Matt's closeness to her and, perhaps, to Elspeth since Elspeth was older. But Matt had not cared enough or was, as Davy claimed, a yellow-belly and a bloody liar and a coward.

Davy would not speak to Matt. Davy had rolled into his bed with all his clothes on and would not speak to Sarah and had frightened Mary Jean and made her cry, and then, to her, to his sister Mousie, had blurted it out. He had shouted that she had been right not to make friends with the bastard stranger, the bloody sailor, who was worthless and a coward.

They were of a size, Matt and Georgie. Mouse thought of each of them with longing. She was afraid of the feeling and yet revelled in it. She had never felt as she had done when Georgie touched her. She knew that he had a power Daddy had never had, Davy never would have. She had felt that power in Matt Shearer too. She resented the fact that he belonged to Elspeth and shared secrets with Elspeth and treated her, Mousie, like a bairn.

Elspeth had come in from the counting-house all neat and strange in her plaid dress, not one of them any longer. Elspeth had shaken Davy and tried to make him tell her what was wrong. It had been left to Sarah to tell Elspeth what had happened. Elspeth had been quiet, too quiet, and had not chided Davy at all.

Elspeth had concerned herself with Mary Jean and had said very little until Matt had come in five minutes later, then she had gone to him and had taken him by the arm and led him outside to talk in whispers, soft whispers in which there was a note of consolation, as if Matt had suffered a grief the way they had done when Daddy was killed, the way Mr Bolderon had spoken that day at the kirkyard.

Elspeth had been so distracted upon her return from work that she had just tossed the four crowns upon the table. The big round coins glinted among the flour dust and the wet patches where cabbage had been chopped and the penny-sized pools of blood from the meat that Sarah had bought from Mr Nicol's earlier on. Mouse wondered where Matt hid his money. How much had been earned that fortnight? When would he remember to dole out her share? He was usually prompt on that score. She had no need of the money. She had eight pence left from last pay-night, eight pence tucked into the toe of a slipper she had outgrown but kept because the pair were of red kidskin and Daddy had given them to her when she was very young, along with a pink scarf which she had long since lost.

Matt had eaten bread and tea. Elspeth had fed Mary Jean, and Sarah had drunk tea for they had eaten earlier in the afternoon. Elspeth picked at scraps and looked at Matt as if she wanted to take him into her arms or tell him something that should not be heard by other ears. Meanwhile Davy lay below the bedclothes pretending he could hear nothing.

Sarah soon put herself to bed. Elspeth had made Mary Jean comfortable and had sat with her behind the curtain while Matt slouched at the table, cheek on his hand, stroking his beard, his blue eyes full of something that Mouse could not name. Mouse had wanted to put her arms about his neck, to slide on to his knee, touch him, comfort him. But she had chosen her attitude and would stick to it because it was easier than changing. Matt looked so sad sitting there at the table, staring at nothing, remembering, perhaps, the big jagged mountains of ice that grew out of the seas where the whale lived.

"Is Davy sleepin' too?"

"Dead to this world," said Elspeth.

"I never intendit t' let the boy down," Matt said. "If it had been a less public place than the Grapes I might have lost my temper an' taken on the swine."

"You were right to turn away, Matt."

"Nah, nah, 'Pet. I was wrong – as usual."

"But if there had been bloodshed it would have brought the Sheriff's man or the Riding Officers. Mrs Figgens would have sent for them. They might have recognised you."

"It wasn't for that reason I turned tail, Elspeth. When I saw the knife it reminded me o' that night at Kennart. God, I'm no' scared o' Georgie Haynes. I'd take him on in a split second if he showed his face here."

"Georgie Haynes'll not come here," said Elspeth.

Hardly daring to breathe, Mouse listened. She could not fathom what Elspeth and Matt Shearer meant to each other but she was more convinced than ever that they had known each other well some time, somewhere in the past.

"Aye, Haynes'll suppose you're protectit," said Matt. "Protectit by a coward."

"Matt, Matt, Davy'll not hold it against you for long. You'll see, he'll come round in a day or two."

"He wants me to tak' him below."

"Oh, no. I'll not allow it."

"He thinks, since I'm the bread-earner, I've the final say."

"It might please an' flatter him," said Elspeth, "but in a matter of days, a week at most, he'd be in worse health than ever. No, no, Matt. You must be firm with him. I'll not have Davy waste away out of stupid pride."

"Pride's not stupid, 'Pet. I wish I could afford more of it," Matt said. "But, aye, you're right. Davy would suffer ill in no time at all if he had t' work below ground again. God, he's so thin an' weak. I fear, even as it is, he might no' be with us long."

Mouse frowned. Stirring slightly, she lifted her knees and put her hands to her face, her thumb into her mouth.

Matt and Elspeth were silent for two or three minutes. She heard the clank of the kettle, the dribble of water, smelled the aroma of a fresh brew of tea. She wondered if Mam and Daddy had ever sat drinking tea at a late hour, talking, just talking. She could not remember now.

"Would he fare better in Balnesmoor?" said Matt.

Balnesmoor; Mouse had heard them mention the name before. She did not know where it was. It was not a name that colliers bandied about or that Daddy had ever used.

"Gaddy would have pulled him round," said Elspeth.

344

"Gaddy, aye."

"Why did you treat her so badly, Matt?"

"I was o'er young t' be married. I blamed Gaddy, your mother, for hastenin' me into it. Even you must admit she acted like lightning after – you know."

"If it had not been for Mam would you not have sought t' marry Anna?"

"How can I say now? Perhaps; perhaps not. I had no choice, 'Pet. Between my father an' your mother I was fixed, like a bullock, by the nose."

"Would you – would you have sought to marry me?"

"No."

"I'm not flattered, Matt."

"I – I liked you, 'Pet, but you were too like your mother, like Gaddy Patterson. It's odd – we all thought so – that *you* were the foundlin', yet you were the one wi' all Gaddy Patterson's qualities, good an' bad."

"Bad?"

"Aye, you'll have your way, come what might. You're loyal but o'er pressin' for a woman."

"Am I, even now?"

"More so than ever."

Silence: Mouse sensed that Matt had hurt Elspeth.

How did Matt know so much about Elspeth Patterson? It seemed that he had been married to her sister at one time. If so, where was the sister now? Puzzling out these mysteries tired Mouse but she willed herself to stay awake. She had a hint of other secrets and the answer to something that had bothered her a lot. Matt, it seemed, had no designs at all on Elspeth Patterson. They would not match, would not, one night, roll and grunt together behind the curtain. The realisation brought Mouse a sensation of warmth in her belly, a strange disquieting feeling.

"Have I hurt you, 'Pet?" Matt said.

"No, no."

"You shouldna be injured by such comparisons. God, every man on Ottershaw admired your mam. Some would have had Gaddy if they had not been feared o' the talk. My father too."

"Lachlan?"

"Aye, the righteous grieve. I remember how my mam worried o'er it when Gaddy was free, after Coll died."

All these names; Mouse was confused. But she was as certain as cheese that Matt and Elspeth had a secret, that some dark cloud hung over them both. Had Elspeth been a lady once? Had matchin' brought her down?

"I never guessed it," Elspeth said.

Silence again: Mouse did not stir this time. She sucked her thumb without a sound and breathed into the palm of her hand.

"Will you ever go back, Elspeth?" Matt said.

"I – I canna," said Elspeth.

"Because o' what I told you about James Moodie? Because he was – and he *was* – involved in murder?"

"That reason first," said Elspeth.

"Did he beat you?"

"No. He was kind. But he was wicked, Matt, in other ways. Do not ask me. I've no wish to speak of it."

"He frightens you?"

"Yes."

"At least, if it comes to it, you *can* go back home."

"What would become o' these children: Davy, Sarah, Mouse?"

"Ach, they're collier bairns. They'll survive."

"Davy too?"

Matt did not answer.

Elspeth said, "Now I'm settled behind the countin'-desk, I think Mr Bolderon might keep me there."

"I doubt if Bolderon'll last long on the Abbeyfield. I've heard from Thomas Rance how his agreement wi' the owner expires soon an' how he canna find capital t' buy in again."

Mouse did not understand this turn of the midnight conversation. She was impatient with it. She did not want to hear of Mr Bolderon and Thomas Rance. She wanted Matt to talk of her again, to lay out like a roll of fine silk some attractive future that would include them all, even Davy.

Matt said, "I think he'll take you wi' him if he leaves here, 'Pet."

"He's said nothing to me on the score."

"He'll be bidin' his time. He's picked you for somethin' other than a paymaster, Elspeth," Matt said.

"He supposes me t' be a widow."

"Let him think it."

"Matt!"

"God, there are worse things than havin' two husbands."

"I'd have to tell him the truth. I couldn't deceive him."

"Oh-hoh! It's in the wind, is it?"

"I – I believe it might be, in due course of time. He's full of attentions and charm."

"Be careful, 'Pet. It might no' be marriage he's after."

"Mr Bolderon's a gentleman."

"I have my doubts about that," Matt said.

"What about you, though?" Elspeth said. "My sister'll seek a divorce in course of time. I know her. She'll want t' be free again."

"Free for the bloody laird o' Ottershaw t' take his pleasure wi' her."

"Matt, you canna defend against divorcement."

Matt did not comment or protest. He said nothing.

Elspeth said, "Will it hurt you t' lose her?"

"Nothin' from the past hurts me now, 'Pet," Matt answered. "But havin' Anna taken from me by the process o' the law would be the least hurt o' all. Hah! Would it not be an irony? I would still be an outlaw, a lost man, but I would be free t' take another wife."

"You? Who would you want t' marry?"

"Mousie, perhaps," Matt answered.

It was all Mouse could do to keep her legs from jerking in astonishment, to prevent herself sitting bolt upright with a cry. She would not have known what words to use, whether to choose outrage or delight from the rattlebag of emotions in her head and heart.

"Och, Matt. Don't tease," said Elspeth.

To Mousie's consternation Matt laughed away his own suggestion.

Minutes later, soothed by levity, Matt told Elspeth that the hour was late and that he felt settled enough to sleep.

Elspeth and Matt Shearer went, separately, to bed.

Sleep might come quick to the sailorman but for the girl in

the nest below the dresser there was only confusion and a night of restless dreams.

In the morning she could not meet Matt's eye. She sulked at her own shyness, said not a word – and everything on the surface was just as it had been before.

It was the night of the day upon which Randall Bontine of Balnesmoor and Ottershaw had stepped to the altar in a far-off kirk in Aberdeenshire, had taken vows of marriage and bound himself to the duty of husband to Suzanne Seaton of Piperhaugh. Though Anna had been conscious of the importance of that day in her life, she had felt less sorrow than she had anticipated, only a kind of bitterness which inured her to the occasion.

It was all so far away, Randall so far away. She told herself that she would feel pain perhaps when Randall returned with his bride and she glimpsed them together, riding in the carriage along the turnpike or coming here to Strachan Castle to visit Alicia and Mr Gilbert. But Anna was no longer convinced that her passion for Randall Bontine was unquenchable as she had once supposed it to be.

The Sinclairs, however, were more in key with the import of the day than Anna appeared to be. Catriona and her mother chattered on about 'the wedding' every time they had an opportunity. Even Sandy, who had fallen into a quiet mood since Mr Rudge's visit to Strachan, had wryly remarked that this was 'the day' and that Sir Randall would know all about it – as if he, Sandy, was an expert in the pitfalls of matrimony.

Bracken had turned sad and yellow very swiftly that season and the hills were not brave with autumn colours but tawdry and leaves from gardens and parks were too wet to whirl in the stiffening wind and coated the grass like paper scraps. Darkness came early. When milking was finished and the cows packed out into the quagmires of the pastures again, Anna wanted only to be indoors by the glow of the fire in the kitchen for the dusk was far, far too melancholy for her present mood. Once she was indoors, however, and had dried her feet and legs and changed her stockings, helped herself to a bowl of broth from the pot and had taken Robbie on to her knee to give him his supper, then she found that she hardly

348

thought of Randall at all and that her ability to visualise the laird and his bride preparing for nuptials had quite waned away.

Even Catriona and Aileen Sinclair could not stir it to life again. It was Sandy who eventually found their remarks annoyingly suggestive and growled at them to find another topic for the supper table since he'd heard enough about bloody Randall Bontine for one damned day.

"La-de-dah!" Cat smirked. "Are ye jealous, then, Sandy? Would ye like t' be the lairdie tonight, eh?"

Even for Aileen, though, that was too pointed a remark and she advised her daughter to be more ladylike or she would get her ears boxed as she used to when she was a bairn.

Anna had heard so much of this bickering, endured so many trivial quarrels between the Sinclairs that the subject of it all hardly seemed to matter. She blotted it out. She thought instead of Robert Rudge and what sort of wedding feast convention would allow to a woman who had been divorced. Would she have a fine, bright, cheerful day for it, and rose petals on her path and scattered on her bed? She thought of Robert Rudge as lover – until Robbie clamoured for her attention and she took him away from the kitchen to play for a half-hour in the dining-room since the master was away and there was nobody to say her nay.

She lit two candles, set up Robbie's wooden skittles and let him roll a wooden ball at them, rumbling and trundling along the floor. Aileen would not object since it was for Robbie's amusement. Anna half expected that Sandy would come to join them, take a turn at the skittles. But he did not. She returned to the kitchen in due course to find that Sandy had gone to his bed.

It was well after ten o'clock, the castle as dark and as silent as such a decrepit building ever got, before Anna discovered that Sandy had not been in bed but had been down in the cellar with the ale keg for company. He had had, by the look of him, a fine time to himself, making free with Mr Gibbie's brew. She had not imagined it of Sandy. It made him seem a true brother to her husband, Matt.

Robbie was asleep in his cot. Anna had taken a bone comb from her box and, seated on the side of her bed, combed her hair, not because she was particularly neat but because it gave her sensual satisfaction, like a tabby washing its fur.

She had a candle in a little brown knobbed glass, a mirror in a wooden frame propped against the wall and, studying her face while she stroked and caressed her dark hair across her shoulders, she wondered at the changes in her and why they were not, that she could see, reflected in her outward appearance. She looked beautiful – she thought – and mysterious, too luxurious for a niche in a servants' corridor. She was unmarked by the disasters that had dogged her, by child-bearing, and did not look weary and sallow and worn like a wife.

The comb whispered reassuringly in her hair. She gave a little sigh that changed into a suppressed gasp as Sandy's visage appeared beside her own, edging it out of the looking-glass, and consumed the candlelight with his shadow. She had not heard him come. She had been so absorbed in her own thoughts that he had stolen to the bedside as soundlessly as a sneak-thief.

She let the mirror drop to the bolster and turned to him. She could smell drink on him. The resemblance to Matt was apparent.

He wiped his mouth with his hand.

"Makin' yoursel' beautiful, Anna, are ye?" he whispered.

"How much have you taken?"

"A taste here, a taste there." Sandy shrugged.

He seated himself by her.

She might have supposed that he had come to offer her comfort if it had not been for his condition. He was half unclad, wore only his breeks. The rope at the girdle was loose. He was handsome now. His boyish quality had gone this past month or two, most of his daft innocence. He was as handsome as Matt had been when she had stolen him from Elspeth – only Elspeth had not wanted him after all and her efforts had led to nothing but grief and pain.

Sandy was unsmiling.

Anna touched the candle glass with her finger, shifting it so that she could look into his blue eyes and read the extent of his drunkenness. He was not out of reason, not blistered with spirits as she had feared. He seemed sharper, though, edged, and spoke in a low, distinct voice as firm as his father's had once been.

"I'm told there's no hope for me, Anna," he began, without preamble. "Marriage between us will always be impossible."

"We both know it."

"But love is not."

"Sandy, I'm promised."

"To Rudge, is it?"

"It was me, not Mr Gibbie, he came t' see."

"I'm not blind, Anna. But he came t' take a look at me too."

"You?"

"Just t' see if you're cheatin' him."

"How can you say such a thing?" Anna protested.

"Rudge expects loyalty. Expects purity. Is that no' a joke?"

"Mr Rudge is a gentleman."

"I know fine what Rudge is," said Sandy.

Candlelight and the confinement of the niche made Sandy seem less threatening. He did not smell sour as Matt had done when he was in his boozing cups. On Sandy the odour of spirits was clean and masculine. His chest and torso were muscular and his breastbone downed with coarse fair hair. Anna wondered how he could have grown into manhood without her being more aware of it.

"Go away back t' your own bed, Sandy."

He shook his head. "I'm named after old Sir Gibbie's brother; did y' know that?"

"No, I did not."

"My father worshipped the Bontines. When I was born he didn't have the impudence t' name me Gilbert so he picked the next best name."

Anna frowned. Was this, after all, just tipsy talk?

She said, "Who gave Matt *his* name?"

"The oldest o' the Bontines; Matthew. He was heritor before old Gibbie. He died young, though. My father remembered him an' thought he was a hero."

"You're named Alexander – after the Irishman?"

"An' stuck wi' it."

"Why – what does it have t' do wi' me, Sandy?"

"Nothin' of consequence," said Sandy.

He hesitated, frankly staring at her breasts. He reached and placed his hand upon her and, when she did not slap him away, reached again and drew down the collar of her shift.

Anna crushed her thighs together. She sank back an inch or two until her head rested against the wall. She was drenched with perspiration. It had been many, many months since she had been with a man, with Randall, and she had desired the pleasure of it too often to reject Sandy out of hand.

She closed her eyes.

Not so many weeks ago she had almost fallen in love with him. Now he was with her, his hands brushing her breasts, his mouth touching her flesh. She responded in spite of herself. She arched her spine and thrust herself to him, offering more. When he caught her around the waist and dragged her down on the narrow bed Anna gave a small urgent gasp and spread out her arms.

"No," she murmured. "No, please, no."

Struggling against instinct, she strove to reason with her instincts. If she yielded to him now she would become his for ever, a prisoner of the man and of the place. With vivid clarity she saw how it would evolve, how Sandy would make use of her and how pride in his conquest of her would change him, cause him to flout and defy his father, his mother and the society's conventions. She might become his woman but never his wife.

She put her knee beneath him and heaved him from her. At the same instant she wanted to comfort him, kiss and caress and hug him to her but she did not dare. She had learned from marriage to Matt and from the things that she had done with Randall that loving was not love, that real love was quick and slippery as mercury in a dish. Deep in her heart she knew that she was not cruel enough to spoil Sandy too.

He came at her again. She struck out at him. He caught her arm, held it, but sought no further intimacy. He looked down at her bared breasts, knees and thighs bare under the rucked shift and at the tears in her dark eyes. Abruptly he flung her arm from him and sat back, crouched on his haunches on the floor, his face level with her own.

"Am I no' good enough for the likes o' you, is that it?"

She swallowed her tears, let no tremor into her voice.

Deliberately she pulled up her shift to cover her breasts and brought her hair down over her shoulders.

"I would do you no good, Sandy," she said.

"I wouldna cast you aside."

"I'm promised to Mr Rudge."

"Christ!" Sandy hissed. "Is it only that sham promise that prevents you?"

"It's no sham," said Anna, with a prickle of anger. "I have it in writin'."

Sandy got to his feet. He hitched his breeks against his waist and stared down at her, despising her.

"Aye, sham," Sandy declared. "You that's such a schemer, Anna, I'm amazed you canna see what Rudge is up to."

Heat and desire had gone out of her. She was relieved by a sudden wave of curiosity. Swinging her feet to the floor she grabbed Sandy by the wrist; he might otherwise leave her unappeased.

"What do y' mean?" Anna demanded. "What's Robert up to?"

"Rudge only wants the mill at Kennart. An' you're his one hope for obtainin' it," Sandy answered.

"Kennart mill? Me?"

"When your sister returns to claim her rightful due then your famous Mr Rudge'll be given his marchin' orders."

"Why should that be?"

"For skinnin' silver from the purse."

Anna saw it all with astonishing clarity. Now that it had been brought to her attention she realised that she would, in fact, have been surprised if Mr Rudge had *not* taken the chance to peel a few pounds from the mill purse while Jamie Moodie was ill. It was obvious that the lawyer mannie, Hildebrand, had learned of the theft and would recommend that Elspeth dismiss the manager as soon as she returned to Balnesmoor.

It was all so clear, so brilliantly clear.

If Mr Rudge was married to her, to Elspeth's sister, his position at Kennart would be secure for life.

Anna laughed aloud.

She saw Sandy's eyes widen.

Aye, she had been correct in her judgement. Sandy Sinclair was too innocent ever to be her man. As wife, as lover she

353

would soon have warped him out of honest shape and brought him only ill luck and unhappiness.

Sandy stammered, "D . . . did ye know? D . . . did Rudge say as much?"

"Kennart mill's my bridal price," said Anna evenly. "Did you suppose, Sandy, a bachelor like Mr Rudge would take a wife otherwise?"

"Good God Almighty!" Sandy exclaimed. "You're worse than he is."

"Aye, that might be true," said Anna.

She felt oddly flattered by the insult, quite warmed by it in fact.

"What – what if Elspeth does not come back?" said Sandy.

"In that case Mr Rudge will marry me for other reasons."

"Phaaah!" said Sandy in disgust. He tore his hand from her grasp. "You're two o' a kind. Both devils."

He stamped away up the corridor, muttering, all his ardour, his youthful passion diminished and spent.

Anna heard the clink of a bottle against a tankard and imagined him, in the kitchen, taking a long swill of whisky or ale to cleanse the unpalatable truth from his mind.

It would take more than liquor to make Sandy understand. Surely, though, he would eventually realise that she was not for the likes of him, law or no law.

Anna sat musing on the side of the cot for a while then reached below the cot and fished out her box. From it she lifted a tub of coal-black ink and a feather quill, a tablet of smooth paper, all of which items she had removed from Mr Gibbie's chamber under the turret stairs and which she was sure he would never misss.

She balanced the tablet on her knee, tucking it against her stomach with her forearm as if it was a school slate. Stooping, she dipped the cut of the quill into the ink and let it drip for a moment, then, making up in patience what she lacked in skill, she penned the date upon the upper portion of the page.

She watched the black ink dry.

She wrote: *"My Deerest Robert."*

She sucked the feather for inspiration and then, piece by piece, completed the letter: *"I long to see you agin. I wish to convers with you at your erliest conven'ce. It w'ld be sutable for you to call on me on Wes'day 1st. I will eckspec you for your dinner. With All My Afekton and My Respek, I Am Your Anna."*

Tomorrow morning, first thing, she would walk with the letter to the mail office and on Wednesday, when Robert came, she would inform him that she had made up her mind, that she would have him for a husband and would settle terms for the marriage with or without her sister's blessing, with or without Elspeth's return.

NINE

Sisters in Sorrow

Keir Bolderon's courtship of Elspeth Patterson was a good deal more subtle than Robert Rudge's wooing of the heiress's sister. Throughout the autumn months, while poor old Snippets languished under Doctor Kidson's ministrations and was bled with increasing frequency, Keir Bolderon's unlikely friendship with Elspeth ripened and changed in character.

It was astonishing just how quickly and how thoroughly Mrs Patterson acquired that air of 'apartness', a certain brusqueness of speech and manner, that separated her from labouring colliers. It was not the power of the post of paymaster that effected the change but rather the suitability of the person, woman or man, for the post. To do it at all demanded a degree of intellectual fibre that Elspeth Patterson had always possessed or, in the course of her secret life as wife to the wealthy Moodie, had adopted as a means of keeping up with her husband.

It was an easy matter for Mr Bolderon to defend himself against the ribald remarks and aspersions that were cast in his direction by fellow engineers and companions in management who were all agog at the notion that a female could do anything as demanding as make up wages and accurately keep books. What intrigued them was the prospect of having such a radical appointment accepted by their own crews, in being at liberty to select some sweet young thing from out of the ranks and, by paying her a few shillings, protect her from the brutalising effects of coal-labour and, at the same time, save themselves money. None, however, had the audacity to try it. None had found a girl capable of it. In consequence they chinned old Bolderon at every opportunity and gave him gyp at monthly meetings of the Coal Owners and Managers Association in the Peveril Tavern in Alloa. Keir Bolderon took it all in good part. He was evasive about the woman, offhand, in fact. If he had gotten on to his high horse, been all kirk and county about it, he would have taken more stick than he got and might have roused the curiosity of his fellows as to the natural attributes of this female phenomenon, brought them riding out to the Abbeyfield not to admire the nice new winding-rope or grimace at the primitive methods still in general use but to squint at and appraise the female paymaster and perhaps try to steal her away.

Closer to home only Thomas Rance was often enough in the company of both Mr Bolderon and Mrs Patterson to observe the flowering of respect and affection between them and to puzzle over it.

Thomas Rance was not, of course, so unworldly as to ignore Keir Bolderon's probable motive. Mrs Patterson was a fine-looking woman, neat about her person, well-spoken and well-educated. She was also attractive to a man in a more earthy, honest sort of way, and it was on the level of a collier that Thomas Rance pitched his judgement of the manager's intentions. Thomas Rance found the nosegays of garden flowers that would appear in a glass dish on the counting-house table rather hard to stomach, found the Frenchified habit of making a 'pic-nic' out of the midday meal went against the grain of his gruff temperament. Indeed, most of Mr Bolderon's little 'attentions' to Mrs Patterson seemed ridiculously out of place in the middle of a coalfield. But the woman herself was more sensible than her employer. She would drift along with Mr Bolderon's games only so far, would then brush aside the candy talk, sweep away the wine glasses, china bowls and lace-edged teacloth and say, "Time we got on with the work, Mr Bolderon, is it not?"; to which question Mr Bolderon would answer with a reluctant nod and pretend, suddenly, to be very busy indeed.

The tenor and circumstances of life on the Abbeyfield did not suit such a genteel wooing. In late August a slump of rock in the main tunnel mutilated a boy and a woman. Thomas Rance led the crew that dug them out. Mr Bolderon carried the writhing victims to the counting-house where rudimentary doctoring was administered until Doctor Kidson could arrive on the scene. There was blood in profusion, screaming, a crowd of wailing relatives gathered about the pallets on which the woman, a mother of seven children, was held down, and the boy, youngest of three, sunk into a torpor and died there on the floor below the high desk where men, come Saturday, would make their marks and take their money. Mr Bolderon tried to hasten Elspeth away from the scene but she was stern and purposeful and, with lips pursed, got to her knees with clean water and a swab and bathed the boy's crushed head, cooled it and crooned to him until his mother took over the task. Only when the boy, a lad of no more than ten, gave up the ghost with a strange little purr in his throat, did Elspeth Patterson step back and find a quiet corner in which she could shed her tears.

In September a coal-oil lamp burst and scalded two haulers, blinding one. Again it was Mrs Patterson who offered comfort until the family could be drawn from the pit and brought to the offices to lead the women away since they were capable of walking, albeit in agonising pain. In September too, coal-hewer James Caldwell expired of natural causes in the base-level seam that ran west from the ladder bottom. Mr Bolderon had gone down to examine the corpse and had supervised its removal to the carpenters' shed where it would lie under a blanket until coffined for burial. On that occasion it was Keir Bolderon who had bowed and shed tears for the dead man whom he had not known well, though not in sight of his oversman or Mrs Patterson but up on the path behind the fences hidden by a drape of yellow and russet leaves.

Next afternoon there was a basket of roast lamb and a jar of pears stewed in burgundy and a fresh lace-edged cloth to keep grease off the table; and Mr Bolderon and Mrs Patterson had wasted an hour in eating, talking and talking all the while on matters more solemn, that day, than gay.

Bewildered by it all, Thomas Rance shook his head and left them to it. He could not fathom what a sensible and educated widow could see in a man like Keir Bolderon who, according to talk, would be out of employment and without a penny to his name come Easter.

Airs, graces and drawing-room manners were not for Mr Rance for, at last, he had forgotten what it felt like to be falling in love.

*   *   *

Early that morning Matt inadvertently brought down a huge rib of coal. Caught off guard by the size of the fall he feared that the rumble would be heard not only by the Ogilvies but by hewers near the ladder. Mouse – Sarah close on her heels – was in the narrow tunnel when the noise enveloped her. She wriggled forward to the trap at once and, receiving Matt's assurance that he was uninjured, crawled past her sister to bawl out that all was fine with the Bennets and there was no cause for alarm.

The rib had peeled from a long section of coal that stretched to the nether end of the slit. For the first time the millstone slab was exposed. Curiously, Matt examined it by candlelight, followed it to the cave's narrowest part. Here, space was so tight that he had to suck in breath and scrape chest and belly on the wall. Mouse scowled through the trap and only when the dust had cleared came down the worn steps to fill the creel with coal to push up to Sarah who in turn would pack the sleds.

Matt said, "God, but there's more."

Mouse glanced at him.

"It wends on under the slab."

"What?"

"It's no splinter this, Mousie. Did your daddy ever explore the high end?"

"I dinna think so, Matt."

Matt rubbed the millstone with his thumb and dislodged even by that light pressure a few glittering grains. He strove to stretch the candle further into the crack but could not and, with much grunting, extracted himself and came out.

Kneeling by the coal pile on the floor, hands idle, Mouse continued to watch him.

Matt put the candle on a ledge, pointed a finger at the girl. "I could've swore I heard you speak, Mousie."

"It was a question had t' be answered."

"Even so," said Matt, "it's a start."

He stood close to her, drawers plastered to his loins, showing the man-shape. He saw where she was looking and turned away, hitching his cloth in embarrassment.

Over his shoulder he said, "I'll ask y' another question then:

359

if I could break down enough o' that slab, Mousie, could you wriggle in there wi' a candle an' see what's to be seen?"

She glanced from Matt to the shadowy region where walls and ceiling converged.

"Aye, I could."

"I'd make sure ye didn't get stuck," Matt said.

"Will the slab break easy?"

"Nah, I doubt it," said Matt. "It may not yield at all."

"Break out the coal, then," Mousie said. "Make a hole for me on the high side."

"It'll be damned narrow."

She gave a little snort. "Aye, but I'm damned wee, am I not?"

Matt squatted, facing across the column of unbroken coal. She did not meet his eye. She busied herself packing lumps into the creel. Above them Sarah rested her elbows on the rim of the trap and peered at the couple.

Matt said, "I'm no collier, Mousie, so tell me what y' think. Will there be a complete seam through there?"

"Might be."

"Who would know?"

"Rance." She looked up. "But we're no' tellin' *him* about it."

"Would Davy know?"

"He might. Let me go in an' see."

"Aye," said Matt. "Seein's one thing but reachin' is another. Look, I canna excavate, Mousie. It would take a full crew o' men to break safe through the slab t' what lies beyond."

"What are you sayin'?"

"I'm sayin' it's too much for me."

"Daddy could've done it."

"Nah, nah. Your daddy, fine man wi' pick an' wedge though he was, would have baulked at this job too, Mousie."

"So you'll give up our pickin's, will ye?"

She got to her feet, lumps of coal dropping from each hand. Matt would not let her go, however. He put his arm about her waist and drew her over the coal, pinning her against him.

"Stop it, Mouse," he commanded. "Stop it."

She went slack against him. No man had ever held her so

tightly before. It turned her legs to jelly just to feel Matt's arms about her.

Matt said, "We'll look before we act, Mouse. I'll do what I can t' knock out crawl space. But, I warn you, if the slab locks off a complete seam then it can be a secret no longer."

She lay against his shoulder, breathing raggedly.

Matt gave her a gentle little shake. "Do y' hear me, Mouse?"

"Aye, Matt," she murmured.

Hector Fotheringham was more astringent than he had ever been before. He did not tell his manager in so many words that the problem of investment had been solved. He indicated in general terms, with that aristocratic vagueness which Keir Bolderon found so infuriating, that surveyors would be taking over in early summer of the coming year. He was not vague, however, when informing the manager that he blamed him for lack of enterprise, considered him something less than the expert he professed to be.

Keir Bolderon did not bother to defend himself. He did not even pursue the line that might have led to an admission by the owner that he had borrowed money from the Falkirk banker. Keir Bolderon had a contract. He needed every last day of the contract to conduct a proper courtship of Elspeth Patterson, to marry her, lay his hands on her wealth and negotiate by purchase a share in the Abbeyfield. It no longer mattered that the situation had deteriorated. Experts notwithstanding, new winnings might not exist and any sort of a contract might, in a year or two, be worth less than the paper it was written on. Somebody – not the lovely Hector, of course – might be throwing good money after bad, and he might be squandering his future to no avail. Blinded by Fotheringham's shabby treatment, Keir Bolderon played the game to the hilt in the fond belief that he might yet run out a winner if only he could catch Mrs Patterson before Moodie's sisters found her or had her declared dead. Time was, to a degree, on his side. He was not, however, elated to receive Olivia Melrose's invitation to 'take supper' at her residence in Hanover Street.

Not so long since, Keir Bolderon's entire week would have been lit bright by the prospect of a rendezvous with the handsome widow. Now, though, he found that the attraction had been but skin deep. All the things he had recently admired had become detestable vanities. Olivia Melrose might affect the manners of a lady but she was no better, really, than he was.

Nonetheless Keir Bolderon journeyed to Edinburgh. He paid a call on Neil McNeil; no walks with the old man now. McNeil greeted Bolderon from the depths of an ancient sedan chair stood before a blazing fire in a room at the back of the warehouse. Sons, grandsons and nephews were much in evidence, giving the visitor the eye, heads cocked like scavenging crows waiting for a ram to die. Not only had McNeil's legs given out but his shrewd brain seemed foggy too. Mr Bolderon stayed only five or six minutes in the trader's company then went away saddened by the sight of such ruin.

In this mood he reached Hanover Street. He was duly admitted to the parlour and greeted by the effusive Olivia Melrose, or, as he thought of her now, Lizzie Moodie. Beneath the silken gown and whispering petticoats, beneath stockings and slippers, under the pearl-decked diadem, Keir Bolderon saw the ghost of a dreary, half-starved lass from Balnesmoor. All her chatter about Edinburgh society's wits and wizards seemed false, sheer affectation. Keir Bolderon knew only too well how the change in his attitude to Mrs Melrose had come about. In his heart he was Mrs Patterson's man, her gallant and knightly defender. Mrs Melrose was their enemy.

Seasoned by years of hypocrisy, however, Keir Bolderon managed to seem as affable as ever. He could not fire himself with ardour, though. Not even frequent glimpses of the smooth, heavy orbs in the bosom of Mrs Melrose's gown could fire his former interest in the widow.

Mrs Melrose seemed unaware that her suitor had 'gone elsewhere'. She was less reserved than before and at once started to share secrets with him, to discuss matters of family business as if he was a friend of many years' standing.

He was told, without having to ask, that Janet had gone home to Dundee to attend her daughter-in-law's lying-in but that she would return to Edinburgh before the November session and that a certain Mr Augustine – no relation to the saint – had agreed to challenge the will and to promote the sisters' cause in the Scottish court.

"Is Mr Augustine – optimistic?"

"Indeed. He believes that Janet an' I have justice on our side."

Keir Bolderon's concept of justice had changed along with his feelings towards Olivia Melrose. He put a handful of questions to her, sufficient to ascertain that the Moodie sisters were no closer to wresting the weaver's fortune from its rightful owner, Elspeth, than ever. Mr Augustine – emphatically no saint – was patently a plausible rogue set on soaking them for months to come. Keir Bolderon did not advance this opinion but allowed Mrs Melrose to chatter away to her heart's content. He hardly heard Mrs Melrose's voice, listened with no more than half an ear to her complaints, to the dismal harangue against her brother and his eccentricities. He was thinking of Elspeth Patterson, of her beauty, her personable habits, her warmth.

Keir Bolderon started as Mrs Melrose transferred herself, quite without warning, from her little tub chair to the sofa by his side. She touched his arm, took his hand. The move was totally unexpected, unprovoked. He glanced towards the closed door of the room, willing the housekeeper or damned schoolmaster or *somebody* to intrude, to save him from embarrassment. The desire that had once been in him had turned to revulsion. It was all he could do not to leap to his feet with a cry.

"Is there somethin' wrong, Mr Bolderon?"

"No. No, Madam. I—I fear only that—"

"I need a man's strength now," the woman said. "I need the comfort an' consolation of an arm about me, a shoulder to lean upon, in a literal sense, not merely metaphorically."

Keir Bolderon swallowed. Her breasts were fully displayed in the neck of the dress. He could see the puckering of flesh as she leaned towards him and tried to lay her cheek against his neck.

He felt a strong desire to shout, "Too late, Madam. Too late. I have found what I want elsewhere," but managed to control the impulse and, suppressing a shudder, patted her soothingly upon the shoulder.

"My servants are discreet," she whispered.

Good God in Heaven! He was being seduced. She believed

that by taking him to her bed she could bind him to her. He saw why she had swung in the wind towards favouring a rough-mannered engineer. She assumed that he would fight for her rights like a husband and lift her again to some new plane of achievement. How could he tell her that she was too old for such tricks and that he had found, among other things, a conscience?

Awkwardly he disentangled himself.

She was disappointed and bewildered.

"Have I offended you, Mr Bolderon?"

"Not in the least, Mrs Melrose."

"Why then do you wish to leave?"

"Because the hour is late an' I have to be up an' about at an ungodly hour tomorrow morning."

"On business?"

"Aye, Madam. Coalpit business."

"Would you not, Mr Bolderon, prefer to be about business of another sort?"

She had not quite given up on him.

Perhaps if he had not met the sister Janet, had not been privy to their machinations – which he regarded as immoral, unethical and unwarranted – he might have succumbed to her blandishments. But he was a man of principle and in love with another.

Olivia Melrose did not want a lover or a husband. She wanted a clerk, a secretary and somebody to wage war on her behalf with the laws of the land. He was a manager of men, an engineer, not a lap-dog to the petty bourgeoisie.

Elspeth would not behave thus. Elspeth would not try to wheedle him into wasting his time and talent on squeezing the law for all it was worth.

Olivia Melrose wanted an answer.

He pushed himself from her, got resolutely to his feet.

He said, "I feel that I should inform you, dear Mrs Melrose, that my connection with the Abbeyfield will terminate in ten months' time. It seems that Mr Fotheringham has found another investor."

Obviously Mrs Melrose had expected something more intimate; shyness, not pragmatism. Really, he supposed, she did not give a farthing for his enterprise. Had she ever understood his predicament? He wondered if it was the hard hand of sister Janet that had thrust Olivia Moodie Melrose into his arms.

"I have an income that requires –" said Olivia Melrose.

"Management?" said Keir Bolderon.

"I do not understand what you mean by that word in this context, sir," said Mrs Melrose who, whatever her faults, was not so insensitive as to withstand such an obvious rebuff.

"No matter," said Keir Bolderon.

For a mad moment he longed to tell her that he could end all her concern, her fretting over the acquisition of money that she did not need and which did not belong to her. James Moodie's fortune would not compensate the Moodie sisters for the sufferings of their early years, the years of struggle and discipline that had fashioned them, that had made them what they were. They could not buy back their innocence any more than he could buy respectability.

He might say, "I know where she is, the heiress."

He might say, "Taking me for a husband is pointless."

He might say, "You and I, Mrs Melrose, are out of the same box."

In his mind, like echoes of thunder, rumbled memories of his own boyhood.

Olivia Melrose started. Her hands worked at the skirt of her gown, drawing it down and down as if he had somehow caught her in an immodest pose. Did she read the truth in his eyes? Did she, of all people, see in him the sorrow of a man who cannot grasp what he has claimed, who is finally victim of a decency he had sought to discard?

Keir Bolderon said, "I'm not for you, Mrs Melrose."

"Stay, though – for a while at least."

"I cannot."

"Why have you changed, Mr Bolderon?"

"I cannot explain it."

"Is it because you've discovered my secret?"

"Aye." It was the simplest answer he could give even if it was not quite true. "Aye."

He was relieved by her anger. She rose like a cloud, all dark and swarming, and struck him a blow across the mouth with the flat of her hand.

Keir Bolderon felt a spot of warm blood on the inside of his lip. He sucked at it while the heat of her fingers spread across his cheek.

"I thought you liked me," she said, already regretting her outburst. "I thought you were a suitor for my hand."

"I wanted only your money."

"In spite – no matter what – you may still have that."

"Only your money, Madam," said Keir Bolderon quite deliberately, "not you."

"Get out," she cried. "Leave my house. Leave me alone."

She reached for the bell on the table but Mr Bolderon needed no servant to eject him. He gave her a bow, rueful and polite to the very last, then, without apology, turned on his heel and left.

Occasionally on warm nights close to dusk Matt Shearer would take himself down to the river's edge, peel off his clothes and walk naked into the water. He would turn on to his back, kick up spray with his feet, thrashing thus for three or four minutes, then would find bottom again and emerge dripping and startlingly clean to rub himself dry on a cloth.

The colliers who observed Shearer's ablutions thought him daft and wondered that he did not catch his death and die. They washed themselves indoors in tubs, basins and buckets and would not have dreamed of bathing in the Forth.

With the coming of the autumn, however, Matt found the shore too dark and lonely after shift and took to the more conventional method of ridding his body of its coating of dirt.

He demanded no more than a blazing fire and a cauldron of hot water with which to fill the bottom of the round wooden tub into which, comically, he somehow squeezed himself. Because the lassies were not kin he had strung another curtain of washed burlap across another corner of the kitchen and would lug the tub behind it and bathe in comparative privacy.

Mouse alone would keek at the curtain. She would see the bulges and bumps that Matt's elbows, knees and buttocks made and would glower at this novelty and tell herself that she disapproved and that Daddy would never have done it, that the old way of skimming off black grime with a wet towel was the best way for a man. Mouse never undressed. On occasions she would quickly slip out of her shift and slip on

366

another but she was ashamed of her body and drew a very fine line between practicality and modesty.

As was usually the case these days Elspeth had not returned from work at the counting-house. Elginbrod would be late up with the tally and Elspeth was obliged to bide until the clerk presented her with his daily totals which she would then record in the coal log and the ledgers. It was meticulous work and Elginbrod's pages were invariably grubby and blurred and difficult to decipher which took more time and made her later home than ever.

Sarah would prepare food or finish off the cooking that Davy had seen fit to start that afternoon and often supper would be eaten and Mary Jean would be fed before Elspeth returned. It was not an arrangement that any of them found particularly comfortable. But there was the consolation of money for, with Elspeth's twenty shillings added to Matt's take, the family were in clover.

While Davy and Sarah skiddled with pots about the hearth Matt took his bath. The simmering cauldron, which had had pride of place upon the fire, had drawn heat from the cooking-pots and created a fog of condensation in the small kitchen. With dirty clothing flung about the place was horrid and cluttered to such a degree that even Mouse sought out a private corner and Mary Jean retired, girning, to her bed to prattle and complain to her rag-doll until Mam came home to give her attention.

Matt had been behind the curtain for three or four minutes before he called out, "Davy, will ye bring me yon bar o' soap?"

Davy answered, "Get it yoursel'," for Davy had not, after all, forgiven Matt for his betrayal. "I'm no' your bloody servant."

"Davy, for God's sake!" Matt elbowed back the curtain and gesticulated to the boy. But Davy was stooped over a pan sizzling with pork fat and dared not, even if he had wished, release his hold on the iron handle lest the four pieces of meat slither into the fire and be lost.

From her seat on the edge of the bed, Mouse said, "What soap?"

"There, wi' the towel." Matt's thick, pale arm jutted from the curtain. "Aye, that's a good lass."

Mouse lifted the wedge of soap and picked her way through the litter. Matt's hand opened to take the stuff but the girl did not give it to him. Instead she insinuated herself behind the curtain and, leaning over his big naked back, dropped the soap with a plop into the suds in his lap.

"God, Matt Shearer, but you're mucky!"

"Scrub m' back, then," said Matt, amused.

Tentatively she touched her fingertips to the flange of muscle that covered his shoulder-blade, then she flattened her tiny, calloused palm against his flesh and rubbed it in a circular motion.

"Mousie!" Davy was alarmed. "Mouse, come awa' out o' there."

"I'm only scrubbin' Matt's back."

"Come out, damn you, when you're told."

"I used t' do it for Daddy."

"Aye, when y' were wee."

"I'm still wee," said Mousie.

"Davy," said Sarah, matter-of-factly, "attend t' the meat."

Scummy black water made a kilt for Matt's loins. His long legs hung out of the tub, almost touching the door. He leaned forward and arched his spine to cover his private parts as the girl slid water over him and, using her hand like a spatula, skimmed grime from his body. He fished for, found and gave her the soap. She smeared it across him, working upwards, not daring to turn her chore into a caress.

Neither of them spoke.

"Take this bloody pan, Sarah," Davy shouted, "till I see what's goin' on."

"In a minute, Davy."

Mouse leaned on Matt, hands laving suds across his collarbones, the column of his neck, down to his chest. Matt stiffened in a bowed position. Hair brushed his earlobe, made him shiver. Mouse was breathing with her mouth open as if the work was hard. She put her breasts against him so that her dress became wet and slithery too. She was so intent on cleaning him that she seemed oblivious to anything other than the job on hand.

Matt stopped her.

"That's – that's enough, Mousie."

The pan clinked as Davy edged it to the stones and a tidal wash of reeking fat crackled and spat and spilled.

"You'll fire it, Davy," Sarah cried. "Hold it up."

Matt put his hand about Mouse's wrist and pinned it against his chest. Her face was against his neck, her mouth by his ear, hair tickling and brushing his cheek. Her breasts were soft against his spine.

"No, Allison," he whispered.

She pushed away abruptly and drew back the curtain just as Davy wrenched his pan from the hearth.

In her corner Mary Jean was watching, the rag-doll rocked in the crook of one arm as if it was a babby. Mary Jean had stopped girning. She sensed tension even if she did not understand it. She kept her eyes fixed on Davy and the cooking-pan for the spoiling of supper had precedent and was a disaster whose import she could grasp.

Davy's agitation found no outlet. Mouse emerged from behind the burlap before he could react. She was wet about the chest and arms, hair clung damply to her cheeks. She looked directly at her brother, smugly plucked the worn grey towel from the bed and returned with it, four or five steps past the table, and hung it like a cloak across Matt's shoulders.

"There!" she said. "See!"

Blue smoke rose from the frying-pan. Torn between Mouse and saving the supper Davy twisted, knelt and did his best to rescue the meat by laving it with fat before drawing the pan away from the heat of the coals. Globules hopped out and burned his wrist. He clanked the pan down, sucked the scald and glowered as Mouse, quite unconcerned, glided to the dresser and took out a dry garment, glided to Elspeth's corner and snapped shut the curtain there.

Matt clambered noisily from the tub. Davy's fears were lost in fussing with supper, with drying and dressing, with Elspeth's return.

Nothing was said, no remark made. From that moment of intimacy, however, came a change in little Mouse Bennet who, without Matt, would be again lost – and this time for ever.

Elspeth glanced up from her writing and, in dismay, saw Snippets Smith standing in the doorway of the counting-house.

It was a quiet morning, disturbed only by the cacophony of the winding-gear. Henning had gone below to sort out an argument about the tally and McCaffray had been despatched to Alloa to take delivery of a sealed letter from Mr McNeil, payment, less all the merchant's discounts, for August coal shipments.

Snippets had shrunk. His cheekbones were like rivets, his eyes sunken. He leaned for support on an ash stick while he balefully observed the female phenomenon seated at *his* desk with *his* ledger open before her.

Elspeth got to her feet.

"Mr Smith," she said. "It's grand t' see you out an' about once more. I trust it'll not be long before you're back at your place?"

The paymaster did not answer. He picked his way across the uneven floor as if a wrong move might topple him and send him sprawling. He came to the desk, turned the ledger and inspected it in silence for two or three minutes, wetting his finger with the tip of his tongue to turn the pages.

"Neat enough," he said pedantically.

"Thank you for sayin' so, Mr Smith," said Elspeth.

He darted a glance at her to see if she intended sarcasm but found her perfectly sincere.

"Where did you learn t' account with such accuracy?"

"From my departed husband," said Elspeth.

Snippets made no comment but it seemed to Elspeth that he did not swallow the lie. She could hardly confess that she had, on occasions, kept the clothbook for her real husband, James Simpson Moodie, who was by no means dead.

"He taught ye well."

"Are you," said Elspeth, "intending t' return before the next paying out, Mr Smith?"

He gave a little sniff, as if checking a tear of regret, and said, "I'm in need o' the wage, Mrs Patterson, or I would not be returnin' at all."

He still had not told her when he intended to resume his duties, to oust her from her warm, dry billet and send her back down the shaft.

"Is your health so broken then?" said Elspeth.

Again he did not answer her. He said, "Mr Bolderon has

been t' talk with me. I'm to take you on as my deputy. At least Mr Bolderon did me the honour of askin' if I would inspect your work an' approve it before I gave my agreement."

"You do not approve of women in the counting-house, do you, Mr Smith?"

"No, Mrs Patterson, I do not. Money should be handled by persons of responsibility an' sound sense, qualities that are rarely found in females. A woman canna control her brain as a man can."

Elspeth said, "Be that as it may, Mr Smith, I doubt if you'll find error in my countin'."

"Mr Bolderon has kept an eye on you, no doubt."

"I do not require t' be supervised, Mr Smith. For your information I do not find this work particularly taxin' – even with an 'uncontrolled brain'."

Snippets Smith tapped the ash stick upon the floor, showing his impatience and his annoyance at the fact that she had spoken back to him. She should have been meek, apologetic, in awe of him. It was not that Snippets doubted her skill in arithmetic and with the pen; he feared that the position he had held for so many years would be devalued in the colliers' eyes by the fact that it could be done just as well by a woman.

Sourly Snippets Smith said, "I see you'll have my job, Mrs Patterson, if I should let it slip even one inch."

She hesitated. She did not want to make an outright enemy of him for she would, with luck, have to work by his side in the months ahead. She was stung by his unreasonable attitude, however, and his condescensions.

She said, "I *have* your job, Mr Smith, albeit as a temporary measure. I don't believe that the Abbeyfield has suffered because of it."

He tapped with the stick, tapped and turned on her.

"I'll be back at my post within the month, Mrs Patterson, for it is the post t' which I was appointed an' from which I've not been dismissed."

Elspeth could not resist. "Never fear, Mr Smith, I'll be here to ease the weight from your ailin' shoulders."

Another man might have seen the humour in it, have realised that there was no barb to the hook. But not Snippets Smith. He was too brittle a person, too uncertain to acknowledge

371

Elspeth's quickness. He made no rejoinder to her remark. He shifted about, using the stick, and shuffled towards the open door as crimped and peevish as if pain still gripped him.

Elspeth watched him go.

For a moment an apology hung in her mouth but she smothered it. Men like Snippets Smith brought out the worst in her, though Gaddy would have seen it otherwise.

She had been, she knew, injudicious. As she seated herself at the desk once more she wondered if Mr Bolderon would not finally side with the paymaster, with a man, find some menial post for her to occupy, one more in keeping with her status and her sex.

"Just let him try," she murmured and jerked the pen from its holder.

A blob of ink fell from the nib on to the ledger.

Elspeth uttered a little tut at her carelessness, blotted the stain and, with the leaf-shaped knife kept for the purpose, began to scratch it out and make the page clean again.

When the wedding celebrations were over Randall Bontine wasted no time in returning with his bride to Ottershaw. It was a busy season, time of the harvest and the gathering of cattle for the trysts. However much Randall trusted his grieve it made him uneasy to be away from the estate and he felt that three weeks was quite long enough.

Suzanne was by no means reluctant to leave the shelter of her father's house and embark swiftly upon her new life as mistress of Ottershaw. She was more in love with Randall than ever for they shared a sexual passion that had to be disguised from modest and decent relatives. Walter, perhaps, had an inkling that his old comrade in arms had made a wise choice, in more ways than one, in selecting his sister. Randall would never suffer from neglect of the playful affection that slips from the privacy of the bed-chamber into all aspects of a marriage, making the fortunate couple considerate to each other and eager for the candles to be lit and the evening to move towards night. Suzanne was certainly no dry stick. Randall was not a selfish lover, demanding without return his pleasure. The first weeks of the marriage were exhausting to both husband and wife. But in Ottershaw a certain amount of decorum was required, a code of behaviour that prohibited too frank a display of love and desire; the servants must not be 'shocked'.

It was with more rue than rile, however, that Henry Hunter caught Sir Randall and Mistress Suzanne kissing over breakfast in the dining-room. He should, of course, have knocked loudly to announce his entrance but he had somehow not expected his master to be 'bristling', as it were, at that hour of a chill autumn morning, particularly in the presence of a dish of grilled trout whose glabrous eyes stared up from the plate, dull and disapproving, like those of kirk elders.

Mistress Suzanne pulled away from her husband and fluttered the bodice of her day-dress, not meeting the gaze of the old steward.

"Beggin' your pardon, Mr Randall, but one o' the Sinclairs is in the servants' hall an' adamantly demands t' speak wi' you," Henry Hunter announced.

"Is it Lachlan?" Randall said, rising.

"No, sir, it's the laddie; Sandy."

Randall frowned slightly. "Does he carry a message from my brother? Is there illness or accident at Strachan Castle?"

"I put the same question t' him but he indicates that his business is wi' you, laird, an' does not concern Mr Gilbert."

In spite of himself, Randall glanced over his shoulder at Suzanne who sat quite meekly, as if the message meant not a thing to her. She toyed with a flake of fish upon her plate and then, as if making a momentous decision, reached for the silver pot and busied herself pouring coffee into her cup.

She had never asked her husband to explain the visit of the girl from Strachan Castle on the night of the Ottershaw ball. She had been afraid of his honesty, of how he might answer her, and realised that his visit to her bedroom that same night was not, perhaps, coincidence. Whatever Randall had done in the past, whatever hints of scandal and depravity were attached to him were none of her concern. Randall would not be the first bachelor to have sown wild oats before marriage.

Randall said, "I shall come, Hunter. I'll see him in the hay yard." As the steward left he turned, said to his wife, "It seems, dearest, that the business of the day has caught up with me. With your permission, may I leave now?"

"Of course, my love." Suzanne did not rise from her place

at the long table though she did look up and force a smile of reassurance. "Shall I ask cook to prepare a luncheon or will you be gone until dark?"

"I'll give my instruction to Hunter after I see what this young fellow wants," said Randall. "He is, by the way, the son of my grieve, now grieve to Gibbie. I cannot imagine what he requires at this hour."

"Trot off and see." Suzanne blew him a kiss from her fingertips, hiding her apprehension well.

Sandy Sinclair waited by the back wall of the old coach-house in that part of the stable yard where once, years ago, his brother had exercised Sir Randall's stallion, Sabre. Now, at this season, the hay crop had been dragged here to help dry it and had been stored in the long lofts above the building. The yard looked untidy and ill-groomed. Labour could not be spared just yet to make it spick and span and Sabre was too long in the tooth to require daily exercising now.

Sinclair waited by the arch at the mouth of the yard, hat nervously clutched in his hand. It gave Randall a strange feeling to see him there; the youngest Sinclair was an amalgam of both father and brother, stalwart yet truculent. His weathered face was flushed with embarrassment. Randall's apprehension increased. Sandy Sinclair was Anna's watchdog; he feared that the young man had brought bad news concerning the girl.

"Did you walk here, Sinclair?"

"I – I borrowed old Maisie, laird."

"Come then, speak your business."

"I seek employment on Ottershaw," Sandy Sinclair said.

Randall raised an eyebrow and hooked his thumb into the straps of his leather belt. Suzanne's civilising influence had not caused him to abandon working-rig for something fancy.

"You're my brother's servant, employed on Strachan. Have you been dismissed and, if that's the case, what reason is behind it?"

"I – I haven't been dismissed, sir. I come here wi'out Mr Gilbert's knowledge an' wi'out my father's consent. I know I should stay at the castle, sir – but I canna. I want t' come back here. Where I belong."

"Where you belong? You belong where you're put, Sinclair."

374

"If – if I canna come here again, sir, I'll have to attend the October hirin' fair."

"Your father will never allow it."

"I'm my own man, Laird Bontine."

"Why do you want away from Strachan? The truth, now."

"I'm not settled there. I never will be."

Randall hesitated. "Look at me, Sinclair."

Sandy obeyed. "Aye, sir."

"Is it her?" Randall said.

"It is, sir," Sandy answered.

"Do you want her?"

"Aye, sir. I do."

"But she will not permit you liberties, is that it?"

"We can never marry."

"Oh, so it's *marriage* you want," said Randall. "No, that can never be."

"I'm in a torment, laird."

"If you find another lass to make into a wife," Randall said, "your torment will vanish."

"I want no other girl, sir, at least none I've met so far."

"Why did you not make your request to my brother? That would have been the proper and correct method."

"Mr Gilbert would not understand, sir."

Randall's eyes narrowed. "Do you think I will?"

"If not you, Sir Randall, who will?"

From the brother, from Matt, the question would have been rank impertinence but Sandy Sinclair was too innocent and honest by half.

Randall said, "I can't order my brother to release a servant."

"But you could ask him, sir," said Sandy.

Asking, of course, would be enough. Servants and tenants were fully aware that Gibbie still danced to the laird's tune and always would, unless Gibbie brought his ship home and made his fortune independently of the Ottershaw name.

"I could, indeed, 'ask' him," Randall said. "But he may not grant your request, Sinclair. Certainly your father will resist."

"It's that, sir, or seek another master."

"I would not want to see you lost, Sinclair."

"Then, please, ask him."

"How can I explain without making Anna seem responsible?"

Sandy Sinclair pursed his lips. Perhaps he was on the point of blurting out that Anna *was* responsible.

Sandy said, "She plans t' marry Robert Rudge."

"Good God! Is that true?"

"Aye, sir."

"When?"

"When her bill of divorcement comes due."

"Rudge?" Randall Bontine laughed wryly. "Robert Rudge, damn me! That sly old reprobate."

"Could I come here – for a while at least?" said Sandy.

"Does Rudge know of her intentions towards him?"

"He has been t' call on her," Sandy said. "She's been to Drymen too."

"Yes, but is it marriage or matching that the damned fellow's after?" Randall said. "Come now, Sinclair, don't look so shocked. You must be aware of his reputation."

"It's marriage."

"Hence the torment?"

"Aye, sir."

"Do you suppose that quitting Strachan will cure it?"

"Take me back, sir, I implore you."

Randall Bontine put his hand on Sinclair's shoulder.

He said, "Well, I know you for an honest worker and I would prefer to have you employed here than skulking about the roads mending wheels for farthings. Yes, I'll consult my brother about it. No doubt he will inform your father."

"Thank you, Laird Bontine. I'll no' let you down."

"By God, I'll make sure that you don't. Now go on with you. Leave the arrangement to me."

Sandy hesitated. "What – what about Anna?"

"Anna," said Randall, "is no longer our concern. Let her choose Rudge. She deserves him, don't you think?"

"Aye, sir," said Sandy gratefully, and without more ado left Ottershaw for Strachan Castle.

Word came down to Anna from Catriona who had it from Aileen who in turn, received it from Mistress Alicia: Sandy was returning to employment at Ottershaw. Anna fizzed like a sulphur fuse and could not see the move as reasonable and advantageous. Sandy, it seemed, had been offered the post of deputy grieve. Lachlan had urged the young man to accept, to return to Ottershaw. Anna lost all sense of propriety. She sought Sandy out at once, away across the bottom field where he had been weeding the late crop of carrots, a crop he would not now take in.

He shouldered the hoe at her approach and awaited her arrival like a sentry.

"I've heard the news," Anna, still thirty yards away, shouted.

"Aye, is it not good news?"

"Good for you. Bad for me."

"I thought you'd be pleased," said Sandy, "at my good fortune."

She stood before him, legs all clay, skirt hems sodden, and planted her fists on her hips.

Sandy stood his ground, leaning on the hoe, the rank uprooted weeds straggled along the rows behind him. Rain was coming in again, drifting across the Lightwater.

"You're abandonin' me," Anna cried.

"It's nothin' t' do with you."

"Could you not have asked me first?"

"For why? You're all set up wi' Robert bloody Rudge. I've nothin', except this place, an' that's less than good enough for me, Anna."

"You'd be grieve here."

"On Strachan! I'd as soon be grieve t'an acre o' sand in the bloody Sahara desert."

"What'll your father do wi'out your aid?"

"Employ two other hands."

"Two?"

"I do the work o' two men here, since you've failed t' notice."

"What conceit. Is Lachlan no' angry wi' you?"

"He's fair delighted. I am too. It's not every day the laird o' Ottershaw asks for a lad t' be deputy grieve."

"It's me, it's because o' me," said Anna.

"Huh!" Sandy exclaimed.

"I'll not be grunted at, Sandy Sinclair."

"Listen, Anna, I'm flesh an' blood. How can I stand t' be

near you, day in and day out, when I'll never have you?"

"If I—"

"NO. DAMN YOU," Sandy shouted.

He turned and scythed with the hoe and tossed up a great pile of the weeds into the wet air and slashed at them as they fell. He threw the hoe to the ground then and, relieved, swung back to face her.

"You ruined my brother, Anna, but you'll no' ruin me."

"Matt brought ruin on himself."

"Aye, perhaps he did. But then again you did nothin' to aid him. What you want, Anna Cochran, you somehow contrive to get. Well, you'll get no more from me. Go to Robert Rudge, press yoursel' against him, make cow's eyes at him. Let him melt. I'm off out of harm's way."

She was used to the stings and insults from Cat and Aileen, to Alicia Bontine's wounding remarks. But they were women and it seemed natural for them to be jealous of her.

It was Randall who had called Sandy away. Did the laird still fear that she would ensnare Sandy as she had ensnared him? Was Randall jealous too? Such foolishness gave her a little comfort.

Leaving the hoe upon the row, weeds all tossed about, Sandy started away across the field towards the castle.

Anna gave a great sigh. She wiped her hand across her face. The air had made her skin wet. She wiped the hand upon her skirts and looked down. Bare feet in the clay. Legs, all unhosed, streaked with the soil of the fields. She had loved a laird and gained nothing from it except the responsibility of a bastard bairn. No, she told herself; Robbie was no bastard. He had been born in wedlock and his paternity had never been questioned or examined. He was a Sinclair, not a Bontine. In due course the woman from Piperhaugh would bear Randall proud sons. The heirs to Ottershaw would be decently established and she, Anna Cochran Sinclair, would still be fettered to the fields; and her son after her. Until that instant, alone on the edge of the autumn pasture, Anna had not admitted that Robert Rudge was her one and only hope. She had thought of him as an alternative to something better, a measure of safety should destiny not treat her as well as she deserved. But Robert Rudge was all she had.

If Sandy was correct and Mr Rudge wanted only to establish claim to the managership of Kennart, then she could not afford to tarry. She must captivate him without Elspeth's power and money. She must make Mr Rudge fall in love with her. She must earn his *respect*, for she had learned from Randall that it was not enough to be desired. Love and playing at love were games for lassies. For a woman with a bairn and a sorry history behind her she needed a man she could trust and who would trust her in turn. Mr Robert Rudge it would have to be. And soon.

Anna nodded and picked up the wooden hoe. She tidied the weeds into a pile, patted them with the heel and then, with the implement over her shoulder, trudged decisively across the field to bring in the beasts for milking.

Anna had made up her mind.

Later Keir Bolderon was to wish that he had been a little less circumspect in his courtship of Elspeth Patterson, that he had had the zeal to go down on his knees before her and, even in the presence of two small chaperones, Sarah and Mary Jean, declare his undying love and whisk her to the altar before she could catch her breath.

It would not have been necessary for him to marry Elspeth, merely to have stated his intention to do so and to receive her promise in return. In the wake of disaster he could not expect her to forgive him or understand that beneath his silence and scheming there was a kind of love.

He should have surrendered the Abbeyfield, flung aside his ambition, given himself honestly and openly to her. On that October afternoon he should have told her the truth. But he did not. He was still wary, and confused. How could Elspeth agree to marry him when she still believed herself to be the legal wife of James Simpson Moodie of Balnesmoor?

Keir Bolderon invited her to bring the children to his house for tea. She accepted willingly, did not hedge. Mr Bolderon spurred his servants to produce sweet fare in a quantity that would have fed half the bairns on the field and not just the pair from the Bennets' cottage. Elspeth arrived promptly at three o'clock. She wore a plain brown outfit with narrow lapels and a round hat trimmed in velvet that seemed so perfectly suited to her that Keir Bolderon suspected it had been brought from her wardrobe in the weaver's mansion. Mary Jean wore a clean pinafore and a starched bonnet with blue ribbons. Sarah was dressed in a small plaid pattern and carried new shoes and stockings which she put on at the gate, hiding shyly behind Elspeth while she did so. Keir Bolderon welcomed them warmly.

It was a dry, dull sort of day and the parlour of the house, though not at all grand, had a cosy glow to it, with a coal fire in the hearth and brass all gleaming, the tea-table set before it. Before tea, however, Mary Jean and Sarah were taken out into the little garden by Dorrith, his servant, to see a donkey he had brought in to amuse them and to feed it cabbage leaves and carrot tops.

Alone with Elspeth for a few precious moments Mr Bolderon was tempted to press his advantage, to blurt out words of love, to propose. Still confused, however, he restrained himself. He was afraid to commit himself to a situation which might strain the tenuous friendship between them. Instead he asked after her collier, learned that Matt Shearer was quite well. He enquired after the health of the boy, learned that Davy Bennet was as well as could be expected. He enquired after the sullen girl-child, was told that Mouse too was in excellent spirits. He might have enquired after the welfare of the household cat if there had been one but Elspeth, at this turn, lifted the conversation away from stilted politeness and asked him directly when he expected Snippets to return.

Mr Bolderon expressed the opinion that Snippets would be back at his desk as soon as he could hold a pen without trembling and that, such was his determination, that might be very soon indeed.

Elspeth asked what would become of her. Mr Bolderon told her that she had performed so excellently well that he intended to create the post of paymaster depute. She asked, very practically, about the wage that the new post would provide. Mr Bolderon, thinking quickly, informed her that it would pay only fifteen shillings in the week, not twenty.

At this inopportune moment Dorrith returned the children

with the information that the rain had just begun, and hadn't she better get on with serving tea since that was her job not being a nursemaid in wet weather?

"Servants!" said Mr Bolderon with a smile. "How odd is the relationship between a man and his cook."

"We had a cook once who—"

Aghast, Elspeth stopped in mid-sentence. Mr Bolderon, flustered too, pretended that he had not heard.

He beckoned to Mary Jean who came from behind Mammy's chair, climbed up on the manager's knee and let him take off her bonnet and duly admire the ribbons of which she was very proud. Sarah, brown and solemn, watched without a word. She would dart a glance now and then at the scones and jams and dishes of jelly that adorned the table.

"Aye, she's a wee pretty thing," said Keir Bolderon. "She has her mother's features but her colouring—"

"After my husband," said Elspeth quickly.

In due course tea was brought in: plates of buttered bread, a bramble pie, still steaming, and a bowl of clotted cream.

Sarah managed a smile when she was invited to sit on the padded bench by Mary Jean's side and help herself to whatever took her fancy.

Crumbs, flecks of cream, droplets of jam flew in all directions. There seemed to be as much adhering to the girls' faces as ever made its way into their tummies.

Keir Bolderon was not offended by their lack of manners. He enjoyed the sight of their appetite for it reminded him of his brothers and sisters and the infrequent treats that had come their way when he was young.

What pleased him, however, was the confidence with which Elspeth coped with the battery of tea-things. She was expert with tongs, could tell a hot-water jug from a teapot and dispensed, at Mr Bolderon's invitation, slices of bread and butter without a hitch. That she had presided over better boards than this Mr Bolderon did not doubt.

In the parlour with Elspeth on that dismal October afternoon a sort of forgetfulness descended on the manager of the Abbeyfield. He was contented. He would have been more contented still if he could have come out with the truth, put his hand over hers and imparted – somehow – the news that she was no longer wife but widow to the tyrant who had brought her to this low pass.

At half past four Elspeth called the girls to her. She wiped their faces with a napkin, told Sarah to fetch the bonnets as it was time they found their way home before darkness came thickly and the rain got worse.

Mr Bolderon experienced a strange sense of loss. He begged them to stay longer. But Dorrith had appeared in the doorway with the big tray in her arms and gave him such a glare that he shrank from it and said that, if leave they must, he would bring out the gig, which he seldom used, and put on the hood and ride them to the road by the field gate to save their pretty clothes from soiling.

Egged on by the girls, Elspeth agreed and Mr Bolderon hastened out of the house to the leaning shed where the gig was stored. He prayed that his horse would not baulk at being put into shafts after so many months of the saddle and generally fretted that the afternoon, which had been so pleasant, would end in farce. But the horse was unconcerned. The gig wheels squeaked on their axles and made the girls laugh. Mr Bolderon said that he employed two dozen mice to run inside the hubs to help the vehicle along. The girls laughed even louder and flung themselves about under the shawl he had brought to keep them warm.

Elspeth did not reprimand them. She sat by him on the front board, under the tar-black hood, while he edged the conveyance out of the back gate and along the dark path through trees and on to the road. It was only a couple of miles to the field gate but Keir Bolderon drove the horse at hardly more than a walk, spinning out the afternoon, making it last. The thought of the long evening, alone in the parlour, filled him with gloom.

Across the river skirts of cloud lifted a little and painted a ghostly sheen upon the water. The lights of keel-boats could be seen, faint against the lading quays. The thatch dwellings on the far shore held firelight in their tiny windows. The Placket clock chimed out five notes. Dusk intensified around the sound and increased Mr Bolderon's melancholy. Only the giggling of the bairns behind him and Elspeth's voice murmuring a snatch of song seemed counter to the effects of weather and the season.

"What's that?" Keir Bolderon said.

"Hm?"

"The air you were singing."

"Och, it's nothing, Mr Bolderon."

"No, tell me what it was."

"My mam used to sing it to me, whiles, when I was young. I never knew its name. She called it the *Sleepin' Song*."

"Will you come again for tea?" Keir Bolderon said.

"If I'm invited, yes."

"Next Sunday?"

"No, Mr Bolderon, not quite so soon. I fancy that would soon turn it into a habit. In two weeks, though, or three, I'd be happy—"

"Two weeks it is," said Keir Bolderon, consoled.

By chance Anna was not paid her half-yearly wage until the middle of October. The sum was due on the very first day of the month. Upon that day, in consequence, her term of employment expired and she was free to leave her master's employment without redress or recrimination if she chose so to do.

All of this Anna discovered by consulting the relevant chapter in *The Pocket Lawyer*. If her interpretation of the clauses was accurate then Mr Gilbert was in default by not summoning her to the drawing-room until twenty-two days after the due day and not paying her wage on time. She had made no great fuss about the delay. Indeed she hardly thought of it for so many other things crowded upon her mind that October that she had no desire to spend her pittance on anything much, except some clothing for Robbie.

Mr Gilbert too had much on his mind. He had returned from the wedding at Piperhaugh to a mess of small debts and a disturbance on his estate – Sandy's departure – that would have to be resolved by the hiring of at least one reliable hand from the local community.

In addition the brothers Pryde had discreetly informed him that all was not well with the affairs of the bank. Quite what this meant Gibbie was not sure. The Prydes had kept their cards too close to their chests for too long to take him willingly into their confidence. Perhaps they were warning him. Perhaps they had had some wind of his duplicity in the matter of the Moodie trust money or – and Gibbie would not put it beyond them – perhaps they sought to lay hands upon it for their own purposes.

Moodie's money was, however, gone. Gone into the hands of Mr Fotheringham who had – though Gilbert knew it not – already spent much of it in buying into the iron works at Carron, not upon the rejuvenation of the Abbeyfield.

If he had been possessed of that fact then Gilbert Bontine would not have been uneasy and distracted but would have been thrown into a great feathery panic. Mr Fotheringham, of course, told Gibbie nothing. The gentleman of Placket was not yet committed to begin paying interest upon the loan which was not, on paper, a loan at all and yield from the share would not be forthcoming until the 'old lease' expired and the 'new lease' was subscribed and signed.

Strachan's income for the capital year was minute. It was far less, because of weather, than Gibbie had anticipated. And now Gilbert had come to the day when, like it or not, he must fork away more of his hard-earned income and pay his servants their wages. He had the bag of money and the book. He summoned the servants one by one, beginning with Lachlan. He paid them all, including Edith Williams, before he got down to Anna Sinclair who had been waiting below in the hall for the signal that it was her turn to confront the master in the ultimate relationship of all servants, that moment of acknowledgement of the fundamental purpose of labour – payment.

Anna entered the room. She wore a shawl and bonnet over her dress and had shoes upon her feet. Gibbie did not even notice her apparel. He sighed as he counted out twelve shillings from the bag and placed the coins upon the table.

The brown leather bag was now absolutely empty and seemed to Gibbie, as he peered into it, oddly symbolic. He glimpsed Anna's hand as it slid the money from the table and into a shabby velvet purse. He looked up, noticed nothing, sighed, nodded.

Anna said, "Thank ye, Mr Gilbert. I will now be terminatin' my employment here."

"Yes, yes," said Gibbie absently.

"Forthwith," said Anna.

"What in God's name do you mean, girl?"

"I'm leavin' too, sir."

"But – but why? You were put here by my brother and he will be—"

"I was put here by nobody," said Anna sharply.

"I have—have a bond—"

"There's no paper document, Mr Gilbert; none I've ever seen nor heard about," said Anna. "If you tell me you've some sort of document between you an' Mr Randall I can tell you it's worthless."

"You can tell me, can you?" said Gilbert, temper rising at the girl's attitude.

"My son an' I are leavin'," she said. "We have no goods belongin' t' Strachan and no debts t' square away. I'm paid to the end o' the term and I'll not be askin' for extra days."

"The agreement?"

"The law o' master an' servant allows me to do as I wish."

"Anna, for God's sake, where will you go?"

"Drymen. To Mr Robert Rudge's house."

"Rudge?" Gilbert exclaimed. "Rudge!"

"I'm to become his wife."

"What if Sinclair – your husband – what if he returns for you?"

"I canna wait for that day," said Anna. "Besides, sir, Matt'll never show his nose here again. He dare not. In six months' time I'll petition for a divorcement. It'll not be denied me nor will the court delay it. I've Mr Hildebrand's word on that."

"Hildebrand? What the devil have you been up to, Anna?"

"Nothin', Mr Gilbert. My position here is – un-ten-able."

"I must consult my wife – and your father-in-law. Wait here."

"There's no need t' consult anybody," said Anna. "I'm not obliged to *ask* for release, Mr Gilbert. I'm declarin' my intention an' I'll be gone before noon."

"To live with Rudge?"

"Aye, sir."

"Does Rudge *know* that you intend to arrive on his door-step?"

"It's at Mr Rudge's express invitation."

"The devil! Stealin' my servants behind my back."

Anna said steadily, "Mr Rudge an' I will be married in due course o' time. Meanwhile I'm to be his housekeeper."

Gilbert did not know enough of Robert Rudge's domestic arrangements to enquire as to what fate Anna had in mind for the present incumbent. He got to his feet, shook his head, tried to lay an avuncular hand upon her shoulder.

Anna stepped nimbly out of reach.

Gibbie could not imagine what he had ever seen in her and why, now and then, he had actually felt sorry for her. A reflection of the attraction she had held for Randall had lit her up for him too, perhaps. All that was gone. She was, after all, nothing but a self-seeking, thoughtless trollop who would bed, let alone wed, any man who would promise her a life of idleness.

"Anna," Gilbert Bontine told her, "you are lettin' me down."

She answered with a short bark of laughter and, allowing him no further opportunity to bully or persuade her to change her mind, turned on her heel and left the drawing-room.

Helplessly Gibbie watched her go.

He had lost control of the one charge that Randall had ever given him, to look after and care for Anna Sinclair and her son. What, in God's name, would Randall say to him? What would he say to Randall?

And, as if that worry was not enough, who would bring in the cows?

"Alicia," he shouted, running across the corridor to the main staircase. "Alicia, what shall I do?"

Anna heard him as she wrapped Robbie into a warm winter coat and roped her bundle to her hip.

She took one last look around the hole in the wall of the corridor which had been her drawing-room and her parlour for so many miserable months and, as the Sinclairs, those who were left, came running out of their niches, alarmed by Gibbie's cry, she found Robbie's hand and led him quietly out of the kitchen door and away across the yard to the field path that would take her, clear of the turnpikes, to Robert's house in

Drymen where she would be safe and welcome and would make her new home.

It had been a particularly arduous day for Robert Rudge. Scarf had ridden in from the big market at Perth with the worrying news that prices had risen once more and that he had not been able to negotiate for wool crops on the ground. Shepherds had suffered from the wet as well as cattle-owners and there was a dearth of mutton all across the country. On Rudge's instruction Scarf had left to try his luck on the Glasgow market where imported wool might be available at reasonable cost, enough to keep the tartan cloths coming from the Kennart looms in sufficient quantity to meet orders.

It was after dark before Robert Rudge got home to Drymen. He noticed that the parlour lamp was lit and as he passed the front of the house saw Anna Sinclair and her child seated in the oak chair, the bairn fast asleep in his mother's arms. He put away his horse with alacrity and hurried into the house through the kitchens.

"What does Mrs Sinclair want?" he asked his grizzled servant, McFadzean.

"She says she's come t' stay, Mr Rudge."

"To stay?"

"Aye – an' if she comes, I go."

"Patience, Mrs McFadzean. Let me see what it's about before you collect your belongings."

He entered the parlour with a smile upon his face.

Anna did not rise. Keeping still and small she clutched the child against her as if Mr Rudge was a slave master who had come to separate them. It was something of an act, of course, but it touched Robert Rudge's heart by its appropriateness.

"I have left Strachan, Robert," Anna said.

"Is there a reason?"

"I canna wait t' be your wife; that is the reason."

"You cannot be my wife until the divorcement."

"I can be your servant. I'll be the best servant you've ever had, I promise."

Robert Rudge did not doubt it.

He hesitated. He was still a little in awe of the power of his present housekeeper, the indomitable McFadzean, whose in-laws, burly tenant farmers scattered along the road to the lochside, might come out with the intention of teaching him a lesson. He had seen evidence of the moral outrage of the wild men of Balmaha and he did not want to risk offending them.

Anna said, crying, "I'll be all that a wife can be, Robert. Dinna turn me out. I've nowhere else to go, me an' Robbie."

Still Robert Rudge hesitated.

If it had been a simple seduction of a simple country lass he would have known exactly what to do. He would have gone down beside her, stooped over her, separated her gently from the sleeping child, would have made the child comfortable on the love-seat, would have kissed and fondled Mama and, in ten minutes or so, would have had her upstairs and out of her skirts and bodice. McFadzean would have frowned and muttered, like the good God-fearing woman she was. But McFadzean was sensible and practical and knew what her master was. She would respect his manliness and his natural needs and would bake one of her beef pies for supper for Robert Rudge never sent away a lassie unsatisfied and unfed.

But Anna had come to stay. Suddenly he feared for his privacy, the clockwork routine of his home and wondered at the destruction that this dark-haired girl had wreaked on the menfolk of at least three families. Dark-eyed, moist-eyed, moist-lipped, hair smooth about her cheeks, her skin pale in the lamplight and her bosom heaving with the emotion of it all, Anna awaited his decision.

He said, "You put me into a difficult position, my love. I'm an unmarried man and there may be complications if and when we seek legal blessing in marriage."

"If – if Elspeth returns," Anna said, "I'll see to it that you remain manager of Kennart."

"Oh!"

"If Elspeth does not come back, an' the Moodie sisters get their claws on the mill then we'll swim t'gether. I'm young an' can do things that—"

"Yes, yes, yes, Anna," Robert Rudge said. "I'm not in need of illustration. I do see the advantage."

"Think of it, Robert, as a contract."

"Yes, Anna, but which of us finds the bargain?"

"Neither of us," said Anna. "Unless my sister comes back."

"You are forcin' me to gamble."

"Have you a room for the child, where he can sleep?"

"I have. Small but snug. You may sleep there too, Anna, until I decide—"

She got up. Robbie was slung awkwardly in both arms. The child stirred, whimpered, clung to her breast, legs dangling. His fingers plucked at the bodice of her frock as if he still sought to suckle at her breast.

Robert Rudge said, "Give him to me, Anna."

He took the boy gently from her arms and carried him upstairs while Anna followed with the candle. Tucked snugly into the bed in the narrow little room under the eaves Robbie turned his face into the bolster and settled instantly into deep sleep.

Anna said, "Now, Robert, where is my bed?"

"I'll have a cot made up here."

"Is that how you wish it t' be?"

"Perhaps, sometimes—"

"Take me now," said Anna.

Robert Rudge puffed out his cheeks and gave a low, soundless whistle. It was not an affectation, a sign of resignation. He wanted her now, wanted her so badly that he could hardly resist. But he gathered himself, said, "Let's pretend, Anna, that you're a lady of quality and I'm a gentleman. We'll have a quiet bite of supper downstairs and then, when the servants have retired, we'll stroll upstairs."

The idea pleased Anna.

She grinned. "Provided the supper doesn't take too long."

"Do you really want me, Anna?"

"Really I do."

Later that night, throughout the night, Anna was to prove her sincerity with such enthusiasm and invention that Robert Rudge, for all his experience with women, felt a little shocked at her verve and, before the candle burned out in its blue-glass dish, submitted to exhaustion and gave himself up to being loved like a lord.

Davy and Sarah, perhaps, should have told Elspeth what was in the wind between their sister and Matt Shearer but Elspeth was so seldom with them now that she seemed almost as much a stranger as the sailorman. Besides, Davy was uncertain as to what part Mouse had played in attracting Matt Shearer's attentions. He seethed with frustration as well as rage at his lack of knowledge on such matters. Sarah, on the other hand, had a woman's instinct for truth and not enough fire in her blood yet to be jealous of her sister. She held her tongue to protect the romance and in consequence the love between Matt and Mousie flourished without impediment.

Elspeth might have intervened. She might have made appeal to Matt's sense of honour. It was not honour that Mouse found compelling in the broad-chested coal-hewer. She hungered to be loved by him, to be changed by his touch and knowledge of him, things that she had realised were possible and attainable since the night she had rubbed her breasts against his bare body.

At home Mouse mooned about in a moist red dream of matching. In the tunnels she laboured like a demon, hastening to and from the nearness of Matt as busy and mindless as her namesake in a harvest field shorn by the reapers. The grieve's son, the arrogant whaler, the outlaw flushed when she called out his name. He answered her without sarcasm or teasing and asked a dozen times each shift how things fared with her and if she was weary and assured her that the drag would soon be over and that he would wait for her by the gate and they would walk home together in the October starlight. He kept his promise too. When they walked thus Mouse felt as if she had gone to Heaven. She kept her tongue still for fear of offending him and let him put his big strong arm about her and help her across the plank bridge, as if she had not crossed it a thousand times without aid. She leaned on him lingeringly and, so far was she gone, even murmured thanks. Within the confines of the cottage Matt and she lived in a state of physical intimacy that some married couples never attained. Matt, however, was afraid of being thought a seducer. He would do no more than administer a kiss upon her brow or cheek and hold her briefly in his arms at the door. Indoors, with Sarah and Davy and Mary Jean, he was careful not to demonstrate how his feelings had changed. He would not allow Mouse to scramble on to his knee or even to touch him. They spoke in stilted and polite phrases but took little part in the general chatter of conversation as if being in love had removed them from reality.

Davy grew more and more sullen, seething with incomprehensible anger. He had never cared much for Mouse yet he was afraid of what might happen to her if she was ruined by this stranger, this coward. Anger and loathing knotted in his chest and his cough returned. He spent his days lying upon his bed, fists clenched and jaw set, and did no housekeeping at all. He wondered what they were doing below, his sister and the sailorman, if they were doing things that were bad, the things he had imagined himself doing but had never found the strength or the opportunity to try.

Elspeth was concerned about Davy. She bought him honey in the comb, which he ate with a spoon, and she sent Sarah to the Placket farm to purchase warm fresh milk which she forced Davy to drink while she watched him, as if he was a bloody infant, too small for solid foods. He could have told her what was wrong – if only he could have found the words.

It was late in the month, towards the Friday of All Hallows Eve, when Matt announced an intention to probe deeper into the millstone cave. It was the first Davy had heard of it and it galled him still more when Matt consulted Mouse and not him about the venture.

Matt had finished his supper and had pushed away the plate. Mouse was seated by him, her thigh brushing his under the table, and Elspeth was soothing Mary Jean, who had had a tumble at the minder's cottage that afternoon and had a bruise upon her brow which made her fractious.

Matt wiped his beard. "Well, Mousie, it seems to me we're runnin' through the seam damned quick."

"Aye, Matt, we are."

"What do y' say, Mousie, if we take a peep into the depths tomorrow?"

"I say we should, Matt."

Elspeth looked up. "Is it not dangerous, Matt?"

"I'll be careful, dinna fret."

"Matt'll take out coal, not rock," said Mouse.

"You'll need fresh candles," said Elspeth. "Wax candles. I

think there are four still in Mr Bennet's box. They'll gutter less an' give more light than tallow."

"I'll take them down wi' me," said Mouse.

Half reclining on the bed, Davy held his hand against his throat to prevent an outburst of coughing. He could hear the seething in his lungs and felt an awful weakness in his limbs at the thought of Matt Shearer breaking down the back of his daddy's cave, changing its shape and nature.

Mouse said, "I'm to go first into the hole."

Davy heard himself speak. "Who says this?"

Mouse answered haughtily, "Matt does."

Davy mimicked his sister under his breath. "Matt does, Matt does." Aloud he said, "Is Matt too feart t' go by himself?"

Sarah said, "Matt's too big for it."

Elspeth said, "Matt, promise me you'll take care."

Matt dismissed her fears casually. "Aye, aye."

Davy lifted himself on his elbows. "You'll be needin' t' brace the roof first, remember."

Mouse said, "Matt knows what t' do."

Davy said, "Matt knows every bloody thing, I suppose."

"Knows more than you," Mouse snapped.

"Thinks he bloody does," Davy retorted.

Matt said, "I'll knock in a lateral prop, two perhaps, from the rock t' the coal wall. I've got timber down there already."

Davy could not bring himself to address the sailorman directly. He said, "Mouse, tell him t' keep the lateral props short. Three feet o' green wood's right for a brace."

"You're all wind, Davy Bennet," Mouse told him. "You've never propped in your life."

"I heard Daddy talk—" Davy began.

"Aye, but I *saw* Daddy do it," said Mouse smugly. "So it's me Matt'll have t' rely on."

"That's enough," Elspeth intervened.

Too late: Davy rolled on to his side, turning his back on his sisters, on the stranger who had usurped his rightful place as head of the family, who cut the coal he should have cut. In his chest there was a constricting pain. Tears swam under his eyelids. He fought not to cough, not to weep.

Oblivious to Davy's distress, Matt went on, "I'll use dry

wedges, of course. I'll take a pick, mallet an' rods. The less I cut the safer it'll be."

"What if Mouse gets stuck?" said Sarah.

"I'll no' get stuck," said Mouse.

Davy hardly heard them now. He laid his head on the bolster, put a hand to the side of his head, fingers to his ear and wriggled his shoulder to hide his face.

"Davy?" Elspeth spoke tenderly, stooped over him, a forearm raised as if to shield him from the light. He wanted to turn, take her in his arms, have Elspeth hold him as she held her bairn. Instead he slashed out petulantly at her.

"Leave m' alone."

"Davy! Oh, Davy!" He heard the woman sigh. "It's hard for you, I know."

She was the only one who understood. Even she could not guess at half of it. He could hear Matt's rumbling laughter, Mousie's sniggers. Matt spoke. The others laughed, even Sarah and Mary Jean. Perhaps they were laughing at him. Laughing at his tears, at his unmanly need to be cradled and cuddled, mocking him for his weakness.

Elspeth touched him. "Let me help you, Davy."

Suddenly all the soft emotions were puffed away like fat on a hot stone. He flung himself round and sat up.

"Get t' hell," he shouted. "Get t' hell an' let me be."

He swung his feet to the floor and stood up.

The others were staring at him, not laughing now. Fury suffused his limbs, bringing with it a false strength, sufficient to carry him past them and out of the door of the cottage.

Chill in the air, the darkness deep; Davy forged on across the plank bridge without glancing back. He heard Elspeth's cry. She called his name. He did not respond. She did not pursue. He needed the cold and the darkness to cool the fever that raged in him. He ran along the path between the trees and turned on to the track that took him down to the workings.

Horses stamped and blethered in the stables. Davy hurried on to the round shape of the coping around the Dead Man. He climbed on to it as if it had been his destination all along.

The shaft was boarded over but the planks had warped. When he knelt upon them and put his face down he could smell the dank pit, could feel the great dark space dropping away below him. He plastered himself belly down upon the planking, holding to its rim as if to a spinning wheel. He had fled from the cottage so that he might weep and rage unobserved. But here on the lid of the Dead Man he found solace and anger and tears went out of him. It was cold, a lovely skin-crimping cold. The blood in his body felt like white snow, his lungs rock-hard and icy. He put his ear to the crack and listened to the emptiness, felt the knowledge of what he must do come to him like an echo.

He grinned, nodded, then got up and went back to the cottage, all calm and assured.

When Mouse spoke to him, he ignored her.

When Matt asked him where he had been, he gave no answer.

When Elspeth said, "Davy, you'll do yourself harm," though, he grinned again as he had done on the roof of the Dead Man and told her, "Not me. Not me," and, shivering, clambered into his bed again and tugged the blanket over his head.

Night terrors had not troubled Elspeth for many months. She slept lightly but without dreams. That night, however, she was trapped in a net of visions, isolated in the millstone cavern. She screamed silently into silence. Sarah was there and Mary Jean. The girls were perched above her like sea-birds on a cliff. They were holding out their arms to her and crying. Silence changed the dreadful dream into nightmare, made Elspeth twist and sweat in the tangle of blankets in her corner. Image followed image: a coiling snake, a stone-grey lizard. Creatures hazy and without form threatened her in the tunnel. In the cave her daughter cowered on the high ledge, crying out for Mammy, Mammy, while Sarah hovered in space like a tern, cawing at her. Then Mary Jean was flapping her arms, cawing too, trying so hard to fly away, fly away, fly—

"Elspeth, Elspeth, for God's sake wake up."

Hand upon her shoulder pulled her out of it. She snapped open her eyes, stared up at Matt, naked to the waist, huge as a genie in the candle flicker.

He frowned down. "What ails you, 'Pet?"

She reached out thankfully and grasped his arm. He was so real, so solid. He connected her with Balnesmoor and the time before she had known James, with the green days of her girlhood on the high hill of Drumglass.

"Matt," she gasped. "Oh, Matt, I was dreamin'."

"A nightmare by the sound o' it."

Mouse suddenly appeared by Matt's side. She placed a hand upon his hip, rubbed herself against him. She seemed tiny as a sprite in her shift, hair, grown long, falling about her shoulders.

Awake too, Mary Jean kneeled round-eyed on the edge of the mattress.

"Bad dream, Mammy. Bad dream."

"Aye, love. Gone now. All gone."

Matt said, "A taste o' whisky will cure you, 'Pet."

Elspeth shook her head, managed a feeble smile.

"I'm fine," she whispered.

"I'll cuddle ye, Mammy." Mary Jean scrambled into bed beside her, snuggling down ostentatiously, arms wrapped about Elspeth's waist. "Go t' sleep now. Soon be the mornin'."

How often had she consoled her daughter with those words. It would, indeed, soon be morning. She tried to imagine sunlight and a clean breeze off the Forth. All that came to mind, though, was the shaft and the tunnel, the trap under the millstone.

She shuddered.

Mary Jean clung to her tightly.

"I'm – I'm all right, really."

Mouse was looking up at Matt, still touching him. If she had been more alert Elspeth might have seen the adoration in the girl-child's eyes, a reflection of her own faraway innocence and the wonderment of being in love. But she was too enervated to notice and, a moment later, Matt and Mouse slipped away, taking the candle with them.

Mary Jean gave her mother a little clumsy kiss upon the nose and Elspeth's tensions slackened. She placed an arm about her daughter.

In the sighing of the wind about the cottage she could almost make out the children's insubstantial voices crying aloud – *Fly away, fly away, fly away* – but whether they spoke to her or to each other Elspeth had no idea.

She rose early, long before dawn, to make ready for the day.

* * *

395

Gossip abounded in the villages of Drymen and Balnesmoor. The weavers of Kennart, who knew old Rudge well, were hardly surprised at this latest titbit. They tutted and smirked, shook their heads at the manager's escapade. Some envied him his 'housekeeper'. Others muttered that this must be the last straw in wickedness and that now, surely, God would punish Robert Rudge. Imagine daring to live out of wedlock with another man's wife in the shadow of the Drymen parish church! The fact that the other man's wife was the notorious Anna Cochran Sinclair added spice to the affair. In drinking-dens along the back roads and in taverns in village squares the talk those nippy nights was all of Rudge and his paramour.

At first Mrs McFadzean, the 'original' housekeeper, did not feel any great resentment towards Anna Sinclair, who, in fact, pitched in with domestic chores and only played the dame when Mr Rudge came home of an evening. But Mrs McFadzean soon found that she could not intimidate Anna as she had browbeaten a string of kitchen maids before her. It was the loss of that contest of wills that turned Mrs McFadzean against the interloper. Anna would not even let her bully the present maid-servant, Isa, a wall-eyed waif from Kennart, too slow to be used in the manufactory and too ugly to find a husband. Anna was very sharp with Mrs McFadzean, told her in no uncertain terms that Isa was not a slave and deserved a measure of civility to temper strictness. Mrs McFadzean was outraged. She appealed to Mr Rudge, who placated her as best he could.

The squabble might have blown over but for the attitude of the elders and kirk-buddies who, through the minister, managed to convince Mrs McFadzean that her soul would be doomed if she dwelled with the vile abomination. So Mrs McFadzean left Mr Rudge's employ and went to be a servant to her brother and his wife who lived in a hovel on the banks of Loch Lomond and was miserable in spite of the five guineas that Mr Rudge gave her as a mark of appreciation for her years of loyal service. Mr Rudge, at that time, would have paid the world to go away if he could have met the world's price.

Love, alas, did not bring a snap and a skip to Mr Rudge's

step. It did not brace him as it would have done a young buck. In fact he crept about the mill and climbed the office stairs as stiffly as if somebody had taken a switch to his back. He did not have the juice left to be severe with workers and traders and might be said to have 'mellowed' under the influence of the woman from Strachan and Ottershaw. If the weavers had known the truth of it they would have been shocked and amazed. The manager of Kennart had finally fallen under the fatal spell of Eros and what had begun as a plot to secure his future had swiftly become a snare from which he could not escape.

Anna was lithe and beautiful, without modesty or scruple, and more inventive than he would have believed possible. The tricks of the amorous art seemed to come to her naturally. She thought nothing of parading herself before him like a nymph, quite unclad. His mind smoked with visions of her and his body ached for her throughout the day at Kennart. She possessed him soul and body. He was more slave to Anna Cochran Sinclair than master. For all that, Robert Rudge had his pride. He gave as good as he got and did not deny her her pleasure by pleading fatigue or distraction.

"Are you happy here, Anna?" he would ask.

"Aye, I am."

"Are you happy with me?"

"I've never been happier with any man, Robert."

Lying upon his back, without nightshirt or nightcap, Mr Rudge would grin like an old wolf. "Will you still marry me, Anna?"

"As soon as I'm free."

His lids would droop. He would sigh with contentment at the prospect of all the nights of pleasure that they would share when they were man and wife. He would give a little start when she bent over him again. He would open his eyes and see her breasts and the soft line of her throat and her rapacious mouth, lips parted and the tip of her tongue showing.

"Will I kiss you t' sleep, Robert?"

He knew what she meant and was astonished by it. But he would nod and lift his head and let her lower her breasts for kisses as if he was bidding them goodnight separately, let her slither down by him, her tongue working little patterns over

397

his chest and neck and belly in a manner never written about even in the most salacious fiction he had read; and he would grunt and clasp an arm about her and hold her very, very tightly as if afraid that she would abandon him in the night or devour him whole.

As for Anna, once she had been rid of the housekeeper and had the running of the neat little house all to herself she too put all thought of Elspeth from her mind. She sharpened herself up to be a wife in the parlour with almost the same enthusiasm as she was mistress in bed. Next year, when she was free, Robert Rudge would make her honest. There would be no fear for Robbie's future. Perhaps she would bear Robert a son or two to round out the family.

They would go to school in Edinburgh, her sons, just like Bontines. She would go on Robert's arm to visit, once the fuss had blown over, might even call at Ottershaw, wearing a pretty silk dress, take tea as an equal with Randall's fine lady, let Randall see what he had lost.

In the meantime she had Robert Rudge – and he was no mean man, just as loving as she wished without becoming all moony and daft like Sandy Sinclair. She tried not to think of Sandy or of Randall. Certainly she spared not a thought for Matt, her legal husband who had vanished so thoroughly from her ken and might for all she knew be decently dead.

Sarah was left with a candle and a water bottle to keep watch at the mouth of the narrow tunnel. She was just out of sight of the Ogilvies' room which, like all the other nooks on the base level, was running out of easy-cut coal and in three months or four would dry up completely.

Sarah did not like being left alone, though she could hear the *chack* of Mr Ogilvie's hammer and the growl of the daughters' voices, and even peep out cautiously to glimpse the shake of candlelight outside the room; that consoled her and calmed her fears.

She was sensible, was Sarah. She knew that Matt and Mouse had important work to do in the secret chamber and that they would be too occupied to keep watch for intruders.

While Sarah kept scout Matt and Mouse, alone in the cavern below the millstone slab, prepared to breach the slit at the rear of the cave. Matt had already made a stout ladder out of timbers and rope and had put up a brace upon which he could rest his chest and arms. He had taken a deep cut out of the coal seam to accommodate his right shoulder, a fall that had been broken and removed during the course of the morning. A ramp of chows led up to the ladder and the ladder, in turn, to crossbeam and the crack.

Sweating in a loincloth, Matt hauled himself to the cross brace and hung over it. He made three grooves in the coal. It was promisingly 'heavy' and dusty and did not splinter into fine edges under the hammer and swelling wedges. He had learned the trick of using dry wood for his wedges and received from Mouse an iron pot of drainage water which he poured over the wedges once they were crammed into place. Expansion forced splits in the solid face and, with luck, the coal would come away in thin flakes to the hammer thereafter.

Hanging on the brace with head and shoulders stuck into the corner was tiring. He had, however, caught a whiff of air from the finger-crack at the joint of roof and wall.

He placed his nose against it, sniffing like a sheep-dog, while Mouse, just below him, asked, "Is it fresh? Is it?"

Matt could not give an answer.

He climbed down from his perch to take a breather. Mousie went up, wriggled on to the crosspiece, took a long sniff and frowned.

"Smells queer," she said, and sniffed again. "Like – like fish."

"I hope we're no' penetratin' the river bed."

"Ah-nah," Mouse assured him. "Daddy said the river was a thousand feet from here, measured on the tide."

"Measured on the tide? What did he mean?"

Nose to the fissure Mouse sniffed and frowned. In fact she had never quite known what Daddy meant by the statement but had accepted the truth of it because of the conviction that he was always right. What she caught wind of through the fine crack was not liquid, of that she was sure. It smelled, now she thought about it, like one of the blocks of salted, rock-hard cod that poor widows bought from Mr Nicol's shop to boil into stew.

Mouse blinked. By her right ear the stub of a wedge made

a little *cheeping* noise as it expanded and swelled. Matt had set the wedges in a triangle, giving three points of pressure. She blinked again as the lowest wedge emitted a creak, and a crack zigzagged across the outer surface of the coal wall. Three or four thumbnails of coal fell from the line to the cavern floor and Matt, who was more nervous than he cared to admit, gave a stifled whoop and jumped back.

Looking round and down Mouse caught the movement and laughed.

"It's workin', Matt. You'll get rods in here an' a slump o' some size quite soon."

"Come down, Mousie."

"When I'm done."

"Come down."

"Make me."

"Mousie, I'm givin' ye warnin' . . ."

She lifted her skirts and showed him her legs. Giggling, she tried to entice him on to the ladder, to put his hands upon her. Matt was too tense and too full of purpose to play games.

Reluctantly Mouse climbed down, making way for the man. With three rods in his left hand and the hammer hung on a thong about his shoulder, Matt squeezed up the ladder to the beam once more.

Twenty minutes later he had effected a cut. It was hardly a proper cut since the coal came down in awkward lumps, rumbling and cascading into the cavern in clouds of dust. He saw now that more expertise than he possessed was needed for 'exploration', and withdrew from the corner in defeat.

"I've done all I can do, Mousie," Matt declared. "It's o'er dangerous for one chap."

"But is there coal, Matt?"

"I canna say what's beyond the lie o' the slab."

"Let me try," said Mouse.

They were both coated with grime, and the initial excitement of discovery had waned. Mouse, however, was not one to give up easily. She scaled the ladder and got herself on to the beam, hunched under the roof.

"Candle," she said.

Matt handed her up a fresh stick, newly lighted, guarding the flame as best he could.

It was small work and fussy. Mouse was good at it. Matt watched admiringly as she stretched herself along the beam, just as high and tight as she could get and, holding the candle-cup in the palm of her right hand, pushed it along the cut as far as it would go.

"It burns," she said.

Her face was hidden by her shoulder. She wriggled, lowering one leg over the brace. From below Matt could see her calf and thigh. He would have looked away if he had not been afraid that she might fall. He felt a terrible affinity with the pit-girl and had to fight an urge to thrust his hands around her, to feel her naked flesh. It was not the time or the place. He concentrated on staring at the high, shadowy crack into which, astonishingly, Mouse had managed to insert her head and shoulders.

"Can y' see anythin'?" Matt whispered. "Anythin' at all?"

"There's no stream o' air, Matt." Her voice was hollow. "But the candle's burnin' clean as a whistle. Aye, wait, I can see."

"What? Is it more coal?"

"A hammer. Give m' up the hammer."

Legs kicking, skirts shanked up, she pulled herself from the aperture. There was fear in Matt that she would crush herself into it, would vanish into darkness out of his sight, out of his reach. He climbed a step of the ladder, hammer in hand. She twisted and leaned back, like a tabby on a tree branch. Her face was small, lambent and fierce.

"Give me that." She snatched the hammer from him. "Now, Matt, hold me tight."

He went up another foot, narrowing himself, placed one big hand about her thigh, the other across her bottom. She wriggled out along the cross brace and knocked away at some obstruction within the fissure. She gave a little squeal. Matt tightened his grip. He heard coal fall, not into the cavern but into space beyond the millstone slab. He knew without being told that they had broken through.

Mouse slid the hammer back to him. He slung it carefully about his shoulder, took hold on the girl again, pressing his body against the slab for support, slipping his hand along her thigh and calf in a firm caress, catching a ruck of her skirt.

She was making tiny sounds in her throat, panting with effort, in almost to the waist.

"Aaahhh!" Mouse exclaimed.

Panic flooded over Matt. "Come back, Mousie. That's far enough."

She ignored him, inched forward. She thrust the candle-cup within the dark place and held it there.

"Mouse, please," Matt pleaded.

Crabbing backwards, she returned. Matt shifted his hands from her legs to her waist, let her pivot on the beam, grinning.

"It's big," she told him, shiny-eyed. "Aye, it's big."

"But is it deep?"

"Miles deep. As far as the light goes, an' further."

She kicked her bare legs in delight at the discovery.

Matt held her. "Can it be reached?"

"It's the line o' this seam, our seam, nippit by the millstone slab. It can be blasted awa' wi' black powder."

"Mouse, I canna risk usin' powder."

"Three or four charges o' black powder an' we've a mile o' big coal for our profit."

"Nah, love," said Matt. "It's too much for us."

"It's ours, ours."

Prudently Matt said, "Come down, Mousie. We've gone far enough for one day."

"But it's ours, Matt."

"We – we'll discuss it wi' the others. See what can be done."

"We found it, Matt."

"We did, aye, but—"

She leaned forward on the perch, hands upon his shoulders, and kissed him full on the mouth. She leaned again, until her whole weight was supported upon him and he was braced hard to hold them both in balance.

"Mouse, you'll have us both off."

"Hold me tight, Matt."

Beneath the cotton garment he could feel her small breasts press against his chest. He was suddenly conscious of his naked-ness and squirmed to hide his arousal. It was as if the fire which had smouldered in him had been fanned into a blaze by the draught from the long seam. He kissed her throat, her chin, her mouth, dragged her to him, her legs about his rib-cage, heels locked behind his spine. Carefully he brought her down.

"Matt, m'darlin', m'love."

"No, Mousie, not here."

"Aye, here," she snapped as he lowered her to the floor of the cavern. "Where else but here?"

"But you've never—"

"I'm ready."

She was not thrusting and demanding. She was female in her heart, in her being, not some creature de-sexed by the nature of work, by the coarse years of labour in the pit. Matt saw that he need not pity her at all. Under the shell was a girl who needed him as Anna had never done, not out of weakness but out of love. This was her rose garden, the bottom of a coal pit was her bower. Where else would he take her? He lowered her to the floor and lifted her skirts. She stared up at him, showing no apprehension. She tore at the buttons and the ragged ribbon that fastened her bodice, drew the garment apart to show him her breasts. Matt unlooped the cloth from his waist and knelt before her. The grime that smeared his torso and chest made his loins seem pale and doubly naked. He was aroused, and not ashamed. He wanted her to fear him just a little so that he might comfort her. He kissed her mouth. He touched her breasts with his fingertips. He put his lips to each nipple in turn, tugging and teasing them, feeling them stiffen and thicken. Slipping an arm about her he lifted her to him. He did not impose himself, let Mouse probe until she found his manhood and joined with it. He lifted her higher. Her mouth gaped. She gave a soft swooning sort of cry. Still he did not press. He let her rest, then felt her surge against him. Her knees clasped his hips. She was wet and soft around him. Only then did he lean into her. She cried out, not like the sound that Anna made or the false passion uttered by girls from the gutters of the Babylon. There was no falseness in Mouse, no resentment. He put his head down, lips parted over her open mouth and shared his breath with her as they rode to a climax.

Matt heard nothing, Mouse nothing.

Far away, beyond the band of millstone grit the sound of trickling sand was lost to the couple on the cavern floor.

* * *

For three hours Davy had waited, seated on a stump by the side of the carpenters' shed, shivering as shadows grew long and the autumn sun sank away down river.

If it had been impulse that had taken him there then it would have cooled too in the waiting time. But Davy had steeled himself, convinced that it was his duty to betray the family for the good of the pit.

It was close to four o'clock when he at last spied Thomas Rance. The oversman emerged from the counting-house and set off across the angle of the yard towards the shaft. It would be drawing-up time soon, Davy realised, and Mr Rance would not have much time to spare to hear a crippled lad's fanciful tale.

He must be firm and convincing.

"Mr Rance," he called out, and scrambled to his feet.

Thomas Rance turned his head.

"Mr Rance." Davy swallowed and beckoned. "A word wi' you, Mr Rance."

It was how Matt would have put it. He felt pleased with himself. His confidence grew. He made the oversman come to him, did not scuttle and creep like a damned putter or rope-boy.

Mr Rance had no expression on his face. That blankness had disconcerted better and bigger men than Davy Bennet. Davy breathed through his mouth, the evening air going down into his lungs as thick and cold as milk on a winter's morning. He must not splutter, cough, must say it straight out.

Mr Rance stopped five or ten feet from him.

"What's wrong with you, Bennet? Are you in need of help?"

"I know where's a seam," said Davy.

Thomas Rance could not prevent a frown of incomprehension furrowing his brow. He came closer. "What's that ye say?"

"A seam, a new seam, a new winnin'."

"What do you know about seams?"

"Daddy found it," said Davy.

He experienced no relief at being rid of the secret.

Thomas Rance put out a hand and clamped it on his shoulder.

"In the base seam?"

He had been believed. Mr Rance had not doubted him. Davy nodded.

Mr Rance said, "Beyond the room?"

Davy nodded again.

"I've been down there on the dead night," said Thomas Rance. "There is no extension to the old seam."

"There is. Damned if there isn't. It's hid. Hid behind a door, a wooden door under the back mound."

"Who put the door there?"

"Daddy."

"Is that why his take was so high?"

"Aye. It would've been higher too if he'd laboured harder. It's a bloody rich store o' coal, Mr Rance."

"Is that where he met wi' his accident, in the new seam?"

"Aye. We brought him out."

"Who did?"

"Mrs Patterson, me an' Mouse."

"Christ!" said Thomas Rance. "Why, in God's name, did you still keep the seam to yourselves?"

"We promised Daddy we would."

"Who excavated the seam?"

"It took none," said Davy. "It's a – a nat'ral fault."

Thomas Rance shook his head. "No, there are no natural faults at that depth. It must be an old diggin', neglected an' forgotten."

"I've bloody *seen* it. I've cut bloody coal out o' it. It's a fault, like a cavern, I tell ye. Under a slab o' millstone."

"Is the man, Shearer, is he cuttin' there now?"

"Damned if he's not," said Davy. "The bastard."

"I should have known it," said Thomas Rance. "How could a sailor hew coal at that rate wi'out experience? I should've guessed it."

"I'll tak' ye down there," said Davy. "I'll show y' where it is."

"It canna be hard to find, Bennet, since there's no road at that level."

"I'll tak' ye down when they all come up at shift's end."

"Why are you doin' this?"

"I want t' cut."

"I see," said Thomas Rance. "It's *your* seam, is it?"

The oversman did not remind him that he was too puny to hew coal, too burned out with the black spit in his lungs to descend into the seams. The oversman put his big hands on his thighs and brought his face close to that of the boy.

"You want Mr Bolderon's bounty, is that it?" he whispered.

"I want t' bloody *cut*. I want *work*."

Whispering still, Thomas Rance said, "Ten pounds, Davy, that's all you're entitled to."

"What am I needin' wi' ten pounds?"

"Be that as it may, Davy," Thomas Rance said, "now you've told me it's no longer a secret, your secret. I'll be obliged to report it t' Mr Bolderon."

"I – I might have told ye a lie," said Davy. "See it first."

"Ah!" said Thomas Rance. "Ah-hah!"

"I'll show ye the door, the way in. I'll tak' ye down."

"It's not a lie, Davy, is it?"

"Nah."

"But why tell me at all, Davy?"

Now that it was done, Davy had no answer to the oversman's question. He could not explain it. Nobody could explain it. No one would ever know why.

Thomas Rance said, "Wait for me in the forge, Davy. Keep warm by the fire. Tell Mr Cameron I sent you."

"What – what'll ye do?"

"We'll go down, Davy, as you suggest, when shift's over an' the levels are cleared."

"You an' me, Mr Rance?"

"Just you an' me, Davy," Thomas Rance assured him.

Elspeth returned late from the counting-house. It was a dry clear night for once. She had not needed to change her shoes to cross the field but had picked her way to the cottage straight and quick. She was not thinking of Davy or of Mouse and Matt, but of the news that Keir Bolderon had given her that Snippets would return to claim his desk on Monday morning and that in future she would be answerable to the paymaster not the manager.

Keir Bolderon had imparted the information with many expressions of regret. He had assured her that, if it had been left to him, he would have paid Snippets off and kept her close by him. In the course of the day he had made one or two remarks whose implication Elspeth could not fail to understand. She felt sure that Keir Bolderon would soon make a proposal. She was not dismayed at the prospect, only by the fact that she must refuse it without explanation.

How could she tell him that she was wife to another man? Marriage was impossible. Not only had she her own horrid secret to protect but she was also obligated to Matt, must on no account bring the light of attention upon him. Matt's very life depended on her silence.

When she reached the cottage, however, Elspeth's anxiety about her own predicament was replaced by worry of a different kind.

Mouse and Matt were alone there. The girl was seated boldly upon Matt's knee, flushed and smug. Matt, in contrast, seemed embarrassed.

It dawned upon Elspeth that Matt Sinclair had not changed. He had taken advantage of Mouse or intended to do so very soon.

"What is this?" she demanded.

"What it seems t' be," said Matt.

"When did—"

"Matt's mine," Mouse said.

Still dirty from the day's work, she draped an arm about the man's neck and kissed him brazenly.

Matt disentangled himself. "It – it just happened, 'Pet."

At a loss, Elspeth looked round.

There was no pot upon the fire and the fire itself had not been raked and set but burned low and smoky in the hearth. Potatoes had not been scrubbed. The ham-bone she had put in a bowl of water to make stock had not been simmered. Nothing at all had been done that day, and Mouse and Matt seemed so wrapped up in this new-found 'love' that they had neglected—

Elspeth took hold of herself.

"Where's Sarah?"

"No' in yet," said Matt.

"An' Davy?"

Mouse shrugged. She tried to buss the man again but this

time, gently, he turned his head aside. "Aye, where *is* Davy?"

Matt put his hands around Mouse's waist, lifted her lightly from his lap and got up.

"'Pet, we never meant—" he began.

"Has nobody thought t' fetch Mary Jean?" Elspeth angrily demanded.

"I expect Sarah's gone for her. They'll be here in a minute or two," said Matt. "'Pet, listen t' me. About my intentions—"

Now that she thought of it, she had seen signs of the attraction between the pit-girl and her brother-in-law. She should have remonstrated with him before now, should not have ignored it. In her confusion Elspeth managed to blot out that problem. She concentrated on the lateness of the hour, Davy's absence and why it was that Sarah had not returned with Mary Jean.

Matt said, "If it's Mary Jean that's got ye worried, I'll toddle down—"

Elspeth rounded on him. "How long have you been here?"

Matt shrugged. "A quarter-hour; a half, perhaps."

"Did you not *think*, Matt?"

"Ach, Davy'll just be sulkin'," said Mouse.

She went to the hearth and rattled the iron among ashy coals. It would be an hour or more before the fire would be hot enough to boil a pot of any kind.

Elspeth snapped, "Did it not occur t'you that Davy has not been out alone after dark for months?"

"I'll awa' an' find him," said Matt. "Mousie, my love, why do you not go down to the minder's an' make sure Mary Jean's safe? I expect you'll meet Sarah on the way." He looked at Elspeth. "Will that calm y' down, 'Pet?"

Elspeth said, "What happened today?"

She did not know why she should make a relationship between exploration of the fissure in the rock and the unusual events of the evening. For an instant Matt was bewildered. He frowned. "Eh?"

"Did you break through – in the seam?"

"We did, aye, we did," said Matt.

"Is it another cavern?"

"Aye." Mouse chuckled. "Packed wi' coal too, Elspeth."

"Did you go into it?"

"Mouse saw it," said Matt. "But, look, we can talk o' this later. I'm starved an' in sore need o' supper. Once we've found the missin' lambs an' boiled the pots we'll tell ye all about it, 'Pet."

"Yes."

"Mousie, off an' fetch Mary Jean."

"Aye, Matt." She discarded the iron poker and rose with alacrity, beaming at him.

Mouse made towards the door but did not do more than reach her hand to the latch when the door opened suddenly and Sarah, white-faced and breathless, burst into the kitchen.

"Where's Mary Jean?" Elspeth cried.

Clinging to the door handle, Sarah shook her head.

"It's – it's – Davy," she panted. "I – I've just seen him at the shaft wi' Mr Rance."

"Rance?" Mouse put a hand to her sister's neck and cocked the younger girl's head up. "What's Davy doin' wi' Thomas Rance?"

"Takin' him below," Sarah answered.

"Christ! Davy's shopped us," Matt said and, grabbing at his coat, ran out of the cottage like a hare.

The horsemen and the winding operator, a young man named Imrie, had been none too pleased to be told to remain at their posts. They had no choice but to obey the oversman, however. Grumbling, they had let down the bucket and left the horses coupled to the gear twenty minutes after the time when the pit was cleared. Even Elginbrod had come up and gone home. Mr Rance wore such a dour expression, however, that none dare argue or complain; and they had done no more than mutter questions as to what the oversman might be up to, dragging the Bennet boy, and him a cripple, down below at this dead hour.

Imrie was even less pleased, some thirty minutes later, to be roused from nodding half-sleep in his upright box near the shaft head by a violent hand upon his throat.

In the glimmer of the lantern he recognised his assailant as the bloody sailorman. Shearer was twice his size and as mad as a baited bull. His eyes fair blazed and there was spittle upon the corners of his lips. He seemed to have lost all his reason, though there was no reek of spirits upon his breath when he dragged Imrie from his stool and thrust his face close to the winder's.

"Did bloody Rance go down?"

"Aye, aye."

"Wi' our Davy?"

"Ben – Bennet, aye."

"Who else?"

"No – nobody."

"Right, then." The hand slackened. Gagging a little, Imrie sagged against the side of the box. "Shout the horses an' bring up yon bloody bucket."

"Wha –wha—"

"*Now.*"

Fearing for his life, Imrie thrust his head from the aperture in the side of the box and called out to the horsemen in their big low-roofed hut twenty yards away. He could see the span of the rope slack across the sky, was too conscious of Shearer behind him, crowding him, to dare issue warning to his companions.

He croaked, "Take up the bucket."

"Louder, damn you."

"TAKE UP THE BUCKET."

After a moment or two the rope stiffened and the roller of the drum began to rotate, the wheels to churn in their cappings of black blubber.

Shearer gave Imrie no opportunity to sound an alarm but he did not bully the winder again. Indeed, now that his will was being done he seemed quite reasonable and rational.

As the bucket came up from the bottom of the shaft he said, "I'm goin' down too. Mr Rance expects me t' be there at the bottom but I nippit home for a bite first. See?"

"What's he doin' wi' Bennet?"

"We're – we're lookin' for a new seam. Davy Bennet thinks he remembers the line."

"Ah-hah!" Imrie was not convinced.

He was even less convinced when the Bennet lassie and Mrs Patterson appeared across the yard. The girl was barefoot but the widow had taken time to toss a shawl over her shoulders, though she still wore the neat plaid frock that she affected when she paid wages.

"Matt," Elspeth called. "*Has* Davy gone down?"

"Aye, with Rance."

"What can we do?"

"Brazen it out."

"Matt, are you certain Davy's—"

"Why else would he take Rance below?"

"But why would he do such a thing?"

Matt made a sound of frustration, half groan, half roar. "How would I know what rattles in Davy's head?"

Cowering by Matt's side, Mouse said, "Are ye goin' after them, Matt?"

"Aye, though I fear it'll do no good."

"I'll come wi' you."

"Nah, Mousie. It'll be enough if I'm there."

"But it's my bloody seam, dearest," Mouse said.

"'Pet, hold her back," said Matt curtly.

He wasted no more time. The moment the bucket swayed level with the platform he leapt into it. He reached and caught the uprights to steady the contraption, and shouted, "*Lower awa'*."

Imrie glanced at Elspeth. He had respect for her. She was Mr Bolderon's depute and, as far as he knew, his sweetheart. She did not contradict the sailorman. Strictly, no man was supposed to descend into the pit after shift hours without a direct order from Mr Rance. Imrie hesitated then stuck his head from the box and called to the horsemen.

"SLACK OUT."

Elspeth clasped Mouse to her. Mouse squirmed in her grasp but the woman held her very tightly and would not let her go.

Mouse Bennet screamed, *"Maaatt, Maaaaaatt—"*

Arm raised, Matt gave the girl-child a punched salute, a farewell, and sank out of sight below the platform's rim.

TEN

Footsteps of the Flock

Davy was a bantam cock again, small and swaggering. He had his triumph and his power as he led the oversman into the trap and assisted him down the steps as proudly as if he had carved out the seam with his own bare hands.

"See," he declared, swinging the hot lantern about.

Thomas Rance had laboured along the tunnels not at one with the earth this evening, not with Davy Bennet scuttling along before him and the weight of his responsibilities dragging on his back like a sack.

The door was hidden, but not well hidden, behind a mound of loose marl. He glanced at Jock Bennet's old room in passing and saw that there had been no coal cut from it in weeks. When the door was exposed and taken from the trap and Davy had climbed expertly into the space Thomas Rance hesitated for a moment. All his pitman's senses were afire. He could hear an empty silence that indicated space. He could smell coal in his nostrils, taste the atomised dust of a day's cut, could taste and smell other minerals too. Air was not especially scarce. The lantern flame did not pale or stifle. He pushed his bulk through the trap and went down the four short steps into the cavern.

Coal by the ton-weight hung on the walls but it was the glittering slab that caught his attention; millstone grit, without doubt. He was astonished to find a slab of such scale and density at this depth and its presence disturbed him. It was not a sinister instinct that told the oversman there was something amiss in the cavern's construction, a mystery and a puzzle of Nature. He understood the physical forces that had formed the seams and levels of the place called the Abbeyfield, the ice and snow-rivers, the quakes and great alluvial washes.

Davy Bennet danced about, swinging the lantern. "See, do

y' see, Mr Rance? I told ye, did I not? Coal an' more bloody coal. Damn me, it's coal wi'out end."

The lad's estimate was an exaggeration. The fore-cavern was certainly not scarce of coal – coal of fine quality at that – but it was limited. Two young hewers could skin it out, Thomas Rance suspected, in a six month, though he could not judge the depth of the seam. He noticed that Bennet or Shearer, perhaps, had peeled the stuff to the rock here and there. All in all the formation was strange. Thomas Rance advanced cautiously along the cavern's narrow floor.

Great ribs of coal lay broken on the floor, ready for transportation; a whole week's take ready to be loaded on the sleds. You could see where Bennet and Shearer had set the candles, mark out their progress along the seam by the smoke-smuts. He had never, ever, seen such a place. It amazed him that he could stand tall in it and that an arm stretched out would not quite express its width.

Davy Bennet tugged at his sleeve.

"They were lookin' on t'day, Mr Rance. Mousie an' him. they found more; a whole seam, Mousie said. A line, a run, a bran' new cut. Up there, I think. Aye, up there."

"How long since your father discovered this seam?"

"Last year, last spring."

Last spring there had been hope for Mr Bolderon's contract. Now it would be Fotheringham and the new partner, whoever he might be, who would reap the benefit of the discovery. Bennet's selfishness had ruined the best manager he had ever worked under, a man who had sympathy for his colliers and who considered himself one with them.

Anger spurted in the breast of the stoical oversman, anger at Jock Bennet, at Elspeth Patterson whose hypocrisy seemed more heinous than that of the dead hewer or even the sailor-man.

Men might be expected to bow to greed, mixed in with pride. But she, the Patterson woman, she must have known what straits and circumstances fettered Mr Bolderon, she more than anyone these past few months. Why had she kept lip-tight about the existence of this seam, this saving discovery? Was this a form of selfishness too subtle for him to understand? Did she, perhaps, require Mr Bolderon reduced before she would

413

consider herself good enough to marry him, for that was what was on the manager's mind, plain as a pitpost. Such thoughts, unrelated to coal, skipped and skittered about in Thomas Rance's mind as he picked his way over the fallen coal, following the lad and the lantern along to the fissure's narrowing.

"Up there, see." Davy pointed.

Shearer had left a little timber ladder conveniently in place and had banged in a cross brace high up between the converging walls. Crumbled coal had spilled down the smooth wall.

"See it," Davy Bennet whispered. "Yonder's where Mousie went through."

Thomas Rance took off his coat. He folded the garment neatly and laid it on the floor and, as he did so, bent and examined the constitution of the elements there. A strange grey sort of sand; he rubbed it in his fingers. It did not adhere to his skin. He sniffed it. It smelled slightly like gunpowder, though not so pungent. Sand, an unusual sand. He blew it from his fingertips, wiped them on his shirt then said, "Give me the lantern, Davy."

The boy was agog. Gradually his brashness and bravado had been diminished by the place itself, by the realisation that he had sided with an oversman. He was in awe of the authority of Mr Rance now and the quiet assurance of the man so different from that of his father. Meekly he handed over the lantern.

Standing close to the boy Thomas Rance said solemnly, "You did the right thing, Davy."

"He would've ruinit it," Davy murmured. "He would've took it all, left me wi' nothin'."

"Step back a pace, Davy," said Thomas Rance.

Now that he was clad in shirt-sleeves Mr Rance's bulk was evident. His arms were thickly muscled and his chest, though sprigged with grey hair, was as broad as that of Matt Shearer. Why, Davy wondered, had he not noticed the oversman's strength before?

"Are y' goin' up there, Mr Rance?"

"I am, Davy. Step back further, lad."

Again Davy retreated. His heels clipped the coal ridge and he tripped. He stuck out his hand and bruised it and sat down

414

upon the ridge and, sucking his palm, watched as Thomas Rance clambered up to the beam with the lantern wire clenched in his teeth. Davy had no part in it. From that moment it was none of Davy Bennet's doing, though that fact went unrecorded and undiscovered.

Thomas Rance leaned over the crossbeam. Still with the lantern wire in his teeth, its barrel hot against his chest, he peered into the crevice that Matt Shearer had enlarged that afternoon. Thomas Rance could smell the same smell as Mouse had done, a whiff from ages past. He heard too a weird, dry trickling sound, like sand in an hourglass.

"What the devil!" he whispered.

Thomas Rance did not doubt that there was space, vast space, beyond the Bennets' cavern. He could sense it with every fibre of his being. Leaving the lantern balanced on the crossbeam, he came down from the perch, found a mallet, rods and wedges, tucked them into his leather belt and, without a word to Davy, climbed up to the crevice once more.

Wheezing slightly, Davy watched.

It happened very suddenly.

It was as if the hoary old tales of egg-shell rock had been true all along. Though the river bed was far off the channel which the flood had gouged out a hundred thousand years ago was not so distant. It had been filled grain by insidious grain in some far-off eon, the long hollows left by melting ice had been packed under pressure. Fire and flood, the earth's hot passions, might all be spent but the debris remained locked below, the ashes of its energy preserved.

To test the depth of the coal seam Thomas Rance inserted a rod into the groove that Matt had gouged out. When the rod met resistance the oversman gave it a whack with the mallet, one cautious jabbing blow. Sand spurted into his face. Sand fell over his chest like a shower of dry water. Sand blinded Thomas Rance. He swung away, slipped and clung desperately to the beam with one hand. Sand hissed and pattered over Davy who flung himself backward and scrambled over the coal towards the trap.

Then, as suddenly as it had begun, the flow of sand stopped.

Thomas Rance dragged himself on to the beam. He rubbed sand from his eyes, spat, and with his face close to the iron examined the point at which the rod had run through. He hesitated, gripped the rod and began to screw it out, inch by inch.

No gradual thunder warned man or boy. The crack was as sudden and sharp as a musket shot. The millstone slab shifted its precarious position and its edge found no support. More tiny grains poured fom the outrun. The slab crunched down and split across its breadth. The lantern and Thomas Rance were instantly lost. Sand that had remained locked in long chambers for a hundred thousand years came forth in a hissing deluge, overwhelmed the man and buried him in a breath. Davy, a moment in the dark, cried out for his daddy before he too was buried. Uncountable quantities of sand swarmed into the worm-holes of the Abbeyfield and slithered with astonishing rapidity along the tunnels.

Deep along the river shore rocks shifted.

Mr Nicol was putting up his shutter when the cobbles trembled. The shutter dropped from his grasp and clattered to the ground and the shopkeeper stepped back in amazement as his hams and puddings swayed and danced on their hooks and lamps and lanterns chattered on his shelves. Behind him the bell in the tower clanked once, then twice, and then was silent.

In the back room of the Grapes Mrs Figgens was uncorking bottles when all the glassware came alive and kegs grumbled on their trestles. She dropped the screw, flung her apron over her head and shrieked in terror, believing that Judgement Day had come at last and that God was after publicans.

On the keel-boat *Matchless*, ploughing from Alloa to Leith, Georgie Haynes felt the heave of a huge wave. He supposed that it was naught but a freak of the equinox or a squall that stroked up the waters of the Forth and did not even glance back at Placket's night-shrouded shore.

Hector Fotheringham had caught his wife as she dressed for supper and, at the precise moment of the disaster, had been pandering with her in the big four-poster. He was caught between passion and curiosity and had to strike the woman under him to make her let him go. He tore from her, bruising her white arms, and threw open the casement and leaned out just as a second tremor disturbed, if only slightly, the solid foundations of the Priory.

Mr Fotheringham realised that an accident had occurred. He thought it might be fire and explosion, collapse of tunnels inadequately shored. Even at that moment the heritor of Placket wrote off the field's income and felt relieved that he had so little capital invested in it and would survive the misfortune no matter how bad it turned out to be.

Behind her husband, by the side of the rumpled bed, knelt Margaret. Half-naked and sprinkled with sexual sweat, she prayed to God to save her from the retribution that might imminently descend upon the wicked colliers, the punishment due to brute beasts who laboured for a living, not to ladies and fine gentlemen who paid their kirk tithes and unfailingly praised His Name from their private pew in Placket kirk.

Keir Bolderon had barely reached his house when the tremor rattled the china plates and cutlery on the table. Dorrith yelled and released the soup bowl which shattered on the flags and spread a great welter of broth across the kitchen. Keir Bolderon stood quite still, still clad in coat and hat, until the vibrations ceased; then he turned and ran to remount his horse and ride as fast as the creature could manage back to the pit shaft.

In the fields that flanked the Rutherford burn doors were opening in cottages and shacks. Colliers, their wives and children came pouring out, except those who had hidden under beds or blankets or who had suffered some minor cut or burn by the shaking of their homes.

At the pithead the horses which had trudged the circular route all day long and had an extra hour added to the drag, shied and sheared at their leathers and turned so fierce for a minute or two that it was all the horsemen could do to bridle them and prevent them wrenching the wheel from its axle and breaking the rope.

Mouse and Elspeth, loitering by the shaft head, heard more than a supernatural rumble, felt more than a shaking of the earth. They could hear a sigh, a roaring suspiration deep below and felt the wind that draughted upward, whirling, from the shaft. They fell to the ground, Elspeth covering the girl-child with her body, as if the pit had turned volcanic and would spew forth molten rock at any instant.

There at the exit the noises were more prolonged and magnified, the upward thrust of wind sustained. Grains and granules pattered like rain about the women and peppered the rooftops of the sheds. The rope came alive, snapping and whipping as if some gigantic thing had grasped the bucket like bait and sought to worry it loose. Beneath Elspeth, Mouse uttered not a sound, not even a whimper, until men began to arrive from the cottages. Even then the girl-child said nothing, did not stir, for the menfolk were also afraid and came no closer than the gable of the shed, all tense and leaning away as if about to flee. It was Elspeth who got to her feet and, now that the flurry of wind had diminished, walked towards the platform. Mouse rose to her knees, arms spread, watching Elspeth step on to the platform.

The sounds had grown, if anything, louder. Elspeth could hear the snap of ladders, the low-pitched rumble of collapsing columns and that all-devouring hiss like the serpent of her dreams.

She had no doubt at all that the river's hidden channel had been breached and peered down into the darkness in search of water. She saw, of course, nothing at all. She frowned, stepped down from the platform and returned to the place where Mouse knelt.

"What is it? What's happenin'?"

"Floodin', I think," said Elspeth. "Somebody run for Mr Bolderon. Go on, somebody fetch the manager."

Two of the Leach boys turned and ran at her command, sprinting away into the darkness of the hedges and trees that bordered the back road. More colliers, including women, filled the avenues between the buildings. They were silent, struck dumb by the sounds that rolled out of the shaft mouth, by the faint but perceptible quivering of the ground beneath their feet.

"It's flood, aye," somebody declared. "We'll need t' get awa' before it wells out o' there an' swamps the fields."

"Will it do that, Billy?"

"Will it no'."

"Aye, yon's the river, the river comin' through the seams."

"Oh God! God save us all!"

Elspeth stood her ground, a hand on Mouse's shoulder. She was waiting for Keir Bolderon, she realised, in the ridiculous hope that he would offer a solution, that he would somehow rescue Davy, Matt and Thomas Rance, that all was not ruined after all. She watched the colliers retreat, some in sudden panic, others reluctantly.

Within minutes she was alone again, alone with Mousie, waiting for the man to come.

Elspeth was relieved when Keir Bolderon galloped into the yard a few minutes later. He drew up, dismounted and tossed the reins to one of the colliers.

"Take her to the stable, Anderson. Malone, tell the horsemen to bring out a fresh pair. You," he turned on a small swarthy hewer, "take word to the cottages. I want the houses cleared. Every man, woman and child. Tell them to collect their best belongings and go down to the village. Shelter will be arranged for them. I want a safety crew assembled in the counting-house in a quarter of an hour."

Peeling off his coat he strode towards Elspeth.

"What are you doing here, Mrs Patterson? I suggest you get away home an' collect the family an' make haste out of the Abbeyfield. The ground's riddled with the tunnels of old workings. I fear there may be a collapse if the flooding is severe."

"It – it started in our room, Mr Bolderon."

"Your room? At the base level? How can you be sure?"

"Davy – our Davy – he took Mr Rance down to show him a secret seam."

"Secret seam? What secret seam?"

"There's a long seam lyin' under millstone. Jock Bennet discovered it. We've been workin' it ever since."

"God in Heaven! Why did you not tell me, Elspeth?"

"Jock Bennet would not let me."

"After he died?"

Elspeth shook her head. She was ashamed of her greed now, her selfishness. The accident, the flood seemed so connected to that original act that it might all have been her fault.

"Matt's down there too," said Mouse, whispering.

"Did the sailor go with Rance an' the boy?"

"He followed after them."

"When did Rance go down? At shift's end?"

"Yes."

"So we must assume that Mr Rance broke through a baffler wall an' let in a flood of water. If that's the case – and he and the boy were caught on the bottom –" Keir Bolderon shook his head.

Mouse looked up at Elspeth, sought her hand. The girl-child's fingers were icy. "Is – is Matt – gone?"

"We can't be sure, Mouse."

Elspeth did not dare offer more hope than that, or more consolation.

"I'll speak with you afterwards, Elspeth," said Keir Bolderon sternly. "I've much to do here, meanwhile."

She watched him stride away. The men had separated themselves from their women. Across the edge of the field lanterns showed, bobbing along the path to the roadway. Some households had already begun to trail towards the village. It was, Elspeth realised, only a precaution. She could not imagine that the earth would open up and swallow the community whole. On the other hand she had read of subsidence on other pit fields. Mr Bolderon would not want to risk a loss of life. In one way the colliers of the Abbeyfield had been lucky. If the breakthrough had occurred during daylight hours then the loss of life would have been considerable.

Thomas Rance and Davy were dead. Keir was correct; there was no hope for them. But Matt – she clung to a faint fond hope that somehow Matt had escaped.

Elspeth drew Mouse away. The girl was strangely silent. There were no hysterical outbursts, no tears. She was pinch-lipped, white-faced and trembling but she had learned to hold in her suffering as a woman must do in the passage from girlhood to maturity.

"Come, Allison," Elspeth said. "We'd best leave it to the hewers. They know what t' do."

"Matt . . . ?"

"Mr Bolderon will bring Matt out."

"He'll come back t' me, won't he?"

"Yes," said Elspeth.

"Matt'll no' desert me. Matt loves me, so he does."

"Allison, we'll have to find Sarah an' Mary Jean, get away from the cottage."

420

"Aye," said the girl, with a nod, and led the way through the sheds towards the field gate. "Matt'll find me, never fear."

Keir Bolderon waited one hour. All sounds had ceased. The shaft was as still as he had ever heard it.

Through the night air he could hear the voices of the colliers as they wended down, still, to Placket. In the counting-house the long trestles that usually supported money tonight held charts of the workings. He pored over them in company with the six-man crew of safety and rescue workers. Thomas Rance would have been the leader of this group but it was to 'rescue' Thomas Rance that the men had been assembled. It was also to determine what event had occurred below ground and how extensive the damage to the workings had been, to learn if coal could be safely drawn from any part of the pit within the week.

Though he worked efficiently, Keir Bolderon had a soft sickness in his heart. Elspeth had cheated him. She had sustained a lie throughout the months of their friendship, even after he had promoted her, after the earning from the 'secret seam' had become inconsequential.

It was not the first time that a hewer had found a pocket of great coal and kept the knowledge of it to himself, risking dismissal if his cache was discovered. Keir Bolderon was puzzled by the location of Bennet's cavern, however, for at that depth and in that strata pressure invariably squeezed out all air spaces.

It was an hour after the tremor before Mr Fotheringham put in an appearance. He came down in a gig driven by a servant and was inappropriately dressed in fawn-coloured velvet and a hat with a blackcock's feather in the band. He came to the counting-house and strode in, striking awe in the men there and causing them to pause in the laying out of their equipment.

Mr Fotheringham demanded to be told what had occurred in his pit. Mr Fotheringham demanded to be told what Mr Bolderon intended to do about it. Mr Bolderon informed Mr Fotheringham that he intended to put himself into the bucket – if the bucket could be retrieved from the shaft bottom – and go down, alone, to the first level and take evidence with his own eyes. Mr Fotheringham shouted at Mr Bolderon. Mr

Bolderon shouted at Mr Fotheringham – and the owner of the pit strode off again, hurling back the command that news be brought to him at his home as soon as it was known.

Ten minutes later Keir Bolderon stood on the rim of the main shaft dressed in a tight canvas jacket and with a coal-heaver's lacquered straw hat upon his head. He had a pick in one hand, a masked lantern in the other, its copper wire glowing orange and strange. A weighted rope had already been dropped down the main shaft, another down the Dead Man. Both had been brought up dry. There was no odour of water, that dankness which would have confirmed flood. And there was, of course, no response to the calling out of names.

"Rance, Rance. Are ye there, man?"

"Davy Bennet. Can ye hear us?"

"Shearer, what say ye?"

The bucket was hoisted slowly. On its arrival at the surface it showed no evidence of moisture or of bruising. It seemed unaltered except for a coating of fine grey grit blown into its weave. By the light of the orange lamp Mr Bolderon inspected the dust, tasted it with a wetted fingertip, found it salty. It did not dissolve upon his tongue, however, and he spat it out quickly, shuddering as if it was alum. He stepped into the bucket and was lowered into the depths, into smothered silence and darkness.

A half-hour later Mr Bolderon's signal was received. The emergency winding-box attendant shouted to the horsemen and the bucket was hauled upwards once more.

Mr Bolderon, pale and perspiring, climbed out.

The hewers were around him instantly – Anderson, Malone, McQueen, Dodd – clamouring to be told what he had found, what sort of state the accident had left, and would there be work for them again here on the Abbeyfield. None asked if he had found Thomas Rance, the Bennet lad, the sailorman.

Mr Bolderon moved away from the shaft and did not look back.

He said, "Have the carpenters build a lid. Put it on an' seal it. Rope off the shaft platform. Do the same at the Dead Man."

"Mr Bolderon, Mr Bolderon, what's happened?"

"The workings are filled with sand."

"*Sand!* Jesus an' Joseph!"

"It lies up to the middle of the second level an', so far as I can see, fills the main roads as well as the secondary. There's nothin' there but sand, lads. The Abbeyfield's drowned."

"An' the work?"

"No work," said Keir Bolderon and, bracing himself, headed for the stables to find his horse.

Mary Jean was fast asleep. Elspeth's arms ached and she had a pain across her shoulders that would not be eased. She sat against the boxes, their 'precious possessions' brought up from the cottage to the inn yard, with a blanket over her knees. Mouse was to one side of her, curled up small, her thumb in her mouth, her eyes wide open. Sarah was on the other; just the four of them now, all that was left of the family.

Within the inn Mrs Figgens was doing a roaring trade in beer, whisky and gin, selling to those to whom uncertainty gave an appetite a wheen of pies and salted fish. The long low building was rowdy and restless like a fair or festival, for there were no corpses to retrieve and no girning widows to console, except the Patterson woman and the Bennets and they hardly counted.

The import of what had happened on the Abbeyfield was discussed hither and thither among jugs and tankards. Roused from their evening chores and chased out of their homes, girls delighted in the novelty and were strumpeting about and flirting with no thought for what tomorrow might bring. One or two of the old wives approached Elspeth, asked a question, offered a word of sympathy and told her of their own sad losses down the years.

Mouse listened without a word. She had drunk a glass of sour milk which somebody had brought her and was sick at once upon the grass. She had put her thumb back into her mouth and, paler and smaller than ever, clung tightly to Elspeth thereafter.

Mouse had not confessed that she had been loved by Matt Shearer. She wondered if she might be carrying his bairn and, in her numbness, speculated on whether it would be boy or girl and whether it would die and leave her as Daddy had done, and Davy, and Matt.

Sarah whispered, "Is Davy lost down there?"

Elspeth answered, "It seems so."

Sarah whispered, "In our seam?"

Elspeth answered, "Yes. Now *ssshhh*, dear, please."

It was not long by the hours of the clock, not much after ten in fact, when Keir Bolderon appeared at the Grapes. He tethered his horse in front of the inn and came through the throng, brushing aside intemperate questions and ignoring the hands that pulled at his sleeves. Whatever news he had for them would be delivered to the assembled workforce in the yard tomorrow morning. He would tell them then that the pit was closed. He would see them paid to the day, to the last earned penny. He would give them all a week rent free in the cottages, and argue for this gesture of charity with Mr Fotheringham. In due course he would send down his best crew to redeem transportable gear from the upper level. But he had seen with his own eyes how deep the sand lay and knew that all the neuks and crannies of the coal seams would be filled with it.

Sand could not be shifted. Fires might burn out, water might be pumped away, but sand remained for ever. The Abbeyfield's life as a producing pit was finished.

"Ah! There you are, Mrs Patterson," Keir Bolderon said with brittle cheerfulness.

Mouse looked up, removed her thumb from her mouth. "Did ye find Matt for me?"

Taken aback, Mr Bolderon had no answer for the girl. He appealed mutely to Elspeth with a little spreading of his hands. He was streaked with coal dirt and unkempt, looked coarser than she had ever seen him. Slipping Mary Jean from her lap into Sarah's care Elspeth got to her feet.

"Is there any hope, Mr Bolderon?"

"None, I regret to say."

"Did you discover—"

The man shook his head. "They'll never be found. The Abbeyfield must be their restin' place."

"I've heard talk that it's sand that flooded the workings; is it true?"

"It is." Mr Bolderon drew Elspeth away. There was far too much interest in their talk from certain sections of the crowd across the yard. Even the women sprawled by the wall were watching him intently enough to read the words upon his lips. "A massive infestation of fine sand. It came, I suspect, from behind the seam that Bennet uncovered."

"How could such a thing happen?"

"That we will never know, Elspeth. We can only speculate on the cause. Thomas Rance wouldn't be foolhardy enough to light a charge of powder. He'd never blast in an unknown seam at that depth."

"Is – is Matt Shearer lost too, do you think?"

"If he was below the second ladder, aye. It's a dreadful sight, believe me. Everything's crushed an' swallowed up. There's naught but a shoal of damned filthy stuff right to the middle part of the level."

"What will happen to them?" Elspeth indicated the colliers, a little less rowdy since the manager's arrival, within the inn.

"They must uproot an' seek work elsewhere."

"Is there nothin' here for them?"

"No, nothing."

Elspeth drew in a deep, deep breath.

She said, "May we return home, to the cottage?"

"I see no reason why you should not," said Keir Bolderon, and then checked himself. "Except – except that there will be strangers here by tomorrow."

"Strangers?"

"Sheriff's officers, inspectors of this an' that." Keir Bolderon looked her straight in the eye. "Men from the Press. The *Alloa Journal* will have a reporter in the saddle even now, I suspect."

"Is it news, what's happened here?"

"News of a sort," said Keir Bolderon. "It'll not have the value of a bloody disaster with hundreds lost but it is news enough for the chickens to scratch at." He paused. "It would be as well if you made yourself scarce."

Elspeth said, "Why? They'll not be interested in the likes o' me. I'm nothing, Mr Bolderon."

"Companion to the deceased."

"I was no more to Matt Sinclair than—"

"Sinclair?"

"To Matt Shearer—"

Keir Bolderon said, "Take the children to my house. Dorrith will find you beds."

425

"I cannot do that, Mr Bolderon."

"What *will* you do?" he said. "Will you go back where you came from now?"

"No, I – I'll find somethin'."

"Elspeth," Keir Bolderon said, "I know who you are."

She stiffened.

He said, "I've known for some months. You're not from Ayr. You're from Balnesmoor in the Lennox. You are – or were – wife to a certain Mr James Moodie, a weaver."

"Oh, God!"

"That's who you are."

"Oh, God!"

He was very matter-of-fact, almost off-hand. "You see, we deceived each other, Elspeth. I could have given away your secret as easily as you kept the secret of the new winnings. It makes us level, does it not?"

"You *knew* and you didn't *tell* me."

Still in that tone of near-indifference, Keir Bolderon said, "I didn't do it to protect you. I did it because I hoped you might fall in love with me an' that you might marry me."

"But you *knew* that I was already a wife."

Keir Bolderon said, "A widow."

He caught her as she staggered.

Sarah started up, jostling Mary Jean, and even Mouse lifted her gaze for an instant. It seemed that Elspeth might swoon but she steadied herself, clutching Keir Bolderon's shoulder, his arm about her waist.

"Come to my house, Elspeth. Shelter there," said Keir Bolderon. "You an' the children will be safe in my house. Tomorrow, when you're rested, we'll talk more of it."

"Talk. *Talk now*. Is he dead? Is James *really* dead?"

"Months ago."

"And yet you said nothing?"

Flushing, Keir Bolderon shrugged. "I – I was in love with you. I didn't want you to leave, to lose you."

"What else have you kept from me?"

"Only that you are still being sought."

"James, my – my husband sought me. That's why I came here, hid here."

426

"No, your husband's no longer a threat. But there are lawyers, a lawyer who seeks you."

"A lawyer? Why?"

"Because your husband's sisters are most anxious to steal away your inheritance."

"I – I don't—"

"Your husband willed his wealth and property to you and your child." Keir Bolderon motioned towards Mary Jean who slept on the old blanket among the boxes. "It's a great deal of money, I believe."

"How long have you known?"

"Months."

"Who told on me?"

"Nobody. It came to my attention through an advertisement."

"You—" Elspeth swayed again but when Keir Bolderon reached out to support her she drew herself away from him. "You *schemed*, didn't you? You wanted my *money*, not me."

"That's true, was true. At first."

Elspeth looked wildly about her. Mouse, Sarah and Mary Jean huddled pathetically at her feet among their little heap of possessions. Colliers squinted at her from the doorway of the inn. Inside, a girl laughed, a shrill braying sound.

It was a cold Ocotober night in Placket on the borders of the Forth; Elspeth could not imagine what she was doing here. She felt as if she was awakening from a dream, that none of it had been real at all. Jock Bennet, Davy, even Matt – none of them had existed, had impinged upon her life except in a split second of time carved out of the night, the time between her flight from Balnesmoor and this moment when she learned that at last she was free of him, of his shame and his guilt and his secrets.

She clenched her fists by her sides and straightened her bowed shoulders. She confronted the manager as if he too was a phantom that had already begun to dissolve and vanish into the dark night air.

"I ask you again, Mr Bolderon, is my husband dead?"

"There's no doubt of it, no doubt."

"Mouse, Sarah, come with me."

Elspeth lifted Mary Jean into her arms and settled the child

427

comfortably across her shoulder, head resting against her hair. She stooped and picked up the heaviest box in her left hand.

"No, please. No, I beg you," said Keir Bolderon. "I admit that I wronged you, Elspeth. But, please, I only wanted—"

"What did you want, Mr Bolderon?"

"My chance," Keir Bolderon said.

"You could never marry a pit girl," said Elspeth. "But by God, you could marry an heiress."

"Where are you going?"

"Home," said Elspeth Patterson Moodie and, without another word, led the girls through the inn yard and out on to the road.

But it was not over and she was not free of the Abbeyfield just yet. In fact she never would be quite free of it, for her time there had not been a dream but as real as her days with James, as real as that long-ago childhood on the green slopes of Drumglass with Gaddy and Coll and Anna. She was the sum of each phase and each had added to the total of the woman she had become.

The shock of Keir Bolderon's revelation had blinded Elspeth to the needs of the girls. Sarah and Mouse had suffered a dreadful loss. It was understandable that when they reached the road and she turned her face towards Stirling the Bennets should hang back. What they had was gone. Only the poor clothes and ribbons and silly tin trinkets in the box remained. The graves must be left behind, the mute elements of labour in the earth, claimed by the earth where Mammy and Daddy lay, and Davy too now, and Matt.

Once she cleared the vicinity of the Grapes Elspeth came quickly to her senses. She could hardly walk away unencumbered, forsaking Placket as she had come to it, with just a bundle and a bairn; hardly walk all the long road back to Stirling with two orphans clinging to her skirts. She stopped. Mouse was crying like a bairn. Even solemn Sarah had a quaver in her voice as she asked, "Are you leavin' us too, Elspeth?"

"No, I'm not leavin' you. I'll take you with me."

"Where? Where?" Mouse cried.

"To where I used to live. To Balnesmoor. It's pretty there, among green fields."

"Is there work?" said Sarah.

"Coal?" said Mousie. "Is there coal at Balnesmoor?"

"I've a house there," said Elspeth. "It's a large house wi' a kitchen an' five rooms."

"Why did y' leave it if it was so nice?" said Sarah.

"I'm no' goin'," said Mouse. "Matt'll need t' know where I am when he comes lookin'."

Elspeth paused, said, "Perhaps you're right, Mouse. In any case we can hardly travel in the dark. We're all tired. We'll need a night's rest first."

"Is it safe t' go back?" said Sarah.

"Quite safe," said Elspeth.

It was strange to cross the Rutherford bridge at that hour on that night. Dogs yapped in excitement about the field, turned loose in the time of danger, abandoned and cast out. In some windows lanterns glimmered, disguising the fact that the cottages were deserted. Over the pit, though, was a halo of light for the rescue crew had lit torches of pitch and coal-oil to illuminate their work. To Elspeth it seemed as if the trees had been set alight and burned in great streamers of yellow and black smoke without being consumed. Even Mary Jean wakened and peered out of sleepy eyes at the sight.

Sarah had been last away. She had closed the door carefully and put a block of wood against the step to cover a hole where rats might slip through. The block had been moved. The door had been opened. The lantern by the window had been taken away. Sarah tugged at Elspeth's sleeve.

"Somebody's there," she hissed. "Inside."

By now they were close to the cottage. Elspeth had all but given in to weariness. She longed to sit down, to put Mary Jean down and rest her aching back. But she saw that Sarah's alarm was genuine and caught at the child and pulled her back. She was too burdened, though, to stay Mouse.

With a cry Mousie dropped the boxes and ran.

"Matt. Matt's come back."

She flung herself against the door, so impatient and noisy in her joy that Elspeth's warning was lost.

Mouse burst into the kitchen.

A tunnel of wan light opened towards Elspeth and Sarah.

Sarah said, "Could it be our Davy?"

Elspeth said, "No."

A shriek from within drew them on. If there was danger or some horrid thing within then they must share it, for they were the survivors, the women of the tribe, and that was their role.

He had not been there long. He had put coals upon the fire but they were black still. He had filled the kettle and hung it on its hook. He had discarded his work clothes, draped a blanket about his naked body. He had found what food there was, a fist of roasted mutton, bannocks, a bowl of salted herrings and had been caught stuffing them into his mouth. He washed the mouthfuls down with whisky and water.

Mouse had not thrown herself on to his lap or into his arms. Oddly, she seated herself opposite him at the table, ridiculously prim and, after that first piercing cry, was almost as solemn as her sister. She stared at him round-eyed, uncertain whether he was really there or if he had come back to her from the grave like a ghost.

Matt said, "It's me, Mousie." He swallowed. "It's me, all right."

Elspeth and Sarah stared too. He was streaked with dirt. Big, muscular and weary, his cheeks bulged with the food. He gave them no particular greeting.

Mouse said, "Where's my brother?"

Matt swallowed. He picked mutton from his teeth with a fingernail. "He was too far down, Mousie. Davy an' Thomas Rance will no' be comin' out."

Sarah shed tears again quietly, a hand to her cheek. Only Mary Jean, who had wakened now, seemed truly elated to see the man. She squirmed in Elspeth's arms, shouting, "Matt, Matt. See Matt," until the man nodded and Elspeth put her down and let her run around the table and stand by him, a hand upon the blanket that covered his knee, smiling up at him in all innocence.

"Close the door, 'Pet," Matt said.

"Why did y' not find Davy?" said Mouse accusingly.

"Sit down all of you," said Matt.

He swilled a mouthful of whisky and put the glass to one side. He drew the blanket over his bare chest, glanced at Mary

Jean and managed a small tight smile for her before he spoke again.

He said, "They were in the seam behind the trap. I'd got down to base level, though only just. I could hear the hammer, for the workin's were quiet, so bloody quiet. Then there was this crackin' noise. Made the ears hurt wi' its sharpness."

"Where?" said Mouse; she still had not touched him.

"In the fissure," Matt said. "One big loud shatterin' crack. That's all I heard until the rush o' the sand o'erwhelmed me."

"Did you see it?" Elspeth asked.

"Aye," said Matt. "It came pourin' out o' the narrow tunnel. It looked like fur, like an animal in the lantern-light. I reached an' climbed the ladder which broke under me. I held on, though. I could hardly see, even though I still had the lantern. I climbed up to the level. I could hear the sand behind me clawin' an' pawin' up the walls. It was then the tremors started an' everythin' started t' fall."

Mouse nodded vigorously. It was as if she had him on trial, was a tiny fierce inquisitor paid to doubt his sincerity.

Matt said, "I didna dare stop. I plunged on along the second level wi' things fallin' all round about me. Another shake an' another. I thought the roof would come down."

"Did the sand reach the second level too?" said Elspeth.

"Aye, washed up like a tide. I was damned lucky, 'Pet. Without bein' aware o' it I'd overshot the ladder an' went on into a long ramp upwards, out of its range. What a fearful tangle o' gear was there. Slipped bogies an' smashed ladders, water swampin' out o' the drains."

"You managed out, though," said Mouse.

"Oh, aye, Mousie. How could I not?" said Matt. "I was near done in but I did not stop. I kept on till I discovered another ladder. Old, it was, all rotted. But it had been fixed wi' ropes an' was still in place. I climbed it, thirty or forty feet, an' came out into a high gallery. I'd lost all sense of direction. The tremors had stopped, thank God. I rested for a while, nursin' my candle in the lantern. Sense told me I was out of reach o' the sand, though I was thoroughly lost."

"The crew would've found you," said Mouse.

"No sayin' who would have found me," said Matt, with a glance at Elspeth. "Besides, I couldna say whether the main

431

shaft had been brought down or not. I forged on. To make it short, eventually I found the bottom o' the Dead Man."

"There's no bucket, no rope in the Dead Man," said Mouse.

"Am I not the one t' tell you?" said Matt. "I climbed up the rotted staves an' shorin'. God, but it was bad. I lost the damned lantern when I was but half-roads up. I had t' climb in darkness, wi' only a faint wee glint o' night sky showin' through the boards t' guide me."

"I knew you'd come back, Matt. I knew you'd not desert me," said Mouse.

"I'd never desert you, Mouse," Matt said.

Elspeth said, "You didn't report, did you? You didn't tell anyone that you survived?"

Matt grinned. "Clever, 'Pet. You were always clever. Nah, I thought t' myself how the pit's done for. There will be no work in the Abbeyfield now, not for us, not for anyone."

"You want everybody t' believe you're dead?" said Elspeth.

"Why not?" said Matt. "I've been outlawed for months, livin' in fear I'd be recognised. If Matt Sinclair lies buried in the pit, Matt Shearer can step away wi' his head high."

"Outlaw?" said Mouse.

"Aye, my sweetheart. I killed a man once."

"What sort o' man?"

"A man like Georgie Haynes," said Elspeth.

Mouse smiled, nodding. She approved of that too. It did not daunt her that Matt, her Matt, had secrets that she could not share.

Elspeth said, "Where will you go, Matt?"

He shrugged. "North or south; it matters not. I'll turn my hand t' honest toil anywhere. I can find a ship, even, if I'm sore enough pressed—"

"Nah," said Mouse. "No ships, no sailin' off wi' the whales. You'll bide home wi' me, Matt."

"Oh, will I?" said Matt. "What makes you suppose I want t' burden myself wi' a lassie like you?"

"You love me!" said Mouse.

"Is that a fact?" said Matt.

"You do, you love me."

"Well . . ." said Matt.

It was Elspeth's turn for revelation now. She told Matt what news Keir Bolderon had given her and explained that she was free to return to Balnesmoor. The family, what was left of it, must part.

"Sarah?" Elspeth said. "You have a choice: will you take the road with Mouse an' Matt or will you come with me? I'll care for you, Sarah, I promise."

They sat about the table watching as the solemn, brown-skinned little girl made up her mind. She put no questions, sought no assurances. She contemplated her fists in her lap for a minute or two and then leaned across and put her arms about Elspeth's neck, clinging at last.

It was still dark when they left the cottage for the last time and crossed the plank bridge over the Rutherford burn. Occupied again, the cottages were quiet and no dogs barked. The halo had faded from above the workings but you could still hear the creak of winding-gear and the high singing sound of taut ropes in the cold dawn air. Was Keir Bolderon there? Elspeth wondered. Did he intend to come to her again, not to let her go? She kept the shawl tight about her, hiding her face, held tight to Mary Jean as they slipped across the corner of the field to the tree line and the back road. She would not have to walk all the way to Stirling. She had money for a coach, for food and lodging for herself and the girls on the journey back to Balnesmoor. It was more, much more than she had had when she came here. Matt had the lion's share of the cash, however. Mouse, true to the end, had argued heatedly that Davy's share should go to her, to her and Matt. Elspeth had given in without argument.

They gathered not far from the wall of the kirkyard. The river had trapped the first of the daylight and stretched out like a long metallic seam below the cloud. There was light enough for farewells, for kissing and tears.

Matt took Elspeth in his arms.

"Tell Anna," he whispered, "I'm a dead man."

"Matt?"

"It's for the best, 'Pet."

"Aye, I suppose it is."

He kissed her on the brow and on the cheek. Mouse watched, frowning and possessive.

433

"My father too," said Matt.

"It'll hurt him, Matt."

"Only for a little while."

He released her, turned, looked at the sky.

"Aye, Mousie," he said. "It's a far piece we'll have to travel before night. Come." He lowered his hands to his thighs. "Jump up. I'll carry you for the first mile. How's that?"

That was the last Elspeth ever saw of Matt Sinclair, the last glimpse Sarah had of her sister. Mouse rode away on the man's broad back, clinging to his neck, giggling again, shapes against the dawn light that tinted the sky to the east. Elspeth watched them go. She felt odd, different, changed now. She did not need Keir Bolderon's protection or his charity. The fact that she thought of him at all was mark enough of her independence. She adjusted the bundle about her shoulders and fastened the knots of the shawl to hold it secure.

She would avoid Placket, cross the back of the hill to the crossroads at Rutherford and rouse the old carrier who had quarters in the farm, pay him to take them to Alloa or even on to Stirling if his horses were strong enough.

She looked at the girls.

"Mary Jean, take my hand."

"Aye, Mammy."

"You too, Sarah."

Sarah Bennet hesitated. She wiped her nose with her wrist and then twined her fingers into Elspeth's and set off trustingly in step along the road to the new place, where she had never been before.

Tom Tolland would not talk, more's the pity. What truths that old devil might have revealed. He could have solved the mystery of what was happening at Moss House now that Gaddy Patterson's eldest had seen fit to return. He might even have been able to answer the most teasing question of all – where she had been and who she had been with. But the steward had always known where his loyalty lay and was, besides, more unsure of his position in the household than ever he had been with Jamie.

Tolland had been startled, not to say astonished, when Elspeth had trailed in very late one night with a child on each hand and a bundle slung across her shoulder to announce that she had returned to claim what was rightfully hers. She had started giving orders as if she had inherited not only Moodie's money but his authority too. Tom Tolland responded as any downy old steward would do – he obeyed to the letter her every command, answered truthfully and directly every question she asked him, and kept his mouth shut between whiles. He gave nothing away even to his friend Hunter who drove to Moss House to offer Sir Randall Bontine's greetings and condolences and to enquire if there was any service that the laird might bestow for the comfort of Mrs Moodie. "Nothing, thank you, Mr Hunter," was the curt reply; and the solemn, brown-skinned child was sent to the kitchen to make sure that Messrs Tolland and Hunter did not settle down to gossip.

Who did she think she was? Some queen or empress? Damned if she did not behave like one, never leaving the house to make herself seen about the village, not even turning up in the private pew at the kirk and it lying empty Sunday after Sunday though the tithes were paid without fail through the offices of the Dumbarton lawyer. The Dumbarton lawyer: oh, aye, he had his privileges, all right. He was permitted entry at any time, day or night. He even stayed once when the November fog was so thick you could have ravelled it into a muffler. But she, Elspeth Patterson Moodie, did not deign to show her face and anyone who went there expecting a welcome was shown the door from the doorstep and turned away, even her dear sister and her man. It seemed that the wife had inherited some of old Jamie's thrawn quality, perhaps a wee touch of his reclusive madness too. Nothing happened in those first three weeks to change the opinion of the good folk of Balnesmoor no matter how they discussed it and dug for scraps of gossip.

The return of Elspeth Patterson Moodie was not the only scandal in the Lennox that autumn. But the other was more remote from the main street of Balnesmoor and came into the village as no more than a whisper on the wind. It seemed that the laird's brother, Mr Gilbert, had gotten himself into a tangle with his finances and was in danger of being declared insolvent. No connection was made, of course, between the Bontines' problems and Elspeth Patterson Moodie's reappearance, for only a handful of people knew where she had been in the

435

missing years and those people were discreet in the extreme.

It was three weeks to the day after Elspeth wandered in from wherever she had been, with her own bairn and some other brat in tow, before her intentions began to emerge.

Anna, of course, had been furious at being rejected; at not being welcomed with wide open arms, wept upon and fussed over on the instant of Elspeth's return. She would lie in bed of a night, propped on an elbow, frowning into Robert's face, now and again rather painfully pounding him on the chest with her fist to demand answers that the chap could not possibly give.

"What's she up to? Why was I turned away? Has she heard about us? Has she found out, from yon lawyer perhaps, what you've done wi' the account books?"

"Anna—"

"Him, Tolland, turnin' up his nose at me, never mind at you. Showin' us the door. God, but I've never been so humiliated. Why did you not *insist* on seein' her, Robert?"

"I'm in no position to insist. She's your sister, Anna, but she is also, alas, my employer."

"Are you just goin' t' bow meekly t' this insult?"

"Anna –"

"My own flesh an' blood. My own sister. She'll not even come out of her damned parlour t' give me a greetin'. After three long years o' separation too. It's an ill an' evil nature that's in her."

"She's takin' stock, Anna."

"Aye, scourin' up all the lies she can from folk that have a down upon us. Lord knows what stories she'll have heard about me."

"Anna, Anna—"

"She does not even know I've a child or whether it's boy, girl or cabbage-stalk. What's more she disna care."

Robert Rudge would sigh, though he rather enjoyed the vigour of Anna's temper and would smother it in due course by taking her in hand and rolling her on to her back, giving her cause to forget, for a while, that his position, apropos Elspeth, was infinitely more precarious than her own. In his heart Robert Rudge respected the Widow Moodie for her refusal to be distracted by folk clamouring for favours. She would be finding out in detail where she stood before she made a move in any direction.

Anna would say, "What's this I hear about Mr Gibbie?"

Robert Rudge would say, "His finances have gone askew."

Anna would nod, as if she knew all about insolvency and the law relating to bankruptcy, and would immediately return to complaining about her sister while Robert Rudge lay recovering from his exertions, hands above his head, thinking that she was beautiful in anger and wondering if it would spoil her shape to bear him children.

There was no such patience in evidence in Strachan Castle. Alicia and Gilbert had not lain down side by side for weeks and neither was in a position to offer the other any sort of comfort. Recriminations were hurled between wife and husband, husband and wife as each day brought fresh travail and a further complication to the situation that they had created for themselves.

It had come to light very quickly that Gilbert had 'loaned out' the Moodie trust fund. The conjunction of events – Elspeth Moodie's return to Balnesmoor and the swamping of the coal pit at Placket – had been as catastrophic as the collision of two planets. Within a week of the event it became clear to Gibbie that he had been a complete and utter fool who had not understood one word of the law of contract and agreement and could not recover a penny of the ten thousand pounds he had given to Hector Fotheringham in exchange for the promise of stock in the mining company. How this palpable crime could be condoned by the law of Scotland was more than poor Gibbie could fathom. But it was – absolutely – and he had no claim or redress against the owner of the company.

What was more, a letter had been received from Hildebrand requesting the transfer of the trust fund to a drawing account in the Bank of Scotland, and Gibbie had been forced to put himself on the carpet before the Brothers Pryde and confess that he had extracted the fund, or most of it, for personal and private use.

The Brothers Pryde had smiled consolingly, patted him on the shoulder, assured him that the Falkirk Farmers' Bank would not go under because of his indiscretion – and, within a day, had had a writ of prosecution drafted, sealed and delivered, arresting all Gibbie's credit, thus absolving themselves from knowledge of or involvement in his acts of embezzlement.

Gibbie had wrung his hands in despair, had wept, had appealed to Alicia for comfort and advice. But now that it came down to it Alicia joined forces with her husband's detractors and called down coals of fire upon his head. It would be only a matter of time, Alicia informed him, before the bailiffs arrived to strip the very clothes from her back and the shoes from her feet and send her out on to the roads in rags to beg bread from strangers to keep her children from starving.

Gulping down his pride Gibbie went at last to call upon Mrs Moodie – and was turned away. He was shocked to the core by this rejection; to be snubbed by the sister of a servant of the Bontines as if he was a thief and an outlaw, not brother to the laird of Ottershaw and Balnesmoor. Quite furious – for Gibbie – he had ridden straight to Ottershaw and thrown the whole sorry story before Randall, had prostrated himself, grovelled, anticipating that Randall would pull him out of the fire, scorched but unconsumed.

Randall had led him upstairs to the library. It was the only corner of Ottershaw that had remained unchanged since Old Sir Gilbert's day, for all the rest showed tasteful touches of the lady of the house.

Once within the library, door closed, Randall had rounded on Gibbie. "If, Gilbert, you expect me to shell out ten thousand pounds to cover your errors then you are even more of a fool than I take you for. I do not *have* ten thousand. I do not have *one* thousand. I will be able – just – to clear my own debt with the Farmers' Bank and absolve Ottershaw from connection with the mess that you've created. But I cannot help you, Gilbert. What in God's name possessed you to dabble in mineral investment?"

"Alicia thought—"

"Alicia! Of course! Damn her vaultin' ambition."

Gilbert bit back a heated retort at this slur on his wife's character. He could not, even now, believe that Randall would not save him.

"How much *can* you raise, Gilbert?"

"I – I have no idea. Not much, not much at all."

"It was a mad, an insane dealin'. You handed your head on a plate to this Fotheringham."

"I know it."

"Now you must suffer the consequences."

"Alicia says it will mean imprisonment."

"Probably."

"Would you see me in prison, Randall; a Bontine in jail?"

"Fotheringham cannot have spent such a monstrous sum on the Abbeyfield."

"I'm sure he has not. Indeed, exploration of the field was not due to begin—"

"Ask *him* for a loan."

"Randall! Fotheringham has already refused me. What's more, I'm told that my bond with him cannot be dissolved, that it's binding to the letter, to the penny. He's not the sort of gentleman to aid me out of charity."

"Gilbert, I would give you alms if I could, man, but it would be no more than alms. You are not the only person in these hard times to feel the pinch of penury. Prices are up and down, down and up, and the cattle—"

"Randall, I will be prosecuted, ruined, shamed."

"I can, perhaps, raise eight or ten hundred pounds."

"Not enough, not nearly enough."

"Mother, if you care to approach her, and Uncle Alexander may be able to find a few hundred more. Then it's up to you to buy off Elspeth Moodie, to plead with her for defrayment."

"She will not see me."

"I expect," said Randall, "that she is otherwise occupied at this particular period. Mrs Moodie will make an approach to you when it suits her."

"Do you suppose that Mr Hildebrand might be able to help me?"

"Oh, dear God in Heaven!" Randall shouted in exasperation. "Do you understand nothing, Gibbie? Hildebrand is *her* agent, her adviser. He wove the damned web. It's Hildebrand that you are up against."

"What shall I do, Randall? What *can* I do?"

"Prepare, I fear, for the worst."

*   *   *

439

Tom Tolland was not the only person in Elspeth Patterson Moodie's intimate circle who seemed to recognise in her certain attributes acquired during the years of her marriage to the weaver. Angus Hildebrand was quite astonished, though he showed it not, of course, by her astuteness and her grasp of just what her inheritance entailed not only in terms of hard cash but in power and responsibility.

She asked about Kennart, inspected the accounts.

She asked about Robert Rudge, digested Mr Hildebrand's opinions of the manager of the mill.

She asked about Anna, heard the sorry story of her banishment from Ottershaw and her motherhood and her flight into the arms of Robert Rudge, the reprobate, and how she resided with him now in Drymen and professed that she would become his legal wife as soon as divorcement was possible.

She asked dozens of other questions, even about her husband and his state of mind and his welfare in his declining months. Mr Hildebrand answered as truthfully and as tactfully as he could, blending fact and compassion in a manner unusual for a member of his profession.

Mr Hildebrand had questions of his own. He put these to his client – for Elspeth Patterson Moodie was his client whether he wished it or not – with great discretion for he sensed that she was reluctant to talk of her months in exile from Balnesmoor and was touchy on the subject of her motives for quitting Moodie and Moss House. He discovered, however, that she had been employed in the Abbeyfield pit and felt an odd imbalance in the circumstances at this information, as if he had lost control to something fateful and supernatural.

"The Abbeyfield, in Fifeshire?"

"Yes, Mr Hildebrand. I was employed there. I dwelled on the field with a collier's family."

"In what capacity, if I may ask, Mrs Moodie, were you employed?"

"In the counting-house."

"Indeed!"

"Do I detect a certain asperity in your tone, Mr Hildebrand?"

"Asperity? Oh, indeed no; not asperity, I assure you, Mrs Moodie. What you detect in my tone is rather wonderment at the mysterious ways in which Divine Providence moves."

"I would not have taken you for a religious man."

"The large sum of capital – twelve thousand pounds to be exact – which your late husband realised by the sale of stocks and assets was placed in trust with a partner in the Falkirk Farmers' Bank."

"For what purpose?"

"To prevent that sum being easily accessible to claimants against the will, in effect Mr Moodie's sisters. It is separate and distinct from that sum which Mr Moodie prudently laid aside to finance the operation of his estates; that is, the mill at Kennart and your domestic offices."

"And from which you are paid too?"

"Indeed."

"And the reason for your 'wonderment', Mr Hildebrand?"

The lawyer explained. He saw Elspeth Moodie's eyes grow round with surprise at the connections that had occurred, linking her to Gilbert Bontine, and Gilbert Bontine to the fate of the pit far off across the Forth.

A vision of Keir Bolderon darted fleetingly across her mind's eye but she could not calculate how the pit manager and the laird's brother had come together in disaster. She did not raise Keir Bolderon's name with the lawyer, however. There was in her a certain slender guilt in respect of the man she had deceived and who had deceived her, and a certain wistful regret that they could not have met under other and better circumstances. She missed Keir Bolderon as she missed James. She was firm with herself, would not yield to silly sorrow. Even so, she could not help but experience James's presence here in Moss House. If it had been her father's intention to bring her round, then he had already partly succeeded. She had no defence against selective memory or the growing realisation that he had, in his way, loved her.

In those first weeks back at Balnesmoor she behaved exactly as her father would have done, with patience and just a hint of autocracy, testing herself in authority to see not only if she enjoyed it but if she could cope with it.

She instructed Tolland to find additional servants, a nurse and a tutor, nobody too grand. She stepped out to inspect the carriages in the coach-house by the stables and to look at the horses that had not been sold. She ordered the old cabriolet to be refurbished and a pair of young carriage horses to be purchased from a reputable dealer and not from the block at Balfron horse fair, thank you, Tolland.

When the time came she held her audiences in the big bright drawing-room and made sure that Tom Tolland's girl earned her keep by dusting and polishing that room until every item within it gleamed like new. She consulted Mr Hildebrand on the state of her immediate funds, had him explain to her in precise detail how she might seek legal redress against Gilbert Bontine for his ridiculous appropriation of her trust fund capital.

In the times when she was not Mrs James Moodie she was still Elspeth Patterson and took delight in being home again, close to the long run of the moor, within sight of the hills above the loch, with the smoke from the village chimneys purling up soft in the soft late-autumn days. She had Mary Jean and Sarah for company, and fine company the girls gave her. Sarah was salved against the pain of losing her brother and of separation from Mouse by all the novelties that money could buy, those things that Elspeth had learned to take for granted during her marriage and might have better appreciated if she had come to them without the burdens of doubt and passion that were the lot of the hill-bred lass.

She would never forget how Sarah snuggled down in clean linen sheets. How Sarah smiled when her head sank into a great feather pillow so deep that she could not even see Mary Jean lying by her side, and how the pair of them giggled and wriggled until softness and warmth overcame them and they fell fast asleep in each other's arms. Nor would Elspeth forget the sight of Sarah and Mary Jean together in the long copper bath before the bedroom fire; how Sarah kept smelling the stopper of the bottle of floral oil that scented the bath water until her seriousness melted into a splashing spree with Mary Jean, though Tom Tolland was none too pleased when he had to roll up the Chinese rug and take it out to the lawn to dry.

Sarah took to soup plates and teapots with curved spouts and the heavy silver knives and forks with which Elspeth adorned the table for her own sensual pleasure as much as the show of it and to teach the girls by example the techniques of gentility.

On the first real day of winter, after a sharp crackling frost which turned the last of the oak leaves yellow on the track and stiffened the crust of the moor under a brilliant blue sky, Elspeth took the children for a walk. They were wrapped up in plaids and tartans, all brand new and perfectly fitted and with new little boots upon their feet. She took them along the familiar path towards the Orrals, that piece of wild country that lay behind Moss House.

Sarah seemed calm and contented and her brown eyes were watchful at the skim of birds across the rough coverts and the high-hung hawks above the rim of the hills.

Elspeth did not venture far that first day. She did not go near the glen where she had met Michael those years ago. Michael was a memory and, no matter how she yearned for it, did not seem real and part of her, not even when she studied Mary Jean and sought the man in her.

The girls were excited to be out, so smart and fashionable in their new clothes. They chatted away as they walked. It startled them, however, when they caught sight of a young man on pony-back and they ran back to Elspeth and gripped her hands very tightly indeed.

Elspeth too was taken aback. It was as if she had slipped through a tear in the veil of time for it was Matt, she thought, who came looming out of the moor-fold not more than fifty yards away, not Matt as she had last seen him, though, but Matt as he had been ten years ago when they were all young and innocent.

Mary Jean too was deceived by the resemblance. She cried out, *"Matt. Me, Matt. See, it's me."*

Sandy Sinclair reined up the pony. He rode it bareback and with only an old rope bridle but he rode confidently and well. He wore only a wool shirt, the sleeves pushed back and the collar open to show his chest. The cold did not seem to bother him in the slightest. He had no hat upon his head and his hair, as fair and fine as Mary Jean's, stuck up like a corona.

"Why, is it yourself, Elspeth? I mean, Mrs Moodie."

"Sandy?"

443

"Aye, it's me. I'll have grown a bit since you – I mean, I mean, since we last met."

He dismounted, held the pony by the rope. Behind him now appeared a small swarthy urchin, bare-legged and suspicious.

Sandy said, "Awa' on home, Macfarlane. I'll come by the farm in a while. We'll no' find strays this far east."

The urchin was gone instantly, vanishing into the fold. He did not reappear upon the breast of the moor, though Elspeth looked for him. He would find his own tracks, secret as a fox's, to the farm that her step-father and Gaddy had once owned and which now belonged to Randall Bontine's shepherds.

Awkwardly Sandy Sinclair stepped forward and tendered his hand. It was a gesture of politeness that Elspeth had not expected. She thought of Sandy still as a daft boy, not as a depute grieve, not as his father's son.

She shook his hand, feeling the strength of it, and then introduced her daughter and Sarah, behaving as if they were already grown into ladies.

Mary Jean said, "You're no' Matt."

"I'm his brother. You can call me Sandy, if ye like."

"Sandy," said Mary Jean, nodding.

If Mary Jean was puzzled by Sandy's likeness to Matt, and by the conjunction of the new life with the old, Sarah seemed to be momentarily stunned by it.

A soft flush rose to her cheeks as Sandy Sinclair bent and took her hand and gave it a shake. She stared straight up at him and let out her breath swiftly.

Sandy laughed. "I'm surprised the wee one remembers Matt."

He would have given all his attention now to Elspeth but Sarah's gaze was disconcerting and he glanced away and then back at her. "My, but that's a fine dress, fine an' warm," he said. "Bonnie, too."

Sarah blushed a deeper hue but did not retreat like a child behind Elspeth.

"I'm employed at Ottershaw again," said Sandy. "We're chasin' out strays before the weather turns bad. Aye, it's done careful now, every beast, every ewe countit an' cared for."

Mary Jean said, "Matt catched whales."

"Matt what?"

It was Sarah who rescued the situation.

To Elspeth's relief she said, "It's not Matt, Mary Jean. Not our Matt. Somebody else."

Mary Jean looked glum, then went forward to pat the pony, a tall strong-looking garron that was too skittish to be a toy for a small child and stamped and whisked his head against the rope. Mary Jean returned to her mother and took her hand.

Sandy said, "I heard you'd come home, Mrs Moodie. Have ye – have ye seen Anna yet?"

"No, not yet. How is she, Sandy? Do you know?"

"How would I know? I'm on Ottershaw now."

"Of course," said Elspeth; the conversation had taken two awkward turns and she was tense, somehow, in the presence of the younger Sinclair.

The chance meeting indicated that she would soon have to concoct a plausible tale and tell Anna that Matt was dead, break the news to Lachlan Sinclair and his wife. She thought of Matt with Mouse clinging to his shoulders, and wondered if Lachlan would have reason to be proud, in time, of both his sons.

"You'll have heard how the laird marrit a woman from the north?" Sandy said.

"Tolland has given me all the news. Is your father well?"

"I see little of him. He has grave concerns at Strachan, so I hear."

Elspeth paused, awkwardness increasing. Sandy Sinclair was too bluff and honest a person to deceive to his face. He was physically so like Matt but in character, she saw, he was Lachlan Sinclair to the core.

She said, "Well, I must get the bairns home, Sandy, before it grows too cold."

"Aye," he agreed. "I'll be needit back at Ottershaw."

"Good day, then, Sandy."

"Good day, Mrs Moodie."

He mounted the pony with a lithe strong motion, and turned it about on its small hoofs as if it was a thoroughbred horse and not just a pack animal.

Sarah's eyes had not left him from the moment that he had touched her hand.

445

He turned the pony and gave the girl a special little salute. "I trust you'll be happy in Balnesmoor, lass," he said with a certain formality that only his wide, boyish grin saved from being pompous.

"I – I will, thank ye," Sarah murmured.

Sandy was gone, riding the garron hard down the ramp of the moor-fold and out of sight.

Elspeth said, "Come on, then. I'm starved for my tea."

"Cake?" said Mary Jean. "Cake for me, Mam?"

"For all of us," said Elspeth, and led the girls by the hand away from the edge of the rough country, while Sarah, looking back over her shoulder, scanned the sleeve of the Orrals for one last glimpse of handsome Sandy Sinclair.

It was brought home to her, in part by the meeting with Matt's brother, that she could delay no longer. She must meet with Anna, with Robert Rudge, with Lachlan Sinclair, must decide what she should do about Gilbert Bontine and the massive amount of money that her father had salted away for her that had been 'lost' in the Abbeyfield. She did not consider it a dreadful irony or a wild coincidence that Balnesmoor and the lands of Placket should be linked in her. She collected into herself all the vagaries of her own strange life and set them alongside its benefits. That she had been found at all in the sheep hut on Drumglass was in itself something wild and miraculous. All that had followed from it, through Gaddy and through James, seemed destined and inevitable – up to this point. She was grown now, alone now, mistress of Moss House, owner of Kennart, employer of weavers and spinners, mother and father to Mary Jean, Sarah Bennet's adoptive guardian. Whatever became of them would depend upon her determination and common sense.

Late that night, after Tom Tolland had slipped away to bed with his girl to keep him warm, Elspeth lit a lamp and put on her heavy robe and slippers and went downstairs.

There was moonlight in the casement on the landing, a great silver swathe of it falling into the hall below, but it did not reach the corridor that branched to the kitchens or to the back room that had served her father as a retreat for so many years. It was here that he had stored his gloomy secrets, brooded upon them, nursed his plots and schemes. It was here that she had first felt pity – and hatred – for him.

The room was locked. She went into the kitchen, silent in her slippers, found the domestic key-ring and took from it the long, bony key. She crossed the corridor, opened the door and, with the lantern held out before her, went in.

Shadows shrank before the light then gathered in the narrow corner behind the ladderback chair that had once been Mother Moodie's throne. It was all exactly as she remembered it, nothing changed: desk, chair, decanters, a bare mantelshelf over an empty hearth. Even the stout wooden chest, iron-bound, still stood below the window, its heart-shaped lock unrepaired.

Elspeth took a deep breath. She got down on her knees, paused, then lifted the lid of the chest. It contained nothing but a shrivelled little bag of lavender. No letters, ledgers or documents of any kind; James had burned them all. She felt no sadness at this loss of the evidence of her birth and her false marriage, only relief.

She gave a harsh sigh, got to her feet again, tipped down the lid of the chest with the toe of her slipper and put the lamp upon the desk. She opened a drawer and found a block of watermarked writing-paper, pens, a knife and a corked bottle of ink that had not dried up. She pulled out the chair, adjusted the lamp, and seated herself.

It was chilly in the room, almost dank. Tomorrow she would have Tolland light a fire. She would have fresh drapes made for the window, the empty chest and the ladderback chair removed. She would bring down the tub chair from the drawing-room, make the room her own.

In the meantime she had letters to write; two letters at least, letters which would signify that she had forsaken the legacy of her childhood, had put the past away and would accept the future that her father had built for her here in Moss House, in Balnesmoor.

He had changed so much that Elspeth could hardly believe that it was only four years since last she had seen him. It was not just that he had grown grey and stooped and lined, he had lost, she felt, his dignity. Stripped of it she saw in him not yeoman but peasant. Even his clothes were lumpy and thread-bare and the horse he had ridden from Strachan, which she had glimpsed from the window, was a limping old mare and nothing like the steeds that had once borne him about the parks of Ottershaw.

She had chosen one of her favourite frocks, a morning dress of beige French lawn with a buckled sash, not too ornamental, and had put up her hair under a plain cap. She knew only too well that her appearance disconcerted him and he did not show her his face, chin up and eyes square, but curled his hat in his fingers and stared at his knobbly shoes with their tarnished buckles.

Elspeth said, "I am not going to tell you a lie, Mr Sinclair. It would be the easy thing for me to do but I have decided against it. What you reveal to your wife an' to your family is a matter for you to ponder. I suggest, though, that you abide by Matt's wishes—"

"Matt?" Lachlan Sinclair lifted his head, the furrow of concern deep as a gash between his brows.

"Aye, it's concernin' Matt that I've asked you here to-day."

"Have you heard from him? Is he—"

Elspeth held up her hand. "Matt's well. He's thrivin'."

Agitatedly Lachlan said, "Where, where's the lad now? Is he here?" He looked about, turned to the tall window as if he half-expected to see his son upon the lawn. "Have ye brought him back?"

Firmly Elspeth said, "Contain yourself, please, Mr Sinclair. No, Matt's not here. Indeed, he'll not show his face in Balnesmoor again. To all intents and purposes, Matt is dead." When he rose in his chair she snapped at him. "Sit yourself down, I beg you. Hear me out."

She told the grieve part of the story, excising certain episodes, refreshing others. She told him of the Abbeyfield and of Mouse, of the in-break of sand and the disaster that had cost two lives and had ruined the pit for ever. Sinclair was too astonished to interrupt. He was well aware that the Abbeyfield was the self-same pit that had sucked in Mr Gibbie's money and changed all their lives. He could not grasp how Elspeth Patterson, let alone his renegade son, had become part of it.

448

Elspeth said, "So, do you see, Mr Sinclair, what a boon it is for Matt if he is thought to be dead?"

"Not him, but this other name," said Lachlan.

"Shearer; yes," Elspeth agreed. "But his identity, by what-ever name, is buried in the sand under the Abbeyfield."

"What shall I do about it?"

"Tell your wife."

"That he's dead? I canna be so cruel."

"Put about the rumour, in that case," said Elspeth. "I shall inform my sister that he's deceased. I'll tell her something of what I've told you."

"I canna kill him, even in my mind."

"I understand," said Elspeth.

"Where is he now?"

Elspeth said, "I don't know. I doubt if we – any of us – will hear of him again, though it's odd how things come round sometimes."

Lachlan Sinclair gave a grunt. "Call it odd, Mrs Moodie, that it's you who'll bring down my master."

"What do you know of that?"

"What I've heard," said Lachlan Sinclair with uncharac-teristic slyness. "It's talk that you'll have him imprisoned."

"I did not ask you here to discuss matters of business. Strachan and Mr Gilbert are associated with me on quite another plane, Mr Sinclair. I felt compelled to tell you of Matt, though, because you've been kind in the past, to me and to my mother."

Lachlan Sinclair pressed his gnarled hands on to his thighs and pushed himself upright. "Will that be all?"

"Will you tell?"

"She'll want t' marry again. Marry Rudge."

"So I believe."

"Is that why you'd have the world think Matt's dead, to suit Anna?"

"The officers of the law will not be on the lookout for a man who's rumoured to be dead. They will not remember his name for very long."

"Is he safe, do y' think?"

"He's safe."

"Happy?"

"She's a fine girl, sharp enough to keep him straight. Aye, Matt will be happy wi' her, with Allison."

"Is this all for Anna, your sister?"

"It's because I do not know what else to do, Lachlan."

He worried the hat with thick fingers, shoulders bowed like an elder at prayer. He had lost all respect in the community and had not the energy to regain it. He was a man at the mercy of his masters, a victim of the changing fortunes of the times. She felt a pang of sorrow in her heart for Lachlan, remembering what he had once been, strict and fair in the service of the lairds, dedicated to unswerving principles. Without them Lachlan was just like Matt, a man nameless and wandering.

"Aye, I understand," he muttered. "It's better if he's thought t' be dead. Better for all of us. Aileen too. I'll not tell her the whole truth, though."

Elspeth said, "I'm sorry."

"What call have you to be sorry for us?"

"None," she said. "But I am, nonetheless."

"Tell your sister, tell Anna she's free. I'll not queer the new marriage for her," said Lachlan Sinclair.

"Very well."

Elspeth put out her hand to ring the bell to summon Tolland to show her guest out. But Lachlan barked, "No, do not do that, Mrs Patt – Mrs Moodie. I can find my own way, thank you."

A quarter of an hour later she had Anna before her; Anna summoned too by letter at an appointed hour. But Anna did not come alone. She would not be separated from Robert now, nor from Robbie. She arrived in the Kennart bob-cart in conglomerated finery with her son struggling in her arms.

Tolland opened the door and Anna marched past him.

"Where is she?" Anna demanded. "Where's my sister?"

"This way, Madam," said Tolland.

There was the whisper of a smile, rueful and amused, on Robert Rudge's face as he trailed Anna into the elegant room and greeted Gaddy Patterson's other daughter.

"Is it not about time?" were Anna's first words. "Where, in God's Good Name, have you been?"

Whatever air of detachment Elspeth had intended to adopt

was instantly gone. "I'm here now, Anna," she snapped back, "an' that's all that matters. Is that your son?"

"Aye." Anna thrust Robbie, struggling, out in her arms as if he was a piglet at a show. "Is he not bonnie?"

"He'll be bonnier still an' a great deal quieter if you set him down," said Elspeth.

This Anna did. She watched her son trot immediately to seek consolation from Robert who took the boy between his long knees and let him turn his face into the vee of his vest from which position, in two or three minutes, he peeped out coyly at his mother and his aunt.

Anna plumped herself down on the couch. She gave her lace-frilled hat a shake and demanded, "Well, what have you t'say for yourself now you've finally condescended t'see us?"

Robert Rudge gave a little casual cough. "Anna and I intend to be married, in case that fact had escaped you, Elspeth."

"I'm Robert's housekeeper presently," Anna added.

"When do you intend to marry?"

"As soon as I can obtain a divorcement," Anna replied.

Elspeth had forgotten how garrulous Anna could be, and how wearisome. It galled her, slightly, that her sister had uttered not one word of welcome or enquired after her welfare.

Elspeth said, "Matt's dead."

For once Anna was struck dumb. She jolted herself back on the couch, hand to her bosom, lips parted. She glanced at Robert Rudge who, stroking Robbie's hair, shrugged his shoulders and, finding voice before Anna, asked the obvious question, "How do you know this, Elspeth?"

Anna had the decency to listen in silence while her sister answered the question with a full explanation of the circumstances. She might hold her tongue but she could not contain her annoyance at the unfolding of the story. She fiddled with her hat, her skirt and finally with the tassle of the couch itself, her restless fingers betraying her agitation.

"You stayed wi' Matt, lived wi' him?" Anna demanded, when Elspeth had concluded.

"Not as you suppose, Anna. I wish to make that very clear."

Robert Rudge said, "Who'll make a record of the toll in the Abbeyfield pit?"

Elspeth shook her head. "I know not."

"No body," said Robert Rudge. "No name upon a stone. Indeed, if there was a name it would be the wrong name."

"All those months an' you never thought t' let me into the secret," said Anna, finding her voice.

"How could I? How could I be sure that James would not find out?"

"Jamie Moodie's been dead for an age."

"I did not know it."

"Aye, but you never tried t' find out."

"A moment, if you please, my dear," Robert Rudge said. "If we might return to the matter of Matt Sinclair's tragic demise; do you suggest, Elspeth, that Anna and I declare knowledge of the death and seek for Anna the immediate status of widowhood?"

Elspeth was grateful to the agent for bringing her back to level ground. She had never much cared for the wolfish Mr Rudge but he too seemed to have changed. It occurred to her that perhaps the changes were not in the men at all but in her, that she was not the same person who had fled from Balnesmoor, that she had become so much more assured that her values had altered accordingly.

She answered, "I would say it would not be wise."

"No body," Robert Rudge repeated. "No proof."

"An' it would get you into hot water, would it not?" said Anna to her sister. "Since you might be accused o' harbourin' a fugitive from justice if it came out you'd been sharin' a cottage wi' my husband."

"Emphatically not wise," said Robert Rudge. "I think, my dearest, that we would do well to leave things as they are, not to sue for divorcement until the appropriate time."

Robbie burrowed his head against the man's stomach and Robert caught the child gently by the arms and swung him up and around and perched him on his knee.

"I'm prepared t' leave it t'your judgement, Robert," said Anna. "But I still think you were selfish not t' send me word, 'Pet."

"I was strugglin' with other things, Anna. I'd reached the end of my tether," said Elspeth. "Besides, I didn't ask you here to quarrel."

Robert fished in the pocket of his coat and brought out a piece of ginger candy which he unwrapped from a paper and held out before him. Robbie plucked it away with his lips like a trout will a fly and hummed tunelessly to himself as he sucked the strong-flavoured sweetmeat in his cheek.

Anna said, "I suppose you'll be wantin' somethin' from us."

To Anna's surprise, and dismay, Elspeth got to her feet and rang the silver bell upon the table.

"No, Anna, I require nothin' at all from you. Since you saw fit to bring Mr Rudge with you this morning, however, I will avail myself of the opportunity to have a brief word with him about Kennart's future."

Anna was silenced by the gravity of the statement. It had not seemed right for her to raise the issue and she was apprehensive now that Elspeth had come straight to it.

The drawing-room door opened. Tolland stood there, dressed in his best and neatly groomed, smarter than he had ever been in the reign of James Simpson Moodie.

Elspeth said, "Perhaps you would care to take Robbie to the kitchen—"

"Kitchen?" said Anna.

"—to partake of some refreshment. You will also have an opportunity to meet the girls: my daughter, and Miss Sarah Bennet."

Before Anna could protest Tom Tolland boomed, "This way, Mrs Sinclair, if you please."

Nonplussed, Anna glanced at Robert who gave her a short but positive nod and nudged Robbie towards his mother. Anna obeyed. She took Robbie by the hand and preceded Tolland from the drawing-room.

The door closed.

Robert Rudge relaxed a little, crossing one knee over the other.

Elspeth said, "Do you really intend to marry my sister?"

Robert answered, "Yes, of course I do."

"Does she love you?"

"Who knows?"

"Do you love her?"

"Are you givin' her away, Mrs Moodie?"

"Would that I could," said Elspeth. "Tell me, who is the father of the little boy?"

"Anna claims it's the laird, Randall."

"Do you believe her?"

"I think Robbie's a Sinclair through an' through."

"But you haven't expressed that opinion to Anna?"

Robert Rudge grinned. "Housekeeper or wife, she's entitled to her illusions."

"You have no illusions, Mr Rudge?"

"Nary a one."

"What if I tell you that I might sell off Kennart?"

"It is your prerogative to do so."

"What would you do then?"

"If you mean, Elspeth, would I still be willin' to marry Anna, the answer is in the affirmative."

"How would you keep her, and Robbie?"

"I do not think you intend to sell Kennart at all," said Robert Rudge. "It's my belief that you want to be sure I'll make an honest woman out of Anna."

"You have an ill reputation, Mr Rudge."

"No, I have a lurid past; quite a different thing."

"Will Kennart make me money?"

"Yes."

"Will you continue to manage it?"

"Along with Mr Scarf, yes, if you wish."

"How much do the mice nibble from the harvest?" said Elspeth.

"Your friend and adviser Angus Hildebrand can, I expect, tell you to the penny," said Robert Rudge. "It's not enough to concern you. Besides, if I have family interests at heart I'll be a mouse no more, will I?"

"Are we forgin' a contract, Robert?"

"So it would seem, Elspeth."

"I'll ask you not to forget that it is my mill, my concern and that you will always remain my servant."

"Oh!" said Robert Rudge, with a little whistle. "You're very direct, Mrs Moodie."

"Not so direct as all that. However, you need not concern yourself that I will discharge you from your present post unless you give me reason."

454

"No skinnin', no flighty behaviour. Honest an' upright?"

"And efficient."

"I'm always that," said Robert Rudge.

"Very well, Robert," said Elspeth. "Now, let me ask you one more question: does the laird of Ottershaw know that he's not Robbie's father?"

Even the wily Robert Rudge was caught by the enquiry. He opened his mouth, spread his hands, pursed his lips.

"I – I—"

"Give me your opinion, please."

"He thinks that Robbie's his."

"Good," said Elspeth Moodie.

She came by appointment and she came in style. It was a far cry from that morning, over a quarter of a century ago, when Gaddy had trudged barefoot down the park of Ottershaw to beg for a place in the parish, to throw herself upon the mercy of Sir Gilbert Bontine out of love for a foundling child.

Now the foundling drove in a handsome cabriolet pulled by two dashing geldings attended by a coachman, of the McGowan clan, who was tricked out in tan and sat up on the board with a whip in his hand, the feather in his hat, the one raffish touch to the rig, bobbing to the rhythm of the wheels on the gravel.

She was alone on the long leather-upholstered seat. The hood was down, for the day was promising fine. She wore a walking-dress of midnight-blue velvet with black cord frogging. Gloves and hat matched in shade and the colour did not seem sombre and severe but daring. She carried in her lap a rolled bag of brown kidskin which went with her when the cabriolet drew up at the front of the house, exact to the line of the stone steps. Hunter bustled to open the door but Elspeth Patterson Moodie waited, the park behind her, until Randall Bontine came to personally bid her welcome and escort her indoors.

The surprise on Randall's face made it all worth the bother, though she was not foolish or vain enough to imagine that the laird would have stepped to her bidding if she had not held aces in her hand against Gibbie. But, given that fact, she was here at Ottershaw and she was not afraid.

"You appear to be – well, Mistress Moodie," Randall said as he led her across the hall and into the long drawing-room on the ground floor.

"I am well, sir, thank you. I am very well indeed."

Randall would have made it his business to learn all that he could of her 'adventures'. He would certainly know that she had lived with the colliers of the Abbeyfield. What would make him uncertain would be the relationship between her job there and Gibbie's downfall. She could not enlighten him without revealing a great deal that he did not require to know about James's sisters and Keir Bolderon; relationships that made it all a bit less coincidental than it at first seemed. She would keep that knowledge to herself.

The woman was certainly pretty and vivacious. She was no long-nosed snob like Alicia but made her warily welcome and, after a few minutes of conversation, offered chocolate or coffee or some other refreshment appropriate to the morning hour. It would have been interesting to spend time with Suzanne Bontine and to expand politeness into friendship, perhaps; but that, Elspeth knew, could never be. Randall would not permit it, not after she had finished with him.

In due course Suzanne Bontine excused herself and left the laird and the weaver's widow alone.

The laird too had changed in the time she had been away. He had grown rather plump, had lost that honed and dangerous edge which was her memory of him. But the hooded eyes were still perceptive and sharp and she felt a little of her girlhood fear of him return for a moment as Hunter closed the drawing-room door.

The smile had gone from Randall's mouth, except for the trace of it that the scar made permanent. He stood by the fireplace, his back to the bright crackling flames, and studied her. His first question surprised her. It indicated that she was not the only one in the room who was apprehensive.

"Did Anna send you?" the laird said.

"My sister is not even aware that I am here."

"So it is not to do with that?"

"It is not," said Elspeth, and added, "not directly."

Randall Bontine seated himself, not upon a chair but upon the top of a huge wooden log-box that flanked the fireplace to the left. The morning mist had lifted and sunlight streamed through the windows, gilding the floor.

Randall squinted at her.

He said, "Then it has to do with Gilbert?"

Elspeth said, "Yes."

Randall said, "Why have you not confronted him?"

Elspeth answered, "There's no need to confront him, no point to be gained."

"It's Gibbie who owes you money, not me."

"Aye, sir, but it's you who can pay, not your brother."

"What has that clever rogue Hildebrand been tellin' you?"

"Quite enough to make me realise that my husband's fortune has been stolen."

"That's a harsh word, Mrs Moodie."

"Stolen, sir, as surely as if your brother had robbed it from a safe-box at pistol point."

Randall Bontine pursed his lips and stretched out his legs. He leaned his head against the post of the fireplace and stared past her into the sunlight. He folded his arms.

Elspeth did not press, waited until he spoke.

"What has Hildebrand told you to do?"

"Mr Hildebrand offers advice, not orders," said Elspeth.

"Is it therefore on Mr Hildebrand's *advice* that you've come to bargain with me in preference to dealing with my brother?"

"Mr Hildebrand does not wholly approve of my intention, sir, and I most certainly have not come here to bargain."

Randall got to his feet and stretched his arm along the shelf above the fireplace. He drummed his fingers nervously. The soldier's enthusiasm for conflict had diminished. His cheeks were flushed and he seemed lacking in gentlemanly assurance.

Elspeth said, "Mr Hildebrand, however, has explained the law to me. He has informed me that Mr Gilbert's bank partners have charged him with breach of the partnership agreement; is that a fact, Sir Randall?"

"Yes, they absolve themselves from blame by that manoeuvre."

"I assume that Mr Gilbert cannot, as an individual, repay the substantial sum of money which my late husband put into his trust?"

"He cannot repay you immediately, no."

"He'll make a monetary offer, a portion of the sum owing; is that it?"

"Something of the sort."

"How much?"

"You must ask—"

"Did Mr Gilbert not ask you?"

"About fifteen hundred pounds," Randall said.

Elspeth nodded; it was very close to the estimate that Mr Hildebrand had made of what Gibbie could garner from his relatives.

She went on, "Fifteen hundred pounds will not be acceptable, Sir Randall."

"Perhaps it might be raised to two thousand."

"I want it all, sir."

"Impossible."

"Within the mandatory sixty days."

"No, it's impossible. The sum went, as you are very well aware, into the coal pit at the Abbeyfield and was sunk with it."

"It wasn't sunk with it; it was sunk with Mr Fotheringham," said Elspeth. "No amount of Mr Gilbert's so-called 'investment' went into improvements or extensions on the Abbeyfield. The fact is that Mr Fotheringham cheated Mr Gilbert, and that Mr Gilbert cheated me."

Randall Bontine could find no words to refute it. She had laboured there, had known the men who had conned Gibbie into throwing his honour and his freedom into an insane gamble for profits. But the Abbeyfield and what had occurred there were immaterial to the present conversation, to the transaction that Elspeth Patterson Moodie had in mind.

Randall sat again, leaning his elbow on his knee, hand to his chin.

"I see that you intend to demand your money and assure that the peace-officers take out letters of caption against Gilbert, to ruin him," Randall said.

"No, I do not," said Elspeth.

"What, then?"

"Your brother, sir, was entrusted with funds and applied them to his own use. He would have taken the profits and not declared them either to his banking partners or to me. The construction put upon this act may be that of fraud, breach of trust or that of embezzlement under the statutes of the laws of Scotland."

"Criminal charges?"

"I'll not see your brother escape through the wide mesh of the civil courts, Sir Randall," said Elspeth. "I will pursue a charge of embezzlement against him, see him arraigned before the judges of the High Court."

"Damned if you will. Gibbie may be a fool but he's no criminal."

"He took what wasn't his."

"He – he didn't know what he was doing."

"Did he not seek your advice?" said Elspeth.

On his feet once more, Randall cried, "If the bloody man had sought my advice do you suppose I'd have let him do it?"

The more distraught the laird became the calmer Elspeth felt. She experienced no malicious satisfaction in seeing Randall Bontine brought to this stage. She did not enjoy it as a form of revenge; it was not in her nature to be vengeful. But she had learned the meaning of power and she would not flinch from using it as her father, as James, would have used it. If she had been nurtured by Gaddy and given shape by the woman, in her too ran her father's strain, undeniable in its intensity and its directness.

"You'd have prevented it, would you, laird?"

"Aye, of course I would. I'd have kicked his backside for even contemplating such a risky thing."

"Risky?" said Elspeth.

"Stupid, foolish."

"Risky because he might not get away with it?"

He spoke to her then as he might have spoken to any servant, not in fury but in reprimand. He jabbed his finger at her. "Do not bandy words with me, miss."

She did not quail from him, did not feel now even a twinge of fear for his position. She straightened and unfurled the leather roll in her lap, let him see within the folds the letters written in Mr Hildebrand's best legal copperplate.

"I'll not bandy words, laird. I'll use the law o' the land as it's given to me as well as to you an' your kind." She checked herself, spoke more slowly, letting the accents of the hill slip

459

from her voice. "Drafts of letters, sir, which will be sent tomorrow to the Falkirk Farmers' Bank, also to the office of the Sheriff of the county who will, without doubt, respond with alacrity since the name of Bontine is invoked, even if the name of Moodie means little to him."

Randall said, "This is revenge. I can smell the stink of it."

"I've no reason to seek revenge, laird. I told you, Anna's affairs are not mine. I want only what I'm due, an' I'll not wait your pleasure to receive it."

"Under law," said Randall, "I'm not responsible for Gilbert's debts, or for his criminal behaviour towards you."

"I know it."

"Take it to *him*. See what *he* says."

"He's your full brother, Sir Randall. He's one of the last of the Bontines left in the Lennox. You'll not escape the taint of it, however it turns out."

"I had nothing—"

"You'll lose esteem, lose trust."

"You *are* blackmailing me. Damned if you're not."

"Is honour not important to you still, sir?"

"I cannot pay that sum, even if I would."

Elspeth said, "I'll accept less than the sum."

"Will you? How much less?"

"Half, or thereabouts."

"I cannot pay half, not without—" He was suddenly still, the hands still, the legs, the head twisted towards her. "What *do* you want?"

"Land," Elspeth said.

"Ottershaw land?"

"Yes."

"Never."

"All the hill land, except the tree plantations."

"Damn you, Elspeth. Never."

"From the boundary line by the Orrals to the mid-line of Drumglass; the moor above the road."

"The road?"

"The oak track."

"It's a fifth part of Ottershaw."

"Less," said Elspeth.

"Who gave *you* Ottershaw's measures?"

"They were contained among my – my husband's documents," said Elspeth.

"Moodie had the lease of the best of the upper grazing from me, and it will be continued, if you wish, for the length of the term." Randall spoke without force or conviction now; she knew that he had guessed her purpose. "No, you cannot have Ottershaw under signature. I'll not sell one acre of it, not to you or to anyone."

"Why not?"

"Because – because, damn it, I have it on trust."

It was quite the wrong word. He stopped as soon as he uttered it, let his eyelids droop.

Elspeth said, "An' my inheritance, Randall, albeit expressed in money and not land, does that not have value too? Is that not my 'trust', what I've been given, what I must use and look after?"

"It's not the same thing."

"Because I'm a woman?"

"Because you're—"

"I laboured in your fields once," said Elspeth. "My sister served in your kitchens; aye, and in your bedroom too."

"I *knew* it would come to that."

"But my husband fashioned a life out of the sweat of his brow and a determination not to be a tenant all his days. He would not settle for less, he would not—"

"Ah, it's Moodie. He left you instructions –"

"He did not. I need no instructions. I want the long tract of hill pasture from the Orrals to the shoulder of Drumglass."

Randall slapped his palm to his brow.

"The Nettleburn!" he exclaimed. "Dyers' Dyke! Of course, of course! This is sentiment, not sense. You're seeking to own your past, to eliminate the memory of—"

"Do not, sir, talk nonsense," said Elspeth. "I seek to eliminate nothing."

"But those places, they are what you want?"

"Yes."

"Where you lived once?"

"Yes, where I lived. Where my mother lived."

"Your mother! She was not your mother. I'd like to know who you really are, Mrs Elspeth Moodie. I'd like to learn

461

your lineage and what heritage turned you into what you are."

"I'm the injured party in a dishonourable case of embezzlement, Sir Randall," said Elspeth. "That is what I am, and all that's material."

She rose, smoothing down the velvet and adjusting her hat. She rolled up the kidskin case with the letters in it and put it behind her upon the table, saying, "I'll leave these copies for you to peruse, laird. I've no doubt that your brother will wish to see them too."

"Twelve thousand pounds is a devilish and extravagant price to pay to satisfy a sentimental female whim."

Anger warmed his words and yet there was still that old ineradicable note of patronage in his tone.

Elspeth, at last, responded sharply.

"Is it sentiment to wish to buy prime grazin' land?" she retorted. "If I purchase an' improve the moor pastures I can run a thousand head of hardy sheep across them and secure a supply of wool to keep the looms of Kennart clacking for years to come."

"Sheep? What do you know of sheep?"

"Enough to make the land pay back what your brother can't."

"No, I'll not submit to it," Randall shouted. "I'll not sell off any part of Ottershaw to save that damned fool's neck. He can go to the gallows for all I care."

"Is that your last word upon it?"

"My very last word, yes."

"In that case, sir, would you be good enough to summon my carriage?" said Elspeth.

But as the laird stalked away to cry for Hunter she allowed herself a faint wry smile for she knew that guilt, Gibbie and the honour of Ottershaw would soon bring Randall Bontine round.

Winter gave her breathing-space and Moss House, in misty mornings and early dark, seemed a haven of warmth and friendliness. It was not that the mistress of the house filled it with 'society' or sought to impose herself upon the customs of the village. On the contrary Elspeth was almost as reclusive as her husband had been in the last years of his life, but with her it was done for different reasons.

Times had changed. Elspeth was aware of it. She did not need to be upon the road, show her face and make her presence felt. It was not that she was more trusting than James had been. She kept a weather-eye on all matters large and small that affected Kennart and its weavers. She was concerned too with the household purse and, while she was not niggardly in providing creature comforts for herself and her children, she did not immediately embark upon a programme of change and alteration. She was content for that cold season to reside in James's house, to adjust to it even though the memories from time to time brought pain.

Moss House was snug and comfortable. The girls revelled in its freedoms, spent the dreary wet days of late November playing by the coal fire in the parlour or bouncing about on the bed in the upstairs chamber or, to Tolland's annoyance, sat by the grate in the kitchen and chattered to the new cook, Mrs Grayling, who was a kindly soul and encouraged them. There was a maid too, not new but 'restored', for Betty had brought herself back when she heard of Elspeth's return. She tended the children now that they were grown with the same firmness as she had looked after Mary Jean as an infant. And there was the coachman, McGowan, and plans to employ a tutor for school instruction after Christmas was over.

Anna and Robert came to tea, came to dinner, came over from Drymen on a Sunday afternoon, as if they were already married and had been 'respectable' for years. Robbie romped about and had the freedom of the house and played blindman's-buff and hunt-the-cat with the girls, for Sarah Bennet had slipped back to taste the pleasures of a childhood missed, and seldom, to Elspeth's knowledge, mooned over her 'lost' sister or the kin she had left on the Abbeyfield.

It was Mr Hildebrand, of course, who brought the news from far-flung quarters. He came frequently to Moss House and talked of purchasing a house in Balfron, for his business in Dumbarton had dwindled so much time had he spent with clients in the spur of the Lennox, and he was growing too long in the tooth to make the journey up the lochside in the sleet and snow. Mr Hildebrand brought news that Randall Bontine had agreed to meet Elspeth's terms, at least in part. Mr Hildebrand acted as go-between in drawing up the agreements of purchase, and haggled for Elspeth over the disposition of the farm of Dyers' Dyke which Sir Randall sought to keep in his possession since the Macfarlanes were well settled there.

To show that she was not stubborn Elspeth had let the farm remain as part of Ottershaw but had insisted on fencing it off, leaving a mere forty acres about the buildings and keeping water rights in the original deed of purchase. She would take possession of the lands and properties above the oak track on the 1st of May and discussed with Robert Rudge how she could juggle credit to buy breeding rams and with John Scarf where such animals could best be obtained.

Mr Hildebrand also brought news from Strachan, told how Gibbie had sought to sue Hector Fotheringham, in spite of Randall's advice to the contrary, and how the Brothers Pryde had withdrawn their charge against him but had asked for his resignation in exchange for a nominal payment; how the Moodie sisters – her aunts, though only Elspeth knew it – had finally surrendered to the inevitable and written off the fees that the venture had cost them; and how the manager of the coal pit had transferred his interest from engineering to mercantile trading and was, so Mr Hildebrand had heard, employed in some warehouse in Leith.

From Matt, from Mouse came no word at all.

Mary Jean – Sarah too – presented a problem in the matter of the lie. It was not in Elspeth's nature to encourage young children to be deceivers but now and then Mary Jean would, in all innocence, let out some remark about Matt that would bring a frown of bewilderment to Anna's face.

Finally Elspeth took the bull by the horns.

The coal fire burned bright in the bedroom and the lamp was like a great round yellow moon on the table by the window. The girls were in their night attire, kneeling upon the bed while Betty sorted out their new-washed underclothing for the morning. Elspeth entered and asked Betty to go downstairs and take supper with cook and Mr Tolland. She settled with the girls upon the bed, drawing them to her affectionately.

"We're going to make a pretend," she began.

"Stories?" said Mary Jean.

"Yes, a story; our story."

"What sort o' story, Mammy?"

"We're going to pretend that Matt's dead and gone to Heaven."

"Is he?" Sarah stiffened and clasped at Elspeth's hand. "Has it—"

Elspeth shook her head. She made a secret little sign with her eyes to Sarah who was quite old enough to understand the need for secrets.

"Matt's with Mousie," said Mary Jean. "Has Mousie gone t' Heaven wi' him?"

Elspeth said, "No, dearest, but there are bad people who would like to find Matt and—"

"*What* bad people?"

Sarah said, "We'll pretend, Mary Jean, eh?"

"Pretend there's bad people?"

"Aye."

How fine it would be, Elspeth thought, if one had to pretend that there was wickedness in the world, if she could be again as she had been when she was young and lived with Gaddy high on the slopes of the hill. But Mary Jean was not without guile and Sarah, as close to her as a sister, could always cajole her and impress her.

Sarah went on, "If everybody thinks Matt's gone t' Heaven nobody will wonder where he is, see?"

Mary Jean nodded vigorously.

Elspeth began to wonder if she was doing the right thing by her daughter, if this tiny deception would not somehow swell and grow into a monstrous lie. She had experienced that process and was frightened of it.

As if picking up the thought from her mother, Mary Jean said, "Aunt Anna asks me 'bout Matt."

"Does she?" Elspeth was not surprised. "What do you tell her?"

"Tell her I loved him," said Mary Jean.

"What else?"

"Tell her he went away wi' Mousie."

"Sarah, is that true?" said Elspeth.

Sarah said, "I told Mrs Sinclair he went away for ever, told her it's what we told Mary Jean."

Elspeth sat back on her heels on the bed. It was such a simple lie that she could not have devised it. She smiled at Sarah and drew the girl to her, stroked her hair, while Mary Jean, not to be left out, rubbed herself amicably against her mother and patted her knee with her hand.

"There, there, Mammy," she said.

"Was that no' right?" said Sarah.

"Perfectly right," said Elspeth.

If only it was so easy to be rid of unpleasant things, to pass them off as lightly as a child does. But memories are stubborn, Elspeth thought, and must be harboured in the heart for good or ill while friends and kindred who once seemed to be the core and centre of life became lost among them, like ewes in the forest.

Rising, clapping her hands, she said, "Into bed."

"Mammy, tell us—"

"Not tonight, dearest. It's far too late for wee lassies to be up. Quick now, into bed."

Mary Jean scrambled under the covers and pulled the blankets up to her nose.

"Sarah, come on," she whispered.

But Sarah lingered and Elspeth sensed that something was troubling the elder girl. She leaned forward and took her hand. "What is it, Sarah?"

"I think about Davy an' our Mouse sometimes. I canna help it," Sarah confessed.

"Do you miss them?"

"Aye."

It was on the tip of Elspeth's tongue to ask if she missed the Abbeyfield, the stink and suffocating darkness of the pit, the back-breaking labour of hauling the sleds; if release from that harrowing existence had not been worth the sacrifices. But the question, however gently put, would have been cruel. Instead she gave the girl another hug.

Sarah said, "You'll not send me back, will you?"

"Don't be daft, Sarah," said Elspeth. "You can stay here with us for as long as you like."

"For ever?"

"Until some young man comes along an' asks you to be his wife," said Elspeth.

Sarah gave a little sigh as if that prospect touched her with its appeal, as if, perhaps, she had some young man already in mind and would live with the hope of it all coming true in the end.

Elspeth left the girls giggling together under the covers and went along the corridor to the stairs.

The house seemed empty now that the servants were gathered in the kitchen. Tonight she felt the presence of James here, not his force, that threatening and obsessional passion which she had feared and hated and which had driven her away, but his loneliness. She shivered slightly as she crossed the hall to the drawing-room.

Lamps were lighted, the fire burned on an empty sort of elegance. She longed to go down to the kitchen, to sit at the big wooden table with Tom Tolland, cook and Betty and share their supper and their companionship. But she could not. She was their mistress and her appearance in the kitchen would disconcert and inhibit them, would be unseemly.

In twenty minutes or half an hour she might reasonably ring the bell and Tom Tolland would serve her dinner in the dining-room where a place had been set at the top of the long, polished table. He might even linger for a moment or two of conversation before he realised his position and left her to eat in peace, to eat alone.

To Elspeth's chagrin he did not reply at once. Indeed, he did not reply at all.

At first she was bewildered and disappointed, believed that her letter must have gone astray upon the road. She was tempted to write to him again but realised that if he had received her first communication and had chosen to ignore it then a second letter would make her seem foolish. She wondered if the formal tone of the original had put him off. She had expressed in it no more than a polite enquiry as to his welfare but had requested his assistance on a practical matter and promised him payment in accordance with the degree of service which he was able to render.

Perhaps he wanted no more to do with her in any circumstances. Perhaps he had found himself an Edinburgh wife.

As casually as possible she asked Mr Hildebrand for news.

Mr Hildebrand had no news to give. Besides, Mr Hildebrand was just a mite less conscientious than usual that snell season for he was nursing a crop of chilblains and a dripping head cold. In any case, he did not comprehend Mrs Moodie's interest in the fellow, for she had neglected to tell the lawyer of her plans and had failed to mention that she had written to the man at all.

Christmas came merrily enough. New Year too. January brought a spell of biting cold, snow towards the end of the month. For a day or two the girls enjoyed the wintry weather. Even Robbie, on a Sunday visit, grasped the principle of making a man out of snow, though his main pleasure in the act seemed to be in knocking the poor snowman's head off as soon as Sarah placed it upon the trunk. But the girls soon grew bored and cross with snow and ice and voluntarily confined themselves to the house and drove Elspeth and the servants mad with their restless energy.

In mid-February rain washed away the snow and a warm wind over the loch brought a thaw. Elspeth drove the girls down to Kennart to stare in awe at the great brown torrent of the Lightwater and to hear the mill wheel thump and thrash in the lade. But Mary Jean did not like such wild din and spectacle and cried and cried until Robert Rudge lifted her and carried her upstairs to his rickety office and fed her ginger candy and let her dabble in the inkpots and spoil half a ream of best quality writing-paper. Sarah, though, was impressed by Kennart's collective industry. She would have wandered about the place, from the forge to the quaking room full of looms and spindles, all day if Elspeth had not coaxed her away, afraid that somehow her ward would come to harm.

March came in calm and grey and patient. Elspeth had not forgotten that she had written the letter but by now she expected no reply. She did not think of him very much except in the late evening hour when she sat alone in the dining-room with empty chairs about her and pondered on why it was that independence had not brought her freedom and why she could not settle to enjoy her privacy and peace. Summer, she told herself, would bring novel occupations, such a mass of things to do that the days – and the nights – would pass in a twinkling and she would not feel that thin little hurt any longer. She would seek out another man to cost the work for her, to execute it too if he was keen and able and agreed to her price.

It was a Wednesday in mid-March. The weather was not bright but it was dry and warm enough for Robbie and the girls to be out upon the lawns, with Betty keeping an eye on them. Robert had had the carpenter at Kennart fashion three little golf sticks and had had John Scarf find a box of feathery balls and the girls and Robbie, shrieking with laughter, were whisking and whacking away to the detriment of the lawn's smooth surface and to the peril of the windows. From time to time, from their chairs in the drawing-room, Elspeth and Anna would see the shape of a child shoot past the window or would look out at some group among the shrubs, three heads bowed in concentration, with Betty not far off.

If confession was good for the soul then Anna, these last few months, had cleansed herself to the point of purity. She was boringly self-concerned, would chatter on to Elspeth about all her loves and losses and talk of men, men, men until Elspeth would feel her head spin and long for her sister to step into marriage and motherhood in the hope that it would take her mind off the triumphs and disasters of her formative years.

"I was young, of course," said Anna. "I knew no better. But I canna say that I was taken advantage of, if you see what I mean. I mean, Matt was one thing but Randall Bontine was another. Just as well, I sometimes think, that Mammy died when she did. I mean, not that she died, do not misunderstand me, 'Pet, but that she died when she did. Doubt if I'd have had the brass neck to let Randall seduce me if Mammy had been about. I was vulnerable, is that no' the word, at that period. Matt was all very well, very amorous, of course, an' mad in love with me but I was too young t' resist a man like Randall."

"Did you try very hard, Anna?"

"Try very hard? How could I have tried harder? I was doomed, y' might say, from the day he first cast eyes on me, when our lips first met. Remember?"

"Yes, I remember," said Elspeth.

She had other things to do, details of business to attend to, but she had not the heart to be brusque with her sister. She

469

wondered, though, how many days she must waste over the years listening to Anna talk about herself.

"I mean, I did it for Matt. In a manner o' speakin'. If I hadn't given in to the laird there's no sayin' what would have happened t' Matt."

"It did not turn out well for Matt in any event," said Elspeth.

"An' what do y' mean by that?"

Quickly Elspeth said, "Matt did not hold it against you, Anna."

"Did he tell you as much?"

"Many times. He always spoke of you with, with affection."

"He loved me, Matt did. But he was spoiled, in my opinion."

"Perhaps he was," said Elspeth.

Through the drawing-room window she watched Mary Jean take a huge, awkward swipe with her golf stick and somehow manage to propel the ball, high and whirring, over the hedge and into the onion beds.

Anna went on, "It's hard for you t' understand, 'Pet. I had too passionate a nature for my own good. I see that now. Not like you. Always chalk an' cheese, you an' me. I mean, I'd never have wed a man like Jamie Moodie – oh, pardon me; I didn't mean . . . In any case, you canna blame the laird for wantin' me, seein' me in an' out of his room every day."

Anna paused. She leaned forward and selected a finger of yellow cake from the tray on the table and put it into her mouth. Elspeth watched her chew. She was still beautiful but the emptiness in her showed sometimes in her eyes which became quite vacant for split seconds of time as if nothing much filled her head now.

Anna sipped tea from a flower-sprigged china cup.

"Have y' seen Sandy Sinclair of late?" she asked.

In fact Elspeth had seen Sandy only five days ago when, rather to her surprise, she had found him in the kitchen chatting with Tolland and eating a veal pie, his garron tied up by the wall that kept the moorland from invading the gardens.

"He – yes, he seems quite settled on Ottershaw."

"I hear Gibbie's off t' Ireland."

"So I hear, yes," said Elspeth.

"Packed off by Randall, like as not, after that stramash wi' the bank."

Elspeth waited for Anna to put a question to her, to enquire about her plans for the stretch of land that she had acquired or to praise her for her astuteness in persuading Randall Bontine to part with it. But Anna seemed incapable of associating her sister with Ottershaw in any way at all.

Anna said, "Lachlan's returnin' to Ottershaw. You'd hear that from Sandy too?"

Elspeth nodded.

Anna said, "Did he ask after me? Sandy?"

Elspeth said, "No, no he didn't."

"Oh!" said Anna.

She dabbed her mouth with a lace-fringed napkin and stared out of the window again.

"Robbie's gettin' tall," she said. "Quite grown up."

Robert Rudge had dropped Anna and the boy off from his gig soon after noon and had promised to return for them by five o'clock, on his return from the bleachfields at Balfron where he had business of some sort that afternoon.

Elspeth glanced at the clock. It was not yet three. She felt impatient, restless, and was frightened that she might quarrel with Anna before the man's return. She tried to occupy her mind with thoughts of all the things that she would have to do tomorrow to make up for the 'social' afternoon in her sister's company, thought too that Anna had got more than she properly deserved in the patronage of Robert Rudge, for the reprobate was thoroughly reformed, it seemed, and hell bent on marriage. She listened to the clock, to the whisper of the pendulum and the *tock-tock-tock* of the weight in its case.

Anna said, "I'm surprised he didn't ask after me. Sandy, I mean."

Elspeth said, "He only dropped in for a bite to eat, Anna, since he was in this quarter. He really had very little t' say for—"

The drawing-room door opened, not thrown open but opened with a swing and a creak. She glanced around. Sarah was there, boots muddy, cheeks red with the spring air, her eyes round and more solemn and brown than Elspeth had ever seen them before.

471

Elspeth got to her feet, held out a hand to the girl.

"What is it, Sarah? Do you want somethin' to eat?"

Hesitantly Sarah stepped forward. It must be something unusual to have brought her directly into the drawing-room. She was a careful girl and would surely have cleaned her boots before crossing the polished hall let alone venturing on to the carpet. In one hand she still clutched the stout little golf stick all smeared and gouted with earth.

Anna hardly seemed to notice the girl. She regarded her entry as a distraction, an interruption to the flow of her conversation. She gave a small *tut*, murmured, "Dirty feet. Dirty feet indoors," and transferred her attention to the plate of yellow cake once more.

Sarah came to Elspeth's side.

Elspeth stooped, her skirts rustling.

"Sarah, what's wrong?"

"It's – it's him," Sarah whispered.

"Who?"

"Come int' our garden."

"Who, Sarah?"

"Mr Bolderon." Sarah burst into a flood of tears. "Mr Bolderon's come t' take me away."

It was at once clear that she had misjudged his circumstances. He was not as she had imagined him to be, all down-at-heel and shabby. There was no evidence of neglect about his person. His cuffs and collar were not frayed or grubby, his coat showed no button strings or coarse patches. His hat had even been blocked and brushed and his shoes shone like two pieces of parrot coal. He was, of course, disconcerted by the effect of his sudden appearance on Sarah Bennet and was profuse in his apologies.

"I really had no notion that I would frighten her so."

Elspeth had hurried to the door before Tolland could come from the servants' hall, had found Keir Bolderon upon the path. Betty was hovering close to him, scowling. Robbie was clinging to her skirts. But Mary Jean was smiling and peeping up at the Abbeyfield manager as if she thought that he might have a fat pony in his pocket and might offer her, there and then, another ride upon its back.

The concern in his eyes seemed genuine. Elspeth had an arm wrapped around Sarah and held her against her skirts.

"She thinks you've come to take her back," Elspeth said.

"Oh, dear, dear. No, no. Please explain to her that I am here by invitation."

Betty came forward, stood, still scowling, by the step while Elspeth explained to Sarah that Mr Bolderon was manager of the Abbeyfield no longer and had no power over them now. Though she remained shaken, Sarah was reassured.

Betty said, "Shall I look after her, Mrs Moodie?"

"Yes, go in with Betty." Elspeth kissed the girl on the brow. "You too, Mary Jean. And Robbie. You may all have some extra cake."

The children were shepherded indoors while Anna, sensing that something unusual was going on, entered the hallway from the drawing-room and loitered there, listening. She caught Keir Bolderon's attention. He was intrigued by the sight of the dark-haired woman and swayed on the balls of his feet to see more of her.

Elspeth was annoyed at the confusion which Keir Bolderon's unexpected arrival had caused. It should have been an occasion of dignified formality. If only he had written to declare his intention to call upon her, she would have made sure that the children were out of the way, that Tolland was in his uniform and that she had been dressed rather more splendidly. The sight of her raised up would have put him at a disadvantage and allowed her to steer the first moments of their meeting more effectively. None of it was possible now. Indeed, Anna would insinuate herself, negotiate an introduction to the mysterious and handsome stranger who had come to visit her sister, would flirt and charm him.

To Keir Bolderon Elspeth said, "May I take it that you did, in fact, receive my letter?"

"Yes, and I must offer an apology for not replyin' to it," said Keir Bolderon. "I did not wish to give a commitment to your undertaking until I was sure of my own position."

"What is your position, Mr Bolderon?"

"I am employed, presently, by the McNeil family of Leith."

"As a mining engineer?"

"Hardly that," said Keir Bolderon.

Elspeth waited but he did not embellish on the exact nature of his occupation.

She said, "Was there nothing left for you at the Abbeyfield?"

He answered, "Nothing at all. It may, however, interest you to know that the pit has been sealed and that a minister was brought to consecrate the ground for the sake of those who lie buried."

Elspeth nodded; she had heard as much from Mr Hildebrand.

She said, "I'm glad it was done in a Christian manner. I take it there was no trace of—"

"No trace of anything or anyone in that filthy sand," said Keir Bolderon. "It may be of small consolation to you but I thank God that so few lives were lost."

Elspeth was aware of Anna in the hallway, hovering like a hawk.

"Mr Bolderon," said Elspeth, "have you come to take on the piece of work which I offered?"

"I cannot say, not until I've surveyed the requirements."

"Will you do so now?"

"If you wish."

"Wait here, please," said Elspeth.

She stepped back into the house, leaving Keir Bolderon to cool his heels upon the path outside. She closed the door a little and swung round. She was harried by the desire to get him away from Moss House, from Anna, from the fuss of conventional introductions. Sensing her sister's anxiety, Anna smiled and made a sign of approval, fluttering her fingers before her face like a feather fan. "Who on earth is *he*? Is he one o' your dark secrets, 'Pet?"

"Mr Bolderon is an *engineer*, if you must know."

She signalled to Tolland who brought her coat and bonnet from the cupboard and handed them to her. She wore slippers not shoes but the weather was dry and she would not take time to change them. She did not understand why she felt so pressed and nervous.

Anna said, "Are y' not goin' to bring him in?"

"Mr Bolderon is a man of many interests," said Elspeth, as

she tied the ribbons on her bonnet. "He'll not have time to waste in Balnesmoor."

"Such nonsense!" said Anna. "Bring him in, 'Pet, till I get a proper look at him."

"Anna, do not interfere. I have business with Mr Bolderon. Plain business. Do you understand me?"

"Nah, 'Pet. I've never understood you." Anna chuckled and shook her head. "Still, if business is what you want, I'll keep the bairns out o' harm's way till you return."

Stiffly Elspeth signalled to Tolland to open the door. She swept out. She beckoned to Mr Bolderon to follow her as she hurried down the path and through the gate into the road. She was relieved to be screened from Moss House by the hedges. Anna would be at the window, watching, speculating.

The meeting with Keir Bolderon was not at all as she had visualised it. She regretted the impulse that had made her write that letter in the first place. What she had she could not lose. In an insecure world she had acquired a degree of security that few women could ever hope to attain. Why did she risk being hurt and rejected, being deceived by this man, by any man? She felt resentment grow in her. Could she not settle for independence? Must she invent a project that would bring Keir Bolderon to Balnesmoor and keep him here for months? Why could she not be happy with what she had gained?

"I'm sorry I intruded without warning, Mrs Moodie."

"Why do you call me that?"

"It's your name, is it not?"

"Indeed, it is my name. But why do *you* call me by it? Was 'Elspeth' only my name when I worked for you?"

She knew she was being childish and churlish but she could not break the mood, remained angry with him for catching her off guard.

Keir Bolderon said, "I'll call you by any name that pleases you."

"Oh, do not be so – so ingratiating. I cannot abide that in a man."

"Can you not," he said, quietly, a statement not a question.

Elspeth marched on, letting him skip to keep in step with her.

She headed along the top road towards the cottages at the

Bonnywell, but broke off into the lane by the Black Bull before she reached the pump. She did not want to give the girls and women there too much to gossip about, for it was not proper for a lady to walk out with a stranger. She was vividly aware of familiar scenes, as if having Keir Bolderon by her side had revived them for her; over there, the kirk; there the kirkyard wall and the place where her family lay at rest. The cottages where James and his sisters had laboured were occupied still by weavers, though very impoverished and dismal they were, and the smoke still rose from the cottage chimneys against the flat, patient backcloth of the hills.

She turned into the lane, walking very quickly.

Keir Bolderon skipped and turned with her, not at all sure whether he was expected to keep step in step by her side or to follow behind like a lackey.

"May I – may I ask where we are goin'?" he said, at length.

"To inspect the site of the work," Elspeth said.

"Ah, yes, of course."

She had walked this lane so often when she was a girl, carrying water and milk from Dyers' Dyke to the hut. She associated it with Gaddy and Coll, with poor Peter Docherty who had loved her and had been loyal but was in the end too weak to save himself from drink. Never had Elspeth felt the din and clamour of the past ring so loud within her. She turned from the lane into the oak track. Bare thorn hedges and the unleafed trees flanked the track but did not screen from view the line of moor and hill. She strode on over the winter litter to the sound of rooks cawing and the distant roaring of a bullock from the valley.

Keir Bolderon settled to her pace. Occasionally he would glance at her but he put no more questions and meekly let her lead him on. If he was puzzled or disturbed by her unusual behaviour he gave no sign of it.

She arrived at the field gate, not the old broken-down gate that she remembered but a new one of stout, clean timbers with posts so recently planted that they had not yet acquired a silky green patina and capping of moss. An iron chain was clenched about the post. She put her hand to it as if she expected it to break at her touch.

"Allow me, Elspeth, if you will."

476

Keir Bolderon found the hook-link, unclipped it from its clasp and pulled the gate open. He let Elspeth enter the field and followed her. He closed the gate carefully behind him, and chained it again.

The hill of Drumglass reared to the west. The hump-backed gable of Dumgoyne was visible too. The moor undulated upwards into the sky. The scar that marked the site of the hut on the Nettleburn was still discernible, though skeletal bracken and rank weeds hid most of it now.

Elspeth stopped. "Here."

"Here?"

"I was raised here, in a sheep-hut."

"Ah!"

"Now I'm owner of all the land your eye can see, from the woods to the sky." She did not speak directly to Keir Bolderon. He stood behind her, by her shoulder. "It's mine. I bought it from the laird. I own it."

Keir Bolderon said, "What will you do with it?"

"Raise sheep on it."

"Elspeth, why did you send for me?"

"I require a person who can manage the land for me."

"I'm no farmer, Elspeth."

"I want it brought back."

"Brought back?" said Keir Bolderon.

"She came over that hill," said Elspeth, pointing. "My mother. She died here. I was found here. I was raised here. I was—"

He touched a hand to her shoulder.

He still carried the man's smell upon him, distinctive but not strong, not unpleasant. He did not reek of byre or tavern and his touch was gentle. She could see his fingers out of the corner of her eye and was surprised at how scarred they were, just like Coll Cochran's or Lachlan Sinclair's. She wanted to turn to him, to have him hold her. But she could not yield, would not submit to the need. She clung stubbornly to a last illusion of freedom, to the old falsehoods that had become the only truths in which she could believe. She did not know how to explain it or why, of all men, he should be the one.

She said, "I want the bogs drained. I want walls built. I want woods to shelter my ewes and stone huts to protect the

477

lambs. I want potato shaws to green the bare ground an'
barley to grow instead of bracken. I want—"

"Tell me what you want, Elspeth."

"I want to build a house, a fine stone house here on the
Nettleburn."

"What's to prevent you?"

She stepped away from him, walked three or four paces.
The grass was thin under her slippers and the hem of her skirt
had become heavy with moisture soaked up from ground that
looked dry. She felt slender and small under the vastness of
the Balnesmoor, unprotected by her dreams.

She turned to him, snapped, "What do you know of it?"

"Oh, stop it," Keir Bolderon told her. "Stop fussing, for
God's sake. Do you suppose I'm so much different from you,
Elspeth Patterson? Do you think I was born into privilege? I
came from a hovel so cramped and filthy that you could scarce
breathe in it. My daddy was a labourer, his daddy before him.
They slaved for the sake of the family, to scratch enough to
feed seven hungry mouths. I saw that as love. But was my
daddy respected for breaking his back in the service of a man
who could not tell a corn rig from a pod of peas? No, he was
despised for his loyalty, my daddy, as we are all despised."

"Where is he now?"

"Oh, dead," said Keir Bolderon. "His daughters are married, his sons dispersed to founder or aspire as suits their
natures."

"What is your nature, Mr Bolderon?"

"To aspire."

"To marry well, to live at ease on your wife's fortune?"

"I'm not the sort who will be idle, whoever I marry."

"Are you not well provided for in this trading-house in
Leith?"

"I'm no damned trader. There's profit but no progress in
that occupation."

"As there was on the Abbeyfield?" said Elspeth.

"On the Abbeyfield I had hopes," said Keir Bolderon. "But
my natural ambitions were turned against me."

"Is that why you courted me, for the influence my money
would give you?"

"Yes, I wanted your money."

"I think I should inform you, Mr Bolderon, that I am well protected against the predations of a husband. I have secured my fortune and my estate, such as it is, against the *jus mariti* by vesting it in a trustee, my lawyer, Mr Hildebrand. Any man who marries me will not have control of my money."

Keir Bolderon nodded as if he had expected no less of her.

He said, "I wanted your money, and then I wanted you."

"Which is it, Mr Bolderon?"

"Both."

Elspeth said, "Why did you not come at once when I invited you?"

"I did not know what to do."

"What was best for you, do you mean?"

"What might be best for both of us."

"Did you doubt that I was good enough for you?"

"God, no! Not that. It did not seem – honest, somehow."

"Does it seem more honest now?"

"As honest as I can make it, Elspeth."

She said, "What will you do for me, Mr Bolderon?"

"Build your house, for one thing."

"Is that all?"

"Whatever else you ask of me that I can do, I will do."

"And the rest?" said Elspeth.

Keir Bolderon was silent. He rubbed his mouth with his hand. He would not yield, could not yield any more than she could. They were true-born Scots and intractable in their loving.

She waited, eyes upon his face.

The wind came ruffling over the crown of the hill and stirred the wasted grasses, moved the boughs of the oaks and the tiny dead leaves that snuggled in the bramble hedge. It brought to her all the small noises of the valley, the sounds from Balnesmoor and the parks of Ottershaw all smoored and mingled and soft as rain.

She would wait no more, give him no more opportunity.

She swept past him, downhill, down towards the field gate and the track through the oaks. Damn him, she would build her own stone house, fence her own fields, tend her own flocks. She did not need Keir Bolderon.

479

She reached the gate, fumbled with the hook-link, shaking it with terrible impatience, shaking and shaking it so that it rattled but would not part. In despair she sank against the gatepost, knowing that he was still above her, motionless and indecisive upon the edge of the moor by the broken ground.

She did not, however, dare to look back.

"Elspeth."

She started when he put his arm about her and held her, held her firmly but tenderly so that she could not escape him on any account. He stretched about her and slipped the link and let the chain fall free. He pushed the gate open.

"Go," he said. "Go on."

She sighed. She leaned against him, her head upon his chest, his arm still about her waist.

"Ask me," Elspeth said. "Please, ask me."

"Ask you what?"

"About the terms of the marriage contract."

He said nothing for such a while that Elspeth peeped up at him. He was smiling.

"How much will it pay me?" he asked.

"Nothing," said Elspeth.

"In which case I accept," Keir Bolderon said and, with a loving hand, lifted her face to his kiss.